FINCH MERLIN AND THE LOST MAP

Harley Merlin 11

BELLA FORREST

ONE

Finch

The golden doors of the Mapmakers' Monastery loomed over me. How long would I have to wait for the entrance to open? I'd only been here a few minutes, and that already felt too long.

All right, Erebus, you've had your fun. Come back now and tell me what the heck I'm doing here.

I stood entranced by the glowing gemstones lodged in the building's spires. Beyond the cliff's edge, the sea crashed against the rocks.

"You'll catch flies if you leave your mouth hangin' open, son." The old Southern lady broke me out of my frustrated reverie.

"Sorry... I've been zoning out, haven't I?" I felt like a schoolboy who'd been caught napping.

"You have. Come sit beside this old girl, keep her company awhile." The old woman patted the seat beside her.

It would've been rude to refuse, and older ladies tended to dig me. Even tough old boots could be softened up into doling out some answers, if I played my cards right.

"What's your name?" I cast her my most debonair smile. "Sorry for not asking before—I think the wind stole away my manners."

She chuckled. "Blanche Dunham. Pleased to meet you." She extended a wrinkled hand. I wasn't sure if I was supposed to kiss it or shake it.

"I'm Finch." I left out my last name and opted for a shake. Both "Merlin" and "Shipton" tended to raise eyebrows, and I wasn't about to give up my state secrets until I knew Ms. Dunham a little better.

"Unusual name."

I shrugged. "Unusual parents."

She laughed like someone who'd smoked twenty-a-day since she was twelve, but it was oddly soothing. "There's a sayin', ain't there, that your parents mess you up, and you mess your kids up, and the cycle goes on. I never had any young'uns, myself, so at least I was spared the weight of naming them. Always thought I'd have gone for somethin' simple, though—a Mark or a Jenny. I suppose you'd be too young to have little 'uns?"

"*Way* too young." My heart almost fled for its life at the thought. "But you're right about parents. Anyway, I hate to ask again, but where are we? Like, specifically? Pretend I'm clueless." *Because I am...*

"The Mapmakers' Monastery," she replied.

I resisted the urge to roll my eyes. "And where is that exactly?"

"Arkoudi, Greece—Asteris, in the ancient days. Right in the middle of the Ionian Sea. If you look, you can see Ithaca. Odysseus's old stompin' grounds." She pointed to a larger island in the distance, partially hidden by the haze that drifted up from the water.

"Greece?" I gaped at her. "Why's it so friggin' chilly?"

"Language."

"Sorry. Why's it so chilly if we're in Greece?"

She smiled. "The monastery. It attracts the winds."

"Very Odyssean, if that's even a word. He used a bunch of winds for something, right? I'm a bit rusty on my ancient Greek knowledge."

"You need to take a look at your ancient literature." Blanche looked across the horizon. "King Aeolos, the Keeper of the Winds, gave Odysseus a bag containing the strongest of winds for his voyage home. They'd almost reached Ithaca when Odysseus decided to have himself a little nap. His men opened the bag, wantin' to know what was inside, set all them winds loose, and it pushed them right back to where they started. Then he got into all that trouble with monsters and witches and cyclops and the like."

I smirked. "An actual, real-life windbag? I know a couple of those." *Davin... here's looking at you, asshole.*

"It's a moral tale, son—it ain't a jest to be taken lightly. There's truth in stories, if you know how to read them. Homer uses Odysseus's error to tell us not to lose sight of our goals till we're over the finish line, else you'll end up beginnin' again."

"Hmm… interesting takeaway. Is this your finish line? Learning to make maps? I mean, that's why we're both here, right?" If she thought we were in this together, she might be more forthcoming.

"Oh yes, son. It's taken me many a year to locate this here monastery, and I ain't leavin' until I've discovered how to draw myself a magical map to reveal hidden places."

"To where, if that's not a rude question?" I asked, keeping it casual.

She sighed wistfully. "El Dorado."

"Great soundtrack. Elton John, I believe. Totally underrated movie."

Blanche frowned. "Eh?"

"Nothing. I babble when I'm nervous." I cleared my throat. "What's in El Dorado for you? Looking for a snazzy pair of gold earrings, or a big chunk of the yellow stuff to take home?"

"Believe it or not, I'm descended from Sir Walter Raleigh. I found out a while ago, and it put me on this path. I'd like to finish what he wasn't able to, all those years ago, when he set out to find that lost city. Unfortunately, he didn't have any magic to help him along, so he never made it." She chuckled wryly. "A bit of gold wouldn't hurt, either, to pay off the mortgage and see myself comfortable for the rest of my days."

"Sounds like a good life plan."

Blanche nodded. "As a young girl, I always thought I'd be some grand explorer, but I found myself in magical administration instead. Not too inspirin', let me tell you. And now that I'm in the winter of my life, I thought it high time I lived out those dreams. They been waitin' on me too long. If not now, then it'll be never, and I ain't willin' to go to the grave without tryin'."

I couldn't help but smile. "That's so cool."

Blanche looked elegant in that way older Southern women often did, not a silvered hair out of place and wearing a full face of makeup. She seemed friendly in a maternal sense, even if she didn't have the kiddos to go with it. I didn't imagine she suffered fools, given how quick she was to call me out on my language. I liked her vibe. To find out that she was a badass granny, using her retirement years to go trekking after the lost city of El Dorado, just made her more awesome.

What am I looking for? El Dorado sounded ace, but gold didn't seem like Erebus's flavor of choice. It was too ordinary, too human.

Riches beyond one's wildest dreams—that probably didn't feature for someone like him, even if he had given himself a physical body to get all snug inside, by draining the Fountain of Youth. It had to be something else. Something more... cosmic. Something befitting a Child of Chaos.

My thoughts flitted toward Saskia and Garrett. They'd be going crazy, worrying about me. Did they think I was dead, crushed under all that rock in the collapsed Jubilee mine? I felt for my pendant—the one Tatyana had given us in case of trouble—but it had vanished. *You slippery-fingered frogspawn!* Erebus must have swiped it without me noticing.

I had to let them know I was safe, and I wanted to make sure *they* were okay. Erebus had promised he'd rescued Garrett and Saskia, but that smoky thorn in my side clearly couldn't be trusted.

I delved into my pocket for my phone and looked hopefully at the screen, but there were no bars to speak of. I waved it around like a madman—everyone knows that's the way to get a signal in a tough situation. But those two irritating words stayed in the top right corner: *No signal.* It wasn't even giving me the option of *Emergency calls only.* Maybe this wasn't a red-alert emergency, but I could've done with a line to the SDC. I just wanted to let the people there know I was alive, if not entirely kicking.

"Human technology don't work here, son," Blanche broke in. "It's designed that way. No mortal interference."

I raised my hands, ready to try out some magical interference. Blanche's shaking head stopped me. "What?"

"That won't work either, if you're wantin' to try a communication spell. The monastery don't want any contact with the outside world."

What, is it a sulky teenager? I got up, took out my stick of charmed chalk, and scraped it against the wall of the monastery. It didn't do a damn thing. No chalk line appeared, as if I had tried to write on glass or something.

"No chalk doors, either?" I sighed.

"'Fraid not, son. All travel and communication magic are banned in these parts." Blanche offered a sympathetic look. "You got folks worrying about you?"

I shrugged. "I just wanted to let them know I arrived safely, you know?" *And that I'm not dead, or strung up like a Christmas ham in Erebus's lair.*

Why would Erebus drop me in a place like this, sealed off from the outside world? Had he deliberately put me here so I *couldn't* get in touch with the people I cared about? That was definitely his style. Let them worry, let me worry, let us all have a big worry party for his amusement.

More to the point, where had he run off to? Now that he had his human form, why wasn't *he* standing on this cliff, waiting to be let into the monastery so he could draw a map to wherever he was looking for?

"What in the name of all that is good and holy is *that?*" Blanche's eyes darted skyward.

A shape bombed out of the azure atmosphere like a UFO on a kamikaze mission. A burning ball headed right for us, streaking along faster than a comet.

A bad joke sprang to my mind, as they often did when I entered panic mode: *I was wondering why my friend was throwing a frisbee, and then it hit me.* Just like this flaming missile would hit us, if we didn't get out of the way.

"Blanche, get up!" I ran to her and picked her up like a firefighter rescuing a damsel. She tried to bat me away, but we didn't have time. Even if we ran for our lives, that object looked like it could obliterate the island, and us with it.

Gathering Chaos into my palms, I forged a springboard of Air under my feet and used it to power us upward. We needed to get as far from that thing as possible.

As I took flight, a protesting Blanche in my arms, I smacked into a wall. Not a real wall, but man, did it feel like it as it connected with the top of my head. A ripple of light spread out, revealing a domed shield that was clearly there to protect the island... or keep us from leaving.

I fell back to earth, too stunned to create a pillow of Air to break my fall. Blanche didn't have that problem—she had me to break her fall. I hit the ground with a thud, staring upward in a daze as the comet grew closer and closer.

Blanche had tried to warn me. This place was completely sealed off from the outside world. It went further than phone signals and magical comms. Now that we were in this bubble, we couldn't get out.

And that ball of burning light was about to strike.

TWO

Finch

The unidentified flying ball of potential death gained speed by the second, glowing faintly blue as it hurtled through the sky. Blanche picked herself up, dusting invisible dirt from the front of her smart navy skirt and mumbling about "foolish heroics" under her breath.

So much for gratitude and helping your elders. Even now, she didn't seem nearly as concerned as she should've. *Maybe she knows something I don't. Maybe the shield will keep it out.*

I sat up and crossed every extremity I possessed as the comet made its speedy descent. If the shield held, it'd shatter into smithereens. I braced for an impact that didn't come. Instead, panic shot through me as the bright ball of light tore through the protective bubble.

I scrambled backward like a weird crab, my ass scraping across the grass in my rush to get away. However, the moment the comet pierced the monastery's atmosphere, it shrank in size. I'd barely moved out of the way when it crash-landed outside the monastery doors—the ones that refused to open. Sparks of blue light showered the ground.

For a second, nothing happened, and I nearly breathed a sigh of relief. But then, a delayed aftershock exploded outward in a violent pulse that sent me flying. Blanche, too. She lifted her hands and her eyes widened, but it was too late for her to use magic. The shocked look on her face would've been comical if I hadn't worried she would break if she hit something.

I sent out a rapid lasso of Telekinesis, catching Blanche with it and using my other hand to create a wall of Air to stop us from tumbling right off this friggin' cliff. It buffeted us toward safety.

With another thud, I hit the ground. I managed to keep Blanche in the air long enough to set her down more gently, but fatigue had begun to set in. It ended up being a rougher landing for the old girl than I'd intended. I didn't entirely know why I had gone out of my way to help this woman, but I supposed I had a soft spot for the older generation. And I didn't want her losing her shot at El Dorado before she'd even made it through those doors.

"Thank you, Finch. That was mighty kind. My reflexes ain't what they used to be." She looked shaky, attempting to fix her elegant up-do. I didn't have the heart to tell her it was a lost cause.

I shrugged. "My pleasure, ma'am." Those words would never slip easily out of my throat.

Now that Blanche and I were safe from a sudden dip in the Ionian Sea, I turned my attention to the aliens who'd caused this stress. Didn't they know my sanity already teetered on a knife-edge? Having to think fast wasn't easy at the moment, after I'd spent a day down a mine tapping all my Chaos resources.

I expected—and, secretly, half-hoped—for little gray men with shiny black eyes. Instead, an absolute beauty and a hulking beast of a man emerged from the small crater they'd made during their landing.

"I told you it wasn't safe!" Beast muttered. "What if the hull hadn't held up? This was a terrible idea. Anything could've happened to you."

Beauty shrugged it off. "What's the use thinking of what *might* have happened? Everything held up fine. Are we in one piece, or aren't we?"

"If we'd taken a dinghy from the mainland, we could've—" Beast started to protest, but Beauty cut him off.

"We'd never have made it through the shield in a dinghy, Luke. It takes great skill and knowledge to reach this monastery. One does not simply row their way in."

The young woman was a small, waif-like creature, with wavy, dark hair shot through with strands of bright pink and a set of odd, pale gray eyes. Her clothes looked like she'd had a run-in with a thrift store: wide-legged, silky peach pants that stopped above her ankle and a ruffled white blouse ripped off from the 1800s. She wore a cropped, pink furry jacket over the top, complete with a brightly patterned backpack. Weird, but it suited her.

"We could've tried!" Beast, who seemed to go by Luke, insisted. He towered well over six feet, with shoulders twice as broad as mine and muscles bulging obnoxiously under a plain white shirt. He had close-cropped brown hair and a chiseled face that might've been good-looking if he'd laid off the steroids. A bit too Neanderthal. He had a backpack, too, though in a much more practical, black style. Lucky them—Erebus hadn't given me any time to pack luggage.

"You should trust me more. I know what I'm talking about,"

Beauty replied. "This was quicker and more efficient, and we only made a little hole in the ground. No harm done." She flashed a sweet smile, and I watched him basically melt into a puddle of adoration. For all his beef and brawn, it looked like this bizarre woman had him wrapped around her little finger.

"That was quite the entrance." I stepped up to make my introductions. "My name's Finch. Still in one piece, though your flying ball came pretty close to knocking off my pretty head."

The girl stared at me before breaking into giggles. "I'm so sorry, we didn't even see you through all the flames licking up the windshield!" She put out her hand. "I'm Melody Winchester, and this is my bodyguard, Luke Prescott."

"Winchester, eh? As in—"

"As in the rifle inventor, yes," she replied, shaking my hand with alarming vigor. I tried to let go, but she held on. "I'm his descendant. It's a hard name to get away from. Everyone says, 'Oh, are you related to the rifle guy?' and I'm always like, 'Yes, that's the one!' Or they say, 'Oh, as in the ones who built that weird house with all the dead-ends and ghosts?' and I'm like, 'Yep, that's me.' Creepy house girl." She laughed louder, practically ripping my hand off. This had to be the longest handshake in history. "I don't mind, so don't worry about asking. Everyone does. Besides, there are worse families to be from, right?"

Oh, sweet girl... if only you knew. "I suppose there are."

"What have I told you about shaking hands with strangers?" Luke whispered. He hit me with a death stare.

"How am I supposed to say hello properly if I don't shake hands? That would be plain rude," she replied, finally releasing me. "My father always said a handshake is the best way to get an idea of a person. You can tell a lot from a handshake, you know?"

"Is that so?" *What's it say when you take forever to let go?* Man, this girl talked a mile a minute. It sapped my energy just to listen.

"Yes, he always said that a person should have a strong, genuine handshake. Weak handshakes equal shifty people, and lack of eye contact means someone has something to hide, or that's what he used to tell me." She smiled proudly.

"Is that why you held on so long?" I teased. "What did you learn about me?"

She cocked her head. "You've got a good, honest grip, but you don't like physical contact. It makes you uncomfortable."

"Well, you're not wrong. Judging by your handshake, you're part boa constrictor." I laughed, and so did she.

"I get a bit enthusiastic sometimes."

"Nothing wrong with that. Pleased to meet you both." I offered my hand to Luke, even though it throbbed from Melody's ridiculous handshake, but he looked at it like my fingers were covered in oozing boils.

"My name is Blanche Dunham." My first new chum shook Melody's hand and wasn't rebuffed when she went to shake Luke's. *Ah, it's like that, is it?* I'd been out of high school for years, but whenever I came across someone like him, it took me right back. He reminded me of Dylan, only less palatable.

"So, you've come to map-make?" I broke the ensuing silence.

Melody and Luke exchanged a secretive glance. "That's right," Luke answered. Simple and to the point. If Melody had answered, I could only imagine what might've poured out of her mouth. The way she rambled had a somewhat endearing quality. Like a hyperactive squirrel.

"You must've led an interesting life, being from the Winchester family?" I tried again. "Although, I thought the magical gene petered out of that line a long time ago." If spending time in the Cult of Eris had taught me one useful thing, it was that knowledge was power. And the months I'd spent cooped up in stuffy study rooms, reading book after book on magical families, would soon pay off.

Luke frowned. "You seem to know a lot about the Winchesters... Finch, was it?"

"That's right," I replied, unfazed.

"He must be a bibliophile, like me!" Melody clapped her hands in excitement. "And you're right. The famous Winchester, William Wirt, wasn't a magical. If he had been, he might not have invented a rifle, am I right?"

I couldn't help but chuckle. "Who needs guns when they can spew magic from their hands?"

"Exactly! So, he wasn't, and the last magical recorded, before me, was two generations before him. Was it two? Anyway, it skipped down the line until I came along, and—poof!—a magical was born. But I think that was mostly my mother's doing. She's a magical, but my father isn't." Luke nudged her, like she'd said too much, but she didn't seem to notice. "They fought and fought about sending me to the San Jose Coven for my magical education. Instead, they brought the preceptors to our house to teach me. Homeschooled—guilty as charged."

"They do that?" Blanche arched an eyebrow. "They never did in my day."

Melody shook her head. "Oh no, it was a special arrangement. I think there must've been quite a lot of money involved, but I don't really keep track of those things. My parents are really protective, and I think they were both relieved and panicked that I became a magical. It could've gone either way, I suppose. The Russian roulette of genetics."

A few of the things she said hit me in a very fragile corner of my mind. Famous magical families, the genetic game of chance... I'd been affected by both. My mind gremlins stayed quiet for now, but they wouldn't for long. My pills didn't have the same edge under pressure and stress. This definitely qualified. If I had to spend a while here, unable to contact anyone, they'd probably wind up going haywire. This protective bubble might've seemed hard to escape from, but it would be much harder to escape my own mind while inside said bubble.

"No need to tell your whole life story, Melody." Luke put a hand on her shoulder. Her cheeks reddened.

"Sorry, I have a habit of talking too much. I'm trying to work on it, but I've always been this way. As a kid, everyone always called me precocious, and I never knew if it was an insult or a compliment. I suppose that was where my love for words began, because I had so much curiosity about that word—precocious. I delved into the dictionary, and I've been addicted to reading ever since. I just have so many things racing through my head, and sometimes they all just come out at once, in a big torrent that I can't control," she said quietly.

"Well, I think it's better to talk too much than say nothing at all," I said encouragingly.

She flashed me a shy smile that made Captain Beefcake glower.

I wonder what you're searching for. I didn't know if her verbal diarrhea would make her a good candidate for gentle interrogation, or if the answers would get lost in the gush, so to speak. Maybe it didn't matter why people were here. Maybe that was none of my beeswax. But inquisitiveness was a trait I'd never grown out of.

I opened my mouth to ask, when a soft scuffling sound distracted me, followed by a groan and the scrape of tumbling rocks. I turned to see a pair of enormous hands grip the edge of the cliff. A moment later, a huge African dude pulled himself over the lip and stood to his full height. If I'd thought Luke was tall, this guy made him look like a midget. The man wore desert camouflage trousers and a black T-shirt. A red military cap topped his head, at an angle.

He eyed us suspiciously and removed the hat to wipe his brow. "Why are you all here?" His accent was rich and deep, flavored with Nigerian pride.

"Same as you, I'd guess," I replied.

"I haven't seen so many before." He pushed his hat into his pocket. "I have come every day, waiting for them doors to open. Not a soul been here, 'cept that woman over there. She been waiting as long as me, to get in them doors." He pointed to Blanche.

"You've been coming every day?" Melody sounded stunned.

"I been trying, though I've not had the right spells till now. I seen a couple more trying too, but they didn't have the right spells neither. I had to bribe me some rogue magicals to give me the right ones, to get past this here protective shield. Looks like I came just in time." A sudden smile broke out on his face, startling in its abruptness.

"I'm Finch." I held out my hand, and he shook it firmly.

"I am Mr. Abara," he replied.

I smiled. "No first name?"

"No, it is Mr. Abara." He peered at me curiously. "No second name?"

"No, just Finch." *Man, he got me there.* It seemed I wasn't the only one playing cloak and dagger. Melody and Luke had their secretive glances, Mr. Abara refused to give up his first name, I wouldn't tell my last name, and Blanche was… well, Blanche.

"I'm Melody Winchester, and this is Luke Prescott—he's watching over me while I'm here." She walked over and shook hands with Mr. Abara, Luke and Blanche following suit.

"Winchesta? As in, the rifle?" Mr. Abara's eyes darkened for a moment.

She nodded. "Yes, and the family who built the famous Winchester house."

"I don't care for gons," Mr. Abara said, his smile gone. "I don't care for weapons of any kind."

"Oh, neither do I, Mr. Abara." Melody looked up at him earnestly. "I wish my family had a legacy that had nothing to do with guns, but we don't get to choose where we come from, I suppose. That's why my ancestor Sarah Winchester built the Winchester house, as a way of appeasing the spirits of those killed by the Winchester rifle. They swarm the place and call it home now."

Mr. Abara smiled again. "Hmm… I didn't know that. At least your family is doing something about it, eh?"

"That's how I like to think of it," Melody replied warmly.

"So, you're here to learn map-making?" All of this historical chatter interested me, but I needed to get to the root of why everyone was here. They all seemed to have a purpose, which meant I was the only one with no idea what to expect.

Mr. Abara nodded. "I am. Same as everyone here, I expect."

"And what is it you want to—" A sound made me stop short. A shrub to the side of the monastery moved.

A figure emerged from the foliage, twigs and leaves stuck in his mane of blond, shaggy hair. He had a red bandana tied around his forehead, giving him the look of a dime-store Axl Rose. Lanky, grimy, and hazy-eyed, he could have easily wandered into that bush after a heavy night, not knowing where the hell he was. His dirty, ripped jeans were covered in slogan badges, like "God Save the Queen," the smiley Nirvana face, and of course, the jagged "A" of a wannabe anarchist. His threadbare T-shirt read "Newquay—Life's a Beach," topping off the punky vibes I picked up from him.

"Wow, how long have I been out?" He ran a hand through his long hair. His accent was distinctly British. "This turned into quite the gathering."

I didn't know if it was his demeanor, or that Davin-esque accent, but he instantly rubbed me the wrong way.

"Have you been there this whole time?" Blanche's jaw dropped.

He shrugged. "I've been here and there, wandering the island, trying to keep myself occupied. This place inspired me to write a stream-of-consciousness piece, sort of Kerouacian, if you want a read. It's just gorgeous here, isn't it? So peaceful, and the water is just beaut. Makes me wish I had my board, to paddle out and lay awhile, you know?"

Please, spare us the open mic night.

"When did you get here?" Blanche demanded, clearly freaked that someone else had been creeping around the entire time she'd been here.

"I came for last month's entrance trials, but I failed miserably, so I've been hanging around since then, taking in the scenery," he replied. "I'm Oliver Huntington-Shaw, by the way. Who are you fine people? I've got to say, it's nice to see new faces. Solitude can be great for the soul, but it can be harmful if it edges into loneliness, you get what I'm saying?"

"Did you say, 'entrance trials'?" I ignored the rest of what he said, which was probably for the best. He'd likely never read a Jack Kerouac novel in his life. He'd probably never listened to Nirvana, or done anything vaguely anarchic, either. He'd gone from probable punk rocker to wannabe hipster in the space of a single meeting.

He nodded. "Of course, mate. You don't get in if you don't pass. I bet they used to take anyone, but that's society for you—always pitting us against each other in the endless competition that is life."

Entrance trials? Ah, crap...

THREE

Finch

"When do these entrance trials start?" I felt more agitated by the second.

Oliver smiled. "Mate, have you been out in the sun too long or something? It's going down tonight, my man. That's if I've got my dates right. It's going to be a full moon party, and we're all invited!"

"A full moon?" I had no idea what day it was, let alone where we were in the moon's cycle.

"Who is this guy?" Oliver snorted. "Is he with one of you?"

I glanced around the gathered group, finding them giving me a weird look. *Don't you put seeds of doubt in their heads, pal.* I'd had enough trouble with the last Brit I'd encountered. I didn't need more reason to dislike this one, too. He'd already given me plenty.

"No, he came alone," Blanche replied. "You are here to map-make, aren't you?"

"Of course, I just don't have all the details. It was sort of a last-minute decision." I gave it my best nonchalance. I wasn't totally lying. It had been last-minute, just not really *my decision.*

Mr. Abara laughed. "Give the boy a break. Everyone's business is their own. He got a reason, you got a reason, we all got a reason. Even if he don't know all the details, he made it through the shield. He's as much right to be here as the rest of us."

"Thanks, man. I wasn't ready for an inquisition," I mumbled.

"Think nothing of it." He clapped me on the shoulder so hard I nearly toppled over.

Our conversation faltered, interrupted by the whirr of a plane engine. I looked up and saw a small aircraft approaching the island, from the direction of Odysseus's rocky Ithaca. All of us watched and waited to see if this would be another member of our expanding party. All the while, my mind raced with thoughts of these trials. What would they entail? I needed some damned sleep before I started running gauntlets and doing crazy things, but it didn't seem naptime had been slotted into Erebus's schedule.

The aircraft slowed as it came near. A door in the side gaped wide, and two figures leapt out before my heart had a chance to jump. Blanche gasped, while Oliver nodded his head admiringly. He'd probably gone base-jumping during his year abroad or something.

Parachutes opened and the figures careened down as they grappled with the pulleys steering their course. Melody and Luke's entrance might have been impressive, but this was old-school impressive. James Bond stuff. As they neared the protective bubble, they sent out streams of Chaos, their mouths moving as if chanting a spell. I couldn't get a good look at them, since they both wore jumpsuits and goggles.

Holes sparked and fizzed in the protective membrane above as it fought against this aerial attack. The holes made a small target for them to hit, and parachutes didn't strike me as very precise modes of transport. I held my breath as they descended farther, almost reaching the crackling holes they'd made. A moment later, they sailed right through, only for the parachutes to catch in the holes as they quickly closed. The parachutists had let up on their Chaos onslaught, which gave the membrane a chance to repair itself at lightning speed.

The two figures dangled like marionettes. They writhed and wriggled to get free, but they were harnessed in tight. I lifted my palms to create a boost of Air. Luke seemed to be doing something similar. But there was no need. Whoever these two were, they didn't need our help. In total sync, like those swimmers with the weird nose-clips, they delved into the pockets of their jumpsuits and took out matching knives. Slicing through the harnesses, they fell in perfect unison to the ground, where they rolled and jumped right back up as if it were nothing. I half expected a "ta-da" or a gymnastic pose to finish off the move.

Overhead, the empty harnesses swayed in the breeze.

"So cool," Oliver said in an appreciative whisper.

As the duo removed their goggles and unzipped their jumpsuits, stepping out of the billowy fabric, I got a closer look at them. Identical twins of the female persuasion, with long, golden hair, olive complexions, and hazel eyes with a matching mischievous glint. *Ugh... twins.* It brought back memories of the Ryder twins. They might not have been identical, but they'd liked to mess with people by changing into each other. I hadn't seen their rampage of mayhem through San Diego, but Harley had told me stories.

"What's the matter? Have you—" the first twin said in an Australian lilt.

"—never seen two sisters parachute out of a plane before?" Number two finished off the sentence in the same Down Under accent.

Creepy...

"Twin sisters!" Melody grinned at them. "That's fascinating. Apparently, magical identical twins have shared—"

The first twin cut her off. "I'm Shailene, and this is—"

"—Fay Basani. You might have heard of us," the second one added seamlessly.

I wracked my brain. "I'm not sure I have."

Both sisters shot me a withering look. "We're the famous Basani twins," Shailene went on.

"Superstars of the Sydney Coven." Fay nodded.

"Responsible for the capture of ten percent of the monsters held in the Bestiary." Shailene grinned at her sister.

"Travelers and adventurers extraordinaire. There's no way you haven't heard of us." Fay shot me another withering look at the same time as Shailene. They just seemed to know what the other was doing.

I shrugged. "I don't read much international news. I must've missed you."

"I know who you are," Melody chimed in. "I've read a lot about you. Is it true that you caught the first Selkies? I know you shouldn't always believe the things you read, but it was such an amazing story that I really hope it's true. It's quite a feat, to wrangle with a sea creature and survive it. They should have the upper hand, in their own territory, so I imagine it's very difficult to achieve."

"You talk a lot, huh?" Shailene smiled.

"You must read a lot, too. Nice to see some articles made their way past Australia," Fay replied. "Which ones did you read?"

Melody paused. "*Magicals Weekly* and their top thirty under thirty."

Shailene looked smug. "That was a good one. Yeah, we were the first to capture Selkies and have them stored in the Bestiary."

"It definitely wasn't easy," Fay added, right on schedule. "They're slimy little buggers, and anyone who says different is lying. They might turn out all pretty on the shore, but they're not pretty when they're trying to escape."

Fay and Shailene looked over the rest of us, their eyes lingering a bit too long on Luke and me. They turned to each other and whispered, matching smirks turning up the corners of their lips. They seemed to be forming judgments, and I didn't know if they were the bad kind or the good kind.

Melody's eyes suddenly widened. "Oh, wow... I wasn't expecting that."

"The Selkie wrangling?" Fay and Shailene chorused in creepy unison.

"No... oh dear, I'm sorry to be the bearer of bad news, but you really shouldn't waste time on fancying Luke, Shailene. Or setting your sights on Finch, Fay. It wouldn't be right for you two to go after unavailable guys." Melody hesitated, apparently oblivious to the personal nature of the details she'd just spilled. "I mean, they're not physically unavailable, but they are emotionally. Gosh, I hope that makes sense? Finch doesn't like physical contact, and Luke... he isn't interested. I'd hate for you to spend energy on them when there are other nice guys out there. I'm sure you have your pick, anyway, looking the way you do."

Fay and Shailene stared at her in disbelief.

Wow... awkward.

"Melody." Luke put his hand on her shoulder, and she blushed furiously.

"Did I do it again?" she whispered.

He nodded. "A little bit, yeah."

It didn't take a genius to realize she had Empath abilities. Given her role as Miss Chatterbox, I felt glad that my Shapeshifting spared me from being Empathed.

Everyone else's abilities would be harder to gauge. I wasn't at the SDC anymore, where you literally pinned the info to your special occasion uniform. These people's behavior didn't do much to expose them, either.

Mr. Abara looked to be playing his cards close to his chest. Blanche was eager to get on with learning about mapmaking so she could find El Dorado. Oliver seemed happy to go with the flow. Melody and Luke worked on their secrets together, as a unit. And the Wonder Twins obviously sought something together. I doubted they did anything alone. That left me, with no idea about anything involving the monastery.

"So, after that bombshell, who's here for what?" I broke the uncomfortable silence. Melody offered me a grateful glance for taking the spotlight off her.

"I'm after Shangri-La," Oliver replied. "I'm going to find it and learn their ways, to discover the secrets of true happiness and a long life. It's my dream to live in a real utopia, a genuine paradise on Earth. And once I've done that, I'm going to write about it."

I frowned. "Didn't someone already do that? I mean, Shangri-La is fictional, right? It's from *Lost Horizon.*"

"He's right, it is," Melody agreed.

"There's truth in stories, mate." Oliver gave a casual shrug. "It's out there, and I'm going to find it, just like James Hilton found it and wrote about it, calling it fictional. If he said outright it was real, people would go flocking after it, ruining that paradise… obviously."

Why did people keep saying that—"there's truth in stories"? As if I didn't know. The Fountain of Youth had been a myth until yesterday. What they were leaving out was the teeny-tiny small print, that there was also danger in stories.

"You're going after Shangri-La?" The Creep Twins snorted at him. "Well, you can expect to have a race on your hands, mate, because that's where we're headed, too."

"Couldn't you all go? I'm sure Shangri-La is pretty roomy," I said.

Shailene snorted. "As if. We're not into sharing glory, unless it's between the two of us."

"May the best explorer win, then," Oliver replied, evidently unbothered. He didn't seem like the sort of guy who got worked up about much.

"That'd be us," Fay shot back.

Oliver smiled lazily. "We'll just have to wait and see."

"What about you?" I nodded to Melody and Luke. "What tickles your geographical fancy?"

Luke hesitated to answer, but Melody came right out with it. "We want to find the Last Unknown—one of the few places on Earth yet to be discovered."

"The Last Unknown? That's not very specific. What if your map takes you to a different Unknown?" I asked.

"It won't." Melody cast a conspiratorial glance back at Luke.

Figuring I wouldn't get much else out of her with Luke the guard dog around, I turned to another member of our party. "And you, Mr. Abara?"

"I intend to find the lost Oasis of Little Birds, otherwise known as Zezura," he replied.

"Never heard of it. What's there?"

He gave me a warning look. "Something I desire. That's all you need to know."

"How about you, Finch?" Melody cut in.

"Me? Oh… I'm… uh, looking for the Fountain of Youth," I lied. I didn't want them thinking I was there to steal their ideas. The Fountain seemed like a safe bet, since it was empty and buried under a mine's worth of rockfall.

I was spared more explanation by the arrival of five more people, coming by sea, sky, and land. One rode up on a four-wheeler, having landed by boat at the other end of the island. He went by the name Bill and came from New Zealand. He instantly recognized the Basani twins. Rodrigo, from Spain, made the same entrance Mr. Abara had, boating to the cliff's edge and climbing up. Lin, from Puerto Rico, came speeding in on a hang-glider, while Giulia, from Italy, rappelled down from a helicopter. Alessandra, who'd come all the way from Brazil, arrived last.

After brief small talk, it turned out they mostly sought the same things—El Dorado, the Lost City of Z, Arcadia, the Aztec home-land of Aztlán—for the same reasons: treasure, long life, or paradise. All the things mortals longed for. Yet none of those places or motivations set off Erebus alarms in my head.

"Do the doors open when the full moon comes out?" I wanted to fill in the gaps in my knowledge. "Do we start the entrance trials inside?"

A ripple of confusion echoed through the gathered group. *Huh, maybe they aren't as clued-up as I thought.*

"Oliver, what happened last time?" Mr. Abara fixed his gaze on our resident hipster.

"Oh, when I said I failed the entrance trials, I meant I missed them completely. I got here too late," he replied. "I don't know what to do past getting through that shield, mate. I thought that was the hard part."

"Anyone?" I said hopefully.

Melody shook her head. "The people who told us the location

said that not knowing what to do is part of the trial. I didn't understand it then—I thought it was just a riddle, perhaps—but now I see that they were right. If that's the case, I suppose our trial has already started."

"All doors open," Shailene said.

"Yeah, we just have to break through them," Fay added.

With that, the Creep Twins strode up to the front doors like a matching set of bookends and started hammering them with Telekinesis. Following their lead, Melody used a gust of Air to sweep herself up to the nearest window. Luke hovered below like an anxious puppy. Meanwhile, Oliver scaled the wall to try to reach the spires at the top.

Bill stepped forward to help, when the gemstones embedded in the spires emitted a piercing screech. Their thrum had been constant up until this point, but this felt different. This sounded like a siren… a warning siren.

Light shot between the gems, red bouncing to red, green to green, and so on. As the shriek built to a deafening howl, a burst of multicolored light flooded the building, knocking back everyone who had tried to force their way through.

Bill sailed backward, toppling over the edge of the cliff. A splash followed. I ran to the lip with Mr. Abara, both of us peering down to make sure Bill was okay. He surfaced and gave a weary wave before turning around and swimming for a dinghy that waited down the shore.

"Is he out of the game?" I glanced at Mr. Abara.

"It seems so," he replied.

A voice boomed from within the monastery. "Welcome, brave travelers, to the Mapmakers' Monastery. My name is Etienne Biset, and I will teach those who make it through these trials. To enter, we begin the first trial—you must solve the riddle of *how* to enter. I hold these trials every full moon, if enough people gather. I don't have the patience to coddle every newcomer that darkens my door. So, I suggest you get on with it."

He had a faint French accent. There was something dangerous about it that scared me and intrigued me in equal measure.

Watching my fellow wannabes gearing up, I sensed things were about to take a turn for the hectic. I had two options: join them or end up like Bill. And I wasn't in the mood for a soaking.

"Let the games begin," I whispered, letting Chaos flow into my palms.

FOUR

Finch

"One more thing." Etienne's voice echoed back out. "I hate to have to simplify what should be obvious, but I must, or none of you will get in. The doors are locked, as you have realized. But the puzzle to solve is this: these doors can only be opened from the inside."

Huh? Stepping outside this monastery without your keys would be a complete pain in the ass.

"I thought it'd be something a bit more—" Shailene began.

"—impressive." Fay finished off the sentence.

"How hard can it be to break into this place?" Oliver asked casually.

If you think it'll be easy, you've never been part of a challenge, pal. I didn't know much about my fellow players' experience, but I'd broken into a few high-security buildings in my time. The New York Coven took the top spot in my breaking-and-entering Hall of Fame, and that had been a real pain.

"Who says we have to break in?" Melody approached the front

door and knocked. Everyone stared at her. Naturally, nothing happened. I liked her outside-the-box thinking, but that was a little too simple.

"What, you thought you could just knock, and they'd answer?" Shailene barked a cold laugh.

Melody reddened. "It was worth a try."

With knocking a no-go, the Basani twins hit the windows first, using a joint attack of powerful Telekinesis to try to wrench the glass from the frames. Oliver went back to scaling the wall, likely seeking a weak spot on the roof. Melody bombarded the front door with Air, while Luke sent twisting silver tendrils from his hand and grasped for the hinges of the front door. The filling in my back tooth started to tug weirdly, as if it wanted to pop right out.

Huh... interesting. Judging by the odd sensation, I guessed Luke to be a Magneton—a manipulator of metals. He'd be paying my dental bill if this baby came out.

Blanche, meanwhile, crouched in front of the side door on the monastery's left wall. A torrent of Water arced through the air and filtered into the lock. Her hands pulled outward, feeding in a strand of bright white Chaos alongside the liquid. I noticed a sheen of frost glitter up the wood of the door and realized she'd turned the water to ice.

It was a decent idea. One I wished I'd thought of, though I lacked the Ice abilities to make it work. Or, rather, the Glacier abilities—a sub-section of Water Elementals who could change the state of water. Ice, steam, the whole shebang.

Rodrigo used Melody's tactic, though he focused his Air powers on the windows, attempting to shatter the glass. I wanted the number of the glazier for this monastery, because those panes proved to be impenetrable.

Lin had scaled the wall alongside Oliver and now tried to take apart the chimney in order to slide down, like some kind of Puerto Rican Santa Claus. Giulia used Earth abilities to shake the foundations of the place—a riskier move, since it could mean breaking the whole building to pieces. Alessandra, on the other hand, used her Earth powers to dig, evidently taking inspiration from *The Great Escape*. I wondered if she'd still be tunneling by the time the rest of us got inside.

Only Mr. Abara and I hung back. He delved into his pocket and took out a pouch of cloth to reveal a small pile of charcoal. He tipped some into his hand and put the pouch back into his pocket. I tried not to stare, but it was hard not to. He closed his hands over the charcoal, and a blue glow shone beneath his palms. When he uncovered it, the charcoal was gone. In its place sat a brand new, sparkling diamond with one facet sharpened to a glinting point.

He's a Geode. Flashbacks to the Jubilee cavern rushed through my mind as I remembered the diamond floor Davin had shattered with his Dark magic. Ponce de Léon had been a Geode too, gifted with the ability to turn rocks and minerals into gemstones.

"Are you just going to watch?" Mr. Abara smirked.

"Huh? No, I'm just… uh… thinking through my approach," I replied hurriedly.

"Good, because nobody likes a slackah." He chuckled as he walked toward the monastery and stopped in front of the only ground floor window not under assault. I heard the toe-curling scrape of the diamond as it started to carve the glass.

Come on, Finch. Get your ass in gear! I wished I knew what this Etienne guy looked like. Perhaps the door accepted verified members of the monastery. I could've fooled the system by Shifting into the Frenchie. Instead, I'd have to rely on a bit of brute force.

Before I could try anything, though, the gemstones atop the monastery screeched again. Light bounced between them, the soft, constant thrum growing until it reached fever pitch. Just as it turned to an unbearable howl, a flood of light spilled across the entirety of the building, sending everyone flying backward. Oliver and Lin hurtled through the air, falling from the roof. The former landed with a thud on the very edge of the cliff, while Lin sailed right over it. The customary splash followed. He was out of the running.

"Lin Garcia and Alessandra Santos are both disqualified." Etienne's voice echoed out of nowhere. How he knew our names, I had no clue. Maybe the protective shield scanned us in some way as we entered. Worrying, *1984*-level stuff, and that made Etienne the Big Brother, watching our every move.

I hadn't even noticed the Brazilian woman disappear over the cliff, but since she was nowhere to be seen, I had to believe Etienne. This task looked easy, but it really wasn't, with those gemstones firing out an expulsion shield every minute or so.

Maybe if we break the gemstones, we'll be able to get in.

Looking pissed off, the Basani twins used Telekinesis to pull themselves up to the roof. Giulia followed them, no doubt wanting a slice of the Basani glory. As a trio, they hammered the gemstones with powerful waves of Telekinesis, Fire, and Earth, following my train of thought. I waited for the gems to break, but they seemed to be made of the same tough stuff as the windows. With every hit, they shimmered brighter, until that thrumming sound rose to a scream again.

The force of protective energy flung the three of them clean off the monastery as another blast surged over the building. The Basani twins lashed out with lassos of Telekinesis, using the strands to grip spires, stopping their descent toward the churning ocean. Giulia didn't have that power. The rest of us watched, no time to react, as she tumbled over the cliff and hit the water with a loud splash.

"Giulia D'Amanzo is disqualified," Etienne announced.

"We have to try to break through, in between those sirens," I said to the sisters. "When it's just a vibration, we're on green. When you hear it shriek, we're on red."

The Basani twins shot me a dirty look. "Stating the obvious there—" Shailene began.

"—genius," Fay added.

How did they do that? Seriously, it was like they had the same brain. The rumors about identical twins sharing powers appeared to be true. They both had a mix of Telekinesis and Fire, and they knew how to use them. I started to feel a bit sorry for the Purge beasts they'd come up against. Poor suckers wouldn't have stood a chance.

More determined than ever, everyone returned to their stations. Blanche kept trying to ice the side door into submission, Oliver took over the role of Santa Claus, Mr. Abara had gone back to his diamond scraping, the Basani twins took the track of gemstone annihilation, and Luke and Melody tried to force the main door with Magneton powers and blasts of Air.

The old adage had it right: the definition of insanity was doing the same thing over and over and expecting different results. Being the spectator had some benefit. Namely, it was obvious to me that none of the current approaches would work.

"We need to focus on one spot, all together!" I shouted above the incoming screech.

"Nice try. You just want us to do the hard work for you!" Oliver yelled back.

Mr. Abara offered a shrug as he carried on with his cutting, and it didn't look like the others had heard me.

"I'm serious! We need to—" I didn't get to finish, as the security protocols swept over the monastery and tossed everyone backward. Mr. Abara bore the brunt of it as an explosion surged out of the marks he'd made and hit him square in the chest. He careened past me, his body curved where the impact had struck him. A few more seconds and he'd be in the water, too.

I don't know if it was compassion or instinct, but my palms lifted on autopilot and tendrils of Telekinesis shot out, wrapping around Mr. Abara's torso. The wrench of his trajectory almost took me with him, but I managed to dig my heels into the soft earth and brace myself enough to keep my footing. As he dragged me closer to the edge, I fell back onto my butt and hauled on the tendrils with all my strength. Mr. Abara paused in midair, a look of surprise on his face. I yanked harder, bringing him back toward me, where he landed in a heap at my side.

"Thank you, Finch," he gasped. "That was a good thing you did just now."

I nodded, sweating. "No worries."

"I mean it." His face contorted, struggling with some buried emotion. "I can't lose this chance."

"Yeah, you and me both."

He got to his feet and held out his hand. I took it and let him drag me up, feeling how sandpapery rough his palm was—the hand of a guy who'd worked hard his entire life. I didn't know what this meant, exactly. Were we pals now? Either way, at least I'd helped the guy out. He clearly wanted into the monastery for a deeper reason than he let on. Everyone else's desires were about money and glory and long life, but I wasn't sure about Mr. Abara anymore. Maybe he had something else in mind. And I wouldn't find out unless we made it into that building.

As the sirens faded to a quiet vibration, everyone returned to their task with gusto, aside from Melody. She took a break and sat on the grass, panting hard. But Luke stepped things up a notch. His hands pressed right up against the door now, his Magneton abilities trying to bend and break every bit of metal that held the thing together. Just like the windows, the metalwork resisted, evidently laced with some kind of secret strength. A damp patch soaked the back of his shirt as he toiled. *Must be nice, having someone to do the heavy lifting.*

"We need to work together!" I yelled again. Maybe they'd listen to me now. I'd saved Mr. Abara—that had to give me some trustworthy points, right?

"Shove off, Finch." Oliver smirked. "Nobody's going to help you, you couch potato. You're on your own, the same as the rest of us."

Couch potato?! I'd started the day breaking into the Fountain of Youth and fighting the slimy blobfish, Davin Doncaster. I bet he couldn't say the same. I was running on empty already—I had no energy to waste here, trying to chip away at this monastery and hope for the best.

I tried to stay cool. "Working solo isn't going to get us inside! We need to find a weak spot and focus on it, TOGETHER!"

"They won't listen," Mr. Abara said. "People like this, they aren't used to working as a team. I would join you, but I understand their reluctance. We don't know the rules of the game. What if only one of us gets the chance to enter? It's not a risk any of us will take. Sorry, my man."

I watched him go, my exasperation rising. The spot on the window where he'd tried to carve out the glass had repaired itself, meaning he was back at square one. Etienne hadn't said anything about allowing only one person inside. He'd said, "otherwise none of you will get in." That suggested there was room for more than one student, but it'd be a waste of good air trying to explain that to the others.

I covered my ears as another siren went off, the screech threatening to burst my eardrums. Each new blast was worse than the last. This time, Luke got the full hit of the security measures. He shot backward like a bullet from a gun, heading right for disqualification.

Melody's head whipped around as he sailed away from her. She chanted something under her breath and lifted her palms. A rainbow of glittering Chaos spiraled out of her hands and splintered through the air. The moment the tendrils touched Luke, a pair of enormous, multicolored wings sprouted from his back. They flapped of their own accord, bringing Luke to a halt. He looked startled to find these new appendages sticking out of his shoulder blades. He craned wildly to get a good look at them. Before he could, they brought him back to earth. He landed delicately on the grass, the wings shrinking and falling away in a flutter of tiny feathers.

What the—? Where had that come from? I knew body manipulation spells existed, using the raw materials of magical flesh to add something, but they were notoriously hard to pull off. Especially viable ones that could make a person friggin' fly! Maybe it was the fact that Melody had a bodyguard, or the vibe she gave off, but I hadn't expected her to be formidable. She seemed the type of girl to need protection, not be the protector. What other tricks did she have up her fluffy sleeves?

"This is—"

"—ridiculous!" The twins threw a temper tantrum, now that things weren't going their way.

"We're famous magicals," Shailene complained.

"We *deserve* to be let in!" Fay scowled at the building. I imagined they were used to having the red carpet rolled out for them. *Welcome to the real world, kiddos.*

Oliver nodded. "Why isn't magic working? What kind of joke is this place?"

My mind cogs whirred as the others got back into it, giving the task all the brute force and magical attacks they possessed. They didn't understand. This was a puzzle, a riddle. If it was as simple as using impressive magic, then it wouldn't have been much of a game, now, would it?

I walked around the right side of the monastery and headed down the wall.

Rounding the corner, I noticed another door. Smaller than the main one, and less obvious than the side door Blanche had commandeered with her Ice tricks. Ivy that looked like it'd been growing there for centuries sprawled across it. The leaves were massive. I crouched and waited for inspiration to strike. It didn't look like anything special. Solid metal, with a narrow gap at the bottom and a thin outline where it fit into the doorframe. I'd seen a million doors like it.

I waited for the next siren to pass before I edged closer, then pushed aside the swathe of ivy to find the keyhole. Sticking my eye right up to the hole, I frowned. I should've been able to see right through into the room beyond. But something blocked my line of sight.

All of the doors only open from the inside...

I slammed my palms into the door, and something jostled slightly. It was a key. The business end of it, blocking the hole.

A shiver of excitement pulsed through me as I put my hand on the door and fed a thin tendril of Telekinesis into the hole. I waited for it to grasp the end of the key, feeling for that familiar tug. But it didn't come. My Telekinesis skirted right past the key, like oil and water repelling each other. Whatever had stopped the diamond from cutting the glass and the gemstones from breaking affected this keyhole, too. Magic wasn't an option in any way, shape, or form.

An idea came to me. I reached up for the largest ivy leaf I could find, about the size of a piece of paper, and pushed it through the narrow space under the door, right underneath the keyhole. Now, I needed something to poke the key with.

I spied a shrub nearby. I hurried toward it, then snapped off a twig and headed right back, jabbing the end into the hole. I wiggled it until the key loosened, then gave it a firm shove. Not too hard, not too soft. A true Goldilocks wiggle. The key fell and hit the ground—and hopefully the leaf—with a quiet *clink*.

A sound made me turn. Blanche stood at the corner of the monastery, watching with interest. I waited for her to say something, but she didn't. She just kept right on looking.

Didn't expect this curveball, huh? I had one of those faces, I supposed, that made strangers underestimate me. Then again, they didn't know I was a Merlin. If they did, maybe they'd have been a little more willing to listen to what I had to say. There was power in a name, but it wasn't always a good sort of power. My surname elicited both responses—good and bad—and, until I knew these folks better, I wouldn't give them the chance to make a kneejerk impression of me.

Feeling slightly pressured now that I had an audience, I tugged the leaf and pulled it out. I almost squealed at the sight of the key resting on the ivy. Blanche stared at me in disbelief. I resisted the urge to punch the air, or whoop, or gloat. After all, I still had to find out if the key worked.

Picking it up, I slotted it into the keyhole and turned it. The door clicked and opened wide, smooth as butter. I nearly lost control of my sphincter at the sight of a man looming in the doorway. The shock made me tumble backward and land awkwardly on the ground. My butt cheeks would definitely bruise.

Tall and impeccably dressed, with sweeping black hair and dark, beetle-like eyes, the man smiled down at me through thin lips.

"Félicitations, Monsieur," he said, his tone almost impressed. "You finally found your way in. Though I would have preferred you to be quicker." He lifted an orb of pure light to his mouth and spoke again, his voice amplified. "The riddle has been solved. All those who remain may enter through the back door."

I frowned. "How come they get to enter?" I didn't mind the likes of Mr. Abara, Blanche, Melody, and, to a lesser extent, Luke, coming in, but I would've preferred to leave Oliver and the Basani twins on the cliff. Their egos could've kept them company.

"This is a team exercise, and all have tried their best. If they have not fallen beyond the perimeter, then they are permitted entry. You would deny them that?"

"No, I guess not," I replied. After all of Oliver's harping on about doing the hard work for me, there was a bitter irony to this outcome. Oliver would be allowed in when I was the one to solve the puzzle. And I doubted I'd get any credit for it. Not from him, anyway.

The others rounded the corner and gaped at me.

"There's no way he—"

"—found the way in!" The Basani twins didn't pull any punches.

I smiled sweetly. "Actually, I did. You can send a thank you however you like—gift card, carrier pigeon, smoke signals."

"Fair play to you, mate." Oliver gave a respectful nod in my direction. "It's always the quiet ones you've got to watch out for, isn't it?"

Huh, whaddya know... I hadn't expected any congrats from him, and I didn't know how to accept them.

"Well done." Mr. Abara gave me another mighty clap on the back, almost dislodging a lung.

"Yes, well done, son. You've done us all a great favor today," Blanche added.

"How did you do it?" Melody stared at me in awe.

I shrugged. "I figured if magic couldn't cut it, we needed to use something a bit more old school. Nothing a twig and a leaf couldn't handle."

"Of course, because wood isn't conductive, especially not where magic is concerned. I suppose we've all come to rely on our Chaos, haven't we?" Melody nodded excitedly. "You must have a very sharp mind, Finch. You could see what we couldn't, though it seems so obvious now that you point it out. I feel like such an idiot."

"Hey, it took some time and observation, that's all. I'm sure someone else would've figured it out if I hadn't," I replied. Even though I'd seen Melody make wings sprout from Luke's back, there was something about her that inspired kindness. A childlike quality.

"No need to be—"

"—condescending," the Basani twins muttered, clearly bitter they hadn't done what I had.

"He's being nice," Blanche chided. "It's not a common trait these days."

I turned to Etienne. "What'll happen to the disqualified folks? They won't drown out there, will they?"

He shook his head. "Do not worry over them. There are boats waiting to return them to the mainland, though I suspect nothing will ease their disappointment." He gestured inside. "Shall we proceed? We've wasted enough time."

I led the way into the building and met the scent of spicy incense mingled with stale stone. Relief washed over me. Maybe I'd finally learn why Erebus sent me here.

FIVE

Finch

My jaw dropped as we edged into the belly of the monastery. It *felt* ancient, with its pristine white walls bordered by vivid blue and gold. Domed ceilings let in the fierce sunlight.

Everything looked like it'd been there for centuries. An artist had painted directly onto those pristine walls, the frames drawn right on the stone, and statues lined the hallways, crafted in the images of famous magical explorers and mapmakers. I recognized Ponce de Léon in the mix, with his pals Sir Walter Raleigh, Marco Polo, Leif Erikson, and Jacques Cartier keeping him company. Small golden plaques hung below the statues, introducing them.

Underneath the domes lay pseudo-courtyards with metal chairs and tables. Many had fountains in the center, water tumbling from a variety of mouths, jugs, and the like. The figures in the middle were easily recognizable as ancient Greek gods and goddesses, in various states of conflict and undress.

"Is it just me, or is it bigger on the inside?" Blanche whispered.

This place had the same effect as libraries and cathedrals—everyone slipped into a stifled hush.

I nodded. "It must be an interdimensional pocket."

"This is so exciting! I've read so much about this place," Melody gushed. "Apparently, there are hidden rooms and corridors all over, leading to secret and lost treasures." She paused. "Why do you suddenly feel apprehensive, Mr. Biset? Is one of your treasures in here? Or should I call you Monsieur Biset? My French isn't very good, so you'll have to forgive me if I butcher the pronunciation."

Etienne shot her a disapproving glance. "You should not poke your *nez* where it doesn't belong, Miss Winchester. I would have thought you of all people would know better, given your own history."

She'd clearly used her Empathy and let the words spill out without realizing she should probably keep quiet. Etienne didn't look pleased about having his emotions publicly ruminated over.

Melody blushed. "I'm sorry, Mr. Biset. I didn't mean anything by it. I have a problem with saying things I shouldn't, but I promise, I'm working on it."

Luke put his hand on her arm and sent a searing look in Etienne's direction. "It's okay, Melody. He knows you didn't mean any harm."

"Let this be your first lesson." Etienne pursed his lips. "This place is a sanctuary. No stealing. No lying. No cheating. And no poking your noses where they do not belong. Oh, and most importantly, no violence. It will not be tolerated, and you will be sent back to the mainland without hesitation." He addressed the last to me.

"Hey, I won't be hurting anyone. I only get violent in self-defense, and even then, as a last resort." Why did he single me out?

Luke, with all his bulging muscles, looked more likely to go ape on someone than I did.

"And why would anyone want to hurt you, Finch?" Etienne arched an eyebrow.

I shrugged. "Occupational hazard."

"Ah, you mean your association with Erebus?" he replied, taking me by surprise.

"Pardon?"

"Are you speaking of your association with Erebus? I know you were enlisted in his service. I imagine that comes with its fair share of difficulties." He eyed me curiously. *Ah, so you don't mind other people's secrets being uncovered.* I held my tongue. I didn't know this guy well enough yet to get smart with him.

"Uh… well, that tends to come with a few hairy moments, for sure." The others stared at me. "But here's a question for you—how come you know so much about us?"

"My defensive shield scans everyone who enters, and my monks are swift in their research," he replied. *I knew it!* "Now, back to you. Did Erebus send you here?" Etienne's voice hardened.

"No, this is all me." I knew I had to lie. "We parted ways after the last job I did for him. Deal done. I won't go into details, but you don't get much choice when it comes to Children of Chaos. They say jump, you say how high." I wished the ground would swallow me up. "Anyway, there's always a chance someone might pick a fight with me. Even if I'm not working for Erebus anymore, I wouldn't want to get soft, right?"

Melody gasped. "Wait… you're… Finch Shipton!"

"Merlin," I corrected. "I don't go by Shipton anymore. I'm sure it's not hard to understand why." I gave a nervous laugh. Everyone was really staring now.

"You're *that* Finch Merlin?" Shailene gawped.

Fay frowned. "I thought you'd be taller."

"Six foot isn't bad," I muttered.

"No way you're Katherine Shipton's son." Oliver shook his head in disbelief.

"Do you want a birth certificate?" I shot back.

Mr. Abara tilted his head to one side. "If you're him, then that means you killed Katherine."

"Exactly." Oliver snorted. "This can't be him."

"Do you want a *death* certificate?" These reactions made me uneasy. I didn't like talking about my dear old *madre* at the best of times, but revealing it all to a bunch of strangers amplified my paranoia. My mind gremlins were having a field day. *They're not going to like you after this.* I might've saved the world, along with my sister, but folks heard the name Shipton and everything that came with it, and I never made my way out of it looking rosy.

"You almost wrecked the San Diego Coven with a—"

"—horde of gargoyles, didn't you?" The Basani twins went on the offensive.

I held my nerve. "That was a long time ago, before my sister came along and made me see things differently. The cult brain-washed me before that. It's not an excuse, but it's the truth. I was exonerated for that after I killed Katherine."

"Have you told that to the people affected by your crimes?" Oliver narrowed his eyes.

"Hey, I've been on trial once. I don't need another one," I snapped. "I know I did wrong back then, and I've been trying to make amends for it ever since."

Mr. Abara took a step closer. I froze, terrified of what he might say.

"A man can only be judged by his efforts to change himself and the world he walks in," he said firmly. "If we judge a person on their past, none of us would appear innocent."

"Yeah, but not all of us have worked for the Cult of Eris," Oliver replied.

"Let he who is without sin cast the first stone." Mr. Abara looked to Oliver. "Is your conscience clear? Can you say you've never done anything you regret?"

He shrugged. "Like I said, I've never been part of a cult that tried to destroy the magical world."

"I *saved* the magical world!" Desperation bristled in my voice. If I ended up stuck in this place, the last thing I needed was a barrage of suspicion and hatred at every turn. I realized with a sinking feeling that the SDC had sheltered me from most of the skepticism surrounding my character and my role in Katherine's demise. And man, was this a hefty reality check.

"So you say." Shailene folded her arms across her chest at the same time as Fay. "Everyone knows you can't trust the media."

Fay nodded. "We weren't there. We don't know what went down in Elysium. We can only go by what the papers and the news say."

"Maybe you fell out of favor with your mother and wanted to take power yourself, not save the world," Oliver added to the triad of pressure. "I heard you worship Erebus. Maybe you killed Katherine for him."

My brain damn near exploded out of my head. "I'm no Erebus worshiper, and I definitely didn't kill Katherine for him. If I'd had my way, Erebus wouldn't have had anything to do with it." I took in a shaky breath, trying to stay calm. "I killed her because she threatened everything I care about. I didn't do it out of selfishness. You'd know that, if you knew what I gave up to make it happen."

"Your mother killed my husband for the Cult of Eris." Blanche's small voice cut through the rising heat of the conversation. Everyone went quiet. Blanche's face rippled to reveal a completely different woman. Still elderly, but more elegant and refined than the squat, overly made-up person I'd met. Her silvered hair was short and sleek, and her features carried a regal beauty that suggested she'd been a stunner in her prime. Cold blue eyes peered up at me.

"You're a Shapeshifter? Goodness, it seems everyone has their secrets, doesn't it?" Melody chimed in with a nervous giggle. "I wondered why I couldn't sense your emotions, but I've learned not to make assumptions about people. There might've been a number of reasons why I couldn't sense yours, though I ought to have used the principle of Occam's razor—the simplest explanation is usually the right one."

Blanche ignored her. "I don't like to show my true image when I first meet new people, but in this case, it's necessary. I don't suppose you recognize me, do you, Finch?"

"Should I?" I asked hesitantly.

"Don't you remember the people affected by your mother's murder spree?" Her entire demeanor had changed in a split second, and I wasn't just talking about her appearance. All her former friendliness had evaporated like a fart in a wind tunnel. Now, she looked at me the way the Muppet Babies had when I first left Purgatory. I always forgot that Harley had been the exception. She'd seen something in me that nobody else had. Evidently, these folks hadn't gotten the memo.

I'm good now... aren't I? Haven't I done enough? Besides, how could I tell Blanche that there were too many to remember? It would've sounded cold.

I cleared my throat. "I'm sorry for your loss, Blanche. But I'm not my mother. I'm nothing like her."

"The apple never falls far from the tree," Blanche retorted.

"This apple did." I knew it was pointless to think I could change her mind so quickly. How was it possible that one word, Shipton, could unravel all I'd done, and all the changes I'd made? It didn't seem fair. Would I always be tarred by my mother's psychotic brush?

"Let us save these conversations for later, shall we?" Etienne reentered the conversation, giving me a much-needed reprieve. "You must prepare for dinner this evening. I will show you to your quarters. Tomorrow, you begin the trials of map-making. Three more await you before you can hold a map of your own making in your hands. I hope you weren't disenchanted by the puzzle to gain entry, for it will only get more difficult from here on out."

I breathed a small sigh of relief. Four trials in total, with one down and three to go. It'd still be a rough journey, I imagined, but at least he wasn't hurling out twenty hoops to jump through.

"Wait, what was the point of the first trial?" I stopped Etienne before he could move off.

He smiled. "I am glad you had the sense to ask. It relates to the idea of Occam's Razor, that the simplest explanation is usually the correct one."

"But I knocked, and that didn't work," Melody interjected.

"Yes... perhaps not *that* simple." Etienne pressed on through the corridors, giving us no choice but to follow.

Mean Girls took the lead—Fay, Shailene, and Oliver—with Blanche keeping her distance from me. I trailed behind with Melody, Luke, and Mr. Abara, none of whom seemed keen to start a fresh chat about my past. I was grateful for the silence. My mind gremlins were making enough noise to last me until this entire thing was over.

Turning the corner into another labyrinth of hallways, I got the shock of my life. A monk in a blue-and-gold robe walked in the opposite direction, hands tucked into his sleeves. I'd always wondered if monks really did that. Now, I had my answer. He gave a nod to Etienne as he passed but didn't say a word to any of us. One thing was sure—he was definitely human.

"There are monks here? That's dope," Oliver said.

Etienne nodded. "This is a true monastery. They are here as a security measure and as caretakers. I don't trust magicals. I have seen too much, and encountered too many, to ever be able to do so. Humans are simpler. Humans are trustworthy."

Someone's got a chip on their shoulder. I wanted to ask why he didn't trust magicals, but after what happened with Blanche et al., I didn't feel like drawing attention.

Fortunately, I was shown to my room first. Maybe it was a prize for being the one to put the key in the lock. Etienne pushed open the door and gestured for me to enter. The room's beauty matched the rest of the monastery, with paintings of verdant landscapes and gods and goddesses plastering the walls. In the middle of the chamber stood a huge stone pillar, carved to resemble a Greek god. A circle of water surrounded the base, which had eerie statues clawing their way out, trying to grasp at the god in the center. I guessed the central statue represented Hades, and those clawing figures were the spirits of the Underworld.

Ah, the stuff of nightmares—perfect. I tried not to shudder, considering the rest of the room was so pretty. Greek writing filled the blank spaces between the paintings. My Ancient Greek was hella rusty. And my modern Greek wasn't much better.

"One of the monks will collect you for dinner," Etienne said, closing the door behind him.

I padded into the room and straight to the bed, sitting down on the surprisingly soft and oh-so-welcoming mattress. I desperately needed it after what I'd been through in the last twenty-four hours. I had a lot of questions, but they'd have to wait.

Must sleep... must rest... must ignore creepy-ass statue.

I had just lain down when said creepy statue vibrated. My eyes darted toward it. Was that supposed to happen? As I watched, the carved face started to move, and the limbs stretched out. I froze in fear.

"So, you managed to get in. Well done, boy!" Erebus's voice boomed out of Hades's mouth, the stone lips moving and everything.

My fear turned to anger. "You better watch who you're calling 'boy.'"

"And you had better watch your tone," Erebus-slash-Hades replied.

"You dumped me on a cliff, and you didn't give me a single bit of information about why! It's a friggin' miracle I'm not ripping your stone head off your stupid stone shoulders right now!" I got up and stalked toward the moving statue. "I'm hoping you've got answers for me. If you've just shown up to taunt me, you can pack it in. I'm not in the mood."

Erebus tutted. "Temper, temper."

"Yes, temper, temper." I glared at him. "How are you even doing this, anyway? Let me guess, Etienne's protective protocols are no match for the Great and Irritating Erebus?"

"It wasn't easy, but I couldn't leave you here without a line of communication. I need to know how you're progressing, so that I can—"

The statue stopped moving, then twisted in a different direction from its original state. Now, it sort of looked like Hades was running away from the creepy hands that reached for him. Something had clearly gone wrong. Likely, the monastery's magical defenses fought against this intrusion.

"Hello? Earth to Erebus, this is Houston, come in." I waited impatiently.

"I will have to figure out another way to communicate with you." Erebus's voice slipped out of Hades's lips. They moved slightly, as though buffering. His voice sounded stilted. "In the meantime, I suggest you get to work and make sure you learn all there is to know about magical map-making. You are not to leave here until you have succeeded in the trials."

"And how long will that take?" I pressed.

"As long as it takes."

"But what am I looking for? What is it I need to find with these maps? I need to know, okay, otherwise I won't know where to start!"

Hades's lips froze. "I… will… be in… touch… again."

"Don't you dare! Tell me what I'm looking for!"

"I… will… find another… way to… communicate." His voice sounded irritated.

"Erebus? Erebus, get back here!" I shouted, but he'd already left. The statue didn't move again.

It didn't make sense. A super-powerful Child of Chaos shouldn't have had any problem breaking through a couple protective defenses. It should've been, quite literally, Child's play. Yet, somehow, the spells had pushed him out.

Did this have something to do with his human body limiting him? I'd have to keep an eye on that, or I'd be stuck on this island forever, in this monastery, trying to learn a skill without any context whatsoever.

As far as Erebus's tasks went, this one was turning into a major headache.

SIX

Kenzie

Taking care of Mom had never been easy. I'd been juggling her needs and my line of work and trying to keep away from the authorities—human and magical—for years now. By now, it had become second nature. I could take it all in stride. Until things took a turn for the worse. This past year felt like ten.

Mom had always been a tough cookie. It used to be that, even through her memory fog, she'd have days or even weeks where she had clarity and knew who Inez and I were. Now, though… we were lucky if she recognized our faces for more than a couple of seconds. If that.

This wasn't Alzheimer's. My mom had a Voodoo curse, old and determined to suck the life out of her. I'd nicknamed it "the Vampire." Not to minimize it, but to cope. A monster was a physical thing—simpler to deal with than an untouchable curse I didn't know how to fix.

So far, nobody had been able to help. Finch's talisman hadn't worked. All the pills from the magical docs hadn't done a damn thing. Even Marie Laveau, badass Queen of Voodoo, had been stumped. Turns out, some things even an awesome, super-powerful sorceress didn't know. She'd told me she suspected the curse predated her, said she was sorry, and turned me out empty-handed. Watching Mom lose more and more of herself, going from total exhaustion and brain fog to flying into sudden bursts of rage and fear which came out of nowhere... sucked. And the changes in her state were near-impossible to predict.

I catalogued my latest batch of burner cells, lifted from here and there in San Diego, when Inez padded out of Mom's room. I looked up from the kitchen table. My little sis. Half my size but twice as ballsy. When she got older, she'd be a force to be reckoned with, that was for damn sure. But right then, she looked so freaking small and lost. I hated that, seeing her fire snuffed out.

"What's up, Nezzie?" I asked gently.

"Mom keeps calling me Rhiannon." Her little face scrunched up. That look, I knew well. She was trying not to cry. There'd be little crescents on the insides of her palms from her fingernails.

"Come sit down. You can help me put new SIMs into these, then put them in boxes." Work is the best way to take your mind off the bad stuff. I'd learned that early on. If I hadn't had my side hustle in stolen goods, I'd be on some kind of meds by now.

"Who's Rhiannon?" Inez bit her lip to stop its shaking.

Mom had called us every name under the sun. On the worst days, she didn't know us at all. She screamed and wailed and stared at us like we were strangers, demanding to know where she was and what we were doing there.

"She probably thinks you're Aunt Rhiannon."

Inez frowned. "We don't have an Aunt Rhiannon."

"She died when Mom was little. You're around the same age she was," I replied. I might've seemed cold, but my way of taking care of Inez involved tough love and constant distraction. We wouldn't make it otherwise. I couldn't appear weak when she needed strength.

I'd have done anything, given anything, to make things better. I'd been so sure about Marie. That letdown had round-housed me right in the gut, and I still hadn't recovered.

Inez got down to business, taking the new SIMs and slotting them into the burners. She'd helped me before. Don't get it twisted —I'd never let her get caught in the same underworld as me. But if putting a few SIM cards into some stolen phones could keep her mind off Mom, just for a while, that wasn't a bad thing in my book.

These cell phones kept us afloat. The local gangs always needed them, since the cops liked to scope out this neighborhood more than most. They were constantly being monitored, and I worked as their middle-woman. Simple supply and demand. Plus, it paid to make friends in shady places. I gave them a way to communicate; they kept me and my family safe. The gang leaders posted members on the street corners to make sure nobody bothered us. Some would even walk Inez to the bus stop when I had too much work to do it myself, so nobody got in her way or tried to hurt her. It made a pretty odd image—huge tattooed dudes flanking my little sis and holding her backpack for her.

Everyone had their shades of gray. If you looked closely enough, everyone had a reason for doing stuff others considered wrong. Most people weren't totally bad. The only person I'd ever met who I could truly mark down as one hundred percent evil was Katherine Shipton, but she'd gotten what she deserved.

"Actually, leave those, Nezzie. You're going to be late," I said, seeing the time on the nearest cell phone.

Inez pouted. "Can't I just stay home with you? Just once?"

"You want to live in this place all your life? You want to live in this neighborhood till you're old and gray?"

"No, but—"

"No buts. Get your ass to school. A real education will get you somewhere, Inez. If I let you stay home today, you'll ask again tomorrow. Sorry, Nezzie, it's not going to happen."

I got up and took her lunch bag off the counter. I shoved it into her hand and fetched her backpack, forcing it onto her shoulders. She'd huff the whole way to the bus stop, but once she got to school, it'd take her mind off home. I envied that. A break from this. Even thinking that way made me feel guilty, but hey, that's life. I'd dropped out to look after Mom. Inez had choices I didn't, and I wouldn't let her give up to be like me.

"Will you walk me?" Inez scuffed her way to the door.

I shook my head. "Diego and Crossbones will be on the corner. They'll take you." I nodded to the huge pile of burners. "I've got to sort through these by lunchtime."

"Will you be home tonight?" She peered up at me as I ushered her out the door. Damn those puppy-dog eyes.

"I'll try to be." I stooped to give her a kiss on the forehead. "Now go on, fill that mind with clever stuff so you can go and be a doctor or something, instead of shifting burner cells for the rest of your life. Or maybe a lawyer, so you can get me out of my messes."

She gave a reluctant smile before hurrying down the creaky stairway and out of the apartment building. That was the beauty of this derelict spot. I could hear every footstep in the empty hallways, and the rusty clang of the front door acted as a readymade alarm. I'd picked this joint for that exact reason. *Ain't nobody going to sneak up on me.*

Turning, I nearly jumped out of my skin. Mom stood in the doorway of her room, giving the apartment a blank-eyed stare. She looked like a ghost. Pale, dark circles under her eyes, her body thin like a baby bird. No matter how much I fed her, she stayed painfully skinny.

"Who are you?" Her words cut me like a knife. "Why are you in my house?"

"Mom, it's me. Kenzie." I stepped toward her, but she put up her fists. *Not now, Mom... please.*

"I don't know any Kenzie. Who are you?! What are you doing here?!" Panic edged her wavering voice. "I'm going to call the police!"

"Don't do that, Mom. I'm your daughter, Kenzie." I edged toward the landline, trying to block her way. She'd threatened this a thousand times, and it never got easier to handle. It wasn't her fault. She was scared. She thought some lowlife had come to rob her blind.

She shook her head wildly. "I don't have a daughter. Who are you?!"

I reached the house phone and opened the drawer beneath it, where I kept syringes of magical serum. A consequence of her almost making it to the phone about six months ago. I doubted the police would take kindly to an apartment full of stolen goods. I hated doing this to her, but the only way to calm her down was to use that serum to put her into a magical sleep. Krieger had given me a whole bunch, just in case. A sweetener to entice me to join the SDC, but this one I could get on board with.

I let Mom come closer. Risky but necessary. The voodoo curse had robbed her of magic, draining what was left of it this past year, or this would've been way harder. Once she reached me, her fists ready to give me a pummeling, I lunged forward and sank the syringe into her arm. It worked instantly, all those magical juices flowing. Mom sagged in my arms, the fight gone out of her. I held her tight to stop her from falling on her face and dragged her to the couch like a gangster trying to hide a body. As gently as possible, I lifted her limp limbs onto the cushions until she looked vaguely comfortable.

She's just sleeping. How many daughters had to plunge syringes into their moms like this? Every time, I tried not to shudder and break down. This shade of gray would never sit well with me. But it helped her, in more ways than one. Every time she woke up from a long, magical nap, she had a slightly better memory. A temporary reboot. It always got worse again, but those moments right after she woke up were some of the best we could hope for. I looked forward to them, in a weird way. It was like having my mom back, the way she used to be, even just for an hour or two.

I sank down on my haunches and looked at her. She looked peaceful. No fear, no pain, no confusion. If I'd been made of tougher stuff, I might've been able to let her go and wish for a higher power, or whatever, to take all her worries away. But I wasn't that strong. I wanted to keep my mom around as long as possible, even if it took away pieces of me. I could live with her calling me someone else's name, or not knowing me at all, as long as her heart kept beating. Maybe that was selfish. I didn't care.

Tears hit me. They didn't come often, and never around Inez. I kept them for the shower, usually, where they mixed with the water and nobody would be the wiser. This time, they came unscheduled. Sinking lower, I held my head in my hands and let the tears fall.

What else can I do? Would I keep stabbing her with needles? Would I watch as she wasted away into nothing? What if she never had a good day again? The bad days hurt Inez more than they hurt me, which messed me up even more. My sister just wanted her mom. I just wanted my mom. And she pulled further away from us with every passing day, every lapse. Big, ugly sobs wracked my chest, and I didn't fight them.

Maybe Harley's right.

Joining the SDC wouldn't just mean being under their watchful eye—it could be a safe haven. Years ago, I'd never have considered it, but covens had changed a lot since my mother's dealings with them. Everything had changed after the Katherine situation. Last time I'd visited the coven, Harley had suggested Mom might be better off in a controlled environment, under Krieger's constant care. And I was starting to agree.

I was gearing up to sob a little more when a knock exploded through the air. My head snapped up. Inez couldn't see me like this.

I got to my feet and smeared my eyes with the back of my baggy sleeves. Why had she come back? Had she forgotten something? If she kicked up another fuss about going to school, I didn't know if I'd be able to hack it. I didn't want to lay into her. That wouldn't be fair. But I'd reached my lowest freaking point. And I worried I might crack.

Still wiping my eyes, I went to the door and looked through the peephole. Ordinarily, I could see anyone there and the hallway behind them. Right then, I couldn't see anything, as if something blocked out the light completely. A sense of dread scurried up my spine like escaped ants.

"Who's there?" I demanded.

A soft chuckle filtered back. "My name is Erebus. I am the one person who can help your mother."

Erebus? Yeah, that definitely sent alarm bells ringing.

SEVEN

Kenzie

———————

"I'm waiting," Erebus said.

I rested one hand on the lock, the other reaching for the shotgun I kept by the door.

"How do I know you are who you say, huh? You could be a security magical!" I shouted back.

"I chose to knock, to be polite. I can break the door down if you prefer a display of power."

I grabbed the shotgun and put it behind my back. "Don't break it down. You think I've got money to burn repairing hinges?"

"Then let me in."

"Or what, you'll huff, and you'll puff, and you'll blow this house down?" I demanded.

"That is entirely up to you, Mackenzie," he replied.

How does he know who I am? I hadn't hung around in Elysium long enough to know this guy, or for him to know me, but I'd heard enough from Harley, Finch, and the others. This wasn't the type of guy to mess with. I'd have preferred police.

"All right, hang on a sec." I slid back the cluster of bolts. Keeping the top one on the chain, knowing it likely wouldn't make a difference, I peered into the hallway.

I expected a misty swarm of shadow. Instead, the most handsome dude I'd ever seen stood in front of me. I did a double take. This couldn't be Erebus. He had a body, for starters. An odd one, sure, but definitely solid. He wore a sharp, expensive suit of dark gray that hugged every carved muscle. His skin and eyes were unnaturally dark, but even so, I didn't believe Erebus stood in my doorway.

"Nice try, punk. Who are you?" I glared at him. "Erebus is some floaty wisp in an otherworld. He doesn't walk around on two feet, and definitely not on planet Earth." Had someone sent this guy? Someone who knew too much about me, trying to trick me? It wouldn't be the first time. Helping gangs came with risks, even though they did what they could to protect me.

"I'm still getting used to human form, if that makes you feel better." He smiled, his black eyes glinting. "But I *am* Erebus. And I can cure your mother, if you help me in return. A fair exchange."

"Fine, so what if you're Erebus? Back up, I mean it. I've got a shotgun, and I know how to use it."

He chuckled. "I knew you would be spirited. I'm pleased you aren't a disappointment, though be careful what you say to me. I like to be amused, but I don't care to be insulted. I am trying to aid you, and I'd hate for us to start off on the wrong foot."

"You shouldn't even have feet!" I raised my free hand, keeping the shotgun tucked behind me in the other. My Esprit—a plain silver thumb ring—glowed white as I brandished it in his face. The light vanished against his all-black eyes in the strangest way. As if he somehow sucked the light right into them. *Weird.* Children of

Chaos had a certain energy to them—a dangerous energy. And this guy emanated that energy by the bucketload.

"What are you going to do with that?" he taunted.

"Whatever I have to. Don't test me." I'd learned a few tricks from my mom before her illness. Magic worked better than a shotgun, though the end result was pretty similar: a stain on the back wall that'd be a nightmare to scrub off.

Erebus sighed. "Don't say you weren't warned." He touched the door with his jet-black hand. A moment later, it burst open, the chain vaporized. An invisible pulse sent me sailing across the living room, where I hit the back of the couch with a thud. The shotgun hurtled out of my hand and slid across the floor. Burner phones and SIM cards skittered off the kitchen table, the half-filled boxes tipped over by the blast.

My eyes shot up as Erebus stepped in. "Cheers for that, asshole! Now I'll have to sort them all again. I'm on a deadline, you tool!"

Tendrils shot out of his hands and grasped me around the waist. They lifted me and put me back on my feet.

"I did try to give you a choice," he said.

"Like I'm going to trust some dude I don't know? Look at the neighborhood you're in. I meet everyone at the door with a shotgun and a warning. What, you think 'cause you rock up in a fancy suit, that gives you the right to bust people's doors open and do what you like? Unbelievable!"

He smirked. "I'll help you put all your pilfered goods back into their correct boxes. But first, how about we discuss my proposition?"

"Take a hike, dickweed," I spat.

His expression darkened. "What did I say about insults?" He tutted loudly. "Either you help me willingly, and I assist in curing your mother, or I *make* you help me, and you get nothing in return.

Be smart, Mackenzie. I may have a human body, but I am still Darkness incarnate. And you do not provoke Darkness. You obey it."

"I bet you say that to all the girls." It took all my courage to give him a bit of backtalk. Honestly, I was crapping myself. I'd dealt with every breed of thug around, and none had struck fear in me like this guy. Mainly because he wasn't all talk, like thugs were. I believed every word Erebus said. I knew I shouldn't disrespect him. Just looking into those eyes told me that danger stood right in front of me.

"Only the ones who struggle to understand the situation they are in," he replied casually. Even his calm oozed menace. I felt it, right in the pit of my chest. That same instinct made people walk a different way at night or lock their car doors at an intersection.

"Why me? Don't say you're feeling generous. I know enough about you. That ain't your style." I fought against the tendrils that held me, but they gripped tighter. A bit tighter, and he'd choke the air right out of me.

He grinned. "Why not you?"

"Because, unless you're in the market for a stolen cellphone, there's not much I can do for you. Are you getting the human itch to go digital? Is that it?"

"You must agree first. Then, I will give you the details of our potential arrangement. I assure you, it has nothing to do with contraband."

I frowned. "How's that fair? Who enters a deal without knowing the details?"

He laughed sharply. "Finch, for one."

"But you had him against the ropes. Finch had to say yes or lose the chance to kill Katherine and save the freaking world. As far as I can tell, you're not giving me any stakes that high." I paused. "Is this something to do with him?"

"Your mother's life isn't a high enough stake for you?" He landed another killer truth bomb. "That does surprise me. As for what you will help me with—as I said, that will have to wait until I have your agreement... or your disagreement. It makes little difference to me. It is less effort if I don't have to do anything in return, but I like to give the option."

I wriggled against his Telekinetic restraints. He watched me strain, an irritating smirk on his lips. He enjoyed his power. People who had it normally did. It annoyed me that he'd managed to put me in this position. I always had an escape route. Always. Then again, I usually knew when I put myself at risk, and prepared for it. He'd come out of left field and taken me by surprise.

He squeezed the tendrils a little tighter. My ribcage ached under the pressure. I had no clue whether he'd kill me. If he wanted me for something, maybe not. But Children of Chaos were temperamental suckers. A dead human meant nothing to them. They wouldn't lose sleep thinking about the families left to cope without those humans. *And he is offering me an olive branch...* a really tempting one.

"Can you really cure my mom?" I needed to know. I'd made a song and dance about doing anything and everything to fix my mom's illness. If I didn't, when the chance lay in front of me, that'd make me a hypocrite.

He nodded. "Help me, and I will help her. Resist me, and you'll help me, while still watching your mother suffer. Surely, the choice is simple? But you mortals are very peculiar, so perhaps not."

There is no choice... Save Mom or don't. That was it, in a nutshell.

I took a breath, pushing against the tendrils. "Fine. I'll help you."

He let me go, to the relief of my gasping lungs. "I am pleased to hear it. I have learned that one catches more flies with honey, so, in return for your willingness to assist me in these matters, I will look over your mother's condition and create a course of action to heal her. As promised. Voodoo curses are treacherous beasts, especially the ancient variety, but I have yet to come across a curse I could not untangle."

He seemed serious, but my wariness turned up to eleven. As he stepped toward the couch, I blocked his path.

"Can't you assess her from a distance, since you're so powerful and all?" I didn't trust him around Mom. I didn't trust him, period, but my mom and my sister made up my entire world. Nobody got near them without my say-so.

He raised an eyebrow at me. A weird image—Erebus with eyebrows. "Do you want me to help her, or is this you saying you prefer to work for free?"

"Fair point." I resisted the urge to call him something rude. He'd warned me about insults, and I didn't want to test that again. My ribcage couldn't take another squeezing.

I held it together as Erebus walked around the couch to my mom. He knelt beside her, and his hands moved up and down inches from her body. Black fumes seeped from his palms, spilling over Mom's sleeping form. If he woke her up, I'd jab him in the back of the head. But, for now, all I could do was watch and wait. Two of my least favorite activities.

I focused on him instead. "Perfect" sprang to mind. His face looked so symmetrical it seemed fake. Every feature could've been carved out of stone and I wouldn't have questioned it. A jaw and a set of cheekbones that could slice a whole fruit salad, a strong nose, strong brow, strong everything. So right it looked wrong, close up. And that Dark energy… it added a razor-sharp edge to him that sent shivers down my spine whenever he caught me staring.

Has he always been able to cross into the real world? If memory served, Children of Chaos couldn't. I didn't know how he'd nabbed this human body. Had he gone down the same route as Katherine, or done something new? No idea. But only Erebus could've made humanity look so terrifying.

"Have you let Finch go? Is that why you're here, harassing me instead?" I broke the silence.

"No."

"Will you ever let him go?" Finch and I hadn't spoken much this past year, but I still considered him a friend. One of my only friends, in fact. Erebus must be up to some shady business, and I didn't want Finch getting hurt in the process.

He chuckled. "Maybe."

"Maybe? How can you say that, after what you just said about sticking to your end of the bargain?"

"You don't know the terms of our agreement," Erebus replied.

"What are you using him for?" I pressed.

"That is for me to know. You need only concern yourself with your deal, not his."

I sighed, frustrated. "Is this human get-up part of your plan? You're not taking over the world, are you? We've already been there, done that, got the T-shirt."

He paused and glanced at me. He didn't look amused. "My human form is part of a personal endeavor, and I have no interest in enslaving mortals."

"What's the 'personal endeavor' then?"

"Personal." His voice bristled with warning. *Time to shut up.* "I have set pieces in motion, and they do not threaten your world, so I suggest you stop asking."

"Am I one of those pieces?"

A creepy smile curved his lips. "You, my dear Mackenzie, are an extremely important piece."

"No one calls me Mackenzie," I shot back.

"As you prefer. I find nicknames crass, that's all." He looked back down at my mom. "By the way, I know how to cure your dear mother."

"You do?" My eyes flew wide, my heart ready to burst. "How?"

"We need to find the one who cast this spell on her."

My jaw hit the floor. An answer... a real freaking answer. It didn't sound like it would be easy, but to hell with easy. I'd walk through Hell itself to save her. Now that Erebus had given me a sliver of hope, I planned to cling to that sucker until we lifted this damn curse altogether.

Do you hear that, Mom? We're getting you out of this. We're getting you out of this!

EIGHT

Kenzie

"Where do we go, what do we do, and who do we talk to so we can get this thing out of her?" I jumped right in. If Mom could be cured, why wait around?

Erebus stood up. "Patience, Kenzie."

"Screw patience. You obviously know how long I've waited for this chance to come along, or you wouldn't have used it to lure me into your deal," I countered.

He folded his arms across his chest, his suit sleeves straining over bulging muscles. "This is no quick task. *You* obviously know that, given how long you have waited for answers. The curse upon her is an ancient, and very well disguised, blood magic curse. You would be hard pressed to find any book, in any library, that contained word of it."

My shock and excitement faded. "Wait, none of this makes any sense."

"How so?"

"Marie Laveau figured it predated her, so the ancient part

makes sense. But why didn't she suggest finding the person who cursed my mom? If it's that straightforward, it doesn't make sense that she never considered it."

Erebus smirked. "There is a great deal about Voodoo that not even Marie Laveau knows. With this particular curse being so well-concealed and ancient in its craftsmanship, she likely suspected a spirit had placed it upon your mother. There would be no use trailing after such an entity, as it would require complicated Necromancy and other difficult magic. A nigh-impossible task."

"You don't think a spirit did this?"

He shook his head. "I know they didn't. I can feel the pulse of life incorporated within the curse. Marie Laveau's Voodoo skills are exemplary, but the 'signature,' if you will, is buried deep, and you must know what you seek. Fortunately, I do."

"I thought you did djinn magic, not Voodoo." I cocked my head at him, beginning to believe him.

"As Voodoo tends to err on the side of Darkness, in terms of magical balance, it is my duty to know it. As such, I have gained all the secrets of this dark craft, from its very inception to the present day."

"Is blood magic the same as Voodoo magic?"

"It is a branch of the same tree. This curse settled on your mother many years ago, likely when you were eight or nine." He gave me a black stare. "Do you remember anyone coming to the house during that time?"

"That can't be right. You must have your calculations muddled, bud."

He arched an eyebrow. "Pardon?"

"That can't be right. My dad was still alive then, and she only went downhill after he died."

My dad had died in Iraq. A United Magicals peacekeeper, he'd stood in the wrong place at the wrong time. Bullets don't care what color you're wearing.

"I assure you, I am not mistaken." Erebus tapped his sharp jaw in thought. "Perhaps you should think of the curse as a slow-working poison, or a cancerous disease. The first symptoms are not immediately obvious, and it can be years before the victim realizes something is wrong. By then, it is usually too late to avoid it. The curse grows stronger with time, sapping more and more strength. The longer it remains, the harder it is to remove."

"But you *can* remove it, right?" I gave him a hard glare. If I'd gotten into this deal for nothing, I'd start firing off shotgun rounds like there was no tomorrow.

"Oh, yes. Have no fear."

Easy for you to say... you're not face-to-face with a human-Child of Chaos hybrid.

"I'll ask again, since you seem easily distracted: Do you recall anyone coming to the house back then?"

I dug deep but came up blank. "We didn't live here then, so it's hard to remember. A lot of my childhood is a blur, with my dad and everything. I need time to think back that far."

"Human memory is such a weak vessel." He scoffed.

I shrugged. "We can't all have big cosmic brains." I sifted through my memories, but one thought kept pushing through. "How come the curse couldn't be detected? A few people looked over her, and they found zilch. Marie wasn't even one hundred percent sure it was Voodoo by the time she finished. It ended up being more of a fifty-fifty situation. I know you said she doesn't know everything, but she must know the feel of a Voodoo curse, right?"

"The individual who crafted this must be a remarkable scholar of ancient blood magic, which is a different branch of the tree of

Voodoo than we know today. The only people who still study and utilize this sort of Voodoo reside in the heart of Africa, in isolated tribes that most people don't even know exist."

"So, are we going to Africa?"

Erebus shrugged. "That depends on where the spellcaster is. They may have left Africa. But, I must reiterate, only they can reverse this curse."

"Why can't you do it, if you're so high and mighty, and you claim to know everything?"

He sneered. "That is none of your business."

"I'd say it is, since I'm your pocket slave."

"This is extremely powerful and complex Voodoo. Its name is 'Death of the Soul.' Going straight to the source is the option with the smallest risk to the victim." He smiled eerily. "Besides, I imagine you want closure, don't you? Do you not wish to look upon the person who did this, and ask them why?"

I looked down at Mom. Since finding out it was a Voodoo curse, not Alzheimer's, that'd been all I could think about. "Yeah... I do." And I'd be taking my shotgun with me, plus a few dynamite spells.

"How does this sound—I will go so far as to help you find the person, on the proviso that you start working for me immediately afterward."

"Are you going to string me along, like you've been doing with Finch?" I still didn't like that. Finch didn't deserve what Erebus put him through.

Erebus laughed darkly. "I only need you for one project, so you need not worry about ending up in the same predicament as Finch. He didn't read the fine print, so to speak. But, for you, I will clarify the length of your service and seal it with an unbreakable blood pact."

"No tricks?"

"No tricks," he replied firmly.

Why don't I believe you? "Fine. Help me get this worm and cure my mom, and I will help you on *one* project."

"Excellent." He wafted his hand through the air and formed a dagger of pure black. I pulled a face as he drew it across his palm. Blood didn't bother me, but I didn't know what would ooze out of him. To my shock, it did look like blood, just darker. On my turn, I held out my palm and let him cut it. It didn't hurt. More magic, probably. With our bleeding hands clasped, he gave me a firm handshake.

"Is that it?" I shook back as hard as I could. His hand felt like a block of ice, cold and smooth and burning at the same time. Sparks of something like electricity stung up into my palm. It made giving a decent handshake pretty tough, but I held on to the bitter end.

"Yes. The deal is sealed. One project in exchange for helping you. Then you walk free."

I eyed him. "Do I get to know what the details are now?"

"It has to do with Finch's current endeavor on my behalf," he replied. "That is all you need to know for the time being."

"You want to throw me a bigger bone there?"

He grinned. "No."

What have I gotten myself into? Erebus had sworn no tricks. But he was a game-player, a master manipulator, through and through. He clearly liked to drop breadcrumbs without giving the whole loaf. I'd have to be very careful.

I still felt I was doing the right thing. By doing this, I could save Mom. My sister could get her mom back. I didn't care about the cost of making that happen.

NINE

Finch

If you could have dinner with anyone, alive or dead, who would you pick?

Talk show hosts always asked that question, and none of the people sitting around this table would've made my list. No offense, but I liked my food with a side of glittering conversation and a few good laughs, instead of an entrée of cold stares and a smattering of suspicion. Melody and Mr. Abara didn't give me any stink-eye, but Luke seemed to have joined the "let's all hate on Finch because he was squeezed out by a monster and is clearly exactly like her" party.

I'd retreated into one of my rarer coping mechanisms—keeping my head down and keeping my trap shut. No jokes. Even when Oliver started going on about his life-changing backpacking experiences in Thailand, I resisted, though I doubted he'd done more than drink cheap beer and lounge around on beaches annoying the locals.

The food, though. *Damn.*

Stuffing every tasty creation into my mouth would have kept me quiet, even if silent judgment hadn't surrounded me. Delicious courses came one after the other, never too heavy. An herby salad with citrus dressing. Moussaka so fluffy it melted on my tongue. Fresh olive bread with fava and tzatziki. Squares of baklava marinated in raw honey. My mouth watered like I had a serious problem with my saliva glands.

All of it had come from the monastery's farm, apparently somewhere inside this huge interdimensional pocket. The courses were served by the human monks, who looked pretty pleased that they had folks to entertain. Perhaps they thought it beat prayer and flagellation, though maybe they weren't that kind of monk.

This is the life. Things felt simple here. I liked simple. It marked a nice change from the hectic pace of the past year. Man, did I deserve a breather.

We all sat at a wooden table on a terrace that hadn't been visible from the outside, with potted lemon trees in full fruit around us and the sunset putting on its prettiest performance. Even the air smelled different here. Cleaner, crisper, filled with the warming scents of citrus and herbs.

"I thought we might take a brief repose until the next course," Etienne said. He sat at the head of the table. Naturally.

"Sounds good to me. I'm about to bust out of my jeans." I broke my silence and gave my swollen tum a rub. "Hey, is that why you wear those robes? No waistline to worry about? I might need one of those soon." I looked at one of the monks clearing plates, but he just gave me a puzzled frown.

Etienne smirked. "Not all the monks speak English, Finch."

"Right." The burn of judgmental eyes hit me again, and my skin prickled.

"Thank you for this generosity." Mr. Abara gave a gracious nod. *Why couldn't I have said that?*

"It is part of the service," Etienne replied. "Aspiring minds must be well-nourished."

"Reminds me of a feast I had in Nepal, before I trekked to Everest base camp," Oliver chimed in. "Course after course, all of it so traditional."

"You climbed to Everest base camp?" Melody looked at Oliver in awe. "Isn't that supposed to be one of the toughest challenges a person can undertake? Was it dangerous? Goodness, how did you handle the altitude?"

He shrugged. "I planned to trek to base camp, but the instructors said my level of expertise was too high for the rest of the group I was with, so they made me stay behind. They didn't want to lower morale, or make the others think they weren't doing well enough. I'll go back one day, though."

I snorted. *Yeah, good one.*

"Something funny?" Oliver glared at me.

"Just a stray piece of bread." I banged on my chest to play up the ruse.

He smiled coolly. "Didn't your mother teach you to chew your food properly?"

I'd had enough of this dingus. "You know what, she didn't. Too busy crushing my spirit. She wanted me so broken that I'd obey her without question. Did your mother ever lock you in a room with a Tarasque on your seventeenth birthday, while it filled slowly with water? Oh, and have that be your so-called present?" I took a deep sip from my glass. "You don't want to know what she did for my eighteenth. There isn't enough therapy in the world for that particular treat."

Oliver sat in stunned silence. *That's more like it.* I took a sly glance at Blanche to see if my tale had softened her up at all, but she refused to look at me. It would take more than one sob story to prove to her I wasn't my mother. All the secondhand apologies in the world wouldn't bring her husband back. Sometimes I felt Katherine had gotten off lightly. She'd died at my hand and escaped trial for all the evil things she'd done. Instead, I seemed to be doing that for her.

"Actually, we fought a Tarasque in France a few years back," Shailene said proudly.

Fay nodded. "They're nothing to write home about. Tough shells, but once you get through that—"

"—they're a piece of cake," Shailene added.

"Yeah, and we were about seventeen." Fay smiled smugly. "That thing is in the Bestiary now."

"No hassle whatsoever." Shailene finished the jibe. A beautiful, savage, arrogant tag team.

I sank back in my chair and clutched my glass for dear life. No matter what I said, I set myself up to fail. Getting us inside hadn't bought me any brownie points. In fact, nobody had mentioned it since, and the Shining Twins acted like it was their divine right to sit there. As if their useless battering of gemstones had been the key, rather than, you know, the actual key.

"Let's start afresh, shall we?" Etienne came in as peacekeeper, no doubt feeling guilty that he'd lit this fuse. "Why don't we go around the table and you introduce yourselves: your abilities, where you come from, etcetera, etcetera?"

"Well, as you already know, we're—"

"—famed monster hunters." The Basani twins jumped straight in, even though they sat in the middle of the bench opposite and nowhere near Etienne.

"We've been traveling the world since we were sixteen, capturing—"

"—all kinds of Purge beasts. Big, small, aggressive, treacherous." Fay beamed at her sister.

"Our names are in the Sydney Coven's Hall of Fame," Shailene went on.

Fay nodded. "We're the youngest to be inducted, and definitely the most impressive. We've got some grisly creatures in Australia, and I'm not talking about the—"

"—spiders and snakes. There are insanely dangerous Purge beasts in Australia, and we've put at least one of each into the Bestiary. Both of us have Telekinetic and Fire powers to help us do it." Shailene gave her sister a nudge, the two of them soaking up the admiration. Not that they got any from me. Their exploits would have been cool, but their arrogance made it impossible to give them any kind of credit. *They need some humble pie for dessert.*

"You said you put ten percent of all beasts into the Bestiary?" I couldn't help myself. A garnish of pettiness would taste so sweet right now.

The twins shot me a withering look, both barrels. "Yes."

"I'll take a look when I'm back at the SDC. I'd love to see the creatures you've captured. Tobe will know which ones came from you. That dude has a brain like an encyclopedia, and he's a good pal of mine. Should be interesting." I smiled sweetly. *Name drop, biatches!* I didn't doubt their skill, but I smelled BS. The BS of embellishment.

They exchanged a glance. "You do that," Shailene muttered.

"Yeah, knock yourself out." Fay's lips curved in a scowl. Maybe she literally wanted me to knock myself out.

"You know Tobe?" Melody shrieked. "That's incredible! Is he as fearsome as everyone says? What about his wings—does he have wings? I would love to meet him one day. Can you imagine what it must be like to live for over a thousand years? How does he feel about that? Have you ever asked him?"

I chuckled. "Whoa there, one question at a time. I'm nursing the start of a food coma here, so I'm a little slow."

She giggled shyly. "Sorry, force of habit."

"He's definitely not fearsome, unless you piss him off. *Then* he gets scary, but most of the time he's a big pussycat. With wings. Big ones. He keeps things in them, like Mary Poppins. Anything you might want, he'll probably have, tucked up there somewhere. As for living that long—he doesn't talk about it much, but I don't reckon it's easy. He's had to watch everyone he loves die and start over, time and time again."

"I'd love to talk to him." Melody sighed.

"He'd probably be down to talk to you, too."

"Why don't you go next, Melody?" Etienne prompted.

Melody's expression quickly changed. Like an eccentric, fluffy tortoise, she retreated into her shell. I guessed she didn't like having the spotlight in larger groups. She probably ran a higher risk of saying something she shouldn't.

She shrugged. "There's not much to say. I'm from the Winchester family. I live in the so-called Winchester Mystery House. I have ties to the San Jose Coven, but I've never visited it. As I said before, I've been homeschooled my whole life, and I suppose I don't get out much." She gave an uncomfortable laugh. "I like to read. I like to learn. And… uh… I have Air and Empath abilities."

"What about those Technicolor wings you gave Luke?" I cast Luke a sly glance. "He looked like the lovechild of an angel and a unicorn."

Melody shifted awkwardly. "Uh… I know a lot of specialist

spells. Transformative ones, mainly. I'm not as good with them as I am with my natural abilities, but I suppose practice makes perfect."

"Give us a show—tell me what I'm feeling," Oliver urged, glossing right over her spell skillset.

She shook her head. "I don't think that would be a good idea. I don't want to slip up like I did before." She nodded to Etienne. "I'm sorry. Sometimes, I forget not everyone has Empathy. The words just come tumbling out before I even know what I've said."

"We all make mistakes," Etienne said, with surprising kindness. Melody's endearing quality seemed to affect him, too. *Yeah, no kidding, you called me out about ten seconds after Melody called you out. Hypocrite.*

"No, go on. Color me intrigued," Oliver insisted.

"Are you sure?" She hesitated and glanced at Luke, who shrugged. It was Oliver's funeral.

"Yes, I'm sure." Oliver sat back and smiled. He evidently hadn't come up against an Empath before. He probably thought himself impervious.

Oh... this will be good.

Melody took a shaky breath. "You keep thinking about the Basani twins. There's all this desire coming off you whenever you look at them. A bit of fear, too. They don't seem to like you, though, so you might be barking up the wrong tree. They feel suspicion and anger toward you. Mr. Abara feels sad and frustrated about something and isn't feeling very comfortable right now. I won't read Etienne in case I say something bad. And... I can't read Finch or Blanche."

Oliver's cheeks turned beet red, while the Basani twins stuck to their nonchalance. But Melody's words about Mr. Abara sparked my curiosity. He didn't look sad. He must be good at hiding it.

"Luke, why don't you tell us about yourself?" Etienne ended the awkward silence.

"Me?" He pointed at his chest. "I'm here to look after Melody. I've worked in her family's service for just over a year. That's it."

Melody nodded. "He's a Magneton."

"Bending spoons like a magician?" I grinned at him and got nothing back. *Tough crowd.*

"There's more to it than that," he replied, unamused.

"I know, I almost lost a filling before." I rubbed my cheek to emphasize the point.

Oliver nodded and tugged on his ear. "And my piercings. Hey, if I threw a fork at you, would it stick?"

He frowned. "What are you talking about?"

"Does metal stick to you?" I parroted.

"It doesn't work like that," Luke muttered. "Don't even think about trying it. I don't want strangers throwing cutlery at my face. I'm not a sideshow."

"Ah, come on. Melody showed us what she can do. Let's see what you can do." I picked up my fork.

Oliver grinned. "Yeah, mate, you know you want to. Just give it a little bend, or make it dangle from your nose. Anyone can do it with a spoon, but I've never seen anyone do it with a fork."

Luke glowered at us both. "I'm not a performing monkey."

I lifted the fork, and the prongs curled over as Chaos spiraled from Luke's hands.

"I mean it," Luke hissed. "Come any closer with that, and you'll need a surgeon to get it out."

Wide-eyed, I sat back in my chair. "Just trying to create a little dinnertime entertainment."

"He doesn't feel comfortable with an audience," Melody said. "That's why I always do most of the talking, isn't it, Luke?"

His expression softened. "Yeah, that's right."

"Even though it always gets me in trouble. I suppose it would be more useful if I had metal in my lips, so he could snap them shut when I ramble." She giggled and touched his arm, soothing the beast.

"I'd never do that," Luke replied quietly.

Mr. Abara's voice thundered across the table. "I come from Nigeria, and I'm a Geode."

This began to feel like Magicals Anonymous. The tension shattered, everyone's focus turning to the mysterious man. He had that effect on people. When Mr. Abara spoke, everyone listened.

He took out his pouch of charcoal and poured a small amount into his palm. He stowed the pouch away, then pressed his palms together, Chaos sparkling. He drew his top hand away to reveal a tiny, perfect diamond. A gasp echoed across the table.

"This is what I meant by dinnertime entertainment!" I exclaimed.

"Whoa. That's huge, man." Oliver's eyes bugged greedily. "I bet you've never been short a quid or two, if you can do that!"

"I don't use it for personal gain." Mr. Abara shot him a disapproving look.

I stared at the diamond in his hand. It reminded me of the Jubilee mine, the diamond floor, and Saskia and Garrett. *I hope they're okay.* More than that, I hoped they weren't panicking about me going AWOL. Harley would be going out of her mind, if they'd told her.

"Can we have it?" Shailene asked Mr. Abara.

He shook his head and turned the diamond back into charcoal. "No."

"What do you do with them, once you've made them?" Fay piped up.

"That is my business," he replied. Nobody dared question him further.

"Blanche, why don't you tell us about yourself?" Etienne moved the conversation along smoothly. I wondered what he'd seen at this table over the years. His skill at navigating potential hiccups suggested we weren't the first unruly crew he'd met.

Blanche set down her glass. "I come from the Kansas Coven, and I'm a Shapeshifter with Water and Glacier abilities." Without prompt, her skin rippled. She turned into Mr. Abara first, then Etienne, before returning to herself. "With Shapeshiftin', the skill changes as you age. It becomes more difficult to turn into people who are considerably younger, which is why I'm not gonna try and turn into some of you young'uns. It takes a toll on this here body."

"Fascinating," Melody said. "I didn't know that about Shapeshifters."

"It's not well known," Blanche replied. "There's a group of us oldies in Kansas, and we used to go dancin' all the time. Well into my forties, I could Shift into a younger figure. One night, we went out and Shifted into slim slips of girls. We wanted to relive a bit of our youth, and my goodness, we were the life and soul. All of those young studs buying us drinks and wanting to take us for a whirl on the dancefloor. We were all married, so nothin' untoward, I might add. Just dancin'. After a few too many wine coolers, one of my friends got stuck halfway between her true form and the one she'd Shifted into. The lovely man she was with—you should have seen his face! I do believe he screamed, staring at this Franken-woman."

A chuckle rippled around the table.

"We didn't try again after that, but we still talk about it." Blanche smiled wistfully. "They keep me grounded these days. My husband and I used to Shift once a year, as an anniversary treat, so we could be young and in love again, but... well, he died almost three years ago. 'Died' is perhaps too soft a word. Katherine had him killed. He had skill as a Necromancer, as well as a Shapeshifter. She took him captive in the middle of the night, as I slept beside him, and... I never saw him again. I received a note through the door, a few weeks later, written in Katherine's hand. It said he'd resisted her, and he wouldn't be comin' back."

My stomach, with all that lovely food, sank. *Did her husband botch Grandpa Prune's resurrection?* She hadn't allowed me in to see Drake Shipton's body, but I took a peek when Katherine thought I was elsewhere. The timeline fit.

Blanche stared at me. All her pain hurtled right at my heart. She wanted to blame someone, and since Katherine was dead, I was the next best thing.

"Oliver?" Etienne prompted.

"I'm from Cornwall, though I'm technically part of the Jersey Coven, in the Channel Islands. There isn't much choice in the UK, unfortunately. If you're English, you're usually part of London or the Cumbria Coven. If you're Welsh, it's the Cardiff Coven. If you're Scottish, it's Edinburgh or Stornoway. If you're Northern Irish, it's Belfast." He sat up straighter, now that he had the group's focus. "I have Air abilities, that's it. I've studied, though, learning as much as I can about spells and hexes to boost what I've got. It's part of the reason I've traveled so extensively. Plus, I'm persistent. A British Bulldog, if you like."

Pfft, more of a Cornish Chihuahua.

"That is what I appreciate about your sort of magical," Etienne said. Oliver had somehow won the big man over. "Now, Finch, why don't you tell us about yourself?"

"I didn't think Oliver had finished," I protested.

"Nah, mate, I'm done. That's all there is to me," Oliver replied. "Let's hear what you're about."

I had two potential paths ahead of me. Be vague and earn more suspicion, or come out with it, warts and all. I might have feared their reaction, but when I looked at Blanche, I knew I had to try again. The only way to wash off the stink of Katherine was to cleanse myself, and that required a bit of a confessional. Where better to do that than a monastery?

Hold onto your robes, lads, this is going to get personal.

"I'm Finch Merlin, formerly Shipton, of the San Diego Coven. I'm a full Elemental, with Mimicry abilities as the cherry on top of that particular cake. I wasn't always a full Elemental, though. After my birth, my mother put a Dempsey Suppressor in me. I had no idea, my whole life, until it snapped when I killed her. Before that, I'd done terrible things in her name, and I got sent to Purgatory for it."

I looked at Blanche, but her face gave nothing away.

"I didn't truly understand how she'd manipulated me until I lost the woman I loved. Katherine had her murdered." I clenched my glass for support. "Harley told me what she'd done, and that's when the penny dropped. Well, it smacked me in the skull. I owe my sister everything. She took a chance on me before I deserved one. She saw that I could change. Her belief in me made me want to change. I never once looked back."

I looked at Blanche again, and I saw a flicker of something cross her eyes. Sadness? Pity? Anger? Hard to tell.

"I devoted my life to Harley's effort to take down my mother. In the last battle in Elysium, I sold myself to Erebus so I could kill Katherine and stop that entire Eris nightmare from claiming more lives." I took a breath. "What I'm trying to say, in essay form, is that I can't change my past, but I've been working so hard to change for the better. I don't want to be like Katherine, ever."

I glanced back at Blanche. "I'm so sorry about your husband. I remember him now, and if it's any comfort, he really dealt Katherine a blow. I wish I could say more to help. I wish I could *do* more. If I could undo every bad thing I did, and undo all my mother's evil, too, I would. But I can't. Even so, please know—I'm sorry."

Silence drifted across the terrace. Even the monks had frozen.

Blanche lowered her gaze. Maybe I couldn't change her mind tonight, but I'd said my piece. A long piece. That was all I could do. The atmosphere had changed, though. I didn't sense quite as much hatred and suspicion as before.

"What about you, Etienne?" Melody came in with a much-needed segue. The silence had nearly killed me.

Etienne smiled. "I suppose it's only fair that I reveal my own truths. It's ironic that my revelations should come after Finch's. He and I share something in common."

"We do?" That surprised me. *Don't tell me you drank Katherine's Kool-Aid?*

"Seeking to transcend our pasts," he replied. "Once upon a time, I worked as a magical assassin. I won't go into the details, but I had some fairly big names on my hit list, and I never missed a target. Never. I killed my client's problems, no matter who they were."

A gasp hissed from the table, as if someone had popped a bottle of champagne.

"How come you're not in Purgatory?" Oliver asked.

"I made many friends among the upper echelons over the years. Through my line of work, that was bound to happen. I made hits for very influential people, serving special magical interests," he explained. "Then, I reached a point in my career where I realized that if I didn't stop, I'd be the one on someone's hit list. And, by then, I had tired of killing. I suppose I found a moral compass, somewhat late in life. So, I came here, telling no one."

"No one bothered to look for you?" I asked.

Etienne shook his head. "I knew too much. It was best if I vanished, and that is precisely what I did. I came here, learned map-making from the previous owner, and took over his position when he retired to New Zealand."

Shailene gaped at him. "How's that fair? If you killed people, you should be in prison, not running this place." Both twins looked likely to burst a blood vessel.

"Life in general is not fair," he replied coldly. "As Monsieur Merlin can attest. The good guys don't always win. The bad guys don't always lose. At the end of the day, we can only look out for ourselves."

"I think that's a pretty selfish way to look at things," Fay said coldly.

Etienne shrugged. "I'm sure I needn't remind you, but you are in my domain, living under my roof. You are here to learn map-making, not to be self-righteous. If you don't like it, you know where the exit is. I warn you, if you think you will accomplish anything by sending security magicals to this island, you will both be in for a very rude awakening."

Etienne made it very clear: he wasn't to be messed with. He'd just told us, outright, what he used to be and how he'd smoothly escaped punishment, which meant he wouldn't worry about us telling anyone or the authorities coming after him. That waved a few red flags. Was he that powerful? I wondered if the Basani twins would even reach the mainland if they tried to bring him some delayed justice.

But if he thought he and I were the same, he was wrong. I hadn't hidden from my actions. I'd stood trial for them and faced the music. I still faced it, in order to make amends. And the fact that nobody had come after him spoke volumes. It looked like it wasn't just the monastery that contained buried secrets.

TEN

Finch

S *leep—who's she? Don't know her.*
 I'd been staring up at the ceiling since dinner. Maybe it was the food giving me a big old dose of indigestion. Maybe it was the unfamiliar setting keeping my nerves on edge. Maybe it was my confessional, dragging up my history and forcing a mirror up to my face. Whatever the case, getting any kind of rest seemed like a distant possibility. I should've been dead to the world by now, but nope... the noggin had gone into overdrive.

The twisted statue of Hades didn't help. Having a huge stone god staring at me didn't exactly make me want to curl up and drift away into the Land of Nod. I could've sworn its eyes followed me. Erebus aside, since he hadn't tried to communicate through the massive god again, it served as a fitting reminder of the monastery's strange past. Etienne had dropped a few tidbits about the history of this place, and Melody had gone wild on the details.

Once upon a Greek tragedy, it'd been the home of the so-called gods and goddesses who'd wreaked havoc on humans, siring children left, right, and center and generally causing a mess wherever they went. Wars, disputes, crimes of passion, the whole shebang. So, it'd come as a shocker to find out that they were just an offshoot of the Primus Anglicus magicals, with a slightly more Mediterranean flair for the dramatic. Hera, Zeus, and the entire roster of famous deities had been vastly powerful magicals, but definitely not gods. Not that this had stopped them from being worshipped as divine beings, and even insisting on it from the puny humans.

There was no Mount Olympus, either. Well, the mountain existed, but the magicals didn't live up there. The location was just a ruse to keep peeved humans from tracking them down. No, they'd lived here at the monastery. According to Melody's endless knowledge, the island used to be bigger, but the edges got nibbled away by erosion, big chunks swallowed by the Ionian Sea over the decades. I mean, this monastery was already massive, but it'd been even bigger back in the day.

Etienne had mentioned that the current building, plus customary interdimensional pocket, had been built on the ruins of the former palace. He'd collected a nifty cache of the Olympians' ancient treasures, unearthed from those bygone times, and stored them... somewhere in this labyrinth. Melody had spilled those latter details, and quickly been silenced, but it'd put a peach pit of curiosity in my brain. I loved ancient treasure as much as the next guy.

Erebus, dude, you've been rubbing off on me. Who could resist ancient Greek artifacts? My mind racing, I wondered if that was why Erebus had dumped me here. Sure, he wanted me to make a map, but what if there was more to it? What if he wanted me to get my mitts on something here? It couldn't hurt to have a look, right? I could think of it as taking inventory, in case he threw a curveball at me. After all, he kept harassing me for quicker deliveries of his underhanded tasks. It would be nice if I could get ahead of him, just once.

Mr. Insomnia might as well do something productive. Hypnos and Morpheus weren't on their way anytime soon. I had learned a lot about the Greek pantheon. As it turned out, Melody had a way of making information stick, even if it came in the midst of one of her rambles. Education by osmosis.

I threw back the covers and put on some real clothes. I'd found what could only be described as a nightie for guys in one of the drawers, and since that was my only option unless I wanted to sleep buck naked, I'd thrown it on. The restrictiveness of denim felt weird after having so much freedom, but I couldn't wander the halls in that nightie. People might start to talk.

Dressed, I snuck out of my room and went on my way. A couple of monks ambled around, even though we were in the wee hours of the morning. I dodged them, slipping into doorways and hiding in the shadows. I could've explained it away as needing to take a walk, but I sensed the monks would feed everything back to Etienne. And I didn't know how I felt about our generous overseer. He might be a changed man on the surface, but I wondered what muddy water rippled beneath his calm exterior.

I came across statues on almost every corner. Carved figures similar to the one in my room, but not as creepy. *Why couldn't they have put one of those in my room, huh?* I'd have taken an Aphrodite or an Artemis, or even a Zeus, over Hades and his eerie grabbers any day.

I rounded another corner, wishing I'd brought string or something, á la Theseus's escape from the Minotaur's labyrinth. *When in Greece...* My mind barely kept track of the turns I'd made in this maze. I thought about retreating before I got completely lost, but a sound stopped me. Whispered voices hissed out of a room ahead, the door slightly ajar. I crept forward and recognized one of the voices—Etienne's subtle French twang.

"What do you think of them?" he asked.

"They don't seem too different from the rest," another voice replied. Peering through the keyhole, I witnessed one of the monks sitting in a chair opposite Etienne. The room had a desk and bookshelves, and though it kept to a simple aesthetic, it didn't look like a place for sleeping. This had to be Etienne's study.

"Really? They don't seem odd to you?" Etienne frowned. "I'm concerned about them."

"How come?" the monk asked.

"It's the timing that concerns me, rather than the individuals." Etienne sighed. "Rumors are going around that a Child of Chaos walks among magicals, in human form. Do you remember Finch mentioning he'd been in Erebus's service?"

The monk nodded. "I think so."

"Ordinarily, the mention of a Child of Chaos wouldn't perturb me, but, as I said, the timing is bizarre."

"Are you saying Finch might be the Child of Chaos?" The monk sounded confused.

Etienne tapped his chin. "I'm not sure. How easy would it be for a Child of Chaos to take on the body of an existing human? From what I heard about the debacle with Katherine, it should not be a simple endeavor. But stranger things have happened."

The monk exhaled. "It's a nuisance that the defensive shield is not more precise in its scanning, but anything more complex would drain the monastery's energy resources."

"Precisely," Etienne groaned. "It is no better than facial recognition. A detailed transformation spell can fool it. And a Mimic would certainly have no trouble tricking the system."

"Do you want us to keep an eye on him?" the monk asked.

Etienne's frown deepened. "Perhaps, for now. He claims his dealings with Erebus are done, but who knows how true that is. Watching him will alleviate some concerns, or at least reveal if he's lying."

So... the protective shield doesn't give him everything about us. He'd mentioned his monks doing quick research, so the shield likely scanned the face of whoever entered, and the monks did the rest, looking it up on some database somewhere. It made for a strange image, trying to picture a monk doing a deep dive into everyone's personal data. Like Astrid in fancy robes.

And he was worried about *me* being Erebus in disguise? I didn't know whether to be flattered or appalled. Then again, he hadn't seen human-Erebus, so he probably had no idea what that would look like. It definitely wouldn't look like me. Now, at least I knew I'd have to really keep my wits about me, if he was going to have monks watching me.

"Is that all that worries you?" The monk shifted in his seat, and I ducked back from the keyhole.

"No." Etienne unleashed a strained breath. "I also heard that Davin Doncaster has resurfaced. I suppose it was only a matter of time. But, if he has grown bold again, then he is a disaster waiting to happen. As ever."

"You think he'll come here?" The monk had flipped from confused to concerned, and I peered back through the keyhole. I had to. If they were chatting about that ass-wipe, I didn't want to miss a thing.

Etienne shrugged. "It's hard to say. He has kept away until now, but he will need to find support now that Katherine is gone. And I do owe him my life, so I suppose that makes me an obvious port of call. Former friendships die hard, when that debt of gratitude lies between two people." He paused. "Part of me is interested in finding out what he wants, and part of me is fearful. He may want to cash in on the favor I owe him. I suppose that is the nature of a debt. They must be paid."

"Would you like me to post monks on the perimeter, Mr. Biset, so you can be informed immediately if Davin arrives?" the monk asked.

Etienne nodded. "Yes, I think that would be best."

"Would you like me to post monks at Finch's door, too?"

Etienne tilted his head. "No. I don't think that will be necessary... just yet. Keep watch over him, and I will do the same. It may be coincidence, and with a skillset like his, I wouldn't want to chase him away if nothing untoward is going on. That said, if my suspicions grow, I may have to take matters into my own hands, to protect the *monastère* and everything I have gathered within these walls."

Huh? I had to get this straight. So Davin and Etienne were friends once, and Etienne owed him his life. And he had a debt to pay, which might bring Davin here? That was confusing and worrying enough. But where had Etienne gotten all his intel from? How did he know about Erebus's recent transformation? Had gossip spread that fast?

More importantly, I'd somehow ended up in Etienne's firing line, thanks to my servitude to Erebus. He didn't trust the lies I'd told. That put me in an awkward position.

Now, I had to worry about Davin trying to break in to see his old pal, and deal with Etienne's suspicion. Man, if Davin and Etienne started working together... that spelled mega trouble for me—a Necromancer teaming up with a former assassin. At this point, I would've given my left eyeball to go back to treasure hunting across the globe. That had been simple by comparison.

Tomorrow morning, I would start training to become a mapmaker. And if Etienne found more reasons to think I was a risk to his little domain, he could easily use that training as a ploy to kill me. But it wasn't like I could just run off and ditch this whole thing. If I failed, Erebus would hang me out to dry.

"Don't you think a Child of Chaos would be more obvious?" The monk's voice brought me back from my despair.

Etienne sighed. "Unfortunately, no. Some have always sought to meddle in the human world. They are slyer than you would think, and a Shapeshifter is the ideal candidate."

The monk nodded. "I hadn't thought of it like that."

"There is a reason the Children have been separated from the mortal realm for so long. It is unnatural for Erebus to wield such power, and it can only spell trouble for our monastery. If Finch harbors any such motives in being here... I will be forced to eliminate the threat." Etienne stared dead ahead, making me reel back from the door.

Did he see me?

He made no move to stand or call me out, but it was all the warning I needed. I was pushing my luck. I tiptoed away, trying to ignore the chills bristling through me.

I was trapped in this monastery with no way out. It was getting clearer by the second that I might not leave alive, if Etienne found out why I was here. "Eliminate the threat" didn't sound like I'd get a slap on the wrist and be let go. And, if he did decide to eliminate me, nobody would ever know where I'd disappeared to.

ELEVEN

Kenzie

———————

W e burst out of a portal. The millionth one today. That's what it felt like, anyhow.

Erebus had me on a wild goose chase, and all I could do was follow. Mom needed this. Inez needed this. I needed this. I'd gotten one of the guys from the corner to watch the apartment, but Mom wouldn't wake for a long time. Maybe not until morning. I felt bad I couldn't keep my promise to my sister, though. She'd get home, see me gone, and be disappointed. But I'd make up for it by curing Mom.

You hear that, Ezzie? When I come home, I'll have good news.

We'd spent the last few hours portaling. It took some getting used to. Portal travel was pretty new to me, and portal sickness was definitely a thing. I'd had to stop a few times to catch my breath, or else I'd have emptied my stomach. Erebus gave me some dumb, impatient stare every time, but at least he didn't have vomit on his slick shoes.

"Where are we?" I stooped again. I had that spit in my mouth—the kind that came right before barf.

"Just outside Shreveport," Erebus replied.

"It's baking hot out here." I squeezed my eyes shut, desperate for this feeling to pass.

He chuckled. "We are in Louisiana. And, you'll be pleased to know, this is our final destination."

"Huh?" I peeked out one eye. We stood in some random field. Nothing as far as the eye could see, except one dingy, janky warehouse up ahead. Erebus had been following a tracking spell through these pain-in-the-ass portals. More than once, I'd wondered if he was just yanking my chain to make it look like he was helping. Then, he could turn around and say, "Well, I tried. Sorry. Now it's time for you to do what I want."

I trusted gang members just enough. Erebus was in the same category.

"This is our final destination," he repeated.

"What is?"

"That is." He pointed to the crusty warehouse.

I shook my head. "Nah, that can't be right. Look at it. There's nobody there." The sun had set, leaving the moon to illuminate this dump. There were no lights on. It probably didn't even have power. Whatever this place used to be, it didn't look like anyone had used it in a long time. The door hung from its hinges, and wooden slats were missing from the boarded windows.

"The spells don't lie, Kenzie." Erebus peered at the warehouse. "This is where the spellcaster is hiding."

"I swear to Chaos, if you're messing with me, you won't like pissed-off Kenzie," I warned.

He smirked. "Haven't we already met?"

"Fine, *super*-pissed-off Kenzie." I folded my arms across my chest. This hoodie wasn't meant for so much humidity. Sweat dripped off me.

"Shall we?" Erebus stepped forward.

"Hang on a sec. How do I know I'm not walking into some trap?"

"You aren't important enough for me to lay a trap," he replied. "And why would I trick you when you have already agreed to do my bidding?"

I shot him a scowl. "Why'd you have to put it like that? If you want to pass as a human—which, let's face it, is going to be pretty hard when you look like that—you need to ease off on the fancy talk. And I don't like the way that sounds. We're in a deal. I'm not your slave. You scratch my back, I scratch yours. Equals."

"Equals?" Erebus laughed so hard I thought he might bust a button.

I glared harder. "You're in a human body now. So, yeah, equals."

"You are funny. A different sort of amusing than Finch. Who knew there could be so many varieties of humor? This human endeavor is very enlightening." His laughter faded. "Now, shall we proceed?"

"In a minute. First, I want to know what this is going to cost me. Don't get me wrong, it's not going to change anything, but I deserve some facts." I held my ground. "What is it you need from me, after this?"

He flicked his wrist. "I suppose it wouldn't hurt to give you more information. I made that error with Finch, not giving him enough information while I had the opportunity, and now I'm contending with the consequences." He heaved a reluctant sigh. "Which, incidentally, is where you come in. There are a few limitations to this body—minor ones, but inconvenient nonetheless."

"Will you be getting to the point sometime soon?"

He cast me a steely look. "Remember what I said about squandering my tolerance." He turned back toward the warehouse. "I'm having trouble communicating with Finch. I took him to a secret monastery and managed to deposit him there, but I haven't been able to resume a connection with him. I attempted and failed, thanks to the fortifications put in place by the owner of the monastery. My powers are restricted by this form, making it almost impossible to reach Finch."

"Why's he at a monastery? That doesn't sound like your kind of thing."

"It goes by the name Mapmakers' Monastery."

"Uh-huh. Is that supposed to mean something to me?" I waited for an explanation.

Erebus stiffened, apparently embarrassed by his next words. "I've sent other servants into the monastery, and all have failed in the art of map-making. Finch is unlike my former servants. He is more capable, and he is much, much stronger. Still, that is no guarantee of success. From those previous attempts, I learned more about the process. Now, I know enough to guide Finch and help him succeed where the others did not. But, in order to aid him, I need to be able to communicate with him. Obviously."

"Still not getting where I fit in." I tapped my foot.

"*You* will go there for me, using your Morph ability, to guide him," he replied. "A magical without your skills might have problems breaking through the monastery's defenses, but a small creature should have no issue. That is why you are the only one who can do this for me."

"Why didn't you just say that at the start?" I'd been expecting something way worse, but this project sounded pretty dope. Breaking into some secret monastery to help out my pal... I'd have agreed a hell of a lot quicker if Erebus had said so upfront.

This way, I got to help Mom *and* Finch. Since he was one of the few people I called friend, it sort of felt like my duty or something.

He frowned. "You like the idea?"

"Like's a strong word. But it's not as bad as I thought it might be." There would be risks, but it wouldn't be my first rodeo. I'd dealt with powerful magicals and places, back when I used to trade in stolen magical goods. I didn't do that anymore, but I still had a knack for getting around magical defenses.

"Mortals continue to surprise me," Erebus mumbled.

"Hey, you're one of us now. Better get used to our quirks." I took a deep breath. "Are we doing this or not?"

"You were the one holding us back," Erebus retorted.

"Well, I'm not anymore. So, lead the way."

I stayed behind him as he set off toward the warehouse. I figured a Child of Chaos in any form was a pretty good shield, if anyone jumped out of this dive.

The stench of rotting wood and rusty metal hit me in the nostrils as we got closer. It looked dark inside.

Following Erebus, I slipped through the gap in the broken-off door. There was nothing inside. Literally nothing. No old machines, not even a crushed beer can or a cigarette butt. No graffiti, either. *That's weird...* Even though it looked empty now, somewhere like this should've had a hint of bored teenagers or some evidence of passing drifters looking for a spot to lay their heads for the night. The absence of anything like that felt wrong. I lived in a derelict apartment block. I knew what an abandoned warehouse should look like.

Erebus put his hand out, and the air shimmered. I waited for alarm bells or sirens, but they didn't come. No snarling guard dogs, either. Erebus knew what he was doing. He tore open a hole in the shimmering forcefield and stepped inside. I followed him, heart in throat. This didn't feel like a safe thing to be doing.

Beyond the forcefield, which I guessed was some kind of inter-dimensional pocket, the warehouse gave way to a makeshift apartment. *So, there is someone home.* They'd just hidden themselves away, off grid, so nobody could find them. Especially magicals. I could tell that from the symbols that glinted on the inside of the force-field. Erebus had untangled one of them like a pro, giving us access without alerting anyone. At least, that's what I hoped he'd done. Wouldn't have wanted to give this punk a heads-up.

A big table sat in the middle of the apartment, covered in Voodoo stuff—dolls, pins, knives, books, bowls full of gloopy liquid that looked a lot like blood. Smears of red stained the table's surface, and one of the knives had rust-colored flakes coming off it. The books were worse. The covers looked... fleshy. Like old skin left to prune in the sun.

Bookshelves were set up all over the apartment, stacked with the creepy, fleshy books. Paintings and drawings mapped out the human body.

The metallic scent of blood lingered in the air. *What has this spellcaster been doing?* I didn't want to think about it too much. But one look at the smeared table was all I needed to get the picture.

"Can you sense them?" I whispered.

Erebus shook his head. "No."

Keeping my eye on the warehouse door, I started to explore. Mangled bits of meat and bloodied animal fur lay in a bucket on the floor. The smell turned my stomach. So did the maggots wrig-gling around in there.

Pinned to the makeshift walls were dried-out lizards and gigantic moths with holes in their wings, the bodies decaying. Everywhere I turned, I saw more death and decay. Creatures, some rotted way beyond identification. And all of it was mixed in with ordinary, domestic stuff. A kettle, a toaster, plates and cups, and a small generator.

I stopped in front of one of the bookshelves. A photo, no frame, leaned against the spines. A familiar face stared back at me. One I hadn't seen in person for years. The last time was at the magical army base, before he stepped through a mirror to Iraq. I'd clung to him so hard, Mom had to tear me out of his arms in the end. I remembered crying all the way back to our house. The one we gave up after he died and Mom got sick.

Why is there a photo of my dad here? The guy next to him had thrown his arm around my dad's shoulders, both of them in full uniform. They smiled like nothing could hurt them.

I looked along the line of books and saw white edges sticking out. I reached for one and tugged out another photo. This one showed my parents, with the same guy jumping behind them. They were all laughing, the camera catching the exact moment Mom and Dad had turned to look at this man. Fear smacked me in the gut.

Frantic, I searched the books, pulling out every tucked-away photo. There were pictures of me and my sister, much younger, playing in the garden of our old house. Birthday parties, Christmases, Thanksgivings, all the family affairs, and this guy was in them all. And one unaware image of me crossing the road in front of our current apartment. The kind of photo you saw in creepy stalker movies. There were photos from the hospital, too, during some of my mom's worst relapses. I wasn't in those. They were just pictures of Mom, asleep in the hospital bed.

What the—!

I reached for another photo, and a creeping sensation edged up my spine. My head whipped around on instinct. A man emerged from the darkness at the end of the makeshift apartment, from behind a rotting wooden post.

He lifted his hands, and red tendrils shot out, lightning-fast. He said something, too, but I didn't understand the language. I'd heard Marie Laveau speak Haitian Creole, but this wasn't it. The only words I picked out were, "*Sisan, sisan,*" before the tendrils tunneled into my chest.

Pain ripped through me like a thousand shards of glass jabbing into me at once. I screamed and sank to my knees. I tried to fight it, but I couldn't control my body. My blood was screaming too. I didn't know how, but it was. As if it wanted to tear right out of my veins.

Darkness threatened. The curse was about to pull me under, but I couldn't let it. I couldn't. If this guy was more powerful than Marie Laveau, then I didn't want to be unconscious around him.

Hold on... just... keep your eyes open.

TWELVE

Kenzie

"**E**rebus!" I screamed.

He was my only shot at surviving this. It was killing me from the inside out. My blood burned; my skin felt white-hot. Tears streamed down my cheeks. Angry, painful ones, with a few bitter ones thrown in. If I died here, who'd tell Inez and Mom what happened to me? I couldn't rely on Erebus for that. He'd just as likely sweep me under the rug and forget about me.

I forced my head to twist around. Erebus stood in front of the smeared table. He looked worried. Red tendrils hurtled at him from the grim stranger. The same stranger from all those photos. The strands hovered a moment, sniffing Erebus out like a cautious dog. As if they weren't quite sure they were allowed to strike.

What the hell was taking him so long?

"Erebus!" I rasped, desperate. He might've been in a human body, but he couldn't be that limited... could he? Beneath all that night-black skin, he was still a Child of Chaos. The Child of Darkness. Voodoo played into his skillset; he'd told me so himself. So why wasn't he doing something?

The red tendrils sniffed him out some more. A moment later, they seemed to decide that they could get involved. With sparks of scarlet flying, they rammed into his chest. Erebus's eyes widened in surprise as he glanced down.

Yeah, they're attacking you, you moron!

I struggled to blink, my eyes blurring. The pain heightened, rising up my throat and threatening to close it altogether. Someone might as well have lit a match under me—every piece of me felt like it was on fire, and every breath got harder to take. If he didn't hurry, I'd pass out. It took all the fight I had left just to cling to consciousness.

Erebus's eyes darkened, if that was even possible. He shot a terrifying glare at the stranger.

"Dedere. Nigrante supervenit aestu. Veni ad me. Frange eo. Qui non cadunt. Et omnia quæ habebat. Veni ad me. Nigrante supervenit aestu. Fiat fluctus influunt. Quod creatio de tenebris ego adsum. Hoc faciunt. Dedere!" Erebus's voice came from the shadows all over the apartment in a deafening roar. Even this asshole had the decency to look afraid.

A dark cloud swelled overhead. It started small and expanded outward. The spellcaster muttered more of his Voodoo under his breath. Red light swirled around him and careened upward to combat the gathering storm. The Darkness swallowed it up, smothering the red sparks until they disappeared. That didn't stop the mysterious man. He kept muttering, clearly panicked now. But he'd pushed Erebus's buttons, and there was no escaping the Child of Darkness.

Hit him where it hurts! I tried to force the words out, but my throat had seized up. My lungs strained, trying to gasp in a breath.

The pain literally stole each one away. I bent double, dragging my nails across the filthy ground.

I managed to glance back at Erebus. Smoke rose from his body, meeting the black clouds. As he lifted his hands, the storm spread wider, obeying its master. Splinters of purple light darted between the clouds, like real lightning but twice as terrifying. As the guy turned to escape, one of those lightning forks crashed down. It bristled with purple-and-black energy, smashing the spellcaster right in the back. He toppled forward and smacked into the ground face-first.

"Don't… kill him!" I wheezed. "We… need him!"

Erebus grinned. "I'm just loosening his tongue, worry not."

The spellcaster tried to stand, a howl ripping from his throat as the lightning bolt shivered through him. I could see the path it took, his veins lighting up and revealing the whole network inside him. Erebus twisted his hand in a circle, bringing the spellcaster around like a puppet on a string. The guy's mouth opened wide, and another bloodcurdling howl ricocheted between the walls. Where the lightning bolt had splintered through him, the formerly glowing veins turned black. They spiderwebbed across his face and throat, like clawing hands trying to strangle him. He staggered on weak knees that gave up on him. He crumpled to the ground again, howling and screaming as the web of veins took over.

How do you like it, huh? I would've really gone hard on the satisfaction if I hadn't been in the same boat. My limbs stopped moving. My chest clenched in a vise. I didn't know how long it'd be before my heart stopped, too. Everything had frozen.

Casual as anything, Erebus walked over and pressed his palms to my shoulder blades. Warmth spread through me, like Deep Heat on a tight muscle. Oddly relaxing after all that pain. As it washed through my body, it unraveled the spellcaster's curse. I could feel it breaking away, loosening up my limbs and muscles. As that weird, fluid sensation hit my lungs, I sputtered—they sensed the oxygen and went into panic mode. I gulped massive breaths, terrified it might be taken away again. But I could breathe and move, all that pain gone in a flash.

I looked up at Erebus. "Th-thank you." He'd saved me. No two ways about it. Much as I hated to admit it. *Maybe you're not so bad to have around in a fix.* I didn't say it—I wasn't going to give him that much credit. But I felt it, blending with the wave of relief sweeping over me.

"I need your abilities, remember?" he replied. "I couldn't let you die on me."

"And here I thought you'd done it out of the goodness of your heart."

He smirked. "I'm still getting used to *having* a heart."

"Don't Children of Chaos have them?" I asked, between deep breaths.

"I suppose we must have an equivalent, but it's not quite the same thing. I've never felt anything... beating in there before. Not for a long time, anyway. I had almost forgotten the sensation." He put his hand to his chest and gave a stilted laugh. A second later, his eyes dropped to the writhing figure on the floor. "Now, shall we see what this wretch has to say for himself?"

I nodded. "I think we should."

Erebus put out his hand. "Come, then."

"Thanks." I took it and let him hoist me to my feet. To my surprise, he held on to my hand a while longer as he led me across the room. I was grateful for that. The pain might have gone, but my knees were hella shaky.

As we neared the squirming rat, things took a turn for the weird. His face contorted, his eyes bulging. Yet, somehow... he looked familiar. My mind scrambled to figure it out. Yeah, he was in those pictures, but that hadn't jogged any memories. So why did he look familiar now? It almost felt like I'd woken from a strange dream and was struggling to remember it. Every time I thought I had it, it slithered away again, back into the corners of my brain.

"Who are you?" Erebus started the questioning.

The guy spat blood onto the floor. "Go to hell!"

"I suggest you make this easy on yourself. I'll ask again. Who are you?" Erebus twirled his hand in the air, and the still-present clouds swept forward.

"Ask all you... like. I'm not... saying anything... to you!" The guy's face scrunched up as a purple bolt hit him in the skull. Pulsing threads of Chaos seared through bone and flesh. Black veins crept into his eyes. He even bit into his own hand to stop a scream. Blood trickled through his fingers.

"Who. Are. You?!" Erebus twirled his hand again, unleashing another bolt. "My patience is wearing thin!"

"None of your... damn... business!" The guy bit his hand again as purple light exploded through him.

"I will ask one more time. If you don't answer, I will scoop out your brain and find the answers myself." Erebus waited. I looked at him, petrified. Would he really do that? Yeah, I was pretty sure he would. "Who are you?"

The guy didn't answer.

"As you wish." Erebus turned his hand halfway, ready to let loose a bolt that would crack open this dude's skull.

"Wait, wait!" he sputtered.

"Are you going to cooperate?" Erebus smiled eerily.

The guy's lips twisted up in a bloodied scowl. "Wyatt. My name is Wyatt. I'm... I'm..."

"You're what?" I jumped in, spitting venom.

His gaze turned to me. "I'm your uncle. Your dad's brother."

"What?" I gasped. "No, you're not. I'd remember you."

"I made it so... you wouldn't," he replied, battling through the pain. "Another trick I... learned from the African tribes. I couldn't have you... coming after me... now, could I? Although, looks like you... found a way. That'll be your... mom's stubbornness. You were... always more like... her."

"I'd say you learned more than a few tricks, Wyatt." Erebus stepped in. "Where did you learn such extraordinary Voodoo magic? I'd commend you if you hadn't chosen to use it against me. You should know, much of Voodoo's strength comes from my side of the coin. Your magic would never have worked."

Wyatt glowered at Erebus. "I spent years in... West Africa, learning all I could, living with... magical tribes. Tribes who still... revere and practice the ancient arts of Voodoo. It's made me one... of the most powerful and... most dangerous Voodoo... practitioners in the world. All anyone knows is... the name Marie Laveau. But her magic... barely scratches the surface. If I'd had more time, I would've... made a dent in you, I'm sure."

Erebus snorted. "I highly doubt that."

"You put that curse on my mom." I pushed in front of Erebus. "Why? If you're really my uncle, why would you do that and make me forget?" Angry tears stung my eyes.

"That's my business," Wyatt replied.

"You better answer her." Erebus narrowed his eyes.

Wyatt grimaced. "Don't blame me if you don't like the answer."

"Just spill it, you bastard!" I snarled.

He dragged himself up onto his haunches. "Not knowing must be killing you. I got away with this for so many years. Nobody suspected a thing. That's the beauty of my artistry—it's so subtle and perfect, it can even fool famous Voodoo queens."

"I mean it! I want to know everything!"

Erebus raised his hands. "Get to the point, unless you want to find out how far I can push torture without actually killing a person."

Wariness crossed Wyatt's face. "The truth is, I loved your mom. I met her first, at a party. I thought my brother might like her friend, so I set up a double date. Then, your parents spent the whole night talking, like me and this other chick weren't even there. And the rest is history."

"Keep talking," I warned, when it looked like he had stopped. "I want to know everything about why you did this. Every detail."

He shrugged, eyeing Erebus's hands. "Your dad and I joined the Magical Forces. He met your mom before his first deployment, and she decided to wait for him. I tried to persuade her not to, but she wouldn't listen. They married when he came back. Anyway, the Forces didn't end up being my style, so I ducked out on an honorable discharge. It wasn't hard. I'd already developed an interest in blood magic, and an injury is easy to fake when you know how."

"Coward," I hissed.

"Who's the brother that's still alive?" He smirked coldly. "I'd rather live a coward than die a hero."

I lunged forward, but Erebus yanked me back. "If you want answers, I suggest you don't beat him to a pulp."

"I came around when your dad was away, in the early days. I kept your mom company, helped with you. Your little sister wasn't born yet. I kept thinking, if I just stayed persistent and showed her I was the better guy, she'd fall for me instead. It didn't work, and I got tired of trying, so I took myself off for my first tribal experience. I came back now and again, met your little sister, but I couldn't stand the sight of your mom playing happy family with my brother. It got harder each time. And then, I heard that my brother had been killed in Iraq. I've never felt relief like that."

I lunged again. "Shut your mouth!"

"Kenzie!" Erebus barked, grabbing me.

Wyatt chuckled. "I'd thought about killing him so many times, but I never had the courage. So perhaps I am a coward. Anyway, a bomb did it for me, in the end."

This time, Erebus preempted my strike and wrangled me into his arms. "Let him finish, then you can have justice."

"Did you not just hear what he said?" I snapped.

"I did, but you asked for a cure. I cannot uphold my end of the bargain if I let you batter him to death before you have the entire story, and the chance to reverse your mother's curse." Erebus kept hold of me as I shot a death stare at Wyatt. "After all, he needs to be alive to perform the reversal. It is not a matter of killing him to break the curse. It would hold, even after his death."

"That's right. You need me, don't you? You think you have the upper hand, but I'm the one with all the cards." He grinned bitterly. "If I don't perform the reversal, your mom will keep deteriorating. So, how about you be a little nicer?"

Erebus laughed. "You may have the cards, but I can make you use them. I can make you dance like a marionette if I wish, but I'm giving you the opportunity to do as Kenzie asks, willingly. It is your choice—continue talking or prepare for another onslaught."

Wyatt's smile faded. "After a while, I went back to your mom, to try and convince her we should be together. I promised to build a better life for her, help her out with the house payments, and make sure you and your sister were safe," Wyatt continued. "But she turned me down. After all that, she refused to even consider it. So I put a blood spell on her. Some of my finest work, if I do say so myself. It eats away, piece by tiny piece, until you forget who you are and there's nothing left of the person you once were."

I wanted to snap his neck. And yeah, I wanted to punch the living daylights out of him. But Erebus was right. If I did that, I'd lose my shot at getting the curse off Mom.

In that moment, all the fire went out of me. My body sagged in Erebus's arms. I didn't want violent vengeance anymore. I ached all over, and I was so freaking tired. Not from the Voodoo he'd thrown at me, but from the years of care, from watching Mom waste away in front of me. I had all my answers, and I had the culprit right here on the ground.

I just want this over with. I just want my mom back.

"Aren't you sorry?" I asked softly. How could someone be so cruel? How could he have ruined our lives, just because my mom didn't want him?

Wyatt frowned. "Sorry? Why would I be sorry?"

"You destroyed our lives."

"Your mom destroyed mine first," he replied simply.

"Are you sure you didn't get whacked in the head on duty?" I gaped at him. "You're a frickin' sociopath. My mom has suffered for years because of you. Some days, she has no idea who we are. Does that make you feel good?"

He smiled a creepy-ass smile. "Revenge is a dish best served cold."

"Yeah? Well, now I'm serving it." I strained against Erebus until he let me go. "You're going to undo that curse, or my pal here is going to scoop out the insides of your skull. As well as anything else he feels like scooping out."

A flicker of fear crossed Wyatt's face. "I won't. Not unless you swear I can walk free."

"What did you just say?" I spat.

"I won't take that curse off unless you swear I can live. I haven't found a way to survive all these years just to die now."

"Wow…" I shook my head. "You really are a coward, aren't you?"

"Like I said, better a living coward than a dead hero," he retorted.

I held back the urge to kick him in the face. "My mom made the right choice. My dad was ten times the man you are."

Wyatt smiled. "That won't bring him back, though, will it?"

"At least he was loved. We still think about *him* every day of our damn lives. Who's thinking about you, huh? I hope you wake up one day and realize how alone you are. And I hope it hurts like a bitch. Maybe then you'll be sorry." I turned to Erebus. "Make him undo the curse. I'm tired of hearing this coward's voice. If he says another word, scoop him."

"With pleasure." Erebus gathered the storm over our heads, ready to strike. Wyatt straightened up, and terror washed over his slimy face. He may have been the worst kind of coward, but his desire to live would work in my favor.

Not long now, Mom. Not long now.

THIRTEEN

Kenzie

W yatt stood on shaky legs and took a moment to gather himself. He didn't look nearly as scary now that all the black veins had receded. But I'd have Erebus hit him with them again if he screwed me over. Once he'd undone the curse, this pathetic flesh bag would go straight to Purgatory.

My uncle knitted his brows together. "If I do this, I get to live, right?"

"Yeah, I guess so," I replied. "Get on with it, before I change my mind."

I watched him closely as he went to the disgusting table and collected all sorts of bits and pieces: a silver bowl, a gold-handled dagger, four rubies, two dried-up lizards, and the entrails of some poor beast. He grabbed one of the fleshy books and heaved it onto the table, upsetting one of the bowls of red goop. I turned away as it spilled onto the surface, but he wiped it away as if it were nothing.

My anger spiked as he climbed a stepladder and took down a

box from the top of a bookshelf. My mom's name was written on the side of it. Like a forgotten prize, or old belongings that never got unpacked, just put up on a shelf.

A thick coating of dust covered the box, and he blew the dust away. The puff sent out a flurry of motes that danced in the sickly glow of the apartment. When I was a kid, my dad told me that they were fairies, keeping watch over us. I stopped believing in fairies a long time ago, but the thought brought tears to my eyes. We'd been through so much, and Wyatt didn't give a damn. He'd only cared about himself. He'd lost his brother, for Chaos's sake, and hadn't batted an eyelid. I didn't need a shrink to tell me he was a few fries short of a Happy Meal. That didn't excuse him. Finch had his demons, and he'd chosen to fight them, not give in to them.

With unnecessary theatrics, Wyatt began. A few flourishes of his hands, sprinkling these herbs and those herbs into the silver bowl. I wanted to throw something at his head. This was serious, not an opportunity to fluff about. But I kept quiet. As long as he undid my mom's curse, I could deal with his stupidity.

With another dramatic twist of his hands, red tendrils poured out, the strands setting fire to the herbs and entrails he'd mixed in the silver bowl. I staggered back as the flames leapt a good four feet before settling into a smoky smolder. Erebus remained unmoved. He'd probably seen worse. Hell, he'd probably *done* worse.

Wyatt dropped the four rubies into the flames. Each time, the flames leapt up again, licking up hungrily. I could feel the heat on my skin. He added the crusty lizards and three types of powder: one black, one red, one white. An acrid scent stung my nostrils as the flames changed color, from blue, to green, to a hellish purple-red. I waited for it to change back to the usual orangey yellow, but it didn't. It stayed that creepy shade and cast the whole apartment in the reddish tinge of an underground dive.

"I whispered these spells to the Primus Anglicus a very long time ago, before they evolved into today's magicals," Erebus said, scaring me half to death. I hadn't realized he'd come up behind me.

"Are you trying to give me a heart attack?" I glowered.

He snickered. "Apologies. I just wanted a closer look. I'm rather impressed, and somewhat flattered, that magic like this has survived to this day. I never thought I would see its like again. Fascinating, isn't it?"

"Yo, head in the game, Erebus. My mom's health is at stake here."

Erebus gave a half-shrug. "Your point being?"

"This isn't some science experiment for me to go all gooey-eyed over," I shot back.

"How would one's eyes go gooey, exactly?" He laughed coldly. "Your mom isn't special, Kenzie. This spell, however, is something very special indeed."

Well, that didn't last long. It looked like his friendliness had done a backslide. That worried me. I needed him to feel like I was still important. If he didn't, how would I get him to make sure Wyatt wound up in Purgatory? His eyes practically had love hearts for Wyatt's work. What if he decided to let my uncle walk free?

I gritted my teeth. I just needed to wait until Wyatt undid the spell; then I could cross that bridge.

Wyatt spoke in that strange language as he wafted his arms like a magician at a kid's party. As he spoke, he delved into the dusty box and took out a cluster of photos. All of them were of my mom. He took out a wool cardigan, too. Pale pink and definitely not Wyatt's taste.

He stole it from Mom. I swallowed my anger.

Finally, he removed a doll. Not one of the raggedy, stitched-up Voodoo dolls from pop culture. This one was eerily realistic. It looked just like her. My mom. Her hair looked like a lock of my mom's real hair. Her face had been painstakingly painted, her lips the same shade I remembered her wearing on dates with Dad. And she wore a smaller version of the cardigan he'd removed from the box.

"What language is that?" I had to distract myself.

"It is an older form of Bamanankan, spoken by the West African tribes who taught him to do this," Erebus replied, his eyes shining.

"You want to stop drooling on me?"

He sighed, ignoring me. "It's a thing of beauty, it really is."

Wyatt continued to speak. One by one, he placed the items from the box into the silver bowl. The flames twisted and turned around each object, devouring them one by one. For a split second, in those flames, I could've sworn I saw my mom. Younger, dancing inside the fire, her laughter echoing beneath the crackle and spit of the flames. That was when it dawned on me. This spell didn't just kill the soul, it captured it, too. Had Wyatt trapped part of her soul in that doll for all these years?

The lights in the apartment dimmed, that reddish hue turning almost black as Wyatt's chants grew louder. Every hair on my body stood to attention. Scary didn't cover it. It was like shadows came from the darkness, slithering across the floor and the walls toward the bowl. I could feel them, snaking over me to reach that pot of Voodoo.

Erebus, meanwhile, had turned borderline manic. A frightening grin was fixed on his face, and his eyes were like saucers. He might as well have been rubbing his hands together. *Maybe he'll snap out of it once this is over.*

The doll exploded. The fragments burst upward and hovered in the air. Hungry flames spiraled out of the bowl and enveloped the fragments until nothing remained. No ashes, no melted strands of hair, nothing.

As soon as it finished devouring the doll, the fire sucked inward before exploding in a spray of red that splattered across my face. I was too shocked to scream, or punch Wyatt in the nose.

"There, it's done. Happy now?" Wyatt wiped the splatter off his face with the back of his sleeve. Sweat glistened on his forehead, mixing with... whatever had just hit us.

"How do I know it worked?" I found my voice quickly enough.

"I can indulge you there," Erebus chimed in. He still sounded manic.

I turned to him. "What do you mean?"

He delved into the pocket of his snazzy suit and took out a mirror.

"What is this, a Disney movie?" I frowned at him, unimpressed.

"Behold." He passed his hand across the mirror. An image appeared. Mom, in the living room of our apartment, waking up slowly. She held her palm to her forehead, looking around in a daze. Just then, Inez came into the frame—we'd been gone so long, with all the portaling, that she must've already gotten home from school. I couldn't hear what they said, but I didn't need to. Mom immediately burst into tears and pulled Inez into a tight hug, clinging to her for dear life. Inez hugged her back twice as hard, tears streaming down her cheeks, too. Mom's mouth moved, and Inez nodded, her little face scrunching up with total, over-whelming happiness.

"Is this a trick?" I whispered past the lump in my throat.

Erebus smiled. "You'll soon see for yourself. This is no trick. Even if it were, you made your promise to me—you bound yourself in blood. You have no choice but to follow me."

"Is it a trick or not?!" I rasped, my own tears about ready to fall.

His expression softened slightly. "What reason do I have to lie to you? To get you to do my bidding? It's not in my nature to force people to my will. I prefer deals, and I have made one with you. This is my side of the bargain. Nothing more, nothing less."

The tears came. It looked so real. Mom holding Inez like they'd been separated for years. Inez burying her face in Mom's shoulder and gripping with all her might. I wanted to be there so badly. I wanted to throw my arms around them both and never let go.

Frustration, relief, happiness, sadness… it hit me in a tidal wave. I could only imagine what Mom was feeling. How much would she remember? Judging by her heaving shoulders, she remembered a lot.

Mom… I'm coming. We had her back! It was almost too much. All these years, hoping and praying for an answer, trying everything on Earth to fix her. And I'd done it. I could barely stand as my body struggled to cope. My hands shook violently as big, ugly sobs wheezed out of me.

Erebus put his hand on my back and returned the mirror to his pocket so I couldn't see Mom and Inez anymore. "You can have your moment later. We aren't done here."

"What?" I peered up through wet eyes. "No, bring them back! Show them again!"

He shifted his focus back to Wyatt, completely ignoring my pleas. "It's time for you to die."

Wyatt stepped back. "You can't kill me. You promised."

"Correction, Kenzie promised. Although, I have a sneaking suspicion she never intended to let you go. Isn't that right?" He shot me a strange, dark smile. "Personally, I really did think about it. But I still feel like killing you." He took a step toward Wyatt, his face twisted with malevolence.

"I want him to rot in Purgatory!" I yelped, dragging Erebus

back. Death was too good for Wyatt. He deserved to waste away in prison so he'd have to think about everything that had put him there. I wanted that to be his punishment, not a quick snuffing out.

Erebus threw me off. But my actions had given Wyatt the split second he needed. His hand shot out and plucked a cluster of bronze orbs from the dusty box where he'd kept my mom's doll. Before Erebus or I could do anything, he hurled them at us. The orbs blew up in our faces, filling the apartment with sour, stinging smoke.

Sparks of light shot through the dense smoke, but I had no clue whom they belonged to. All I could do was wave my hands in front of me and try to dissipate the smoke.

A rush of Air tore through the apartment, clearing the smoke in one skilled move. Blinking the last of it from my eyes, I looked around. Wyatt lay dead on the ground, his gaze blank and empty. Erebus, however, was also on the ground, coughing and groaning. I ran to him and skidded to his side.

"Are you okay?" I tried to help him up, but he flicked me aside.

"I am fine." He got up by himself and dusted off his suit.

I stared at him, concerned. "Are you hurt?"

"Me? Of course not. Children of Chaos don't get hurt by mere mortals." A subtle wince gave him away. He looked exhausted. Sweat dripped down his face.

I looked at Wyatt's dead body. It wasn't what I'd wanted. I'd wanted him to rot in prison. By the looks of it, he'd wind up rotting here instead. I felt sorry for the poor sucker who might find him. Even interdimensional bubbles wouldn't hide the smell forever.

"Hey, you said it yourself—you've got limitations in this body. You can admit Wyatt got one over on you. It's only me here. Who am I going to tell? And it's not as if Wyatt's going to be saying anything anymore." I intended to be comforting, but Erebus didn't take it that way.

"What did you say to me?" His eyes burned with rage.

I fumbled for the right words. "I'm just saying, humans are weak. We make mistakes. That's what makes us human."

He waved his hand, and a portal tore open beside him. Without a word, he grabbed the scruff of my hoodie and dragged me through it so hard I thought he might strangle me. I half expected to step into his otherworld, where he could punish me for running my stupid mouth. Instead, I stepped into my apartment in San Diego.

Mom and Inez sat hugging on the couch, just as the mirror had shown. Their heads snapped up as I entered, both of them confused.

"Mom!" I sprinted to her and wrapped them both in my arms.

"Kenzie." Mom hugged me back. "My sweet, sweet girl. There you are. Let me get a look at you."

I shook my head. "I need to hold you for a minute, make sure you're real."

"Of course I'm real." She chuckled against my cheek. "I've missed you so much. I don't know where I've been, but I've missed you... both of you. I keep trying to remember, but... it's all so fuzzy. It keeps coming and going in waves."

"Don't worry about that now." I gripped her tighter. "You're back, and you're okay, and that's all that matters."

"Do you know where I've be—"

Mom's words died on her lips. One moment she was right there in my arms. The next she was gone. I reeled in horror, turning to Inez. But she wasn't there anymore, either. Frantically, I patted the couch, as if that'd make them reappear.

Erebus cleared his throat. He stood by the kitchen table with a blue glass bottle in his hands. White light churned inside it.

"What did you do, you son of a bitch?" I glared at him, tears running down my face.

"Call this my insurance policy," he replied calmly. "Only I can let them out. This is djinn magic—if anyone tries to get them out, or if this bottle is broken, they both die."

"Why?" I seethed.

He smiled bitterly. "Let this be a lesson to you, to shut up and do your job. Never doubt my strength again, or I will smash it myself." He set the bottle on the kitchen table, dangerously close to the edge.

He might not have been as powerful in this form, whether he wanted to admit it or not, but it hadn't taken anything away from his vindictive streak. The one he was so famous for. I'd over-stepped a line, and it didn't matter if I'd meant to. He was punishing me for it. I'd never hated him more. There was cruelty, and then there was "tearing a daughter away from her mom minutes after she'd been cured" cruelty. He had it down to a fine freaking art.

"Something to say?" Erebus taunted.

I clenched my jaw. "No."

"Good, then get started. I have a few things I need you to get to Finch, as quickly as possible. The clock is ticking..." He gave the bottle a tiny push, bringing it closer to the edge of the table. "For everyone in this equation."

FOURTEEN

Finch

W hat a glorious day to have no idea what I'm doing.
Stuffed full of goat cheese and thick, buttery toast
from the monastery's Michelin-star monks, I walked alone to my
second trial toward map-making. I'd managed to dart back to my
room before things kicked off, making an excuse about needing to
meditate and get in the right mindset. Very Zen, very un-Finch.
Oliver had appreciated it, though.

"Mate, it's so important to sharpen your mind. Nourish your
body, nourish your mind, and the rest will take care of itself."
Those were his parting words of wisdom to me. I wasn't about to
start up a fanfare, throw a friendship party, and buy matching shell
bracelets, but I felt the frost thawing a bit. The Shining Twins had
even passed me the salt when I'd asked, instead of pretending I
hadn't spoken. So, it was all good. You know, aside from the threat
of Etienne killing me in my sleep, or in one of the upcoming trials.

I'd gone back to my room in the hopes that Erebus might show
up for a little pep-talk about what I was doing here. I'd waited as

long as I could, but I didn't want to be late to the second trial. Breaking into the place had been the first, so I guessed it had to be classed as the second one in our required quartet.

Where are you, Erebus? I stalked back along the corridors, peeved that he hadn't even bothered to check in.

His continued absence nagged at the back of my mind. This wasn't like him. He loved summoning me and leaving warnings when I least expected them, but my bathroom mirror remained unfrosted and my windows had yet to receive a bloody handprint. Usually, that would've been a comfort, but I started to wonder if the Great and Powerful Erebus wasn't so great and powerful in his shiny new body. Which, oddly, made me feel about ten times more alone and on edge than I already did. A reliability came with Erebus's constant harassment. Without it, I was just... drifting out here.

You know what would put the icing on this cupcake of anxiety? Davin. I hadn't been able to get that colossal turd out of my head after eavesdropping on Etienne last night. It wasn't like I expected to turn a corner and crash into him. It was just the idea that he could show up and try to shove his way in that made me want to take my chances and throw myself off the island cliff. I was a good swimmer. I'd make it.

Were they still friends? That hadn't been clear. I'd sensed loathe-love vibes from Etienne, with an emphasis on the loathe. Which begged the question: What had they fallen out over? Would their past disagreement be enough to keep Davin away? Man, I hoped so. Sure, I wanted him dead, but alone on this island with no backup, trying to kill him solo, wouldn't have been my smartest idea. Especially not if he had a reluctant friend in Etienne Biset.

A few minutes later, following the instructions I'd hastily written down on my napkin, I pushed through a blue door and found myself in a courtyard. A real one, with the interdimensional pocket thrumming overhead. The warm Greek sun beat down on yet another beautiful, half-naked deity in the center of the courtyard, with water spewing out of a delicately held jug. Seriously, this monastery should've come with at least a PG-13 rating.

Up ahead sat a row of chocolate box outbuildings, with lemon trees on either side of every door and hanging baskets adorning the white stone walls. I checked my napkin. Trial number two would take place behind door number four. I hurried across the courtyard and opened up the door to find... a pottery studio.

Huh. Plot twist. I'm actually here to make a wonky mug for Erebus.

The place had a very calming energy. An indoor fountain bubbled peacefully. Kilns stood at the back of the studio, and huge crates filled with reddish clay were stacked against the far wall. On a few small tables nearest to me lay every pottery tool imaginable.

The others sat behind pottery wheels, and I saw one spare for me. They shifted on their stools like awkward kids on the first day of school, exchanging confused looks.

"I'm Finch, and I'll be your rep for today." I broke the nervous silence and grinned at my new classmates. "We're starting with pottery at ten—please try not to reenact *that* scene from *Ghost*. It just makes everyone uncomfortable. After that, we'll do a little aquarobics in the pool to get those limbs loosened up, then a casual game of shuffleboard, and finish off with afternoon tea in the orangery."

I waited for them to laugh. Instead, their eyes darted past my shoulder, and my heart sank. *He's behind me, isn't he?*

"Very amusing." Etienne stepped through the doorway. "Why don't you take your seat so we can start? I wouldn't want to keep you from aquarobics."

Wishing the ground would swallow me, I crossed to the last

pottery wheel and sat down. Melody covered her mouth, her shoulders shaking as she stifled her laughter. *At least someone found it funny.*

"Are we really doing pottery?" Shailene didn't sound too impressed.

"Yeah, what does pottery have to do with map-making?" Fay nodded like one of those bobbleheads.

"I'm glad you asked." Etienne took up his position at the front of the class. "However, before I answer that, please collect your clay, water, and tools. I will explain the rest once you have everything you need."

We did as we were told. Naturally, Shailene and Fay made a run for the clay, as if that would ensure they got the premium stuff. It looked like a circuit class, the two of them dashing from the crates, to the tool tables, to the ceramic pots of water, and back to their seats in record time. Since Etienne didn't have a stopwatch, I guessed we weren't being judged on how quickly we could obey his instructions.

Back in our seats, our tools collected, we waited for Etienne to give us more tasty tidbits.

"The second trial in your journey toward map-making is a vital one," he began. "A mapmaker must be able to perform, even in the most adverse conditions. Your lives might depend on it."

"Map-making is dangerous?" Oliver asked the dumb question. I was secretly glad, considering I'd been about to ask the same thing.

Etienne gave him a hard look. "It is more dangerous than you could know. Imagine freezing to death on an expedition in Antarctica, with nothing but your map-making skills to get you to safety. Shivering, your extremities frostbitten, your body so cold you can barely speak, you know that all of your colleagues will die if you don't draw the right map. What do you do?"

Oliver looked sheepish. "Learn how to map-make in any condition?"

"Very clever." Etienne smirked. "Map-making is not simply about making maps, though many think so. They are usually the ones who fail. I discovered the craft during a mission to a tiny island off the Irish coast. The island was hidden from sight and near impossible to sense with magic. I'd been instructed to find my target, and it took months of relentless work.

"When I found him, I took the time to speak with him. After spending so much effort tracking him down, I admired him too much to just off him and go home. He told me he had dedicated his life to finding the lost island of Avalon so he could restore Arthur's crown to his family, the Pendragons. It's supposed to have remarkable healing properties, and his wife suffered from a terminal illness. I realized then that a rival family had sent me to kill him so he wouldn't get his hands on the artifact."

"The Le Fays?" I interjected.

Etienne peered at me with curiosity. "Yes, as a matter of fact. I suppose it makes sense for you to know that, considering your historical ties to those families."

"Did you kill him?" Oliver leaned over his pottery station.

"I am getting to that," Etienne said. "This man mentioned that he studied at this monastery, only to fail the trials. But that hadn't dampened his resolve. I stayed with him for a week, learning of map-making and how it could help a person find what they most desired. Hidden places, hidden objects, and secret realms. By this time, I'd grown tired of my job and the endless misery of it. I took no pleasure or pride in it anymore."

"Did you kill him?" Oliver repeated.

Etienne rolled his eyes. "No, as a matter of fact. I let him live and came directly to this monastery. I entered on the full moon, as you did, and partook in the trials. I succeeded and befriended the former owner, a man by the name of Julien Millepied. He allowed me to stay and learn from him, and then passed the mantle to me when he retired."

"The French sticking together, eh?" Mr. Abara grinned.

"It didn't hurt that I was French," Etienne replied.

Oliver's hand shot up. "Are you sure you didn't kill the owner?"

"I didn't. When I left Mr. Pendragon on that island, I left that life behind me." Etienne's voice bristled with annoyance. "I have not killed anyone since, nor do I plan to."

Is he really a changed man, then? I frowned at him. It was quite the tale, and I didn't know how much to believe.

Before I could dwell on it further, Etienne opened his arms and declared: "Let the second trial begin."

He walked to one of the nearby shelves and took down a… gas mask. Pulling it over his face, he twisted knobs fitted into the walls. I'd assumed they fed the kilns, but apparently not. I stiffened as a low hiss drifted across the room, spilling out of grates that ran along the skirting board.

Luke leapt up as if he'd been prodded in the ass with a red-hot poker. He lunged forward to scoop Melody into his arms. She shrieked as he lifted her and sprinted for the door. He yanked on the handle, but it didn't budge. The twins followed suit, running to the windows to throw them open, without success. The door and the windows were locked, and we were stuck in here with the gas spreading across the floor.

I didn't budge, though that didn't mean I wasn't just as scared as the others. I already knew it would be hopeless trying to escape, or Etienne wouldn't have had a gas mask handy. We were supposed to be stuck in here, with no way out. This was a trial, after all. If we could run out of it, what would be the point? Etienne would probably mark it as an immediate fail. And none of us wanted that.

"Remain calm and get to work," Etienne instructed, his voice muffled by the mask. "The gas is not deadly, but it's a mind-altering poison. You must navigate its effects to cling to reality and craft a vase worthy of putting in the kiln."

A mind-altering poison? What the hell did that mean? Poison bottles had skulls and crossbones on them for a reason. Poison, by its very nature, was dangerous. So, how could he say it wasn't? And if it *didn't* kill us, what would it do to us?

"Luke, use your Magneton ability on the window locks!" I shouted. He should have more luck than the twins. Running out of here would've meant instant disqualification but ventilating this room a bit couldn't hurt.

Luke turned and pretty much dropped Melody on the floor. He stared at her, like he wasn't sure what had happened. And then he crumpled into a fit of hysterics. All-out, tears-streaming, gut-wrenching belly laughs. He sank on the ground beside Melody and stared up at the ceiling, forming his hands into puppets and making them talk to each other.

"What do you think, Mr. Whiskers?" he asked his right hand. "Do you think Lukey cheated in the egg and spoon race? They said he did, but he knows he didn't. He didn't put his thumb on the egg. Nope, no way. He didn't do it, did he, Mr. Whiskers?"

I opened my mouth to shout him out of his stupor… when the gas hit me.

FIFTEEN

Finch

A volcano of giggles spewed every which way. Infectious, the gas left no survivors of its onslaught of hysterics. I'd never seen anything funnier than Luke talking to his puppet hands.

"Mr. Whiskers! Mr. Whiskers! His hand is a cat!" I howled, banging my pottery station so hard that a big lump of clay fell right off and landed with a satisfying slap. That set me off again. Reeling in my chair, I scooped the clay up and dropped it again. Another wet slap echoed through the studio. I couldn't breathe through my howls of laughter. I picked up and dropped the clay again and again.

"Throw it against the wall! Make it splat!" Melody giggled uncontrollably, unaffected by being dropped like a ball of clay by her supposed bodyguard.

I took the lump and flung it against the wall. It stuck like a jellyfish, and Melody collapsed in a heap, screeching in delight. I sagged against the pottery station, my shoulders shaking violently with laughter.

Oliver toppled right off his stool, which made us all scream. Even the twins held on to each other and wept ecstatic tears, while Blanche sat underneath her pottery table, staring out like an owl. The gas had hit her a little differently. Her eyes darted back and forth as she gripped the table legs, looking like a troll waiting for the Billy Goats Gruff. Mr. Abara had stood in an attempt to escape the gas, only to slide down the wall and sit with his head buried in his knees, his laughter booming louder than anyone else's.

"Do you remember that unicorn, Fay?" Shailene hiccupped. "Do you remember us chasing it, and then it charged right into a tree and got stuck?"

Fay crumpled into her sister's shoulder. "It kept trying to wiggle its way out! Remember its butt just wiggling and jiggling?!"

"A twerking unicorn!" I shrieked, banging my fist against the pottery station. Everyone howled in response, all of us useless. My body felt loose and free. Man, it was good to just friggin' laugh!

"I never went to Nepal!" Oliver cried, wiping tears from his eyes. "I told everyone I was going, then I went on a package holiday to Ibiza, sat on a beach, and drank my weight in watered-down margaritas!"

"You said the guides told you your expertise was too good to climb with the group! And you never even went there!" Shailene exploded in hysterics, setting off a domino effect. I sank to the floor; it was too damn funny to stay on my stool.

"I know!" Oliver roared, slapping his chest.

Luke lifted his puppet hands. "You know what, Mr. Whiskers, you're right. I did cheat in egg and spoon. I held my thumb over that egg like there was no tomorrow and ran for my life."

Everyone collapsed.

"Mr. Whiskers never lies." Melody covered her face, her laughter coming in stifled gasps. "I like Mr. Whiskers. He can stay."

"Mr. Whiskers is just his hand!" I chimed in, my whole body shaking.

"Then Mr. Whiskers has always been here." Melody grinned like a loon, reaching out to stroke Luke's hand. "It's like that time I found my mom talking to herself. She kept saying, 'No, you're the pretty one. You shouldn't be wasting your time here.' I thought she was talking to a ghost, but now I think she was just giving herself a pep-talk."

We all screamed with unbridled joy.

"Hey, we've all done it. I give myself a pep-talk every morning," I shot back, holding my stomach as my ribs started to ache. "I'll have that six-pack by the end of this! Laughter is the best exercise. Screw your crunches and squats."

"I like my crunches and squats," Luke shot back, giggling.

"I bet you do. How else are you going to not fit in your clothes? Seriously, man, you could always buy a size up, you know?" I threw back my head and bashed it on the table, but that only made me laugh harder. Luke, too.

Melody grasped Luke's hand. "He likes to show off his muscules."

"Mus-cules?" Luke dissolved into a fit.

"You're too cute for muscles," Melody explained, curling up in the fetal position as the giggles hit her again.

"I fought for my muscles." Mr. Abara sobbed into his knees. "Real men don't squat."

The laughter began to hurt. "You should put that on a T-shirt!"

"Who says I haven't?" Mr. Abara shot back.

"You know, I accidentally turned Katherine into a minotaur during one of my 'lessons' with her—she had massive, bulging, furry muscles and... and hooves! And she stank like a cattle shed." I totally lost it. "Man, she beat me so hard, I had to sleep on my stomach for weeks!"

Everyone whooped, clinging to the nearest solid object to bear the brunt of their laughter. Only Blanche remained unaffected, looking around the studio like a startled creature, her neck turning so fast she was in danger of whiplash.

"Hoot for me, Blanche!" I urged.

"What?" the twins chorused, leaning on each other for support.

"She looks like... an owl!" I screeched, wrapping my arms around me.

"She does!" Melody howled, burying her face in Luke's side.

"What kind of owl do you find in the kitchen?" I couldn't resist.

Oliver rubbed his eyes on the back of his sleeve. "I don't know, what kind of owl do you find in the kitchen?"

"A tea t-owl!" I erupted in a violent bout of giggles, and everyone followed suit.

Mr. Abara put up his hand. "What do you call a baby owl swimming?"

"I don't know, what do you call a baby owl swimming?" I set him up, as any good comic sidekick would.

"A moist owlette!" Mr. Abara bellowed, hugging his knees as he gave in completely to the gas.

Now I understood why the Irish called a good time a "gas." This was exactly what the doctor ordered. A bonding experience that laid us all bare, reducing us to weeping, laughing lumps.

"A... moist... owlette!" Melody gasped, sounding near death from euphoria.

I looked around the studio at the others, finding them in similar states of disarray. Then, my eyes locked onto a creepy figure in the corner, his head covered by a gas mask. The laughter died on my tongue, replaced by sudden paranoia. I'd forgotten Etienne.

What if he's trying to kill us? What if there is no trial? What if it's just death by laughing gas? My eyes widened until I started to feel a bit owl-like myself. I twisted my head this way and that, expecting hidden monks to slither out of the gas and end us all. We were vulnerable. We wouldn't be able to fight back.

My mouth dried up, the paranoia threatening to suffocate me. I couldn't get air into my lungs.

Crap, crap, crap... snap out of it! The more I tried to focus, the more clarity slipped away. I wanted the happiness back. I didn't want paranoia. It shivered through me, twisting everything I saw. The laughing faces of the others turned into manic grimaces, the dream quickly changing to a nightmare.

"Melody, do you know something?" Luke's voice distracted me. "You are the single most important person in my life. Without you, I'd have no purpose. You're more than a job to me."

Melody giggled. "Are you drunk?"

"I don't think so." Luke pinched himself, as if that would tell him.

"I can read you, remember?" Melody chuckled. "You try to keep your emotions hidden away, but that only makes them louder."

"It does?" Luke looked horrified.

Melody nodded. "I try to switch my Empathy off, because it can be invasive, but it's really hard. That's why I like being around people like Finch and Blanche, because I can't feel their emotions at all."

She turned to look at me. "But, even though I can't read you, I know you're a good egg, Finch. I know everything you've done— the good, the bad, and the ugly—and this person you've become is the best version of yourself you will ever be. You've worked so hard. It shows, it really does, no matter how the stories get twisted.

Just be careful around Luke—he doesn't like having competition for the alpha spot."

She collapsed in another fit of giggles, but Luke didn't look amused. In fact, he stared at me angrily. Like he'd been hit with the same bout of paranoia that I had.

I'm not going to take your girl. I tried to say it, but the words wouldn't come. The gas locked my throat in a vise. I couldn't do anything but sit and stew in my own paranoid juices.

"I lied when I said I'd been on the island this whole time," Oliver chimed in. It took Luke's attention from me, which hopefully meant I wouldn't get blasted in the face by his cute "mus-cules." "I didn't get here in time last month, that was true. But I went back to Athens instead of waiting here. I spent too much time there, so I missed the first deadline. I was supposed to be on a European tour, but I ran out of dosh. So, I stole diamonds and conned tourists in Athens to build up my bank account again. I think about those people a lot. I think I ruined some holidays."

It looked like the effects of the gas had changed from hysterical to introspective, making our truths spill out like the Exxon Valdez disaster, oil spreading everywhere. My paranoia grew each second. I didn't want my truths spilling out. I'd already told them everything I wanted to.

"Do you remember when we almost got killed by that gargoyle?" Fay glanced at her sister.

Shailene nodded. "You'd think gargoyles would be easy, but they can be slimy little buggers. I still think about those fangs sinking into your neck, sis."

"Me, too." Fay fidgeted awkwardly. "I always wonder what it'd be like if we just gave up on this monster-hunting business."

"We make most of our money from advertising contracts. Energy drinks and stuff, in the magical world." Shailene rested her head against her sister's shoulder. "We always talk about giving it up, don't we?"

Fay nuzzled her sister. "We just want to travel the world and have fun, see what these countries have to offer, instead of jumping from mission to mission. Always on a deadline."

I know how that feels...

"But we can't," Shailene said. "We've created these awesome personas, and we've got to live up to the hype. If we don't, we lose the contracts, the money, the lifestyle."

"Mum and Dad wouldn't be happy," Fay said softly.

"Who else will pay for their matching Lambos?" Shailene sighed. The laughter was fading from each person in the room, it seemed.

Mr. Abara had been looking at Oliver. "You stole diamonds, Oliver?"

"I did. I'm sorry for it, but you see these gigantic rocks on people's fingers, and they're so easy to take. I needed the cash." Oliver sank back, swamped with an air of depression.

"I dream of a world without blood diamonds," Mr. Abara said grimly. "Most of those rocks you speak of—they come drenched in the blood of child soldiers forced to defend the diamond mines of Africa. It's why I traveled to Sierra Leone in the first place, using the disguise of a military officer. If I had my way, I'd stop it all. No more child soldiers, no more mines, no more rich people buying these stones without knowing where they came from."

I hadn't expected Mr. Abara to be a savior type. I hadn't yet pinpointed what kind of guy he was, and that came out of left field.

"I have seen more death and destruction than you can imagine," Mr. Abara continued. "I was a military man, hired to oversee the mines. I wear the uniform, even now, but only so I can protect those children. Change comes from the inside, you know? But it hurts me every time one slips through the net. I remember every face."

"That's rough," I said genuinely.

Mr. Abara nodded. "I'm also terrified of mice." It had no relation to what he'd just said. He just blurted it out, riding the gas wave and following it wherever it went.

"I used to be like you, Oliver, when I was a young'un." Blanche finally spoke. "I Shapeshifted at carnivals that came through, playing games with cards and cups that ordinary folk could never win. Then I'd Shift back, once they knew they'd been conned. No one ever caught me. A couple of times, I Shifted into sideshow folks—bearded ladies, lobster-handed guys, giant women. I changed into a mermaid a couple of times and conned rich men with a fishy fetish. That was more of a long play, though. I had to meet them on the shore and make up stories about only being able to touch land at midnight. They bought it, and they'd leave me jewelry. A few proposals, too, but I always disappeared before it got too intense."

Wow... disturbing. I balled my hands into fists and tried to concentrate on reality. Fighting this gas wouldn't be easy. A gentle hiss told me that it still seeped in through the grates. I didn't trust what it was doing to my body. The gas took me farther and farther away from the job: to make a vase and not get killed by Etienne.

"What do you fear most, Finch?" Etienne asked suddenly. *Speak of the devil.*

I startled, but my addled brain latched onto his question. I tried to push my reply away, but the gas had me by the *cajones.* I couldn't refuse.

"I... I'm worried my life will go by before I prove I've changed. I have crazy feelings for this girl, but she's already with someone. It's as if someone put him through a 'perfect man' machine and poured in everything a woman wants. I don't belong in that picture. I don't belong with someone like her. That's my biggest fear, I guess. That I'll never fit into any picture at all."

I thought about the photo in my room, everyone neatly paired up. Even though Garrett and Astrid were book-ending the image, they'd grown closer. And no one stood in their way. They belonged together. I couldn't envision myself with Ryann. Or anyone, for that matter. My love ship had sailed. Either that, or it was permanently docked in the harbor, filled with holes and unseaworthy.

"I'm afraid of losing the one person I care about," Luke added quietly. "I'm afraid something will happen, and I won't be able to save her in time. I've heard from my colleagues about people dying in their arms. I couldn't bear that."

Melody turned away from him. "I'm afraid I'll break under pressure, that my brain will burn up and leave nothing behind. I'm afraid I won't live up to expectations. Or that I might become a target, that I'll never get a say in my own life, ever again."

Huh? What did that mean? What troubles could a happy-go-lucky bookworm have, to make her feel like that? Did she have exams coming up or something? They could be hard, sure, but getting worked up to that extent felt like overkill. Unless there was something else going on that I didn't understand.

"I'm afraid we'll keep living this life, and that, one day—" Shailene began, breaking off my hazy thoughts.

"—it'll kill one of us, and we'll be separated forever. We came into this world together, and we want to go out together, but there have been so many near misses. I'm afraid we might not grow old together," Fay finished.

Mr. Abara nodded. "I'm terrified the world will never change, and I won't be able to save children from being forced to take up arms. I'm terrified I won't be able to make a difference."

"I'm scared I'll never amount to anything," Oliver murmured.

Blanche ducked farther under the table. "I'm scared that I'll die without achieving what I set out to do. More than that, I'm just terrified of getting older. I have so much life behind me and so many stories, and there's less time between me and death than there has ever been. You feel mortality when you reach my age. I'm scared of that ticking clock."

I glanced back at the eerie figure of Etienne, smugly observing in his gas mask. What was the purpose of this? My hazy mind kept changing the word into "porpoise," making me think about dolphins. But that was the gas talking. *Focus, Finch!* Why would Etienne do this?

Realization struck me. This was a ploy to uncover potential spies or liars among us. Panic struck, like overly affectionate lightning hitting the same spot twice. How did I prove I didn't have a hidden purpose? Had he already read into my gut-spilling? Technically, I was here to learn map-making, but I was also here for Erebus.

Maybe, for once, it's a good thing he didn't give me all the deets. What I didn't know, I couldn't reveal to Etienne. Not that it made me feel better about Etienne's devious prodding and poking.

The laughing gas had hoisted us so high, we only had one way to go... on a slippery slope downward.

SIXTEEN

Finch

L aughter gave way to tears, and tears gave way to stony silence before the laughter started up again. Whatever this gas did to us, it came in distinct blocks of mania. And Etienne seemed to love every moment, chuckling away behind his gas mask like a psycho killer toying with his victims.

What's that thing Harley used...? I rifled through my head. My brain felt stuffed with impenetrable fuzz. I grasped at thoughts and memories, but they spun away the moment I got hold of them. It was as if the gas only wanted us to feel what it wanted us to feel and say what it wanted us to say.

Come on, Finch! I'd gone through worse as a teenager. I'd been trapped in dark rooms that filled with gas before, without a speck of pleasantness about it. Poison gas, thick and smothering, with every intention of killing me. And a clock on the wall, ticking down the seconds before I passed the point of no return. A literal death stopwatch. This should've been child's play in comparison.

I struggled to remember my training and the bits and pieces I'd picked up along the way. Just then, I had a Euphoria moment. Not a Eureka moment. That was what Harley had used, and the thing Katherine had trained me to use, to slow everything right down.

I squinched my eyes closed and forced myself to sink into that deep mental state, grasping for my best memories and holding them with everything I had. They had to be recent, since the older ones were blocked off. I pictured myself on the swing outside the Smith house, talking to Ryann. The next moment, I switched to me and Harley in the car, driving back to the SDC, my belly full of pie. Those would do. I just needed enough of a Euphoric state to take the edge off this gas.

"Why do you still wear the uniform?" I heard Oliver ask, but he sounded distant.

"Looking the part is the only way to protect the children," Mr. Abara replied.

"Do you still work for the mines?" Blanche cut in.

Mr. Abara sighed. "Yes and no. I keep up a ruse, to gain access while I save as many children as I can. I pretend I'm taking them away to be punished for disobedience, then I take them to a sanctuary. There's a cell of us, working together, but the work is slow."

"That's risky, isn't it?" Shailene said.

"It is, but it is necessary." I heard Mr. Abara take a deep breath. "If I have to give my life for this cause, then so be it."

I focused harder on my memories, tuning the others out. Rising like a zombie, I felt my way to my pottery station. I had a spare chunk of clay—one that I hadn't splatted on the wall. Fumbling, I found the pedal to spin the pottery wheel and placed the lump of clay on top. I dipped my hands in water and pressed them to the clay, pushing the pedal to get things moving. My body didn't want to listen, but the slightly Euphoric state helped. Soon enough, I fell into the rhythm of the pottery wheel, giving me a bit more autonomy over my limbs.

"What's he doing?" Melody whispered, returning to giggle mode.

"Making something," Luke replied.

"Is that what we're supposed to do?" Melody paused. "I think it is. Someone told us... Make something? A... vase, right? Is that right? I can't remember. My head is so cloudy."

I heard movement but didn't open my eyes. Not yet. I needed to ensure the gas wouldn't overwhelm me again. The scrape of stools followed, Luke's and Melody's, from their positions next to me.

"We should do that," Shailene chimed in.

"Help me back to my station," Fay replied. More shuffling echoed in my ears. Two more stool scrapes, then three more. Everyone had returned to their stations, unless my ears were playing tricks on me.

I finally dared to look. Sure enough, everyone sat staring at the pottery wheels like they were alien artifacts. Mr. Abara set to work, copying what I was doing. I didn't mind. We all needed to get through this. Blanche got on with it, then Melody and Luke, then Oliver and the twins. Satisfied, I glanced back at Etienne. He'd kicked his legs up onto a nearby table, his arms folded across his chest. *Impressed, Monsieur?* I couldn't tell through his gas mask.

We weren't out of the woods yet. On the other side of Melody, Luke stumbled onto a problem. Metal pottery tools whizzed through the air toward him, sticking to him like flies on crap. He had to duck a few of the sharp ones, though they spun, homing-missile style, and hurtled back at his face. His Magneton ability seemed to be glitching thanks to the gas. It was surprising that it hadn't happened before, when he'd been totally out of control, but I guessed the gas worked in mysterious ways.

And man, was it funny.

"You need to calm down, Magneto!" I crumpled in a fit of hysterics, tumbling right off my stool and hitting the floor. I didn't even feel the impact. I just drew my arms around myself and wheezed, my ribs aching as the giggle train pummeled me.

"It's not my fault!" Luke shouted. "I don't know how to turn it off!"

"You don't have a switch for that?" I stared at the ceiling through blurry eyes, unable to control my body. The temporary Euphoria had worn off.

Melody reached forward and cupped Luke's face. "Focus on me. Breathe with me. Ready? In… and out. In… and out." He made a hilarious show of breathing with her, his eyes fixed open as he huffed and puffed.

"Why are you staring at me? You have to stop, or I'm going to lose it. Be natural. Take relaxed breaths," Melody urged.

"I *am* being natural!" Luke protested. He took a few more breaths, and the stuck-on tools fell away, clanging to the ground.

The sound snapped me out of my hilarity. I focused on the whirr of pottery wheels, that soothing rhythm, and clambered back onto my stool.

My crooked pot sat lopsided on the pottery wheel. It wouldn't be a beauty, but I was going to finish this clay bastard if it was the last thing I did. Etienne wanted to see us concentrate despite the poison gas. That brought a few interesting questions to mind—if he wanted us to get through this, what sort of situations did he expect us to run into while map-making?

I should've worried, but I kind of appreciated what Etienne was trying to do. He had pushed us to our limits. Every limit, so we'd never be in a scenario we couldn't map-make our way out of. And, somehow, it was working. Paranoia nagged at the back of my head.

He could have used this to learn our secrets, too, but I was pretty sure I hadn't said anything damning.

I dipped my fingertips into the water and pressed them to the clay pot, letting the wheel move slowly under the pressure of my foot on the pedal. The clay wobbled and swayed as if alive, but that only made me press my hands more firmly, to stop it from running away. And, hey, it took my mind off the gas. Physical therapy of sorts. All I had to do was look at the pot and watch it take shape. A hollowed-out middle—good. A narrower lip around the top—even better.

I smoothed my hands around the center until the motion gave a womanly curve to the vase. I hadn't intended to go saucy with my clay creation, but I'd take anything my hands could manage right now. Maybe this said more about me as a potter than it did about the gas, but I'd leave the psychoanalysis up to Etienne.

"I think I did it!" I gasped in surprise. A few minutes had passed while I devoted all my attention to Madam Vase. It was the ugliest damn vase I'd ever seen, squat and wavy and leaning to one side, but I couldn't complain.

Etienne got up from his perch and came to investigate. "Very good, Finch. It will make a fine centerpiece on your countryside kitchen table."

"You think I have a kitchen? Or a table, for that matter?" I replied. "And I'm a town mouse, not a country mouse." I didn't know whether to take his words as a straightforward compliment, or one with a backhanded bite to it.

"Mouse? Where?" Mr. Abara shrieked in alarm.

Etienne chuckled. "There is no mouse, Mr. Abara. I was just admiring Finch's handiwork. It is a beautiful example of the ceramic arts."

"Wait... that's it?" I frowned. "I completed the second trial?"

"I asked you to make a vase, and you have... more or less." Etienne patted me on the shoulder. *Yeah, definitely a backhanded compliment.* I'd take it. I had completed the second round.

I sat back proudly and watched the others, keeping the effects of the gas at bay with more Euphoria. Nobody seemed to have a background in pottery. My monstrosity looked almost skillful compared to some of the blobs on show.

"Done!" the twins chorused. Surprisingly, their vases hadn't come out the same. Fay's looked short and stumpy and would have struggled in a line-up of vases, while Shailene's had turned out taller and more elegant.

"Me, too," Oliver said a few moments later.

The twins scowled at him, casting withering looks at his limp vase, floppy and covered in dents.

"I am done," Mr. Abara announced. His vase looked like him: big, bulky, and masculine. It also looked the likeliest to actually hold water.

"I'm done, too." Blanche raised her hand. Her vase was conical, with a thin neck. Again, not a far-off clay equivalent of Blanche herself.

Melody nodded. "I'm finished. I'm not quite happy with it, but I think it should be structurally sound. The base is thick, and there are no air bubbles, so it shouldn't explode in the kiln. I think it'll hold water." Her vase was Best in Show. She'd even put flourishes on the sides by carving thin lines and crimping the top.

We all had our ducks in a row, except Luke. The pressure felt palpable. All of us stared at him, watching him struggle to manipulate clay while tools flew at his head. It felt like sitting in an exam room, waiting for the last person to finish so we could all leave. Pottery might have come easily to Melody, but her skillset hadn't rubbed off on her hired muscle. And the more nervous he got, the worse his control over his abilities became.

I noticed a carving tool jiggling on my workstation. A second later, it hovered. I lunged to try and catch it, but the handle slipped through my fingers. Targeting Luke's vulnerable vase, it hurtled toward him, pointy side first.

Instinct brought my palms up, a tendril of Telekinesis spiraling out. The shimmering end caught the carving tool just before it destroyed Luke's work, and I yanked back. At lightning speed, it spun back the way it came and clattered into the wall.

Why did I do that? I didn't owe Luke anything. He hadn't exactly been friendly toward me. But something about Melody's frightened expression made me step in. She needed Luke; that was obvious. Maybe I was trying to stay true to my word, to be a better man. Or maybe I'd gone soft. Either way, I'd kept him in the running. He finally finished his vase and looked at it proudly.

Etienne applauded, the sound going off like a gunshot. "*Bien,* everyone. You have all succeeded in stage two of the trials."

"We have?" Luke sounded shocked. I couldn't blame him—his vase came out the worst, even without being destroyed by errant tools.

"*Oui,* you have," Etienne replied, clearly amused. "You are dismissed. The doors are no longer locked. With that in mind, I suggest you take the remainder of the day to rest and recuperate while the gas wears off. I wouldn't advise beginning the third trial while it is still in effect."

"What's the third trial?" I sounded like the teacher's pet. All eager, bright-eyed, and bushy-tailed. My head felt anything but— the room still swam around me.

Etienne laughed. "You will find out in due time."

I hated to admit it, but I liked this. I'd never been top of the class, and while my vase was a pretty sorry excuse, I'd finished first. Now that I'd had a taste, I wanted more. I wanted to find out what came next and get through that, too. This had started as a pain in my ass, but curiosity had taken hold, and that reluctance turned to determination without my noticing. I loved a challenge.

"I'd put that on my shelf." Melody cast a shy glance at Luke.

"You're just being nice," Luke replied.

Melody shook her head. "No, I mean it. It's interesting. Why have a boring, normal vase when you could have something personal and handmade?"

They were an odd pair, but they intrigued me. Everyone did, to an extent. Blanche had killer stories. Mr. Abara seemed less mysterious now that I knew what made him tick. The Basani twins reminded me of everything I hated about covens and magical elitism, but they wanted freedom. And Oliver... well, he was Oliver. Like a kiddie pool—not much depth.

And don't even get me started on you. I looked at Etienne, who returned my gaze with a cool one of his own. Did he have it in for me? Was he just biding his time?

"Do you have a concern, Finch?" Etienne asked.

I shook my head. "Just thinking about what I said."

"Ah yes, the inevitable hangover from this gas." Etienne removed his gas mask and smirked. "There will be regrets."

"You can say that again," Luke muttered, embarrassed.

I couldn't believe I'd talked about Ryann to these people. Then again, I hadn't exactly expected a sneak attack of mind-altering poison. That girl definitely had a firmer hold on my heart than I'd thought. The whole experience renewed an incessant itch to see her again.

Ah, Ryann... why did it have to be you?

SEVENTEEN

Kenzie

———————

After leaving me with a whole bunch of instructions for Finch, and revealing some more about the monastery and what went on there, Erebus vanished with a rush of air that knocked the blue bottle off the kitchen table. I vaulted from the sofa, reaching the table with a second to spare. My hands gripped the slick glass tightly. It almost slipped through, but I held it to my chest and twisted my body around, my back hitting the ground with a thud.

I lay there, panting. Rage coursed through me. I hated Erebus. I'd never hated anyone more. But he'd pulled all the right strings to force my obedience. Namely, Mom and Inez in this bottle. He'd snatched away any choice I might've had, despite the fact that I'd already given that up when I made the blood pact.

Asshole... total asshole.

I took the bottle to the TV, tucking it behind the screen where it'd be safe. It felt weird to be alone in the apartment. Even when

Inez went to school, Mom was always here. Technically they were still here, the light of their souls swirling inside the glass.

Erebus had barely answered any of *my* questions about the monastery mission; he'd just made sure I had the details he wanted me to know, then vamoosed.

A knock at the door echoed through the apartment, making me jump. Erebus wouldn't bother knocking.

I crept toward the door and picked up my shotgun. "Who's there?"

I peered into the spyhole and a wave of relief barreled through me. Ryann stood on the other side, glancing over her shoulder like she expected gang members to jump her.

"Kenzie? Is that you?" she asked nervously.

I put down the shotgun and opened the door. "What are you doing here?"

"Harley sent me to bring you into the SDC."

I frowned. "Not going to happen."

"What? Why not?" She tried to look over my shoulder, but I blocked her view.

"I'm busy," I replied. "Why's Harley calling in the troops?"

"Everyone's freaking out about Finch. The whole SDC is looking for him. She's got security magicals all over the place, searching for Davin, too. He's already at the top of the most-wanted list, but she's drawing in more and more departments now, including the Magical Secret Service. And Harley's worried that someone might be targeting people who know Finch. She thinks you might be vulnerable."

I smiled bitterly. "She's worried about Erebus, huh? Or just Davin?"

"Both, I guess." Ryann looked at me curiously. "You know about Finch and Erebus, then?"

I shrugged. "I've recently learned more than I wanted to know."

"What do you mean?"

I gestured inside. "Come in. There's a lot to explain." An idea popped into my head. "But you might have come at the best possible moment."

"Oh?" She followed me inside, where we sat at the kitchen table.

I leaned forward on my elbows. "Before I say anything, swear you won't breathe a word to Harley. Tell her you're guarding me here or something, because of my mom's condition. If you don't, I can't tell you what's going on."

Ryann frowned. "How can I swear that if I don't know what's up?"

"You'll have to wrangle with your conscience, I guess. Decide if you want to know, or if you don't."

"Is it about Finch?"

I nodded. "Oh yeah, and then some. I've got answers. Not many, but more than anyone else."

She rubbed the back of her neck. "I... suppose I could keep quiet, if it's for Finch." She sounded worried. That worked in my favor. If I could buy anyone's silence, it was Ryann's. I'd seen her and Finch together—there were sparks, for sure, even if she wasn't in a position to admit it. I knew she had a dude, but her fidgeting gave her away. It clearly wasn't just Harley freaking out.

"You swear?"

Her frown deepened. "Tell me why Harley can't know."

"This is Erebus we're dealing with. If he finds out other people are involved, he might... destroy something I care about." I nodded to the bottle by the TV, and I couldn't stop my voice from shaking. "He's got my mom and sister trapped in there. Djinn magic that only he can undo."

Ryann's eyes shot wide. "What? Why?"

"You say that a lot, huh?" I said dryly, before launching into the brief version of what happened today. I didn't stop until I reached the part where I'd accidentally called Erebus weak, and he'd shoved my mom and sister in that bottle. It sent a sharp pang through my heart, though I tried not to show it on my face. I didn't need anyone's pity.

"Wow." Ryann blinked slowly. "And I thought I had a bad day."

"I'll never whine ever again, after what I've just gone through." I sighed. "And it doesn't end there. Erebus told me where Finch is. He's safe, but he's far away."

Ryann leaned closer. "Where is he?" She stank of desperation. *Poor sucker.*

"I need you to promise," I urged.

This time, she didn't hesitate. "If your mom and sister are at risk, I won't say a word. Just tell me where he is."

"He's at a place called the Mapmakers' Monastery." I recalled everything Erebus had told me before disappearing—there'd been a lot of stuff to remember. "It's this weird, isolated, coven-like place, run by some French dude named Etienne Biset—a shady assassin-turned-mapmaker that nobody knows much about. Well, Erebus might, but he didn't give me much to go on. Just a name and a quick backstory."

"A monastery? Why would Erebus send Finch to a monastery?"

"Forget about the monastery part. It's more about the map-making, from what I picked up. Erebus told me Finch is there learning to draw magical maps to hidden places—again, no details on why. There are some trials, and they're hella weird and scary and confusing. So, it's safe to say that Finch has gone from the frying pan into a big-ass fire."

Ryann stiffened. "He's in danger?"

"Depends how good he is at the trials. Anyway, Erebus has sent servants before, but Finch is somehow different. Erebus has faith in him, as odd as that sounds." I paused. "But that doesn't mean he doesn't need help."

Ryann nodded. "Go on..."

"Erebus told me that the art of map-making has something to do with Light magic. I asked Erebus why he didn't just get his wifey to help—that Lux chick—but he said she ain't sharing. He wasn't really up for answering the questions *I* had, but I got the feeling they had a spat, and I didn't want to push it. Basically, Erebus wants Finch to succeed. He's learned from previous attempts what works and what doesn't, and he gave me the job of helping Finch out. I've got a whole damn list of things to say, do, and look for."

"And you want me to help?" Ryann looked eager.

"I need you to be my eyes here. Morphing is a strange ability. There's a crapload of power to it, and it leaves my real body vulnerable. I need you to watch me, and this place, and that bottle, while I'm Morphing out to find Finch."

"Oh." She sounded disappointed.

"Look, Erebus is a sneaky son of a gun, and I don't want my body sitting out, exposed. More than that, I don't want anyone following my trail, for their own sakes. I'm not giving Erebus any excuse to tell me my deal is void." I stared at her. "I need that backup, so I won't be wigging out over what's happening to my body while I'm gone. You're the safest bet."

"Why's that?"

"If Erebus says anything about you, I can just pretend I wiped your mind. One of the benefits of being magic-free. I'll explain that I needed a bodyguard, but I'll tell him you don't remember anything. Then, he can't complain or twist things to suit himself."

Ryann sighed. "I'm starting to develop an inferiority complex."

"You should take pride in the fact that we need you. I need you for this, and so do my mom and sister," I replied gently. "Finch does, too. If anything happens to my body while I'm trying to communicate with him, he'll be trapped on his own there, with no clue what to do."

A glint sparked in Ryann's eyes. "If he succeeds, will he come home?"

"By the sound of it, yeah." I smiled.

Ryann tapped her fingers on the table. "Will you tell me everything you find there? Like, what the heck Erebus has Finch running around after?"

"Sure. You'll have your mind wiped, remember?" I flashed her a wink. "What's the harm in revealing a few details?"

She smirked. "I like the cut of your jib, Kenzie."

"Huh?"

"It means I like your style." She chuckled, but some nervousness stayed.

"Does that mean you'll help me?"

She nodded slowly. "I don't like not being able to tell Harley he's alive, but I get why." She glanced at the bottle by the TV. "My family and I were trapped once. I know how it feels."

I felt like a weight had been lifted. With Ryann here, I didn't feel so alone anymore.

"Text Harley, tell her my mom's having an episode and you've decided to stay here to watch me. Tell her I said I don't want anyone else dropping by, so my mom doesn't get worse with a bunch of strangers hanging around—something like that." I hated using Mom as an excuse, but it had to be done.

Ryann whipped out her phone and began typing. "Done," she said a few moments later.

"Let's see what she's got to say." We waited in awkward silence.

Her phone pinged shortly after, and Ryann's eyes scanned the screen. "She says that's fine, to keep checking in, and she hopes your mom comes out of it soon."

Guilt twisted my gut. I got down off the kitchen stool. "Then we have our bases covered. Let's do this. You might be in it for the long haul, if that's okay with you? It's going to take a while on this first run."

"I'll stay as long as you need me to," Ryann replied.

I walked to the sofa and lay down. Ryann followed and perched on the armrest, looking at me. *No pressure.* Closing my eyes, I let the apartment drift away and sank into the center of my consciousness. Slipping into the minds of creatures came as easily as breathing, but I'd have to travel a hell of a way to get to Finch. It would kick my butt, for sure. I'd have to sleep for a week once this was over.

My body thrummed with Morph energy, my mind lifting into space, detaching from my physical form. It latched onto a seagull flying over the apartment. I took the reins instantly, the bird's mind giving way without a fight. Bouncing my consciousness from one animal to another was tricky, but I'd learned the skill a long time ago. And it was the only way to cover this kind of distance in a short period of time.

I soared on the warm currents of air that surged upward, feeling the strong wings carrying me through the sky and on toward Greece. That was one good thing, I guessed… at least I knew where I was headed. I'd have to hop from one animal brain to another to get there as fast as possible, calling on all my Morph stamina. It'd take me a day or so, but I wasn't going to stop until I reached Finch.

EIGHTEEN

Finch

A couple of days passed with no whisper of trial *numéro* three on the horizon. Aside from a massive headache, a need to cocoon myself in sleep for a whole day, and a throat as dry as the Mojave Desert, there'd been no severe aftereffects of the laughing gas. I could only imagine the hysterical scenes if dentists suddenly decided to switch out nitrous for whatever Etienne used on us. It'd definitely make root canals more interesting.

On the morning of the second day, I sat on a different terrace—this place had them by the bucketload—overlooking the calm Ionian Sea. The air shimmered like liquid in the sunlight, making the edges of the monastery's protective shield undulate like a living, breathing organism. Orange and lemon trees surrounded a cluster of tables and chairs, emanating a sweet, citrusy scent. Had I been poetically inclined, I could have filled books and books with the romantic inspiration this monastery provided. All of them would've been targeted toward Ryann, but I'd have been subtle about it. Anyone's eyes could be as dazzling blue and soothing as the rippling ocean, right?

Does she have blue eyes? It was hard to picture her face, not having seen her in a while. I knew the pain of forgetting all too well. Adley's face had become a hazy shape to me now, and I didn't even have a photo to remind me what she'd looked like.

"More goat cheese, Mr. Merlin?" One of the monks bowed so low I thought his spine might crack in two.

I shook my head. "No, thanks, or I'll never fit through the door. I'll take some coffee if it's on, though."

"Of course, Mr. Merlin."

Their coffee was dangerously addictive. It tasted rich and bitter and spicy, flavored with cardamom. I could've downed ten jugs, but then I would be jittering around the hallways, babbling like a monkey.

I turned my attention toward my fellow challengers, who'd picked their own tables, although Melody and Luke hadn't appeared. The Basani twins occasionally shot death stares at Oliver, then at me, then at the others. I didn't know what they were up to, but I knew their type. They were probably scheming to get everyone else disqualified. A charming way to finish off a delicious breakfast of goat cheese and honey.

"Morning!" A cheerful voice reverberated across the terrace. I turned to find Melody and Luke stepping out of the nearby cloisters. Melody, of course, used the chipper voice of a true morning person. Luke just followed, rubbing the sleep from his eyes. I hadn't really seen anyone yesterday, thanks to the effects of the gas. A few of them had emerged from their rooms to eat, but they hadn't been very talkative. Neither had I. But today, everyone seemed more like themselves.

"Morning," I replied. Since I was the only one to reply, Melody made a beeline for me and sat at my table. *My, my, aren't I popular?*

"It's a little chilly this morning, isn't it?" Melody smiled as the monks hurried over to feed her.

I shrugged. "Blanche said the monastery attracts the winds."

She cast a sly glance at the Basani twins. "I mean them. I felt it the minute I stepped onto the terrace. There's a cold wave coming from them. Funny enough, it's fear—it has a distinct sensation, which is hard to explain. I suppose it's similar to that creeping feeling you get when you feel like you're being watched."

"What are they afraid of?" Luke yawned and stretched out.

"They're terrified they're going to fail. I can sense spite too, and a very potent dislike for everyone here, which usually leads to vindictiveness," Melody replied. "I'm sure they're not bad people, but they seem to feel there's a great deal at stake for them." She lowered her voice a touch. "And they *really* don't like Oliver. Most of their emotions are geared toward him, though they have a few icy notes for you too, Finch. Likely because you finished the second trial first. Well done on that, by the way. I liked your piece. Very avant-garde."

She was pulling my leg, and I duly laughed. "Best thing I've made since my finger-painting of the Eiffel Tower in second grade." I paused. "But why the beef with Oliver? Can you delve any deeper?"

Oliver scraped his chair back, closer to my table. Unfortunately, it looked like he'd been in earshot. The Basani twins, on the other hand, were on the other side of the terrace—well out of the way. "It's probably because they remember me, mate. I swindled a lot of cash from them a couple of weeks ago, in Athens. I wasn't sure they recognized me. But I'm guessing they've caught on. Trouble is, they can't hurt me for it. It wouldn't look too good if they admitted, in public, that I'd conned them, would it?"

I snorted. "Looks like they're plotting their revenge, though. Slow and steady."

"They can plot all they like; it doesn't faze me. They aren't my first cheesed-off marks, and they won't be the last." Oliver shrugged, the prince of happy-go-lucky.

"Why aren't you crapping bricks right now? You know that as soon as you're off this island, they'll tear you a new one, right?"

Oliver smiled. "In life, you've got to take the rough with the smooth. They're not killers, so what's the worst that can happen? I take a beating? I've been there before. Bodies heal. Fortunately, I'm not a Purge beast, or I *would* be in trouble."

I went back to sipping my fiercely strong coffee and realized Luke hadn't taken his eyes off me. He glowered at me like he wanted to throw the cup in my face, or worse. *Speaking of a beating...* He clearly hated sitting at my table. But that was the beauty of Melody—she was the glue that bound us together, whether we liked it or not. So, I guessed she was more like a naughty kid with a stolen tube of superglue, spilling it liberally wherever she went.

I met his gaze. *Yo, you should grovel at my feet for saving your lump of pottery.* I almost said it but held my tongue. Was he pissed that I'd had to save the day and pull him through the trial? Luke was used to doing the heroics. He probably didn't like it when his ass needed to be saved, even if it was just a tiny show of kindness.

"Have y'all tried these?" Blanche interrupted our unspoken animosity with a plate of segmented oranges. "I've never tasted anything like 'em. They're so juicy, I could eat a hundred and never get tired of the taste. Here, have one."

She offered the plate around. We all took a slice, since it'd have been rude not to. The oranges were the juiciest, tastiest oranges I'd ever put in my mouth. My taste buds buzzed. *Why does everything taste so much better here?* I worried we might be stepping into "Land of the Lotus Eaters" territory. What if all this delicious food turned us crazy, like it had done to my mythical pal Odysseus? Well, I could think of worse ways to go.

"How are you feeling today?" I asked, devouring another segment.

Blanche's cheeks reddened. "I haven't had a hangover like that since I was a young woman, after drinking moonshine. I suppose that's another problem with gettin' older. The body doesn't bounce back the way it once did. Better than yesterday, though."

"If I grow old as gracefully as you, I'll be more than happy," Melody chimed in. "Although, I don't imagine I'll have as many awesome stories to tell."

"It was a different time when I was a young'un. We knew how to live, since we weren't glued to screens." Blanche chuckled, then turned her gaze to me. "We also learned, at an early age, how to forgive. I was wrong to distrust you, Finch, over what happened with my husband. I've been in the middle of a dark patch since he passed, and I suppose it's blinded me to what's proper. I should've known not to judge on first impressions. I'm sorry for it, son. Truly, I am."

I smiled back, sensing another thaw in the air. "Nothing to apologize for. I understand what that can do to a person. I've had my fair share of dark patches over the years. What do you say we forget it and start fresh?"

"I'd like that," she replied softly.

"Glad to hear it." I took another proffered orange segment, though it felt more like an olive branch. "What does everyone think the next trial is going to be?"

"I've been worrying about that." Blanche chewed her lip. "I hope there aren't any more mind-alterin' parts coming up, or I won't have the energy to continue. If our second trial was to overcome mental obstacles, then perhaps the next will involve something physical? Or magical?"

Melody nodded. "It stands to reason Etienne wants to test all of our facets: physical, mental, magical, and... I'm not sure. Etienne is the only one who knows what's in store for us, and he seems like a very mysterious sort of man."

"Couldn't have put it better myself," Luke said, giving her a dopey smile. I rolled my eyes.

"Mr. Abara, what are you doin', sittin' over there on your own?" Blanche called out suddenly. Mr. Abara had taken a seat on the periphery of the terrace, scribbling something in a notebook.

He looked up, surprised. "I'm just getting my thoughts in order."

"Well, don't be a stranger. Come and join us," Blanche replied. It wasn't a request so much as a demand.

Mr. Abara closed his notebook and slipped it into his pocket before obeying Blanche. As she was the elder of the group, it would be hard to refuse her. Take the orange segments, for example. I'd already eaten a whole orange without realizing it.

"What are we talking about?" Mr. Abara plonked himself down.

"The next trial," I said.

He nodded. "I wonder if this is Etienne's way of keeping us on our toes. He gives us some time to lull us into a false sense of security, and then—bam!—hits us with the next trial."

"That's what I'm thinking. A sneak attack," I agreed. I'd taken a shine to Mr. Abara. He was a tough old nut, but after the other day's poison gas debacle, we all looked at each other with different eyes. Secrets had been unearthed and weaknesses had been revealed, and our motivations had become a bit clearer. His had showed him to be the most noble one among us for sure.

"What if it has something to do with all these so-called gods?" Melody gestured toward a reclining Dionysus. "They're built into the fabric of the monastery, so perhaps they're supposed to play some part in our trials."

"Wouldn't that mean we've got some tough magic coming our way?" Luke replied. "They were offshoots of the Primus Anglicus, who were the purest magicals in existence, from what you've said."

Melody's eyes shone. "You *do* listen!"

"Of course I do," he murmured shyly. "I listen to everything you say."

"As long as these statues don't come to life and start swiping at us," I said. I had a horrifying vision of a stone god wearing nothing but a fig leaf staggering toward me.

"Aren't you descended from the Primus Anglicus?" Mr. Abara jabbed a militant finger at me.

I nodded. "Guilty as charged, yeah. Not that it'd help much. My Primus Anglicus blood is like cordial—it's watered down a whole lot."

"Is that what helped you kill Katherine?" Blanche peered at me with sad eyes.

"Apparently. So maybe it has its uses." I forced a smile, though that topic of conversation made me edgy.

"Is anyone else freaked out by the statues in their rooms?" Oliver interjected.

"I was about to say that!" Melody replied. "Everywhere I turn, I feel like Aphrodite is watching me."

I pretended to pout. "Aw, you got Aphrodite? I got Hades, complete with creepy souls trying to grab at his ankles. Do you want to swap?"

She laughed. "Maybe the women have women, and the men have men?"

"I got Zeus," Mr. Abara said proudly.

"Artemis," Blanche added.

Luke gave an embarrassed smile. "I got Athena, I think, but that might be because I demanded the room next to Melody's."

"I got Hermes, and he's dangling from the ceiling, so I'd say I drew the short straw. Hades is pretty bad, though. Let's hope it's not an omen, eh?" Oliver snorted. "But mine sways in the breeze. I woke up last night and thought he was coming right for me. I've never moved so fast in my life. I spent the rest of the night in the bathtub."

"Ah, so you're interested in the mythology of this place, then?" One of the monks appeared, bearing refills of coffee. He'd clearly been eavesdropping on us.

"There's no better place to develop an interest," I replied.

"Have you heard of Prometheus?" The monk went around, filling our cups.

We all chorused yes.

"He was the first sentient Purge beast created by the Grecian branch of the Primus Anglicus," the monk explained. "Wise and just, he didn't like how the gods and goddesses behaved with the humans. The story goes that he created mankind out of clay and stole fire to warm them, inciting the wrath of Zeus."

I shuddered. "Don't mention clay."

"Apologies." The monk chuckled. "In actuality, Prometheus was so angered by the gods and goddesses, and their treatment of humankind—who existed for a long, long time before he came along—that he tried to forge a forcefield across the towns and villages that these pseudo-deities preferred, using other Purge beasts to fuel it. A Bestiary of sorts. Perhaps the first of its kind, and an inspiration for the Bestiaries that came after. When Zeus tried to visit one of his favorite human ladies, the forcefield kept him out. Enraged, he traced the forcefield back to Prometheus and struck up a deal with Erebus to take the beast to Tartarus, where he would spend eternity having his liver pecked out by one of Erebus's personal monsters—a dark-winged eagle."

"Is he still there?" I didn't remember seeing anything like that on my visits to Erebus's otherworld, but it didn't surprise me that he'd accepted a tantalizing deal like that.

"Oh no, Purge beasts have longer lives than most magicals, but they aren't immortal," the monk replied. "He endured the torment for around two thousand years before his Chaos dissolved. He did many other things prior to the forcefield incident, usually to benefit mankind, which forged his name as a savior of the human race."

My heart sank. "So Purge beasts can die of old age?"

"Certainly. Those like Prometheus can exist for around that two-thousand-year mark, while the lesser sorts don't live as long— maybe fifty to one hundred years, if nothing gets them first."

The monk finished pouring and drifted away, leaving me with a bitter taste in my mouth. *Tobe...* It seemed silly to grieve when he probably had another thousand years left. That was a hell of a lot longer than I would get, but I hadn't realized that Purge beasts could just disappear, dying the same as everyone else.

"What's wrong?" Melody asked.

I shook my head. "Nothing. I'm just thinking about a friend."

"I wonder what else the myths got wrong," Mr. Abara mused.

"They're probably all twisted, since the so-called gods were the ones writing the history books." Oliver put in his two cents.

"Zeus must've been an Electro." Luke drank his coffee and pulled a face.

Blanche nodded. "Artemis may have been a Lunar, able to manipulate the tides, nocturnal creatures, and the minds of people.

I've never come across one, but I read about them once. I thought they were hokum, but perhaps there were powers back then that don't exist now, thanks to all of that waterin'-down of the bloodlines."

"That must mean Hades was a Necroman—" Mr. Abara shrieked mid-sentence and leapt up onto his chair. A tiny mouse scuttled across the terrace, weaving between table legs. I'd never seen anyone move so quickly, especially not a man of Mr. Abara's heft. It reminded me of the old wives' tale of elephants being terrified of mice.

I couldn't help but laugh. Until the mouse made a break for me and scurried up my boot, disappearing up my pant leg.

I screamed like a banshee and leapt to my feet, dancing and jumping and shaking my leg. The mouse wouldn't come out, but I could feel the little thing, its tiny claws digging into my skin. Then it bit me, sending me stumbling across the terrace. I whacked my leg on the nearest table to try to get the friggin' thing out, but I didn't even know where it was. I just got a bruise for my troubles.

It bit me again, and I ran for the monastery. If I wanted to get this thing out of my pants, I needed to tear these suckers off, and I wasn't about to do a breakfast striptease for my new pals. Not with all the cheese and bread I'd been eating. I heard them howling with laughter as I sprinted inside the building, but I was too peeved to care.

I reached the nearest hallway and was about to tear off my pants when the mouse shot out of my pant leg and darted forward, stopping in the middle of the corridor. It waited, staring up at me with wide, beady eyes, then hurried toward a branching hallway on the right. It paused again, its tail flicking.

"Come here, you little punk!" I yelled, taking off after the mouse.

I followed it blindly down hallway after hallway, losing track of the turns. Every time I thought it had vanished, I found it waiting for me around another turn, staring at me weirdly. Soon enough, I was well and truly lost in the monastery labyrinth. The mouse stopped. Its beady eyes met mine.

"What are you doing?" It was dumb to expect the mouse to talk back, but I wanted answers. It turned in a circle before darting down the next corridor. I'd come this far; I couldn't give up on nabbing this rodent now.

But as I ran after it, a thought crossed my mind. *Is there some magic going on here?*

The mouse stopped again and stared at me with bulging eyes, flicking its tail as though... beckoning me to follow?

Are you a Morph?

I hadn't seen any other beasties inside the monastery, apart from the odd fly here and there. But, even if I had, I doubted they'd have had this sort of sentience. It was acting with intention, almost like someone else was in the driver's seat. Which meant this wasn't a normal critter.

And I only knew one Morph... Kenzie.

NINETEEN

Finch

———————

I ran after the furry pest like my life depended on it, even
though it dragged me farther and farther into the monastery.
And all the eerie mystique therein.

Here—wherever 'here' was—the comforting, vacation-style
aesthetics vanished. The coolness of the airy corridors, with their
picturesque pseudo-courtyards, had disappeared. The air grew hot.
Really hot. I tried to convince myself it was from running, but the
atmosphere felt thick. My shirt clung to me in all the wrong places,
sweat dripping from my forehead.

Statues stood here, but they didn't have the sleek, art-gallery
quality anymore. They looked evil, and I felt their stone eyes
boring right into my soul. A couple times, I nearly shrieked after I
rounded a corner and came face-to-face with a creepy carving.

The light couldn't penetrate down here, either, without
windows. That suggested I was underground. No more Mr. Nice
Monastery. I'd crossed into the underworld.

"Where are we going?" I hissed at the mouse. I didn't actually expect it to talk back. But a tail flick, or a blink for yes, two for no... that sort of thing would've been nice. A better question would've been, "Why are you here?" but I didn't imagine I'd get much of an answer for that, either. Still, it left me wondering. And worrying. Why *was* Kenzie here? How had she even found me?

The mouse paused and stared at me. Maybe I was seeing things, but I could've sworn it was giving me a withering look. A second later, it kept on, its little claws tapping on the cracked stone floor. I huffed out a sigh and went after it. *In for a dime, in for a dollar.*

The mouse led me down a spiral staircase, the horror-movie kind, with flickering torches in sconces and shadows lurking around every curve. It gave off a clear "do not enter" ambiance. Even I might've backed off if I hadn't been so sure this mouse was Kenzie. And she clearly had something to show me. I mean, it *had* to be Kenzie. No other Morph would be able to give me the kind of "you're an idiot" look she could, even through a critter's eyes.

At the bottom, a long, narrow corridor stretched out. A massive door sat at the farthest end, a few smaller halls branching off from the main one. The mouse veered with a startled squeak, disappearing into a shadowy alcove carved right into the wall. It poked its head back out, squeaking again. It wanted me to follow... quick. I sprinted for the alcove and tucked myself right back into the darkness.

Not a moment too soon.

A gaggle of four monks appeared on the stairwell, chattering loudly amongst themselves. Not very monk-like, but I wasn't here to judge.

"Excellent serving this morning, Felipe. Michelin-standard, I'd say," one said.

"Why, thank you. I like it so much better when there are new people around. An unpopular opinion, maybe, but it livens up the place," Felipe answered. He had a faint accent. Maybe Spanish, or Portuguese.

"No, no, I agree," a third chimed in. "The monastery can get stale when it's just us monks, monkeying around." He barked a donkey laugh that almost made me snort and give my location away. I clamped my hands over my mouth.

Only the monk leading the group remained silent. He had a certain gravitas to him, which made me suspect he might be one of their spiritual leaders. He paused in front of a small door, just shy of the alcove. Taking a hefty-looking key from under the neckline of his flowing robes, he slotted it into the keyhole and opened the door with a creak.

He ushered his boisterous followers inside and closed the door behind him. I waited for the mouse to make the first move. I wouldn't budge until I knew those monks weren't going to come back out. A second later, the mouse zipped out and hurtled down the corridor. I went after it, a little slower. Big human legs weren't as swift as little mousey ones.

The critter skidded to a halt in front of the massive door at the end of the corridor and slipped smoothly under it. I hurried to the door and twisted the wrought-iron handle, but it didn't turn. I gave it a shove, just in case age had made it stick. But it still didn't move.

Of course it's locked...

I put my palm to the lock and slid in sneaky tendrils of Telekinesis. Usually, this was basic stuff. But the lock had other ideas. A dead, dull sensation slithered back through my hand, rendering my Telekinesis useless. I realized magic wouldn't cut it. Just like the monastery's exterior hadn't given in to magical commands, this door seemed to be on the same wavelength. That was a problem, but not a major one. At least, I hoped not.

It's time for some WWOFD—what would old Finch do? I scanned the corridor for inspiration and fixed on the door the monks had entered. I'd bet my life that hefty key would open up the mama-sized door. Even from my brief glimpse, it'd looked like a skeleton key—capable of opening all the doors along this corridor. I might not have been a locksmith, but I'd cracked open enough doorways to know what would likely work. And I didn't have any other bright ideas.

Sidling up to the door in question, I crouched down and peered through the keyhole. The monks knelt on the floor beyond, in a shadowed chapel with candles setting it aglow. They mumbled in ancient Greek. I spotted the lead monk, the one with the key around his neck.

Closing my eyes, I pictured the monk Etienne had spoken to in his study. He was clearly one of the ecclesiastical bigwigs, if he was in with the boss. My body rippled with Mimicry, taking on the image of that monk. I glanced down to find myself dressed in blue-and-gold robes. Time for a dose of amateur dramatics.

I wrenched open the door, gasping and spluttering. "Help! I need help! I can't... breathe!" My voice matched the favored monk perfectly.

The guy with the key looked up, alarmed. "Everyone, stay at your prayer," he urged as he raced down the central aisle toward me. Only then did he realize who I was pretending to be. "Mikhail, what's the matter?"

"I... can't breathe." I staggered into the hallway and collapsed. The monk hurriedly shut the door behind us and knelt in a panic, looming over me. The key was in my grasp. As he cradled my head and tried to check my airways, I slipped my Esprit out of my pocket. It transformed into a blade, the edge sharp. Grabbing the monk by the shoulders, my eyes bulging, I made a decent show of choking as I cut the rope around his neck on the sly. The key fell into my hand, and I quickly put my Esprit and the key into my pocket.

"Calm down, Mikhail. Try and follow my breathing," the monk instructed.

"I think… I'm having… a panic attack," I whispered back. Dutifully, I followed the in and out of his breathing. Soon enough, I pretended to recover.

"Are you feeling better?"

I nodded slowly. "I… think so."

"What happened to you?" The monk looked at me worriedly.

"I don't know. I made it halfway down the stairs when it hit me," I replied, staring up in desperation. "Don't tell Etienne about this, please. I don't want him thinking I'm weak. This has never happened to me before. I'm sure it's nothing."

The monk frowned. "Do you want me to walk you to your chambers?"

I shook my head. "No… I can make it. It must be the heat down here. It's very strange. But, please, pretend this never happened. When you see me again, I'd prefer it if you didn't mention this. I am so very embarrassed."

"Of course, Mikhail. I've seen the heat get to many monks. You wouldn't be the first," he replied soothingly.

"I'm already much better," I assured him. "I'm sorry that I burst in. I panicked, that's all."

The monk visibly relaxed. "Not to worry, Mikhail. You work too hard; it was only a matter of time before it got the better of you. This is why we're supposed to implement relaxation into our routines, but you've never been one for that."

"Perhaps I ought to try." I gave a dry chuckle.

"Do you mind if I leave you? We were in the middle of a very important chant, and I don't want to abandon them in the midst of it." The monk glanced back at the prayer room. "That is the trouble with new acolytes—they need constant guidance. But I know I don't have to tell you that."

"Go on. I'll be quite all right." I smiled weakly. "Thank you for your help. I must have given you a scare."

"I think we've all grown used to being startled once or twice. As followers, didn't we spend our first few months in a perpetual state of terror, learning all about the realities of Chaos magic and the history of this place?" He smiled back, though fear flickered across his eyes.

This monastery definitely had secrets. That was the trick with a beautiful façade—the surface convinced you that everything was fine, regardless of the grim mysteries that lingered below.

"That we did," I said, to keep up the ruse.

"If you feel unwell again, just wait in the room opposite. I'll come and tend to you in half an hour or so." The monk helped me to a sitting position before getting to his feet.

"I will, though I'm sure I'll be fine. And, again, please don't mention this again. My pride could not bear it."

"Mention what? Nothing has happened here today." He gave me a sympathetic look and headed back into the prayer room. I waited a few moments after he'd closed the door before racing for the locked door. I had thirty minutes to figure out what mousey wanted.

Taking the key from my pocket, I slid it into the lock and turned it. A satisfying *click* echoed back. At least my little performance had been worth it. The monks would probably gossip about it later, but I'd hopefully have the key safely tucked back in one of their pockets by then. And they weren't going to call out Etienne's right-hand monk, right to his face. At least, I hoped they wouldn't, when I'd specifically asked that lead guy not to. Loyalty among monk bros, right?

The mouse waited by a tall candelabra, flicking its tail impatiently.

"What are you giving me that look for? *I* can't slip under doors," I whispered.

The critter twisted around and set off at breakneck speed into the darkness. Unfurling my palm, I lit up a ball of Fire. Its soft glow spread outward, and I almost backed up against the door. A narrow walkway extended over a black abyss. Maybe the precipice had a bottom, but I couldn't see it.

Welcome to the real Hades—it's a hell of a place.

Steeling my nerves, I followed the mouse across the walkway. It didn't seem concerned with the imminent death on either side as it scuttled onward. *Don't look down, don't look down...* Only when the walkway stopped did I realize it was a bridge. But a bridge to what?

A scream echoed through the darkness. Not a human scream. Something more bestial. The hairs on the back of my neck stood on end, and a shudder ran through me. But I couldn't back out now. The mouse continued running, and I followed.

More walkways ensued. Some traversed pure darkness. Others crossed streams of molten lava, bubbles spewing bright orange globules. That surprised me—some powerful magic was being used down here, for the place to have lava running through it. I mean, I wasn't *that* far underground, so it couldn't be the natural kind. Other walkways crossed pools of steaming water, geysers skyrocketing upward and splashing the bridges. I hissed as a few specks hit me, blistering my skin. The hallways that led here were practically Baltic compared to this. My T-shirt might as well have been a second skin.

I raked my forearm across my forehead to try and get rid of the slick mess but only smeared it around. Even the mouse's fur was drenched. It stopped more often, as if to catch its breath. *Not so smug now, are you?*

Beyond the boiling springs, a circular platform opened onto a huge pool of dark water, with nothing visible beyond. Bobbing casually at the edge of the platform was a small boat. The mouse jumped into it, prompting me to do the same. I couldn't be shown up by a rodent, after all.

"You want me to row, right? I doubt you've got the upper-body strength." I sat on the middle bench and picked up the oars, facing forward. It would've been easier to row sitting backward, but I wanted to be able to see where I was going. As soon as I dipped the oars into the water, a glowing line appeared beneath the black surface. It seemed to be guiding me.

Huh... handy. Following the glow, I rowed the boat merrily, merrily across the black pool until my arms started to burn. The heat hadn't let up, but at least it didn't melt the oars.

About ten minutes later, another platform appeared, an island in the black pool. A single door stood on the island, without any walls to hold it up. It was literally just a door.

"How do you know so much?" I eyed the mouse, but it just flicked its tail in reply. Even the monks would've had a hard time navigating this place. I followed the glowing underwater trail to the island and moored the boat on a waiting post before awkwardly clambering out.

I walked up to the door. To my surprise, it was already slightly ajar. It gave immediately and swung wide. I was a little surprised it wasn't locked, but at least I didn't have to go and steal another key. Pitch darkness faced me.

The mouse darted through my legs and sprinted into the gloom, so I went after it. I'd trusted it this far—because I trusted Kenzie.

The door slammed behind me and the space lit with golden light, though I had no idea where it came from. My jaw dropped, and a gasp escaped my throat.

I stood in a chamber filled to the brim with incredible ancient treasures: jewels, crowns, scepters, golden boxes, magical weapons, papyrus scrolls, silk clothing, and leather-bound books that gave off Grimoire whispers. Put together, everything in here must've been worth billions.

I moved toward a golden chalice embedded with rubies the size of my eyeballs. My fingertips had barely touched it when mousey decided to gnaw on my ankle. I jumped back, hopping on one leg as I rubbed the bite.

"Could you not?" I snapped. It scampered up the mountain of treasures and stopped on a small pendant wrapped around the base of the golden chalice. I peered at the object. It was spherical and made from dull bronze, with ancient Greek writing etched into the globe. It hung on a slim bronze chain and was probably the least appealing thing in the entire room. They had crowns, for Pete's sake! *I'd look good in a crown.*

"What?" I waited for the mouse to do something. I could've sworn it rolled its beady eyes as it nudged the pendant, squeaking faintly. "You want me to take this?"

The mouse squeaked again.

"You know, you could've done that from the start. Squeaks are more useful than tail flicks." I shook my head and stepped toward the pendant. Unraveling it from the chalice stem, I slipped it over my head and let it dangle against my chest, under my soaked shirt. It didn't feel particularly powerful.

I eyed a stash of gold coins in a nearby varnished box. They didn't look hexed. Drawn like a magpie to the glitter and gleam, I scooped up a handful. You know, for my troubles.

I yelped when mousey bit me again. "I could crush you, Kenzie. I know it's you!"

The mouse stared at me, unimpressed.

"Stop biting me and tell me why you're doing this. I don't care if it's all in squeaks—throw me a friggin' bone!"

The mouse lashed its tail.

"Oh, I've pissed you off? Well, tough." I reached for the gold coins again, and the mouse darted up the mountain of treasures and leapt at my face. I flailed wildly to try and protect myself. "Dammit, Kenzie!"

The mouse glared at me from my shoulder. It squeaked right in my ear, clearly agitated. I didn't speak vermin, but I got the picture. I could only take the pendant. The rest had to stay here. *But... why?* Couldn't I just have one little trinket, as a souvenir?

Shaking my head, I left the room. Kenzie stayed on my shoulder, clinging like I was a two-dollar donkey ride. I didn't like the feeling, but what could I do—fling her off and watch her mouse-paddle to the other side? *Good thing I like you, Kenzie.*

Fifteen minutes later, I was back in familiar territory. Still underground, but no longer lost. I'd left the key against the side of the wall, by the prayer room in that long corridor, so the lead monk would think it'd dropped off him when he'd come to help me. I rounded the corner that would lead me back to the surface and almost barreled into a familiar figure.

Luke blocked my path. Sweat drenched him, and I knew it wasn't from his daily exercise regimen. He smelled of the monastery's underworld, like campfire mixed with a touch of brimstone. I glanced anxiously at my shoulder, where Kenzie had been sitting. But she wasn't there anymore. She'd clearly seen Luke and made a run for it, knowing it'd beg a few questions if I had a mouse pal perched there.

"Did you follow me?" The words tumbled out before I could stop them.

His forehead crinkled into a frown. "You're not the one who should be asking questions, Finch. I may have lost track of you along the way, but I knew you'd reappear. What were you doing down there?"

"None of your business," I shot back. If he'd lost track of me, hopefully that meant he hadn't seen the whole charade of me Shifting into Etienne's sidekick and stealing the key, or anything after that.

"It is my business if you're up to something." He got right in my face. "It's Etienne's business, too."

I held my ground, though he could've knocked me flat with one shove. "I had a mouse problem. I fixed it. All peachy."

"You think I'm going to believe that?"

"Believe what you want. I'm telling you the truth." I eyeballed him. "What's your problem, huh? I thought you were here to watch Melody, not me. What I do in my spare time has nothing to do with you."

I held his gaze and watched suspicion harden his features.

"Why are you following me?" I asked again.

His eyes narrowed. "Because I don't trust you."

"Have I given you reason not to?"

"I'm looking at one right now." He squared up, and I braced for a hit.

A cluster of monks emerged from a nearby door, chattering. They went quiet as they saw us facing off.

"Shouldn't you be starting your next trial?" one asked.

I glanced at him. "I don't know, should we?"

"Yes, I think you should. Hurry. Mr. Biset doesn't tolerate latecomers!" the monk urged.

"This isn't over," Luke whispered.

"No, it's not," I hissed back. But we couldn't go for each other's throats in front of the monks. And I didn't want to miss the third trial. Turning on my heel, I stormed away from Luke, listening to his footsteps echoing mine.

This monastery got weirder every day. And Kenzie's sudden appearance didn't help. She knew a lot, but how? I turned to whisper to her and remembered she'd vanished when Luke showed up.

My hand slipped over the pendant under my shirt. *What is this for?* Yet again, I had an endless stream of questions and not a single answer.

TWENTY

Kenzie

———————

I jolted awake. It was dark out, but lights illuminated the room. Opposite me, some police drama played on the TV. I sat up and swore loudly. Being a Morph came with limitations, but they'd never pissed me off the way they had today. Frustration was an understatement. I'd wanted to tell Finch why I was there and what to do. He'd probably figured some stuff out for himself by now, but seeing him so annoyed left me feeling worse.

This isn't going to cut it, long-term. I had more intel to pass on, and trying to squeak or tail-whip or bite my way through wouldn't be enough.

"Kenzie?" Ryann's voice dragged me out of my funk.

"Alive and well." I sat up and froze. Ryann looked well and truly freaked. "Did something happen to the bottle?" I darted toward the TV table. The bottle stood where I left it, safe and sound.

She shook her head. "It's not the bottle."

"What's the matter? You look like you just met Crossbones in a dark alley."

"I'm going to pretend I know what that means," she said, clearly rattled. "A message came for you while you were out."

"What message?" I waited for her to give it to me. Instead, she pointed toward the bathroom with a shaky hand.

"I was in there when it appeared."

I looked at the bathroom. "When what appeared?"

"You'll see." She turned back to the TV, staring blankly.

I headed for the bathroom. My knees shook, weak and weary. After Morphing for a long stretch, it took my limbs a while to recover.

I pushed the door open, and my heart damn near stopped. Blood across the mirror spelled four words: *Davin spy. Monastery breached.*

It wasn't much, but I understood. This wasn't a message for me —it was a message for Finch. Erebus sent it for me to relay.

Davin had a spy in the monastery. Probably one of the people I'd seen. Sure, it could be a monk, but that Etienne dude would've figured them out by now. From what Erebus told me, he wasn't a dumbass. More likely it was a newcomer, sent by Doncaster under the pretense of learning map-making. Ryann came to stand in the doorframe.

"Does it mean something to you?" Ryann asked quietly, as I wiped away the blood with a towel.

I brushed by to throw the towel in the washer. "Yeah, unfortunately."

"Is Finch in trouble? Is Davin there?" Ryann asked.

"I didn't see Davin, but I'm guessing he's got a spy in the mix," I replied.

Ryann wrung her hands. "Do you think he's targeting Finch? Garrett said they fought in the mine. What if he went to the monastery to finish what he started—to kill Finch?"

"Before you start wigging out, take a breath. Davin's a big-picture guy. He's not going to break through all that security just for Finch. He'd wait until Finch left." I sat beside her. "Which means Davin is targeting the monastery, not Finch."

Ryann nodded. "You're right... sorry. I keep thinking of Finch getting hurt, or worse, and my brain starts racing."

"You haven't mentioned any of this to Harley, have you?" I had to be sure.

"No. I've been checking in, and she's none the wiser."

"Good, one less thing to worry about. Davin might not be after Finch directly, but that doesn't mean Finch isn't in danger," I continued. "The problem is, I went as a mouse this time, and I couldn't communicate well. I managed to bite him in the right direction, but I need to spell this out somehow."

Ryann turned to the TV, where a commercial advertised some tropical drink. Bright birds burst from a slow-motion splash of the colorful liquid. I hated commercials. What did birds have to do with liquid sugar?

Her eyes widened. "What if you could be specific?"

"Huh? What do you mean?"

"What if you picked an animal that can mimic a human voice?" She pointed to a macaw flapping across the screen.

My brain blew. "Holy crap... that might work! I can't make animals talk like me, but I can use what they've got to imitate some words. Enough to get a message across." I leaned forward to get a better look.

"An African gray might be your best shot. They're known for mimicry," Ryann replied, jittering with excitement. "I've seen videos of them saying rude things, and they have quite the vocabulary when they want to."

"But where would I get one? They're not exactly hanging around Greek islands."

She smiled. "A zoo will have one, though, and I bet Greece has at least a few of those."

"A parrot jailbreak. I like it. You know, you're way more interesting than I gave you credit for." I grinned back. It'd add a bit more flying time to get to the island again from whichever zoo was closest, but if it kept Finch from getting murdered by one of Davin's spies, I'd flap like the wind.

TWENTY-ONE

Finch

———

By the time Luke and I reached the ground floor, we had a pretty impressive escort. The fretting monks corralled us through the corridors like two stubborn bulls until we reached a big, golden door in a cloistered square. Flowers bloomed everywhere, filling the air with overpowering perfume.

The door in front of us looked exactly like the one I'd stolen a key for. I hoped there'd be no fire and brimstone beyond this one.

"Hurry!" the monk urged.

"All right, all right, we're going," Luke grumbled. His mood hadn't improved.

I tugged on the iron ring, and the door opened smoothly. Luke barged past me to get inside first. *Sourpuss.* I resisted the urge to trip him and followed. We entered a strange, round space, with elegant metal staircases leading up to three additional floors with sweeping circular balconies. A glass dome arched in place of a ceiling, and an enormous gemstone glinted at the apex.

This place had shelves upon shelves of glass cases filled with weird plants. Big ones, small ones... And no two the same. One pulsated slowly with bluish white light, emitting bioluminescent spores that fluttered inside the case, trapped. A huge one, higher up, had vibrant purple petals and a center of serrated barbs, ready to clamp down on some unsuspecting creature. It reminded me of the ones that grew in Mexico, after Harley Purged the revamped Gaia.

"You're late," Etienne scolded. He stood before the class, an eyebrow raised.

"Sorry. We got lost," I replied. It wasn't exactly a lie. Besides, the monks had nodded effusively and rambled on about how easy it was to lose your way in this place, after I'd fed the same story to them. Which hopefully meant they weren't suspicious about it.

His eyebrow lifted farther, to almost comical heights. "And what, pray tell, did you do in order to get lost? Was it something more important than learning the divine art of map-making?"

Luke stiffened at my side. *Nothing to say?*

"We did some morning cardio to work off all the food you keep plying us with." I swooped in to save our asses. It wasn't much of an excuse, but hopefully he'd buy it. "If we'd realized the next trial would start soon, we'd have put it off."

"Sit down before I disqualify you for lateness." Apparently satisfied, Etienne gestured to two empty workbenches.

While most of the room looked like a botanical library, the ground floor reminded me of an antique chemistry lab. The kind Dr. Frankenstein might be spotted in, resurrecting sewn-together zombies. Each workbench had a worn, wooden surface, with rows of bottles and test tubes in racks. Some tubes contained clear liquid, while others held vivid purple, neon green, and viscous red. I wanted to yell, "It's alive!" but I was already in Etienne's bad books. I doubted he'd appreciate my comedic genius.

A terra cotta pot sat on each bench, a sapling peeking its way out of the reddish soil. Tiny, fruit-like buds, with a faint orange hue, clung to the barely developed branches, but they didn't look like citrus trees, nor did they smell like them. The saplings gave off a sour aroma.

"What are you, huh?" I touched the branches and recoiled. They felt searing hot.

"You might be wondering what this trial entails," Etienne began. "Last time, you learned to overcome mental obstacles to focus on a task. This test is more about chemistry."

Melody's hand shot up. "Chemistry? I wouldn't expect a lot of chemistry to be involved in map-making."

"You could be forgiven for thinking that." Etienne gestured at the nearest pot. "But chemistry and map-making are very similar disciplines. The right formula in chemistry can lead to a break-through in science, just as the right drawing can lead to a hidden place in map-making. The wrong quantities, the wrong drawings—both lead to catastrophe."

"Yeah, but drawing the wrong map isn't—" Shailene interjected. Of course the twins had to wedge in their opinion.

"—going to kill someone," Fay added.

Etienne smiled coldly. "Observe, then pass your judgments. Everything I present to you will transfer to your endeavors as a mapmaker. You may either open your mind and potentially succeed, or close it and surely fail."

The Basani twins shrugged. "We're listening."

"Good." He walked to a small cauldron on his workbench. Several glass bottles stood beside it. "These vials contain poisons and deadly toxins."

"Please don't release another gas," Blanche begged, her eyes fearful. I felt my own shiver of dread. The pottery experiment had been a nightmare, one nobody wanted to repeat.

"Fear not. That part of your learning is over." Etienne chuckled. "The purpose of these is to show you that, in the right combination, poisons and toxins can actually give life and Chaos. They are created to harm, but you can use chemistry to alter their function, as long as you are precise. If you get one drop wrong, however, you will create something far worse than the sum of its parts."

"So this is a precision test?" Oliver leaned lazily across his workbench.

"Goodness, you're all inquisitive today." Etienne sighed, clearly frustrated. "It is more about understanding that combining the right quantities of poison will create a powerful elixir, strong enough to counteract the killer effects. I am teaching you the importance of equilibrium."

He picked up a glass pipette and dipped it into the cauldron, where he presumably had a potion pre-mixed. Vibrant blue liquid shot up the glass tube. Bringing it over his pot, he dripped eight drops onto the soil of the orange-colored sapling.

The tree grew in front of our eyes, the thin trunk quickly fattening and twisting skyward until it was taller than Etienne. The branches extended, like someone unfurling from a long sleep. The fruits swelled into orbs that looked a lot like the oranges I'd eaten at breakfast.

Awed gasps hissed around the room, including mine. This was way cooler than getting gassed in a pottery studio.

"This is the task." Etienne grasped the cauldron and poured the remains into a sink. The blue liquid disappeared down the drain.

"We have to grow a fruit tree?" Mr. Abara asked.

"In simplistic terms, yes," Etienne replied. "You have the same bottles of poisons and toxins on your benches. You must deduct the correct combination for the life-giving potion, to help the saplings grow until they bear fruit."

How hard can that be? I meant that with the height of sarcasm. He'd made it look super easy, although we hadn't seen the work that went into that cauldron, and I knew it'd be anything but straightforward.

"You have three days to achieve this goal," Etienne continued. "You may come and go as you please, to eat and sleep and so on. The door will remain open all day and night, and your pots are individually marked, so they cannot be switched around. Do not even attempt to cheat, as there are magical measures in place to prevent it. As always, if you fail in this task, you will be removed from the island."

I peered at the racked-up bottles, which were helpfully labeled: *cyanide, arsenic, belladonna, black mamba venom, cottonmouth venom,* among many others. The worst of Mother Nature's poison pantry, neatly lined up. I glanced at the others, who looked similarly perturbed. Oliver, Luke, and Blanche kept their distance from the bottles.

I raised my hand, like a good schoolboy. "How will we know if we're getting it right or wrong?"

Etienne smirked. "The trees will tell you."

TWENTY-TWO

Kenzie

I snapped out of another round of Morphing, panting hard. Not
because of the energy required to keep this up, but because of
what I'd seen. I'd been a literal fly on the wall in that weird workshop. Like a zoo for plants, with a chemistry lab at the bottom.
And, right now, I was terrified for Finch. More than I'd ever been.

I'd gone for the fly first, as I already had control over its mind.
It had been the last creature I'd piggybacked on before entering the
head of the mouse, meaning I could jump easily back to the island
where my fly friend lived. Just one mind leap and I was there.
Almost as simple as the return journeys, where I just zapped
straight back into my head.

Before I went for the parrot, I'd wanted to scope out what Finch
was up to and get the lay of the land, so I'd know exactly how to get
to him when I had the parrot. Plus, it never hurt to listen in on
things. I'd hoped it might be obvious who the spy was, but even
watching, unnoticed by everyone, I hadn't picked up on anything
odd.

"Kenzie?" Ryann hurried to my side. "Are you okay?"

I nodded. "I'm fine, but Finch isn't."

"What do you mean?" She pushed a glass of water into my hand.

"He's on the third trial, and it's a crazy one. A load of poisons and toxins are supposed to make a tree grow. One wrong drop, and I'm guessing it's lights out." I gulped the water.

"Poison? What if there's an accident? Did it sound like it could kill him?"

"I have no idea."

Ryann went to pour me another glass and almost knocked the jug over. She was a big, jittery mess. Her eyes had a haunted look, and she'd gnawed her bottom lip raw with stress.

I leaned forward and poured my own water. "You care about him, huh?"

"I'm… his friend, and he's like an extended member of my family. Of course I care," she replied, her voice shaky.

"There's more to it than that." I stared at her, but she wouldn't look me in the eye.

She shook her head slowly. "I want Finch home, but… it's just because I'm his friend. Same as you."

"Then why are you acting like you've taken fifty caffeine tablets and downed them with a chaser of energy drink?"

"He might die, Kenzie!" she sputtered. "When I heard he'd gone missing after the cave-in, I damn near lost my mind. That's why I'm here, with you, keeping my mouth shut—you've got answers. You've got a way to bring him home."

She clearly liked him. He was my friend, and I wasn't losing control of my senses because he was in a jam. Was I scared for him? Sure. Was I knocking over jugs? No.

"I won't judge you, Ryann. Finch is a good guy. Shady past, sure, but he's different now. Do you know how many times he watched my mom so I could take Inez out to the movies? He'd bring food over, too, in case I hadn't had time to buy any. And some of that happened before he moved away from the dark side. If you like him, good for you. He's one of the decent ones, and they ain't easy to come by."

Ryann's shoulders sagged. "It's not like that."

"Why, because you've got a guy already? People fall in and out of love all the time. It doesn't make you a bad person, if you've got a thing for Finch. As long as there's no crossover, what's the issue? Dump the guy and get Finch when we bring him back."

She stared at me like I'd just told her to nuke the SDC. "It's not like that! I love Adam."

"How much?"

"A lot," she replied firmly.

"Do you love Finch?" I dangled the bait.

"I… no. I mean, yes, but not that way." She fumbled through her reply. It gave away everything. The poor girl had a battle raging in her heart. "I'm just worried about him because, you're right, he's a good guy, and he's Harley's brother, and my family adores him. I don't want him to get hurt. He doesn't deserve all of this."

I eyed the bottle with Mom and Inez inside and decided to let her off the hook before she started knocking things over again. "I have good news."

"You do?" She gave a relieved sigh, either because I'd switched topics, or because she was genuinely thankful for some sort of silver lining.

"We don't need to go for the zoo option. I spotted a pet shop on the mainland with parrots. One can squawk in English, which should make things easier. I don't know any Greek, and I doubt Finch's is up to snuff. I can hijack that one and fly the bird to the monastery," I replied.

"I'd been panicking about that," Ryann admitted.

"Me, too." I flashed her a reassuring grin. "I'll have to pace myself. All this Morphing is doing a number on me. I'm already dog tired, stretching my mind to and from Greece, even though I have a direct route to some of the creatures there now. But Erebus wants me listening in on everything, all the damn time. And it's not like I can run outside the monastery for a breather. The moment I let go, I end up back here."

Ryann frowned. "Are you okay?"

"For now."

"Is there something I can get you? A way to keep you powered up?"

I shrugged. "If there is, I don't know what it—"

The door burst open. Both of us froze, then turned slowly as Erebus strode in with a swagger.

His eyes narrowed on Ryann, and a smirk tugged at his lips. "Hmm, yes… there she is."

Ryann looked like she wanted to disappear between the sofa cushions.

"This is Ryann." I jumped in. "I've enlisted her to watch my body while I'm Morphing. You can't be too careful in this neighborhood. Lots of gangs creeping around, and they don't all like me. Don't worry, though, I'll wipe her mind after it's over."

Ryann nodded. "That's right, Erebus. Is it just Erebus, or Mr. Erebus?"

He shrugged. "Either is fine. And I don't care what you do, as long as it garners results and doesn't bring the coven authorities to your door."

"We've got a plan, and it's keeping everyone away," I assured him.

"Make sure it stays that way." He wandered the apartment,

surveying it. "I'm not here to micromanage you. You know what's at stake if you disappoint me, which is motivation enough, I imagine. I'm here for your report."

I nodded. "Right, yeah, of course." I quickly gave him the details of Operation Parrot. All the while, Ryann squirmed. Seeing Erebus in his normal form would terrify anyone, but seeing him like this, human and cocky... it was the stuff of nightmares, especially for a non-magical.

Erebus laughed. "That would certainly be entertaining to watch."

"Nice to see you having so much fun at my expense." I scoffed. I couldn't help it.

"I hope that wasn't sass, Kenzie." He eyed me, still amused.

"Not at all." I dove right into the rest of the intel before his mood soured. "So, right now, Finch is in the third trial. It has to do with mixing up poisons to make a fruit tree grow."

Erebus groaned. "Yes, I remember the previous attempts. They all failed. All of them."

"But you've got the formula, right?" I pressed.

"It is not as simple as that. Etienne changes the type of plant each year, in rotation, which each require their own unique potion." Erebus leaned against the wall. "Perhaps the two of you can put your heads together and figure out the formula."

Ryann and I exchanged a confused look.

"That's a joke, right?" I asked, baffled.

"You'll have to find a solution, one way or another. Lots at stake, your mother and sister, etc. It doesn't bear repeating," Erebus replied firmly.

For someone so desperate to see Finch succeed, he wasn't putting in a whole lot of effort to make it happen. *He* was meant to be the omniscient one. *I guess you're lacking the omnipotent part, even with a human body, huh?*

"Do you have a list of the potions that Etienne has for each plant in rotation?" Ryann came in with a blinder. That was a damn good question.

Erebus smoothed down the lapel of his suit jacket. "No."

"As a Child of Chaos and all, can't you find a way into the monastery and get the list? It'd be a quick in-and-out job. Maybe he's even marked the one he's using." Ryann was on to something, but Erebus couldn't be the one to do it.

"His human body means he's limited, so he can't go into the monastery himself," I explained.

Erebus glared at me. "Need I remind you about that bottle?"

"I wasn't making a dig, Erebus!" I blurted out, panicked. "I'm just explaining to Ryann why we have to do this without you. I didn't mean anything by it."

"Let's hope not," he said.

"What if I said the plant had little orange fruitlings?" He had to know a few plants.

Erebus frowned. "Orange, you say?"

I nodded. "And when Finch touched them, it was like they were hot or something."

"Hmm… if they were hot to the touch, then it could be a weeping orange willow. Very rare species." Erebus rubbed his chin, thinking.

Ryann grabbed my arm. "I can help. I'm on good terms with a couple of genius chemists at the San Francisco Coven. I met them last year, while I was helping Astrid implement Human Relations into the curriculum across California. We've got a chat, and we still talk all the time and meet up. I'm sure they'd help, and they've got access to rare botanicals. Plus, it means nobody at the SDC will get wind of it."

Erebus snorted. "Very impressive. Glad to see someone is thinking outside the box. A shame you're so painfully non-magical, but I give credit where it's due. You're certainly resourceful." He paused. "No wonder Finch likes you."

Ryann blushed furiously beside me, though her embarrassment quickly morphed into confusion. I felt it, too. If Erebus knew Finch liked Ryann, then it meant he knew *exactly* who Ryann was and what she meant to Finch. Even Ryann didn't know about Finch's feelings. Well, she hadn't until now, anyway.

I realized that I'd put Ryann in a lot more danger than I thought. Any other human, even Astrid, Erebus couldn't have used as leverage against Finch.

I'm sorry, Ryann.

"I should be going. It looks like you've got plenty to keep your-selves occupied in my absence," Erebus announced. "I look forward to my next update." He twisted his hands and disappeared in a whorl of black smoke, leaving Ryann and me in the apartment.

I turned to her. "You need to go, and not come back."

"What?"

"Leave. I mean it. You can't be involved anymore." I nodded to the spot where Erebus had vanished. "You're on his radar now, which means you're in a crap-storm of danger. If I'd known he knew you, I never would've asked for your help."

Ryann put her hand over mine. "I'm not going anywhere."

"You don't get it, Ryann. He'll use you however he can. He'll use you against Finch." I didn't repeat the secret about Finch's feelings. Ryann clearly understood.

"That doesn't matter right now. We need to keep this between us and focus on getting Finch out of the monastery any way we can." Her expression hardened, showing no fear. She had ovaries of steel.

"Look at you, not giving a crap about the E-man."

"He's strung Finch along enough. Let's finish this—you and me. Let's bring our boy home."

She might've been tough, but I still wanted her as far from this mission as possible. Only problem was, I probably couldn't do it without her. She had chemists on call, and she was already up to speed on everything.

I relented. "I should get back to Morphing."

"I'll make those calls." She scooted across the couch, giving me room to lie down.

"Let's hope they've got a formula for us, huh?"

She smiled. "I'll bug them until they find one."

There it is... that desperation. I lay back and closed my eyes, preparing for another trip to Greece. Now that I'd connected with creatures over there, I could jump right into their minds, no matter the distance. So far, my main three were the mouse, the fly, and a seagull, who were never far from the monastery. But that part was the only thing that had gotten easier.

Now that we'd discovered Erebus knew Ryann, this job had gotten way more complicated and dangerous. And it was too late to turn back.

TWENTY-THREE

Finch

W here the hell was I meant to start? I'd spent ten minutes staring at the labels on the bottles. Nobody else had made progress, either. Everyone seemed to be waiting for someone else to make the first move.

"The trial *has* begun," Etienne prompted. He'd left his gas mask at home today, which gave me a sliver of comfort.

Come on, get your logic hat on. I looked over the vials and tried to come up with a plan. *Blue... I should go for blue.* The liquid in Etienne's cauldron had been a vivid azure shade, so it seemed like a good place to start. I reached for a bottle of dark blue liquid labeled "sea serpent excretion" and tipped it into a clean beaker.

Everyone's eyes darted toward me. I'd broken the tension, firing off the proverbial starter gun. I felt them watching and tried to ignore it. I needed to focus on what I was doing. And yet I had no idea what I was doing.

I picked up another bottle, a paler shade of blue, labeled "box jellyfish nematocysts." I poured that in, moderating the amount.

Leviathan blood followed it into the beaker, then a couple of clear substances to lighten up the mixture. Soon enough, I had a liquid that didn't look too far off from the one Etienne had used, at least going by color.

With a deep breath, I put a pipette into the mixture and drew some out. I carried the pipette to the shrub. My shaking hand hovered over it, unable to make that oh-so-important squeeze.

"Nothing's going to blow up, is it?" I glanced at Etienne.

He smiled oddly. "No… at least, it shouldn't."

"Okay, comforting." I closed my eyes and prepared to squeeze the bulb of the pipette.

"Are you sure you want to do that?" Luke's voice stayed my fingertips.

My eyes opened to find Luke standing in front of me, arms crossed. "Huh?"

"Are you sure you want to do that?" he repeated.

"How else will I see if it works?" I replied curtly.

He shrugged. "It just doesn't look like you've given it much thought."

"I'm not a chemist, Luke. It's trial and error." Why was he riding me? Was I on the right track, and he wanted to stop me? I narrowed my eyes at him.

"I just don't think you should be so blasé," he shot back.

I held on to my temper. "Who's being blasé? My hand's friggin' shaking!"

"Perhaps it would be best if everyone concentrated on their own plant," Etienne cut in. "You must all find your own means of creating the right formula. In such small proportions, nobody will come to harm, as long as you don't try to ingest the chemicals."

Yeah, so butt out. I returned my attention to the pipette and gave it a defiant squeeze. A few drops tumbled into the reddish soil. The air stilled with anticipation, and everyone gaped at me. I waited, begging the sapling to shoot up and give me some plump fruit. Seconds passed, but the sapling stayed the same. *Come on, little shrub...* Etienne's tree had grown instantly, but mine didn't do anything.

Then, the tiny fruitlings started to shake. I stepped back, praying that I'd lucked out and gotten the formula on my first try.

But then, the orange seedlings began to cry. They started small, with snuffling that could've been rustling leaves. The sound grew slowly into an all-out bawl. The seedlings shook harder, their sobs turning into an eerie howl that cut right through me. It was the bestial scream of someone who'd lost a loved one. They sounded so heartbroken and pained, like I had tortured them.

"I'm sorry! I'm so sorry!" I gasped, tears springing to my eyes.

The sobbing spread, hitting everyone with that agonizing sorrow. Melody went first, sinking onto her stool as her shoulders shook. Luke went to comfort her, but he was crying, too. Mr. Abara wiped his eyes on the backs of his sleeves, and Oliver stared dead ahead with tears streaming down his cheeks. Blanche leaned over her bench and held her head. The Basani twins clutched each other, weeping at the tops of their lungs. Even Etienne wasn't immune. He sat on the edge of his bench, his tears flowing down an otherwise calm face.

"They are weeping orange willows," Etienne said. "They are a native hybrid of weeping willows and orange trees, found only on this island. If the formula is wrong, they will cry. If the formula is right, the trees will grow and blossom and prompt the fruitlings to turn into fully formed fruit."

"How do I stop them?" I asked through blurry eyes.

He sighed heavily. "They will cease when they are ready."

"Will they do that every time?" Melody whimpered, holding Luke's arm.

"No. As Finch said, it will be trial and error." Etienne pushed away from the bench and made for the door. "I do not care for the weeping, so I will leave you to your work. But, as a parting detail, I should tell you that the closer you get to the right formula, the better the trees will react. They are your guide. Listen to what they have to say."

He left without another word, while the rest of us waited out the heart-wrenching sobs of my sapling.

"I'm sorry. Please, stop crying," I pleaded, caressing the little orange fruitlings. They still felt hot to the touch, but I could handle it to comfort them.

Gradually, their sorrow subsided, but I didn't know if I had the heart to try again. That sound wasn't just creepy, it was devastating. Like all the losses I'd ever experienced, balled up and shoved down my throat.

Forgive me, buddies. I've got to make you grow. Steeling myself, I cleaned out the beaker and started fresh. This time, I chose only the clear liquids and poured them into the beaker. I planned to add serpent excretion last, to give it that blue color. However, as soon as the ricin hit, the whole thing turned red.

"Crap," I muttered under my breath.

"You won't find the right formula through blind luck, Finch." Luke was at it again.

"Why don't you concentrate on your own formula, huh? It doesn't look like anyone will swoop in and save your ass this time, so you'd better hop to it," I snapped back.

Luke looked ready to lunge, but Melody pulled him back. "He's right, Luke. We need to figure this out, and we only have three days. Chemistry is a very exact science, and it's going to take a lot of work to get the correct formula. Come on, let's see if we can make any deductions."

He flashed a suitably venomous glare before leaning over Melody's bench with her, listening to the interesting facts she had to say about each bottle. And, man, did she have a lot to say. I pretended not to listen as I went back to the drawing board.

What did I do to get him this riled up? Yeah, he'd found me in the underbelly of the monastery, and probably thought I was up to no good, but why all the sudden anger? Surely, if he was suspicious, he'd have been better off buddying up to me to get answers. Maybe he thought I intended to hurt Melody, though I had no idea why. Then again, when it came to Melody, he didn't seem to know what rationality was when he was around her.

"Did you know ricin is taken from the beans of the castor oil plant?" Melody rambled. "That's where its name comes from —*Ricinus communis.* The oil is extracted, leaving the ricin in the fiber. It causes cell death and is most effective when inhaled or injected."

Melody was an assassin's fever dream. If Etienne ever decided to return to his old life and didn't feel like using magic, she'd be his girl. While I worked, she rambled about batrachotoxin and how the natives of Western Colombia took the poison from the skin of frogs and laced their darts with it. Hence the name "poison dart frogs."

All the while, Luke smiled at her, observing her like a lovesick puppy. She could have been talking about cow crap, and he'd have kept on grinning.

I mixed another batch of poison, leaving out the ricin and adding the serpent excretion to the rest of the clear liquids. It looked like the right color, but that didn't mean anything. *Trial and error, right?* I drew it into the pipette and carried it to my shrub.

"Fire in the hole!" I shouted.

Everyone covered their ears. After dripping the blue liquid into the pot, I dropped the pipette and followed suit. The seedlings shook, quicker than before. Even through my hands, I heard their sorrowful cries. They twisted in my chest like a knife, bringing another wave of tears to my eyes. I'd need to down a gallon of water, unless I wanted to risk dehydration.

As the sobs subsided, I returned to my bench and dumped out the mixture. Everyone had stopped to have their own sad moment, and they were slowly coming out of it. This was probably why we had three days for this task. With all the crying, we'd be stopping and starting like a rusty old Chevy.

A couple of hours and a whole load of tears later, frustration set in. We all had notebooks, and they were full of failed attempts. This was hopeless. Even having the color as a guide wasn't helping. Plus, there was always the possibility that Etienne changed the color on purpose to trick us. So, I threw everything at my poor shrub. Every color, every combo, every quantity I could think of. Nothing did a thing to calm the seedlings' cries. If anything, they grew louder.

"I hate these plants." Mr. Abara sighed as he dumped a beaker of failed mix into the sink. "What do they have to cry about, anyway?"

"I'm getting very tired." Blanche stretched her arms.

Melody nodded. "Who knew chemistry could be so exhausting? Maybe the fumes from all these chemicals are making us sleepy. Some of them are neurotoxins, so it's not impossible."

"You're saying that now?" I teased. "What if this is just a slower version of that laughing gas?"

"This is ridiculous." Mr. Abara sat on his stool and folded his arms across his chest. "This is not possible. Etienne is fooling us."

"I guess we just have to keep trying." I didn't have anything more encouraging to say.

Everyone got back to it. Shouts of, "Fire in the hole!" became our way of warning the room of another imminent howl of misery. It burst through the lab every few minutes, with all of us ducking and covering our ears. I'd stuffed some cotton balls down my ear canals, which took the edge off a bit.

When I leave for the night, I'm going to find wax. When near Ithaca, do as Odysseus did with the sirens' song, right? If I didn't find a way to block out that heartbreaking sound, it'd finish me off long before the frustration did.

I returned to my mixing like a regular Julia Child, keeping an eye on the Basani twins, who were whispering to each other. Nobody else seemed to have noticed; they were too engrossed in the task. I made a show of pouring liquids into my beaker.

Oliver crouched on the ground, writing failed attempts on a piece of paper with his back to his tree. With him totally oblivious, the Basani twins struck. Using thin strands of Telekinesis, Fay whipped some of his bottles off his desk. Meanwhile, Shailene nabbed bottles from Etienne's desk and switched them with Oliver's. All in the blink of an eye.

You sly little witches! Oliver got back up and reached for one of the substituted bottles, his eyes fixed on his beaker. *Read the damn label!* I tried to urge the thoughts into his head, but I wasn't a Telepath. At their benches nearby, the Basani twins sneered, waiting for Oliver to screw up.

I didn't want to help that lazy wretch. But I didn't want the Basani twins getting any satisfaction, either. This put me in a true pickle. *Ah... life was easier before you came along, conscience.*

I threw out a rapid strand of Telekinesis and flicked the substitute bottles off the table, including the one Oliver was about to pick up. They hit the ground with a splintering *crack*, startling Oliver and the others. He stared at the broken bottles.

"Did you do that?" He looked at me, mouth open. I had my palms up, so I was the obvious culprit.

"I did, but only to stop you from making a big mistake. You need to keep an eye on your stuff, Oliver. There are snakes around." I shot a dark glare at the Basani twins. "You two need to back off. We're all equals here."

The twins paled. "Who's to say *you* didn't switch his bottles?" Shailene retorted.

"You just did. I never said anything about his bottles being switched." I flashed a cold smile.

Their mouths opened and closed like beached fish.

As the dust settled, most of us returned to work. Oliver recovered his stolen bottles and held them close, shooting furious looks at the twins every few minutes. Only Blanche didn't pick up again. She made her way over to me, and I stopped what I was doing.

"That was a wonderful thing you did, just now," she murmured. "You didn't have to help him, but you did. That's commendable."

I shrugged shyly. "I couldn't let them sabotage him. He might be an ass, but they're bigger asses."

"Your language, Finch. It would make a nun blush." She tutted playfully.

"That's tame compared to the stuff I used to hear," I replied.

Her expression softened.

"Nowadays, I just do the opposite of whatever Katherine would've done," I told her. "What are you going to do once you pass all these trials and find El Dorado?"

"I appreciate the assumption that I'll pass the trials." She grinned, but then her expression calmed. "I'm just trying to feel alive before death comes for me. It'll be a slow trek to the grave if I just sit around, doing nothing."

"I think that's admirable. I hope I have the energy when I'm your age... if I get to your age." I heaved a sigh.

She peered up at me, sadness in her eyes. "I hope you find a way to enjoy life someday. You learn what's important when you lose someone. It changes you. Take it from an old lady: there's no sense in life if you're not livin' it and doin' everything you can to stave off death. Just existin' will leave you hollow, son."

I let out a dry laugh. "Believe me, I'm trying."

A nearby rustle distracted me from my impromptu therapy session with Blanche. A parrot landed on the windowsill, ruffling its feathers and throwing back its head.

"Numbskull! Hey! Numbskull!" it croaked. It was definitely looking at me. "Numbskull! Hey!"

This parrot had Morph written all over it.

"Sorry, Blanche. I'm just going to take a closer look at that... bird." I got up and crossed the room.

"Hey!" it chirped.

"Yeah?"

Its black beak opened wide. "Marlin! Marlin! Numbskull!"

Marlin? Wait... if this was Kenzie, she'd only be able to use the parrot's vocabulary to speak to me. Marlin and Merlin. Coincidence? No chance. This parrot was definitely for me.

"What do you want?" I whispered.

"Take a leak! Take a leak!" it croaked.

I leaned closer. "You want me to go somewhere private?"

"Bingo! Two fat ladies!"

"Who are you calling fat?" I put my arm out, and the bird hopped right on. Turning around, I saw everyone's eyes firmly fixed on me. "I'm going to give this to Etienne. No idea how it got in. But if this thing keeps squawking, and those buds start crying again, my ears will hemorrhage."

I hurried out of the room before anyone could question me. I took the parrot into the flowery square outside and ducked into the shadow of a cloister. Only then did I turn to the parrot.

"Kenzie? Is that you?"

The parrot nodded. "Numbskull! Bingo!"

"What are you doing here? Did Harley send you?" I had so many questions, having starved so long for communication.

"No! Numbskull!" the parrot cawed. "Airbus!"

"Airbus? You mean, Erebus?" My heart lurched. "Are you working for him?"

"No time! Spy! Donkey spy!"

I frowned. "Donkey? What donkey?"

"Donkey! Faster!"

"I don't know what you're talking about," I muttered in frustration.

"D'oh! Caster! Donkey! Caster!"

My eyes widened. "Do you mean Doncaster?"

"Bingo!"

"Davin has a spy here?"

It nodded, ruffling its feathers. "Yes! Bad spy! Bingo!"

"Do you know who it is?" I pressed.

"No! Spy! Bad spy!"

"Come on, Kenzie, you have to give me more. You're killing me."

"Poison!" she croaked.

My frown deepened. "Poison? What do you mean? Is he going to poison someone?"

"No! Poison tree! Grow!"

Understanding hit me. "You know how I can make the tree grow?"

"Later!"

"You know, but you can't tell me now?" I prompted.

"Soon! Later! Got to go! Ciao!" The parrot flapped away, leaving me to stare after it.

As I sank back into the shadows, I let Kenzie's stilted words mingle in my brain, trying to make sense of them. First and foremost, Davin had a spy in the monastery. He wasn't just thinking about getting inside, he'd already done it, albeit vicariously. Secondly, but no less importantly, Kenzie might have a way of making that tree grow.

The timing worried me—the same way it had worried Etienne. And the same way it clearly worried Erebus, if he'd gone to the trouble of enlisting Kenzie. That stuck in my throat. What had it cost her? I couldn't think about that now. I'd have to ask her later, if she came back. Until then, I needed to focus on what I could do something about.

Why had Davin sent a spy? Once again, Davin seemed to be meddling in Erebus's business. It left an aftertaste of suspicion in my mouth, foul and unrelenting. If Davin was hellbent on getting in Erebus's way a second time, there had to be a reason. Maybe there was a deeper connection between the Prince of Darkness and the perpetual British stone in my shoe.

Either way, this had just added a guacamole of crap onto this never-ending, layered dip of difficulty.

Trying not to lose my mind, I headed inside. But everything had changed. I couldn't look at the others the same way. Not now. Any one of them could've been the spy, even Etienne. Especially Etienne, given his old ties to Davin.

I glanced at Luke. He ranked high on my list of suspects, especially since he'd followed me around and gotten all annoying about my potions. Almost like he wanted me to fail.

"Hey, numbskull!" Luke shouted over the weeping, as I returned to my bench.

"Talking to yourself again, Luke? First sign of madness, you know," I retorted. Childish, but deeply satisfying.

He scowled. "I guess you and that bird are kindred spirits. Same size brain."

"Actually, African grays are famously smart, so I'll take that as a compliment." I gave him a cold stare. "That one probably had a bigger vocabulary than you'll ever have. Maybe you should ask it to teach you some really hard words, like 'Neanderthal.'"

"What did you call me?"

"Ah, so you don't know what that means. It's hard to explain. I could get you a mirror, if you want me to show you." I knew I shouldn't bite, but if he worked for Davin, I wanted to get in all the digs I could before I exposed him.

Melody put a hand on his shoulder. "He's just teasing, Luke. Come on, let's get back to work, shall we?"

He might not have realized, but Melody was as much his defender as he was her protector. I'd noticed it a lot. Subtle gestures here and soft words there, to calm him down. But if I discovered that he *was* the spy, nobody—Melody included—could protect him from my wrath.

TWENTY-FOUR

Finch

D ay one was a bust. Kenzie hadn't come back, and the monastery had lost its charm. I couldn't even enjoy the tasty food, since it came with a hefty seasoning of suspicion. I observed everyone during those quieter moments, waiting for someone to slip, but I wasn't that lucky. They went about their business, same as ever. Only *my* situation had altered.

On day two, I entered the lab before dawn. I hadn't slept a wink. The slightest sound had woken me during the night and put me on edge. Fearing I might be smothered didn't encourage a good night's rest. Not wanting to stare at spooky-ass Hades until the sun rose, I'd dragged myself out of bed to face another long day of screeching saplings.

Mr. Abara slept on the floor. He'd evidently tried to pull an all-nighter and failed miserably. Melody and Luke stood at their benches.

"Where's your parrot?" Luke sniped right in.

"It flew off," I replied. I'd worried over Kenzie all night, so it was a bit of a sore point. I wanted to know what sort of deal she'd struck with Erebus, and I wanted to know how to solve this tree problem. A hint about the spy's identity would've been helpful, too. But she hadn't returned.

"Don't do that, Luke," Melody said softly.

He looked puzzled. "Do what?"

"Antagonize him," she replied. "Can't you see he's tired?"

"We're all tired," Luke retorted.

"I know, but he doesn't look like he got any sleep at all. I don't know what's gotten into the pair of you, but you don't have to snipe at each other all the time. You're not in competition, remember? We can all make it through." Her tone wasn't patronizing, just honest. And Luke didn't make any more comments, so it must have gotten through to him.

After an hour, I was back in the rhythm of failure. Pouring, mixing, crying, dumping—like a kindergarten sandpit for wannabe mapmakers. *That sound will be the death of me.* Or, at least, my ears. The crying didn't get any easier to deal with, and I hadn't found any wax. I'd thought about jabbing a candlestick in each ear, but common sense had won today. Tomorrow might be a different story.

"Here, I thought you could use this." Melody approached with a steaming cup of coffee. I took it gratefully, but I paused as I brought it to my lips.

What if it's you? What if you've poisoned it?

"Can you take a sip first, to check if it's too hot? I think I ate something I'm allergic to. My lips are on fire, and I don't want to burn them right off," I lied, handing the cup back.

She chuckled and blew on the rich, black liquid. *How could someone be so innocent?* The mind boggled. Tentatively, she took a sip and held the coffee in her mouth before swallowing. "Not too hot, not too cold. The Goldilocks zone of coffee." She passed it back with a winning smile.

"Thanks for that." I took my first sip, like a man possessed. *Caffeine...*

"No problem. I don't usually drink coffee, so I imagine I'll be buzzing soon." She grinned and leaned against my bench. "Mom and Dad never allowed anything that could be considered addictive."

"I'm not going to have Winchesters banging on my door, blaming me for their daughter's caffeine addiction, am I?" I took another gulp, praying it'd wake me up. Playing with chemicals while borderline catatonic wasn't a good idea.

She shook her head. "I hope not."

"How are things going?" I nodded to her workbench, where Luke sat scowling at me.

"Terribly. Etienne said this was about logic, but there's no logic to this whatsoever. How can there be, when he hasn't given us any clues? If we knew the properties of these chemicals, it would be much simpler."

I arched an eyebrow. "You sounded like you were rattling off everything there was to know about them yesterday."

"I know where they come from, and how they affect the human body, but I don't know which ones cancel out the others. My knowledge of chemistry still has some gaps, it would seem." She gave a sweet sigh. "I can't understand why he hasn't given us any information. In the real world, we'd have books to aid us. So why not here?"

"I guess it wouldn't be as much of a challenge." I gave a wry chuckle.

"What are you talking about over here?" Luke finally gave up his scowling and came to investigate. Or keep tabs on Melody. Poor sap. He would have a hard time in life if he couldn't let the girl he liked chat with other people for more than a minute. That was major stalker territory.

"How impossible this trial is," I replied. "And the evils of caffeine."

Melody giggled. "Finch asked me to make sure his coffee wasn't too hot. Who knew it could be so delicious? Then again, everything here is."

"Do you think there's something in the water?" I mused.

"Magic, you mean?" Melody's eyes widened.

I shrugged. "Maybe."

"Are you okay?" Melody turned suddenly to Luke. "You feel agitated."

Ah, the perils of falling for an Empath. Wade had been through that proverbial gauntlet, and it hadn't ended so badly.

Luke stiffened. "Yeah, I'm fine. It's just… this task, you know? It's frustrating the heck out of me. Every time someone fails, we all suffer when those trees start wailing. I don't know how much more I can take."

"You know what you can do to make it stop?" I met his gaze.

"What's that?" He walked right into my freshly laid trap.

I smiled sweetly. "You can give up. Walk out of here, leave the island, and never listen to those trees again."

"You'd like that, wouldn't you?" A muscle twitched in his jaw.

"*Moi?* Of course not. I'd hate to see Melody all on her own, without her big, bad bodyguard to keep her safe. That's why I saved your wet lump of pottery." I paused for dramatic effect. "But you're more than just her bodyguard, aren't you? At least, you'd like to be."

Melody gasped. "Finch! That's nonsense!"

Luke's cheeks reddened.

"Is it, Luke?" I taunted him more. "I might not be an Empath, but I don't have to be."

My assholery served a purpose. Luke was gaga for Melody—Tiresias himself, the blind prophet of Apollo, could've seen it. And he seemed set on antagonizing me. I needed to use those traits to my benefit. First, to get a confession out of him that he was Davin's spy. Maybe Davin had threatened Melody's life, and that was how he'd ended up doing Davin's bidding. Secondly, I just loved pushing this guy's buttons.

"I think we should get back to the trees. Someone still hasn't woken up yet, by the looks of it." Luke's voice held a warning. "He's babbling like an idiot."

Melody followed him back to their workbenches, looking confused. The cogs were definitely whirring in that incredible mind of hers. For someone so smart, she wasn't bright in the field of love. She had to be naïve not to see how much Luke adored her. I hoped she didn't get caught in the crossfire if Luke was Davin's spy.

I shook myself. I couldn't fixate on Luke. Really, it could be any one of these people. I'd seen enough to know appearances could be deceptive. Appearing like good folks didn't mean they weren't hiding dark secrets. Davin had tricked far nicer people in his time.

After the second day's epic failure, I worked right through the night and into day three. Mr. Abara and Blanche joined me in the all-night brigade, though they'd passed out around four, waking every time the saplings sobbed. I'd kept at it, and now I felt loopy, like I didn't know reality from dreams anymore. Which was probably why I was high-pouring arsenic into a tumbler like a cocktail wizard and singing "The Final Countdown."

Staying entertained kept me marginally sane as the pressure mounted. I was nowhere near mixing the poisons right. Luke had stopped biting when I taunted him. Kenzie still hadn't come back. And Davin's spy was out there somewhere, watching and waiting.

As if summoned, the rest of the challengers walked in, with the exception of Melody. The Basani twins went straight to their workbench, whispering in hushed tones. I carried on with what I was doing, keeping my ears pricked.

"Are you sure you know what you're doing?" Shailene murmured.

Fay nodded. "I think so. I'm still rusty with the Morse code. And it was foggy on the sea last night."

Morse code? What?! Had they been talking to someone? My chest gripped with dread. Who had they been talking to?

"What if it's not right? What if he was wrong?" Shailene urged.

Fay shrugged. "At least it's a start. It's not like I could say a whole lot. If you want to be sure, you learn Morse code."

He? What he? My mind went into overdrive. Naturally, my first thought was Davin. People didn't always need power in order to make a deal with him. I mean, he was usually the one pursuing the power. But what if he'd made them an offer they couldn't refuse? Money, maybe? I wasn't sure what might be tempting enough to make them tick.

I watched the twins intently, until Shailene looked over and I dropped my gaze like a damn stone. I had to keep my eye on them, that was for sure. If they had someone helping them from the outside, that rang a massive alarm bell.

"Are you okay?" Melody walked in with coffee, followed shortly by the rest of the challengers. Without being asked, she took a sip before handing it to me. "You don't look okay. Did you know that exhaustion can have the same effect on the body as alcohol?"

"I didn't." I took the coffee and downed half in one go.

"Too much coffee isn't good for you either. Have you been at this all night?" She sounded worried.

"Oh yes-indeedy, not that it made a difference. These trees keep on crying, and I keep on torturing them. I started out feeling sorry for them, but now I just want to put them out of their misery." I didn't know if it was fatigue or paranoia or what I'd just heard from the Basani twins, but I found myself staring at Melody as I drank the coffee. As if something on her face might make her stick out as the spy. What if the twins were too obvious? What if I was getting my wires crossed? I couldn't rule anyone out just now.

"Have you come up with anything yet?" I asked.

"Not yet," she replied.

"You haven't found any secret books that contain the answer?"

She looked away quickly. "Books? Why would I have found a book?"

"I don't know. You seem to know a lot about poisons, and I doubt that information is just in your head." I toned down the intensity so it wouldn't look like an outright accusation. Although, she was definitely acting shiftier. "I figured you like to read, so a book would be your go-to."

"Nope, I haven't found any book, and I haven't found any solution," she mumbled.

Mr. Abara groaned. "You're not the only one. None of us are any closer to finding the formula."

"I'm starting to think you were right." I lifted my mug to him, still trying to seem normal. "What if Etienne is messing with us? I mean, it feels like this is a setup for failure. He waltzed on out of here and has probably been giggling himself stupid in his study, thinking of all the screeching we've put ourselves through. For nothing, I might add."

"I don't like violence." Mr. Abara padded over to join the coffee crew. "But, if that's the case, I might have to throw one punch. For honor's sake."

"Get in line." I laughed wearily. "Is the room spinning, or is it just me?"

Melody patted my back. "It's you, Finch. Why don't you take a break, at least until you've finished your coffee?"

Take a break? Why would you want me to take a break?

"I'm seeing colors." I stared up at the lights, which were ringed in fog.

Melody frowned. "Are you colorblind?"

"No."

"Then, you can always see colors." She stifled a giggle.

"I mean, I can *hear* colors. Ah, dammit, I don't know what I mean." I sagged against the workbench and propped myself up on one hand. "This task has finished me off, lads and ladettes. I don't know how anyone gets to be a mapmaker, frankly. I wonder what Etienne's pass rate is. Zero, probably. Hey, do you reckon that's why he ended up with this place, because he's the only one who ever passed?"

Mr. Abara grimaced. "If that is true, maybe there will be two punches. If he stands between me and my goal, I'm not going to be happy. It is more important than a set of trials."

"Changing the world, right?" I smiled up at him.

"Precisely."

"That can't be an easy task, though, can it?" I started along a line that I hoped might make him slip up. "You'd need backup to put something that huge into action."

Mr. Abara's eyes narrowed. "What do you mean?"

"It'd take power and resources, wouldn't it?"

"Not necessarily," he said stiffly. At least he was meeting my gaze, but that didn't mean much. It might have been a ploy—being bold to make me think he had nothing to hide.

"No? So, you're in this solo?" I arched an eyebrow. I remembered him saying he worked in a cell.

Mr. Abara folded his arms across his chest. "There is a cell of us," he confirmed. "We all have the same goal. I'm just the one finding a safe haven."

"Who else is in your cell?" I pressed.

"You wouldn't know them," he answered gruffly. Tension bristled between us. He clearly didn't like me asking so many questions. But why? Surely, he should've been all too happy to tell all about his savior work? He seemed willing to do a lot for his cause. Maybe Davin had offered to help him with his task in exchange for him being a spy. That kind of power and influence couldn't be sniffed at, and I knew Davin had ties to the upper echelons of magical society. Their money could've helped Mr. Abara a hell of a lot.

"So, you don't have sponsors or anything like that? Charitable aid, that sort of thing?" I tried to keep my expression as casual as possible.

"We don't welcome outsiders. They can't be trusted." A glisten of sweat shone on his upper lip. A sign of deceit, maybe?

"Map-making wasn't always like this, you know. They taught it freely in the olden days, but I suppose there were more places to discover," Melody chimed in. It smacked of a diversion tactic. "Magicals used to use it to find objects and artifacts that had been stolen during conflicts or lost over time. So, I suppose you could say they used it as more of a complex tracking spell, which was probably why less secrecy surrounded the art."

"Greed is a powerful motivator," Mr. Abara said. "The desire to hoard a treasure and make people jump through hoops to get it, for the sake of making it elite. That is why I don't associate with that sort of person, Finch."

Melody nodded slowly. "I agree with you, to some extent, but sometimes it's important for places to stay hidden. If map-making wasn't so difficult to access, then those places wouldn't stay hidden for long. They'd be overrun by people. Is it important to you, Mr. Abara, that the place you're looking for remains a secret to the majority of the world?"

"It is," he replied, visibly mulling it over. "I suppose you're right. If map-making were free to all, there'd be no place like the one I'm looking for. You're wise beyond your years, Melody. Very smart."

"Having these trials weeds out the time-wasters, too," Melody went on. "You need a dedicated cause to go through this. I think we all have one, or we wouldn't be here."

Mr. Abara smiled. "If I fulfill my cause, I'll die a happy man."

And what would you give for that cause? And what would you give, Melody, to find your hidden place? The light in Mr. Abara's eyes was intense with hope. But hope could lead to desperation. Making a deal with Davin wouldn't mean his heart wasn't in the right place. Look at what I'd done with Erebus. And Mr. Abara certainly looked like a man with a mission. I didn't exactly know what a lost oasis had to do with child soldiers, but if he knew, then he'd do everything to achieve that.

"There's one place on Earth that has never been mapped. It's called the Last Unknown. That's why I'm here," Melody explained. "It has a lot of other names, in many different languages, but the Last Unknown has a ring to it. It makes me feel like an explorer, discovering the last true mystery on our planet."

"If it's unknown, how do you know it exists?" Mr. Abara asked.

"There are countless legends surrounding it, and I've always found them fascinating. It's ancient—even the old magicals of bygone days only whispered about it. And, if it exists, it can be found by map-making." She gazed at Mr. Abara and me, and I realized the two of us had leaned closer, drawn by the mystique.

"What's special about this place?" I asked. Maybe that would give me an indication of where Melody's motivations lay.

Melody nodded. "It's wrapped in myth, so nothing is certain, but... we have reason to believe it's where the last true-blooded descendants of the Primus Anglicus lived."

I snorted. "Inbreds, you mean?"

"No, not inbreds." She rolled her eyes, amused. "There were many clans and global branches of the Primus Anglicus, so they wouldn't have had to inbreed. It's thought that they fled there to escape persecution. It's likely ruins by now, after so many centuries."

"Who was persecuting them?" Mr. Abara seemed equally intrigued.

Melody rubbed her chin. "Nobody knows. It could have been other magical factions, or self-preservation of the true bloodlines. We can't know, because no one ever found where they went."

"Do you think the gods who used to live here might've gone there?" I pointed to a statue of Hermes precariously balanced on an upper balcony. What if Davin was searching for old bloodlines?

"Again, nobody knows. It's the last true mystery." She smiled, clearly reveling in our interest.

A more interesting mystery than the one I'm dealing with. I could've listened to her all day, if I had the luxury of time. I was still fumbling in the dark with the formula, and everyone seemed suspicious. Even Oliver seemed suspicious, simply by working alone. He hadn't really made any bonds with anyone. Was that on purpose?

Was he keeping to himself, so he didn't slip up and reveal he was the spy?

I looked back at my workbench, pretty disheartened by the trials, the spy, all of it. I'd created every formula combination I could think of, writing them down as I went along, and the saplings blubbered at every attempt. Like they were mocking me.

For the first time since starting these missions for Erebus, I was genuinely stumped. No light at the end of the tunnel, no leads to follow. I really didn't know if I could pull this off. Options and time were quickly running out. It boiled me up inside. I needed to succeed, for all the usual Erebus-related reasons—i.e., him hurting people I cared about. I needed to find Davin's spy before they decided to take me out. And I needed to free myself from Erebus's service, or I'd only have more of this to look forward to. But I was no closer to achieving any of it.

"Finch?" Melody peered at me. "Are you okay? You disappeared for a minute."

I nodded. "Just tired."

Yeah... tired of all this uncertainty. Tired of Erebus. Tired of it all.

TWENTY-FIVE

Kenzie

———

I snapped out of my latest Morph. Finch was on his third and last day of the poison trial, with twelve hours to the midnight deadline. I'd watched him from afar, zipping back and forth between my apartment and Greece. Now that I had a connection to the African gray, it was easy to slide back into the mind of the bird. But, right now, I needed a breather. I didn't want to draw attention to him, not with a spy in the midst. Any weird activity might've encouraged the spy to strike.

Still, it sucked that I'd had to make it look like I'd left him on his own. With no news to give him, watching had been my only option. I'd even been there as he slept, guarding him. If anyone had tried to slip in and hurt him, I'd have raised the damn alarm. But no one had. Plus, he hadn't slept much.

"How is he?" Ryann was obviously done with subtext as she crossed the apartment. With so much at stake, and us on a strict deadline, Finch was the primary concern. I was just the mouthpiece—for information we didn't have yet.

"Really tired," I replied.

"And you?"

I smiled grimly. "Really tired. Tell me you've got some good news. We really need it right now. He's failing on his own. This task is freaking impossible. Etienne hasn't given them any clues or anything; they're all failing."

She whipped out her phone. "Well then, you came back at the right time."

"What do you mean?"

"I'm waiting on a call from one of the San Fran chemists," she replied.

I stared at the phone. "It's two o'clock in the morning. You sure they're going to call?" The time zones were killing me. Being ten hours behind Greece made things a lot more difficult. If we had to wait until a decent hour in the morning, Finch would lose another seven hours, at least. Hours we couldn't afford to lose.

She nodded confidently. "I spoke to her half an hour ago and she was still hard at work with her team. They haven't slept much, I don't think."

"Neither has Finch." I stretched out my stiff limbs.

"He's not sleeping?" A worried frown furrowed her forehead.

"Nope. He pulled an all-nighter, and he's pretty much on the edge of insanity. I heard him singing 'The Final Countdown,' if you want an indicator of his mental state." I tried to muster a smile but couldn't. This wasn't funny in the slightest. "He's not doing too hot, Ryann. This task has him stressed to his limits."

"I'll see if I can get an update." Ryann tapped furiously at her phone, jabbing at the screen.

"Whoa there, don't crack the damn thing. We need it." I was only half teasing.

She smiled nervously. "Sorry. I guess Finch isn't the only one stressed."

"They don't know what this is for, do they—the chemists?" I didn't know everything she'd been up to while I'd been out Morphing.

She shook her head. "No, they think it's for a paper I'm writing on the use of poisons that's going to be published by the California Mage Council. I asked them to put a rush on it because it's going to publication tonight, with the promise that they'd be credited for all the chemistry work."

"You don't think they're going to be pissed off when it doesn't come out?"

"I'll just tell them I handed it in too late." She shrugged. "Who knows, maybe it will end up in some publication."

I smiled at her. "Looks like you've picked up some of Finch's more devious qualities. Such a bad influence."

"Hey, these are all mine," she replied. "Sometimes, in law, you have to play a little dirty to get justice for those who deserve it. This is no different."

"Tough girl Ryann might just be the best one yet." I sank back into the couch and wished I had time to drift off. My body ached all over, and my brain… was pretty much a write-off at this point. Spending so much time inside different creatures wasn't good for anyone.

The phone rang, and Ryann swiped the screen violently. "Marisol?"

"Yeah, it's me," a voice replied, on speaker. "Sorry to call so late, but I guessed you were still up, since you've been texting back."

"I'm not sure I'll get any sleep until I've got everything together for the editors," Ryann replied, cool as a cucumber. I knew there had to be a reason "lawyers" and "liars" sounded so similar.

"Yeah, same over here. We're so eager to get this in on time. It'll be a huge benefit for getting subsidies and grants. Getting money out of the covens for chemistry is tough. It'd be easier to turn lead into gold." The chemist, Marisol, cackled like she'd made the joke of the century. Ryann gave her a polite chuckle in response.

"Does that mean we're on target?" Ryann pressed, still keeping it chill.

"Pretty much, yeah. I've got a team of three, and we've been doing live tests since you called yesterday—honestly, I've got a spreadsheet as long as my leg with all the experiments we've done. It's taken a lot of effort and resources, but we think we've finally cracked it," Marisol replied.

Ryann glanced at me, an anxious smile forming. With that sort of manpower, or womanpower, they'd clearly been able to tweak quantities better and faster than Finch. Plus, they already had an in-depth knowledge of chemistry.

"Can you tell me what the formula is?" Ryann asked, nodding at the notepad on the table. I leapt to it, snatching up a pen.

"I'll just attach it in an email, though I might have to send it in the morning when I've had some sleep. I think I left my brain in the lab," Marisol said. In fairness, she did sound tired.

Ryann paused. "Yeah, that's totally fine, but would you be able to tell me the formula now, so I can jot it down? I'll need to hand a list to the editors so they can double-check they get the spellings and quantities right. Not all of them are used to scientific stuff, so the sooner they can have the information, the better."

"Oh… right, of course. I hadn't thought about that. I forget that not everyone's a chemistry nerd." Marisol barked a laugh. "Do you have a pen handy?"

"Yep, I'm good to go." Ryann winked at me.

"Okay, so everything has to be mixed in this order. It's six drops of cyanide, four of arsenic, seven of black mamba venom, one of cottonmouth venom, two of cone snail venom, five of box jellyfish nematocysts, five of ricin, two of tetrodotoxin, eight of batrachotoxin, three of Leviathan blood, one of Charybdis blood, and one of Scylla blood. Finally, ten drops of sea serpent excretion. When it's mixed, you can add any quantity you like to the soil— more means a big tree, less means a smaller tree." Marisol went quiet for a moment. "Did you get all of that?"

Ryann looked at me, and I nodded. I'd written it down, just as she'd said it.

"Yeah, I got all that. Thank you so much, Marisol. I can't wait to see the article published," Ryann said. "And, just to be clear, what did this formula do when you tested it?"

"Something extraordinary," Marisol whispered, as if it were a secret. "It seems to speed up development, even though it's formed from so many poisonous substances. We now have a weeping orange willow crushed up against the ceiling of the lab, after you told us to bring a sapling in. Actually, we were hoping to call it the 'Tree of Life' formula, if that's okay with you."

Ryann grinned excitedly. "Of course, that's no problem."

"Would you mind if I continue looking into it? My team and I are very eager to see what else this formula can do." Marisol sounded just as excited.

"Sure, knock yourselves out," Ryann replied, punching the air silently. "And thank you again for the quick turnaround. I know it hasn't been easy. Next time I see you, pizza's on me, okay?"

Marisol chuckled. "We'll hold you to that!"

"Okay then, I'll let you sleep, and you can send that email in the morning." Ryann had already started dancing a jig.

"Speak to you soon. And thank you for this opportunity."

"I'm the one who should be thanking you," Ryann replied.

"Speak to you soon." She swiped the "end call" button and did a rock-star slide across the kitchen floor.

I jumped up, forgetting how tired I was. "So, we really got it?"

"We got it!" Ryann whooped, shimmying and shaking.

I laughed and pulled her to her feet, and the two of us burst into a dance around the kitchen table. I may have twerked, but that'd stay between the two of us. Ryann went wild, giving it her best moves, waggling her phone over her head like a trophy. We'd just won the big leagues.

"We can bring our boy home!" Ryann sank down onto a stool, howling at the ceiling like a wolf.

"You bet your sweet ass!" I sat down beside her, grinning like an idiot. "I've been freaking out so hard. He's got like twelve hours left, and he's totally clueless."

"And now we've got the goods to get him through!"

I sighed with relief. "I never listened in chemistry class. I don't know my periodic table from my elbow. Man, I could kiss those nerds."

Ryann nodded. "I know what you mean. I just want to smother them with love, and then smother Finch, and then smother you, and maybe even Erebus."

I shot her a mischievous look. "I'm sure Finch wouldn't mind a bit of smothering from you."

"Not this again." She rolled her eyes. "Erebus doesn't know what he's talking about. I've been thinking about what he said a lot, and I've come to the conclusion that he was just trying to worry us. He probably wanted us to think he's got some leverage on Finch when he doesn't. There's nothing more to it."

"What about what *I* know?" I smirked.

"And what's that?" She arched an eyebrow.

"That he's crushing on you, and you're secretly crushing on him."

She shook her head defiantly. "You've been in that bird brain too long. Finch doesn't think about me that way—he's been through a lot. I doubt he ever wants to fall in love again, after what happened last time."

"What if the right girl came along?" I nudged her arm.

"Then I'd be happy for him." Her face tightened subtly.

"What if the right girl came along at the wrong time?" I poked the bear some more.

Ryann sighed. "If you're talking about me, you're barking up the wrong tree. He's a friend. I'm his friend. That's it."

"You just did a power-slide across the kitchen floor. Not what just a friend would do." She could deny it all she liked, but she still showed the signs of someone who cared a lot more than she let on.

"You twerked," Ryann pointed out. "Look, I'm thrilled we've cracked this, and I'm excited that we helped Finch. It's like finishing an essay at the eleventh hour, just in time to hand it in." She stared down at the table. "I mean, come on, this entire world owes everything to Finch—it's nice to pay some of that back."

"What if you knew he liked you?" I had to ask.

She shrugged. "It wouldn't change anything. I'm with Adam, and I love him. I can see a future with him."

"You can't with Finch?" For some weird reason, a lump formed in my throat. A secondhand sadness for my pal.

"I... told you I don't think of him like that," she replied after a moment. "And Finch is hardly ever around. He's always away on missions, and even when he's at the SDC, he's in his own world half the time. Adam is... stable. He's sweet, and he's reliable, and he's constant. That's husband material."

"And if Finch's missions end after this?" My voice cracked. *Get it together, Kenzie! Geez.*

Her gaze hardened. "I love Adam. I *know* Adam. I could try for years with Finch, to get to know him better, and never scratch the surface. I know it's not his fault, and I'm aware I sound like a total bitch, but I like what I can understand. And I don't understand Finch."

Maybe you should try harder. I couldn't bring myself to say it. It wasn't Ryann's fault. I knew what she meant. Finch was a tough nut to crack. I just wanted him to find some happiness after so much misery and struggle.

"Adam must be a hell of a guy," I said instead.

Ryann offered a small smile. "He really is." She paused. "Finch is, too, but he's not my guy."

"No… I guess not."

"Do you have someone?" Ryann held my gaze.

I snorted. "Me? God, no. Me and guys are like oil and water—we don't mix. I've been around too many and heard too much of what they brag about. It's ruined guys for me."

She chuckled. "Maybe you haven't found the right one."

"Adam got a younger brother?"

"Sadly not."

I nodded. "Well, since my love life is hopeless, we should get this show on the road. I won't get a boyfriend out of it, but I'll get my friend back, and that's enough for me." I glanced at the couch. "So, as Finch would say—it's Morphin' time."

TWENTY-SIX

Finch

Mr. Abara all but frog-marched me to my room, since I'd turned into the walking dead. I'd been on guard the whole way, in case he tried to jump me in the corridor. But he hadn't; he'd delivered me to my room and stopped just shy of tucking me in. That didn't let him off the spy hook. He might've been biding his time, waiting for a less obvious moment to strike. Paranoia mixed with sleeplessness did not a sane Finch make.

Twenty minutes ago, I'd slumped forward on my workbench and almost sent my tree flying. Melody saved it by flinging some mad spell at it, lifting it up in a vortex of rainbow light and setting it back on the table. Naturally, Luke gave me an earful. As if I'd asked her to help me. I was grateful, sure, but I didn't deserve a bunch of crap for her decision. Especially not from him.

After labeling me a risk, Melody and Mr. Abara had joined forces to get me to nap. And I hadn't been about to try and say no to Mr. Abara. He could've slung me over his shoulder and carried me if I'd refused. He almost had. I wondered if they were trying to get me out of the way, so I'd be sure to fail and they could skip back to Davin and tell him the good news. But which one had first suggested I get some rest? My weary mind couldn't remember. It could barely remember my own name. All this suspicion and uncertainty on no sleep was driving me mad.

So, naturally, sleep didn't come. *Evasive minx.* It was like turning in for an early night, then lying in bed for hours, unable to drift off. My frustration levels peaked. Who could've slept, knowing they had half a day left to figure out an impossible formula?

Maybe I should bash my head against Hades to knock myself out. That way, I'd be able to sleep through the deadline. Hope was the worst part of this. That vain sliver of possibility that it could still be done. It would make the disappointment of failure hurt so much more when that axe fell.

I turned over in bed and nearly screamed at the sight before me. A massive bird had just flown into the window, banging on the glass with its beak. It took a moment for my exhausted brain to realize it was the parrot—a.k.a. Kenzie.

"Son of a nutcracker!" I hissed into my pillow. I quickly got up and let the bird in. "You almost gave me a heart attack!"

The parrot cackled. "Good news! Good news! Numbskull!"

"You don't need to keep calling me 'numbskull.' I know you're talking to me." I put my arm out, and it hopped on. "And, pardon my French, but where the hell have you been? You tell me there's a spy, then flap off like that? Not cool, Kenzie."

"Windbag! Good news!" the parrot croaked.

"I'm not a windbag! You abandoned me." I pouted. "And where'd you learn a word like that? Actually, while I'm at it, how are you even speaking English? Shouldn't you be squawking Greek?"

"Focus! Marlin!"

I sighed and sat on the edge of my bed. I supposed the minutia of the parrot's linguistic skills didn't matter. "Fine, what's the good news? I'm guessing that's what you're trying to say, right?"

"Bingo! Good news!" The parrot nodded. "Formula!"

My eyes widened. "You've got it? Ah man, this is going to be hard, isn't it?" Trying to decipher parrot-speak with something so specific would be a nightmare.

"Listen! Numbskull! Pen!"

"Right, a pen." One-handed, I grabbed my chemistry notebook and pencil. I hadn't left my notes in the lab for anyone to set their peepers on. "Okay, shoot."

"Right order! Get it right!" the parrot chirped. "Six! Sewer snide!"

I frowned. "Huh?"

"Six! Sewer snide!"

"Six drops of cyanide?" In my sleepy state, Kenzie's parrot-speak somehow made more sense.

"Bingo!"

I wrote it down and waited for the next linguistic challenge.

"Four! Ass lick! Seven! Black snake!"

"Okay, so that's four drops of arsenic—at least, I hope that's what you're trying to say. And seven drops of black mamba venom, yes?"

The parrot nodded. "Numbskull! Good work! Pretty Polly!"

I smirked. "Thanks."

We went on like that for at least ten minutes. As exasperated as it made me, I had to admit this was hilarious. If Erebus could've seen me now, he'd laugh all the way out of his skin suit.

The parrot hopped up and down my arm. "Last one! Last one!"

"Holy crap…" In my sleepy state, it only just dawned on me what this meant. This wasn't a game, even though it'd lightened my mood a bit. After this, I'd have the friggin' formula in my hands!

"Ten! Sea snake! Goop! Sea snake!"

I wrapped my arm around the parrot and squeezed carefully. "Ten drops of sea serpent excretion?"

"Genius! Bingo!" It cawed happily in my awkward hug.

"And that was the last one?"

The parrot bobbed its head. "Last one! Last one!"

"How much do I put in the soil?"

It rubbed its face against mine. "Big! Big tree! Small! Small tree! No problem!"

"I owe you, Kenzie!" I smushed a kiss into the parrot's feathery head. "I mean it. When I get back to San Diego, I'm buying you whatever you want. Name it, it's yours. Crap, crap, crap, you actually did it! You absolute beauty!"

"Go! Tick-tock, tick-tock! Go!" the parrot croaked.

"You're coming with me, right? This is all you—you've got to see if this works." I lifted the parrot onto my shoulder, but she flapped off to the window.

"Ryann!" it cawed.

My heart lurched. "What?"

"Ryann too!"

"Ryann helped you?" Stupid, tired tears brimmed in my eyes.

The parrot nodded. "Go! Waiting! Go! Tick-tock!"

She's waiting? I didn't have time to decipher what Parrot Kenzie meant.

"Go!" it croaked, its feathers ruffling.

"All right, I'm going!" I headed for the door. On the threshold, I turned back. "Thank you. You've saved me from going insane. Thank her, too, when you see her."

The parrot chirped. "Thank her yourself!"

"*Now* you can do full sentences? Unbelievable." I flashed a smile. "Wish me luck."

"Good luck! Punk!"

Laughing and crying in a weird mania, I sprinted out of my room and back to the workshop. I wanted Kenzie to come with me, but I understood why she'd flown away. Etienne would suspect cheating if I suddenly turned up with the formula *and* a parrot. Still, I wished she could see her work come to fruition. Literally.

Her work and Ryann's. Knowing Ryann cared was definitely a nice little boost. I couldn't help the spring in my step.

"You're supposed to be sleeping," Mr. Abara scolded the moment I burst through the door and ran for my workbench.

"I had a power nap, I swear." I grinned up at him and started racking up bottles in a neat line, in the right order. "And it worked wonders."

Everyone's necks craned to look at me.

"What do you mean?" Melody peered over. "Did you figure it out?"

I laughed like a madman. "Let's find out, shall we?" Terrified someone might try to stop me, namely Luke or the Basani Boasters, I hurried to create the mixture, but not so fast that I'd make a mistake. Keeping a steady hand, I dropped various liquids into the beaker, sticking to the instructions.

As the last drop of sea serpent excretion fell into the mix, I frowned at the beaker. It was bright red. *You sneaky French snake...* Etienne *had* tried to lead us astray, giving us the wrong color.

"Good luck with that," Shailene taunted.

"It's red, dumbass. It's meant to be blue. That's all Etienne gave us," Fay cut in.

I met their gaze. "You think that was a clue?"

"Of course it was," Oliver chimed in. "That's what we've all been aiming for."

"Exactly. If you think he gave us *any* clue, you're playing the wrong game." I picked up the beaker, swirled it, and dumped the whole thing into the soil. Just as Kenzie had said—a big amount meant a big tree, a small amount meant a small tree, and I wanted the biggest damn tree I could get. Just to rub Etienne's face in it.

Immediately, the trunk grew thick and spiraled up, and didn't stop until it reached a good seven feet. The branches extended outward like a ballet dancer's arms, leaves growing along them. And those sobbing, wailing little seedlings swelled, no hint of sorrow. The fruits puffed until they hung like big, orange balloons, around the size of a kid-friendly bowling ball, and the branches sagged under their weight. The scent changed, too, going from that foul, decaying smell to a sweeter, citrusy aroma.

"That's what I'm talkin' about!" I whooped and hollered until my throat went hoarse. "Finch Merlin, knocking it out of the friggin' park!" It wasn't polite to gloat, but this felt unbelievably good. Relief washed over me like I'd taken a nosedive into the Ionian Sea. I could already taste the drink I'd toast my victory with. Of course, I'd think of my little birdies and have a glass for the pair of them. I couldn't have done this without them.

"You've got to be kidding." Shailene gaped at me.

"How did you do that?" Fay added.

Oliver nodded. "How did you know Etienne was pulling our legs with the blue thing?"

"He made it clear we need to figure everything out ourselves," I replied, punching the air like a man possessed. "He never intended to give us a helping hand, in any way, shape, or color."

"Will you give us the recipe, before Etienne comes back?" Blanche got up hesitantly.

"Yeah, share the love," Luke demanded. "You wouldn't even have a plant if Melody hadn't saved it. You owe us."

I raised my eyebrows at him. "Oh, do I? I thought this was every man, or woman, for themselves. You didn't seem keen on sharing ideas before."

Screw all of y'all. I had my favorites, sure, but any of them could be Davin's spy. Trust no one, and never be disappointed. That had been my mother's motto, but it rang true. I couldn't risk that British oxygen thief getting his mitts on the map-making skill before me. Every person eliminated from the island narrowed my suspect pool.

"What, you're not going to share?" Luke challenged.

"That's not good sportsmanship." Oliver folded his arms across his chest.

I shrugged. "You've got the same tools as me. You've still got time—figure it out for yourselves." They didn't have a nifty little parrot with all the intel, but they didn't need to know that.

The atmosphere changed as everyone huffily returned to their work. I'd become *persona non grata*, which was fine by me. After all, I wasn't here to make friends. I was here to get myself out of Erebus's servitude. Preferably alive.

I was admiring my freshly made orange tree when footsteps sounded. I looked over to see Melody, Blanche, and Mr. Abara making a beeline for me.

"Torture me all you like; you won't get the recipe." I was only half joking.

"No torture here, boy." Mr. Abara grinned. "Just wanted to congratulate you. Well deserved. You're the only one who managed to stay up through the night. If this win belongs to anyone, it's you. You worked hardest. It's only fair."

Oof, nice guilt trip. And he didn't even realize.

"My sentiments exactly. You've earned this." Blanche nodded, though she looked nervous. "I'm not gonna lie, I wish you would help us, but that would be cheatin'. What would we learn? Nothin'. I just hope I can manage it in time."

Melody patted me on the shoulder. "You see what a little rest can do? You were working too hard, frying your brain. You just needed a bit of sleep, and your mind did the rest. The mind is wonderful like that. I'll never stop being fascinated by the way it can piece things together."

"I couldn't have done it without the coffee." I flashed them a guilty smile.

"I might have to break my promise to my parents as the deadline gets closer," Melody replied. "Perhaps coffee is precisely what I need. I'm usually good at puzzles, but this is unlike anything I've ever had to contend with. Give me a crossword, and I'd have been out of here two days ago."

"If I don't make it, promise me you'll use that map-making for good?" Mr. Abara sounded so sad I almost gave him the recipe there and then. He wanted to save child soldiers and change the world, for Pete's sake. At least, that was what he'd told me. It could've been a lie, and even if it was true, that didn't mean he wasn't the spy. So, I held my tongue.

"Hey, you've all got it in you, somewhere," I said. "The day isn't over. You've still got time to get it right."

Mr. Abara brightened. "I haven't given up yet. I'm not starting now."

"That's more like it." I smiled, feeling like crap.

"Let's show Etienne what we make of his tricks." Melody giggled, a bit of fire back in her voice.

Blanche nodded. "At least Finch has given us one thing."

"What's that?" I frowned.

She smiled wide, her eyes twinkling like that wild young woman of her heyday, causing a ruckus wherever she went. "At least now we know it's red."

TWENTY-SEVEN

Kenzie

I might've left Finch to it, but I wasn't ready to Morph out of there. I'd helped him with the formula, but he had another, bigger monster to wrangle—Davin's spy. And he couldn't go snooping himself with these trials going on. The best thing about folks staying in a monastery under the searing Greek sun? They left their windows open. AC hadn't reached this island, which worked just fine for me.

Still in parrot mode, I flew the monastery's perimeter, searching for the rooms of the other challengers. A hallway connected Finch's room to another branch of the residential setup, its windows open to let the breeze in. I almost flew past it, when a familiar figure made me land on the ledge and hop into the shadows. Etienne himself. He paused beside an alcove in the corridor. A second later, a monk emerged from the darkness, giving me slimy sidekick vibes.

"Have you any updates for me?" Etienne whispered, casting a

glance up and down the corridor. He missed my vantage point completely.

The monk shook his head. "No, sir."

"Have you kept an eye on him?"

"I have, sir. He's spent most of his time in the botanical library. I believe he took a brief respite but has since returned to his task."

"Do you know if he's any closer to solving the formula?" Etienne shot another look down the hallway.

"He seemed exuberant when he ran past, but he has otherwise been morose. So, it is hard to say," the monk replied.

"Have you noticed anything strange? Anything that might tie him to Erebus?" Etienne pressed.

The monk paused. "No, there haven't been any recent breaches or odd behaviors. He hasn't tried to go to the underground chambers since we found him and Luke wandering around down there. Either he is very sneaky, or he is telling the truth about Erebus."

"Hmm... continue to watch him and come to me if anything changes. I *must* know the instant he solves the formula, if he does manage it."

"Of course, sir." The monk bowed and hurried down the hallway. Etienne also went on his way, traveling in the opposite direction of his monk friend. I darted through the window and followed him at a safe distance, keeping to the high ceilings, where I could hide at a moment's notice.

I trailed him through countless halls and passageways, until he halted outside a narrow wooden door. The surrounding wall looked slightly curved, like a spiral staircase that might lead to a tower or a spire. I hung back in the rafters as Etienne unlocked and opened the door, slamming it behind him.

What's he up to... and what the hell is up there? I flapped down to the door to see if I could jostle the handle open. But my beak and talons weren't good enough. I'd reached a dead end. I tried to listen through the keyhole, in case I heard him talking… either to himself or someone else. But silence came back.

Even so, his behavior was suspicious. He'd watched Finch all this time, though his monk clearly hadn't been as thorough as he claimed, or he'd have heard me squawking. But *why* was he watching Finch, and who was he watching him for? Himself? Davin? I wouldn't get any answers right now, though Etienne might reveal his true colors once Finch solved the formula.

Back to plan A. I found an open window and soared out. Etienne reeked of ulterior motives, but that didn't mean he was spying on Finch for Davin. After all, if he was, he would've known Finch still worked for Erebus.

Flying back to where I'd entered the hallway, I swept along the outer wall until I found the first room belonging to one of the other challengers. It would be hard to sift through their stuff with talons instead of hands, but I had to make the best of it.

I knew instantly that this room belonged to Melody, from the array of fluffy jackets in her wide-open closet. You could tell a lot by a person's room, even on first glance. Melody was messy—seriously messy. Clothes, books, and jewelry lay strewn everywhere. The bed was unmade, with last night's pj's flung carelessly over the twisted sheets.

I scoured the place for anything of interest. My beady parrot eyes spotted a journal on the desk, and I quickly flew to it. Using my beak, I flicked through a couple pages, but found nothing interesting. Just a blow-by-blow of what she'd done with her day, down to what she'd eaten and the products she'd used to wash her face.

Disappointed, I bent over the edge of the desk and tugged the drawer handle until it skimmed open. Another book lay inside. I hopped down and flicked it open, using my talons to brace the page. Weird writing covered the paper in neat handwriting. I wracked my brain but couldn't identify the language. A flat, bottle-green lens sat beside the book. Curious, I picked it up in my beak and dropped it on the page. Nothing happened.

Perhaps I didn't have the right tool to read it. I knew about lenses like this, which could unravel a code or translate a language. Harley and Finch had used one on the Merlin Grimoire, back in the Katherine days. But no way could I crack it in parrot mode. All of my Chaos abilities were back in San Diego, stuck in my real body. I couldn't channel through my feathery friend.

Still, it was a start. Finch would definitely be interested to hear about it. Although, how would I communicate this level of detail to him? Maybe I'd have to lead him here physically, so he could check it out himself.

Could Melody really be the spy? From what I'd seen of her, she wouldn't say boo to a goose. Then again, that might make her the perfect spy—nobody would suspect her. I did an idiot check of the rest of her room. There were no other oddities to speak of, unless you counted her fashion sense.

Exhilarated that I might've actually found something impor-tant, I moved on to the next room. This must belong to Mr. Abara. It was as regimented as the man himself. And he didn't have much. One of the monks could've told me the room was unoccupied, and I'd have believed them. Mr. Abara had a spare T-shirt, some fresh underwear, and a pouch of coal, but not much else. There were pictures, too. Shrivel-edged Polaroids of grim-faced kids in dirty, torn clothes, some wearing military caps. A couple tried to smile, but it looked like they'd forgotten how.

That supported his story but didn't mean he wasn't hiding something. I ransacked his room as discreetly as possible, worming into every nook and cranny I could find. Nothing in the drawers, nothing on the tables, and nothing on the desk, other than his military cap. I'd seen him with a notebook, but I couldn't find it—he likely had it on him at all times, which was annoying. Ransacking a room was one thing, but plucking a notebook from someone directly might get me in trouble.

Reaching his closet, I hopped onto the top shelf and riffled around in the dark. My talon hit something solid, and the sound of skittering metal followed. I'd knocked it right out of the closet to the floor.

Fluttering down, I landed beside a signet ring. It boasted a big diamond in the middle. Not strange, considering Mr. Abara's skillset. But this didn't look new. And it didn't look like something he'd wear, either. In fact, I'd seen a very similar one on Finch's finger, though his had a red stone. I'd asked about it once, and Finch just gave me a vague reply of, "It gets me from A to Z." Which meant it had to be some sort of portaling stone. But why would Mr. Abara have one? And who was on the other end?

Once again, frustration nagged me. I didn't have the right skills to use the ring now. But it definitely wasn't normal to have a personal portaling stone. I picked up the ring and stowed it away so Mr. Abara wouldn't notice it missing and freak out. I didn't want any potential spies jumping ship before I'd told Finch.

So far, I'd searched two rooms and found two secrets. I thought about going to Finch immediately, but I needed to check the rest, in case I found something more damning. After all, a ring and a strange notebook could mean anything. It was better to be thorough, and have all the intel, before I went to Finch. Though relaying everything would wear out all the vocab this parrot had.

I found the next room. It wasn't immediately obvious who it belonged to. Very neat, very tidy, everything in its place. The only weird thing was the cage underneath the window, where two pigeons cuddled together. *Who likes birds?* I couldn't remember anyone specifically mentioning them.

I set to snooping. I pried open the wardrobe first and found prim cardigans and crisp blouses. Stylish but demure. The Basani twins wouldn't have been caught dead in stuff like this, which left Blanche.

I flew to the desk. A packet of elegant stationery lay on the surface, with a cartridge pen beside it. Very Blanche. Peering closer, I tried to make out the indentations in the top piece of paper. I'd seen people do that in spy dramas. If I'd had hands, I could've brushed over it with a pencil or something. But I lacked fingers... and a pencil, for that matter. So, it all just looked like nonsense.

Other than that, and some makeup items in pristine order, Blanche didn't have much going on. A disappointment. But I'd find something else in one of these rooms... I just had to keep looking.

The door opened. Panicking, I flapped behind the curtain above the desk and shrank as much as I could. A monk entered the room. Did Etienne have monks watching everyone?

However, as the door closed, the monk's skin rippled. The robes and shaven head disappeared, revealing Blanche. She had come back, using her Shapeshifting to avoid notice.

Shouldn't you be in the lab?

From my vantage point, I couldn't see much of the room. Just the desk and the path to the door. Blanche headed for the desk and sat, making me shrink farther into my hiding spot. She picked up the pen and started to write. Intrigued, I peered through the gap in the curtain and watched.

Dear D, the letter began. My heart almost burst in my feathery chest. "D" could only be one person, given the secretive context. Blanche had been way down on my list of possible spies. It was all I could do not to squawk in shock. My mind raced. I had to know what she was saying to that creep.

Dear D,

Finch has completed the task. I don't know how, but he may have an insider. He couldn't have figured it out alone. Thanks to your help, I'm not far off myself. A few more tests, and I will have it—I think I know which formula Etienne has decided to use from the list you gave me, though it has taken me longer than expected to work through. Once that's done, I will proceed and take what you've asked for.

Yours faithfully,

BD

This will break Finch's heart. "D" was definitely who I thought it was. And when I said I was looking for something more obvious... well, this was it.

I'd watched Finch with the other challengers. He and Blanche had developed something of a bond in their time here. Now, I realized she'd played him to gain his trust and cast his suspicions elsewhere. And, damn, she'd done a good job. I was reeling, and I didn't even know the chick.

Blanche rolled the letter into a cylinder and pulled a small metal tube from her pocket. She slid the message inside and went to the pigeons, taking one out and setting it on the windowsill. My guts churned. *That's what they're for...* Evidently, she'd found a way around Etienne's communication ban. Very clever. Seriously, who used carrier pigeons these days?

The message throbbed in my brain. What had Davin asked her to take? Whatever it was, that was the least of my problems right now. Outing her was the only thing that mattered.

I had to act fast to stop that pigeon. Leaving my parrot behind the curtain, I Morphed right into the mind of the carrier pigeon. It'd be harder to communicate with Finch, but if I had the evidence tied to my ankle, maybe he'd get the message.

No sooner had Blanche tied the tube to my pigeon leg than the African gray burst out of the curtain, squawking at the top of its lungs. Blanche shrieked and released me. Seizing the opportunity, I flew right out the window. She lunged for me, but my feathers slipped through her fingertips.

TWENTY-EIGHT

Finch

E tienne stared at my giant tree, arms folded. He'd come back five minutes ago and had been staring since.

"Is that what you were after?" I prompted. I couldn't have been happier, though I tried to avoid stepping into smug territory. I'd actually done it, with a little timely help. I'd completed this task, and now I could get on with actual map-making. Etienne had mentioned four trials, and I'd succeeded in the first three. Only one more to go, though I might well be the only one proceeding to the final stage.

Etienne glanced at me. "Yes, though I might've preferred it smaller. Nevertheless, it seems congratulations are in order."

"The bigger the better, in my opinion," I replied, trying not to smirk.

"Hmm… perhaps."

"So, what now? Do I get a couple days to rest, like before?" I asked.

Etienne smiled slyly. "No. Now, you move on to learning the

actual skill of map-making. I must say, it's been a long time since someone managed to complete this task."

"You didn't exactly make it easy." I gave him a hard look.

"What would be the point of that?" He returned his gaze to the tree. "The question is, how did you do it?"

I fidgeted nervously. "Uh... I don't want to say out loud. You know, in case people overhear."

"Very smart, Finch." Etienne leaned in. "One of the former candidates reverse engineered the formula from the soil of my example, the same way you did. Nobody ever thinks they can touch my creation, but I do not explicitly prohibit it."

"Since it was sitting there, I thought you wouldn't mind." I covered my tracks quickly, using his words to form my excuse. "And reverse engineering is the only way to do it, without any clues."

"Excellent work." Etienne stood to his full height and spoke to the entire room. "The last three days of the trial are dedicated to learning the skill of map-making, but, as I said, people rarely make it past this task. I ordinarily use those days to restore order to the monastery, but it looks as though I will have to delay that. Please pick all of the oranges from your tree and follow me."

"All of them?" I stared up at the bulbous fruit.

He chuckled smugly. "It would appear bigger is not always better." He looked at the others. "After we've all watched Finch pluck the oranges from this monstrosity, you may all stay and study the monastery's books and archives for the next three days."

"We're not getting booted off the island?" Oliver looked surprised.

"Call it a courtesy, for your efforts during this trial. Of course, you can be 'booted off' if you prefer," Etienne replied.

Mr. Abara gave a short *humph*. "The trial isn't over yet, Etienne. We have eleven hours until midnight."

"You're quite right. I apologize for being presumptuous, but it does not appear any of you are close to finding the formula." Etienne wrung his hands in annoyance. "Nevertheless, my courtesy will remain, if you don't succeed."

"We will," Melody declared.

Etienne shrugged. "I admire your continued confidence. Let us hope it is well founded. Now, Finch, if you don't mind? We are all eager to see you pick the fruits of your labors. Without magic, if you please."

So I can be your personal clown? Cheers, Etienne.

With some difficulty, I grabbed the pot and attempted to lower it to the ground. The thing weighed a ton. My arms shook as I maneuvered it to the floor, finally managing it in a low, painful squat that made my thighs burn.

Even then, the fruit was too high. With no shred of pride left, I clambered onto the workbench and reached for those plump oranges. Tugging them loose, I placed each at my feet until there were none left on the tree. I had a grand total of eight—not a bad haul, if I did say so myself.

"Do you have a basket or a bucket?" I jumped off the bench.

Etienne shook his head. "No."

"Then how am I supposed to carry them? Can I use magic now?" They were huge. I'd never fit them all into my arms. Not without making orange juice, anyway.

"That is up to you to figure out. And no, you may not. It is important for all magicals to understand the value of working without magic." He was enjoying this a bit too much.

I squinted at him. "Is this another task?"

"No, Finch. This is merely common sense," he replied dryly. "If you don't have that, then you really shouldn't be here."

"Fine." Pulling the edge of my T-shirt, I fashioned a pouch for the fruits and duly gathered them. All eight. Satisfied, I grinned at Etienne. *How d'you like them oranges, huh?*

Etienne didn't say anything. He walked away. I stared after him a moment too long before realizing he intended me to follow. After sandwiching my notebook between my elbow and my ribs, I did just that.

Etienne led me through the monastery at a rapid pace. Eventually, we reached a narrow door lodged in the wall. Wandering alone with someone who could well be Davin's spy didn't make the journey comfortable. I wasn't about to forget his little friendship with the biggest pain in my ass since I sat on a nail at ten years old. It was better to be prepared. I kept my Chaos ready to go, pumped up on the adrenaline. The fear took the worst of my fatigue away.

Pulling out a set of keys, he opened the door and went inside. I walked after him, still ready to fight if I had to. A second later, I almost lost that burst of fire in my belly. I stood, faced with a spiral staircase that twisted all the way up to a platform.

Etienne ascended in a casual stroll. My body, on the other hand, really wasn't up for a climb like this, even with the rush of adrenaline. But I wouldn't be beaten by a set of steps. I hurried up the staircase after him until we finally reached the platform.

A gasp escaped my lips. I stood in a domed room with a single desk in the center. There were no walls, just glass on all sides, like a lighthouse without the lamp. It gave me some unsavory flashbacks to Ponce and his Cuban retreat, but this was different. The view stole my breath, though that could've been the climb. The shimmering ocean stretched all the way to the horizon, and beautiful islands peppered the water. The whitewashed island houses glinted in the sunlight, looking almost fake, like part of a dreamscape instead of reality. Even after I left this place, I knew I'd remember this view from time to time.

"This is where you will start your journey. You have completed three challenges, and here lies the final one—learning the art that will grant you a map of your own making." Etienne gestured to the desk. It had a solitary, blank sheet of paper in the middle, along with a quill and a pot of ink. Suitably old school. A wicker basket sat next to it, where I immediately dumped the oranges, alongside a plate and a knife. *Ooh, I could do with a snack.*

"So… map-making *is* the fourth trial?"

"Indeed. Please, be seated."

I took a seat and stared at the paper. "Are you going to guide me through this?"

"I will start you on your journey, then leave. I can't be in the room while you conduct your first map-making episode."

"Why? Is it going to get weird?" I joked stiffly, still wary of being alone with this guy. But if he wanted to leave, maybe that meant he wouldn't turn on me. It made for a puzzling scenario. Did this mean he wasn't in cahoots with Davin? My brain turned into an elastic band, bungeeing back and forth.

He didn't seem amused. "It may. That is why I cannot remain. One's first map-making event is deeply personal and often strange. I would only be a distraction, and there can be no distractions."

Comforting…

"Moreover, I don't wish to be involved in any oddity that may occur," he went on. "It has happened before, when I stayed to watch over my students. In fact, that's what swayed me toward being absent."

"What happened? Sounds juicy." I batted my eyelashes at him.

He sighed. "One of my former students confessed her love for me during her first episode and almost kidnapped me to force me into marriage. She was ferociously strong, both physically and magically. A mammoth of a woman, in more than one sense of the word. She did, in fact, sling me over her shoulder and carry me down those stairs. She used a binding curse to prevent me from fighting back, and it took twelve monks to stop her from taking me away. You should have seen the carnage. She barreled through them like a rampaging bison. Many have never been the same. It's why they all get somewhat antsy when new students arrive."

I stifled a snort. "The ladies love a Frenchman."

"Mm, a little too much in this instance," he replied, with a hint of a smile. "There have been other episodes, though none so severe. One gentleman thought he was an eagle and attempted to smash the roof and fly away. Fortunately, he had Air abilities, so he likely wouldn't have come to any harm. He had to be tranquilized, in the end. Another young lady thought she was Arachne incarnate and decided I had turned her into a spider out of spite. You should have seen the way she scuttled around this room. Horrifying."

"Throw on a Grecian robe, give it some good lighting, and I see how you'd pass for Athena." I grinned.

Etienne chuckled with *actual* amusement. "Perhaps the lighting was particularly good that day. But I don't wish to endure a repeat."

"So, what do I do?" I picked up the quill to take a closer look. I felt more comfortable knowing he would be gone soon.

"First, you must eat one of the oranges. That is how you start. They are infused with the poison mixture that made them grow, and ingesting that poison will allow you to commune with Chaos. It provides the medium by which Chaos will flow through you, for the map-writing part of the process."

I shook my head. "I've already got Chaos flowing through me in spades. I've worked hard on figuring out the balance. If I add more… I don't know what might happen."

"It is the only way to learn the skill," Etienne said simply. "Either you do it, or you don't. That is your choice."

"I *have* to eat an orange?"

He nodded. "Once the poison is ingested and the flow is initiated, the brain tends to have a strange reaction. I won't lie—the more powerful you are, the stronger the reaction."

Well, that's just peachy…

"What's the worst that could happen?" I mumbled to myself.

"I've witnessed many effects: clucking like a chicken, mentally regressing to a five-year-old, attempting to abduct a Frenchman and force him into marriage. That kind of thing." Etienne's eyes glittered with mischief.

I took a breath and reached for an orange. "Let's hope for the mental regression. That shouldn't make too much of a difference."

Etienne laughed. "I wish you luck, Finch Merlin."

It seemed odd that he was so friendly all of a sudden. It should've made me feel better, but it left me more uneasy. Was this some kind of weird subterfuge to get my guard down? I had no clue, but eating a mind-bending orange would probably ramp up the paranoia a few extra notches. *Great.*

"Yeah, like luck is going to do me any good." I shot him a worried look. "Thanks to you, all I can think about are mammoth women and spiders."

He turned serious, without warning, like he'd flipped a switch on his face. "Whatever happens, I will return in a few hours." Without another word, he turned and made his way down the spiral staircase, leaving me alone with my oranges and my horrifying thoughts.

TWENTY-NINE

Finch

A lone, I picked up one of the oranges. *Nice and firm...* I brought it to my nose and sniffed. I don't know what I expected. It smelled like a normal orange. Maybe sweeter. A bit more... artificial, like it was trying to be something it wasn't.

"You'd better behave yourselves, gremlins," I whispered aloud. It wasn't just my influx of power that worried me. My mind was a mess at best, a warzone at worst, thanks to my delusional disorder. Adding a mind-bending poison orange to the mix was a recipe for disaster.

I peeled it slowly, digging my nails in. No knife necessary. The flesh gave easily and released an overwhelming citrus aroma.

"Do I eat the whole thing?" I turned, hoping Etienne might still be around. Silence echoed back. I shrugged. "Go big or go home, right?"

Putting the rind on the dusty plate, I started to chow down. Segment after segment. The juice burst in my mouth, sour and sweet all at once. I had to hand it to the poisons—this thing tasted incredible. Way better than the oranges I'd had at breakfast, what felt like a million years ago.

After I polished off the last segment, I sat back and waited for divine inspiration. My nerves rattled in full force, not knowing what might come next. I gripped the seat of my chair to calm down. *It's going to be fine... it's all going to be fine.*

I felt totally normal. I glanced down at my hands to make sure it hadn't crept up on me—like, maybe I'd turned into a werewolf or something. But they were normal, too.

Huh... I reached for the bowl and picked another orange, then set it on the table as a standby in case I needed more to get this process going.

The minute I started twiddling my thumbs, the weird started. Slowly but surely. My body suddenly felt light, and my hands lifted off my legs involuntarily. I pulled them back down, terrified they might detach and float off into space. *Oh boy...*

The sunlight shining through the domed ceiling transformed into golden liquid, tumbling right through the glass and pooling on the floor, the Grecian landscape beyond melting into it. Blues and greens and whites blended into the gold until the vivid waterfall crashed into the room with me. I stayed frozen in my chair. Only when the orange rolled and danced of its own accord did I stagger back, knocking the chair over.

The seven remaining oranges started bouncing around, squeaking wildly as they jumped out of the basket. I stumbled away as they hurled themselves off the edge of the desk like orange bombs, heading directly for my face.

"I didn't mean to eat him! I had to!" I howled, backing up against the balcony railing. They landed on the ground with squishy thumps, gathering their forces before they made another attack on the orange-killer.

Meanwhile, the vibrant cascade swept across the floor, splashing against the glass walls and warping everything it touched. The glass itself shimmered and wavered, and cracks spread across the dome. Big chunks melted, dripping in glinting droplets that hit the ground with a less-than-liquid *clink*. Spouts of fire shot up from every falling droplet until the room felt like a sauna. No, not a sauna—like the center of the damn Earth. *Is it hot in here? Did it get hot?* I tried to fan myself with my hand, but my fingers had gone long and floppy, almost two-dimensional.

"What the—!" I shrieked at the sight of them. I needed to get out of here. Screw the map-making. I didn't want to see what happened next.

"Oh, Finch?"

My head whipped around frantically. "Who said that?"

"Over here!" A tiny, puffy creature, somewhere between a sugar-glider and a hedgehog, emerged from under the desk, its too-big feet padding right through the golden flood. It stood on two paws, with two more tucked against its chest like the Pomeranian of the T-Rex world.

My eyes bulged. "Who are you?"

"You call me your mind gremlin." It chuckled, covering its face with its paws. It had the sort of voice I'd have expected the original Pikachu to have. Sickeningly sweet.

"*You're* my mind gremlin?" The orange poison was clearly having a laugh at my expense.

It nodded. "Oh, yes. It feels good to be out of your skull. Now I can do some real damage."

"Nice to meet you, but since you're a figment of whatever's in those oranges, I'm going to get going—I can't do this. You'd know that if you really were my mind gremlin," I rambled, edging toward the staircase.

It giggled.

"My mind gremlins don't giggle!" I barked as it approached. Terrifyingly cute. "They're big, tough, nasty little bastards!"

"Who said I'm not?" It blinked its shiny black eyes, snuffling its little pink nose. "You can't run from me. I have a snug little nest in your head."

I shuddered. "I did *not* need that imagery, thanks."

It pointed out a tiny paw. "He's out to get you. Kill him before he kills you!"

"What?" I whirled to find a figure crouched on the stairwell. Well, what remained of the stairwell. The whole thing wiggled like jelly, appearing less than structurally sound. And the figure looked all wrong, like Picasso drank one too many pints before painting a portrait. Still, his eyes and nose were sort of in the right place. Just enough for me to recognize the man trying to sneak up on me.

Luke.

I hurried backward, glancing at the fluffy ball. It was gone.

"Are you... real?" I gasped, my body descending into the jitters.

"I've come for the recipe." Luke rose to his full height, and he didn't stop there. He grew until his head touched the ceiling.

I pressed flush against the wall and squeezed my eyes shut. "I told you! Figure it out yourself!"

"The day will end in a matter of hours." I heard Titan Luke thud closer. "Do it for Melody. She needs this. I need to do this for her."

"Bullcrap!" I yelped. Closing my eyes didn't help. Colors swam across my eyelids, filled with all the monsters I'd ever faced. Every beast from Tartarus, every creature from my missions for Erebus, every boxed-up demon from the Bestiary. Even Tobe made an appearance, flying at me with fangs bared and black eyes, his talons outstretched to shred me. My eyes shot open, only to see Titan Luke looming over me.

"She has a purpose, Finch. Give me the recipe!" Luke's eyes glowed red.

"No way!" I tried to hold my ground, but the floor melted under my feet like I'd waltzed into a Dali painting. "You're not doing any of this for Melody. You're working with Davin—his spy! I know you are! He wants you to learn map-making and kill me as the sprinkles on top of his evil little cupcake of doom!"

Luke paused. "Davin? Who's Davin?"

"Who's Davin?" I mimicked. "Like you don't know. What's he got on you? Did he say he'd hurt Melody?"

"Why are you shouting?" Luke stepped toward me.

"Don't move, I mean it!"

Luke kept moving. "Whoever Davin is, I'm not working for him. I'm doing this for Melody."

"That's what I said. You're doing this to stop Davin from hurting her. I've seen your puppy dog eyes. I know you love her. You'd do anything for her, and I'm guessing the buck doesn't stop with working for a known murderer!" I shivered against the wall.

Luke took another step, and I attacked. My Telekinesis hit him in the chest and knocked him to the floor. Only, the strands were wrong—not clear and shimmery. They came out as oiled-up ropes, with black droplets falling from them and leaving a dark smear across Luke's chest.

It's not real, IT'S NOT REAL! Where the drops fell, craters formed, and the edges fizzled as if from acid.

"I've asked nicely." Luke stood. Lifting his hands, he tore the metal handles off the desk drawers with his Magneton abilities. They darted through the air, clamping my wrists against the glass. I struggled, panting as they turned into snakes and slithered up my forearms.

Desperate to get them off, I sent two fireballs upward, melting the slithery handcuffs into pools of smaller snakes that tumbled to the ground. Their tiny mouths lunged at my boots, nipping and biting at the leather.

"Stop! For the love of Chaos, just stop!" I bellowed. "It's over, Luke. I'm on to you."

"On to *what*? You're not making any sense." Luke readied for another blow, pins and nails hovering, waiting on his command.

How was I supposed to do anything in this state? I couldn't even get back to the desk with golden liquid crashing through the ceiling and melting everything inside. Not to mention the threat of that weird puffball jumping at me. Was this another one of Etienne's tricks? A way to screw with me? He was probably watching on a camera somewhere, having the time of his life.

"You're the spy. That's why you were following me," I replied, trying to get ahold of myself.

"I followed you because you acted suspicious," Luke said. "Maybe you're the one keeping secrets. Bit weird, isn't it, that you just *happened* to come up with the right formula?"

"Don't flip this on me." I unleashed a barrage of Air, the poison transforming the currents into horrifying specters who huffed out vast breaths, their mouths gaping in silent screams. I wondered, in the midst of this twisted reality, if the poison was showing me the truth behind our abilities—revealing them like it supposedly revealed hidden places. Or was my head just upping the weird to epic proportions?

Either way, Luke slammed into the glass. More melting chunks dropped to the floor. Fire sparked up, and the temperature surged to an unbearable level.

The blow made Luke shrink to his normal size, and his features settled into their usual positions. I sagged against the wall, my floppy limbs hardening up until they felt like lead weights.

"Just give me the damn recipe!" Luke jumped up.

"No!" I sent another surge of Telekinesis at him, trying not to look at the fizzing craters that appeared underneath the pulsing strands.

"I'm not a spy! I don't even know who Davin is!" Luke fought back with his pins and nails, forcing me to shield myself with Telekinesis. The oily sheen was worse up close, coming in full Smell-o-vision. An acrid, gasoline-like stench hammered my nostrils, making me choke.

"Liar!" I snuck a ball of Fire underneath the Telekinesis shield, the sparking orb narrowly missing Luke's head.

"On the stairs," a small voice whispered. My head snapped to the side. The little fluffball rested on my shoulder.

"Can you not?!" I reeled in shock. "It's bad enough when you're *in* my head. Don't pop up out of nowhere!"

The fluffball dipped its head, snuffling sarcastically. "You'd miss me if I left. On the stairs, Finchy. Get the first jab in, twist up their guts, blast them sky high. You know you want to." It vanished during my blink.

"On the stairs? What do you mean, on the stairs?" I looked at the stairwell, dodging another onslaught from Luke and his endless array of stolen metalwork.

"What are you talking about?" Luke yelled. "What's gotten into you?"

I glowered at him and prepared another set of fireballs to fry this spy. "Oh, wouldn't you like to know!"

Blanche appeared at the top of the staircase, bringing the fight to a sudden halt. By the looks of it, neither Luke nor I wanted her getting caught in our crossfire.

"Oh dear, is this a bad time?" She lingered on the top step, fidgeting nervously.

"Like you wouldn't believe." I exhaled. "Doesn't Etienne lock doors?"

Luke eyed Blanche. "Actually, he does. I had to break in."

"Perhaps we should trade lockpickin' tips. You didn't quite lock it again behind you," Blanche replied, offering him a sympathetic glance. "Not that it would've mattered. I'm very proficient in the art. Another trick I picked up in my misspent youth."

I sighed, trying to focus. "Let me guess, you're here for the recipe?"

"It's just... we're almost out of time, and I'm no closer to figurin' it out. I thought I had it, but the trees kept sobbin'," she replied. "I can't fail, Finch. I've put so much into findin' El Dorado. If I don't succeed... I'll be kissin' that dream goodbye. After my husband died, it's all that kept me goin'. I don't know how I'll cope, without a purpose."

I frowned. "How did you know where to find me?"

"I followed Luke, who followed you and Etienne. I waited outside awhile, to muster the courage to beg for this," Blanche explained. "Please, Finch. Just give me the recipe. I need it so much." The note of desperation in her voice didn't sit right with me. No, the desperation wasn't the problem... it was the note of command in her voice.

Is it the poison? I stared at her. Nothing made sense in this warped world. More troubling was the fact that Luke was staring at her, too. His face mirrored what I felt: confusion.

A pigeon exploded through one of the windows in a flutter of wings and coos. It wheeled overhead before flying toward me at lightning speed, its coos getting louder. Almost like it was angry about something.

"You all see that, right?" I hissed.

"Of course we do," Luke shot back. "It's a freaking pigeon."

Blanche's face paled. "Yes… I do believe it is. Quick, catch it!"

I ducked away from the bird, but it divebombed my head. Sharp jabs hit my skull. Blanche lunged to stop it, but Luke held her back. She struggled in his arms.

"We have to catch it!" she urged. Now she was more desperate. But why?

"Let Finch do it," Luke replied firmly, still holding her.

"No! He can't!" Blanche howled.

I frowned in total bafflement at the bird. It flapped close to my face, sticking out its leg. A metal cylinder hung on its ankle. *A carrier pigeon…* Realization struck.

"Kenzie? Is that you?"

It cooed furiously and gave me a peck for good measure.

I reached out and untied the cylinder. As I removed the lid, a note slipped into my palm. I unfurled it, and Blanche's eyes widened.

"That's not for you!" she snarled. Luke gripped her tighter. I saw him shivering and realized Blanche was using her Ice ability on him, drawing moisture from the glass above.

My eyes skimmed the note, and my heart sank.

BD… Blanche Dunham. "It's you… you're the spy."

THIRTY

Finch

"You might've lived if you'd given me the formula," Blanche snarled. "But you won't stand in my way."

She grabbed Luke's wrists, and ice frosted up his forearms. He wrenched them away as if burnt, releasing her—and allowed Blanche to unleash hell at the same time. Water surged from the ocean beyond the glass walls and smashed through the roof, sending glass and liquid shattering in all directions. My addled brain couldn't handle it, not knowing what was real and what wasn't.

"Fight, Finch. You have to fight." Puffball sat on the edge of the desk, jabbing a paw at Blanche. *That's not real... is it?* Either way, the fluffy creature was right. I had to fight the enemy I could see and ignore the rest. For now.

I lifted my palms as Blanche made a bid for the notebook on the table—the one with the formula. Oily tentacles of Telekinesis shot out and grabbed the notebook. I yanked it away, and the book sailed into my outstretched arms. I wedged it quickly into the belt of my jeans.

"No!" Blanche hissed. She launched a torrent of Water at me.

I stood, facing the wall of writhing liquid. It took a moment to kick my brain into gear. *Fire with Fire, Water with Water...* Still holding the book, my hands twisted in the air as I focused on the oncoming torrent. I had to bend it to my will. I was stronger than her. I could do this.

The water, seconds from slamming into me, came to a screeching halt. I balled my hands into fists, and the water obeyed. It twisted in on itself, creating a huge, churning orb. With a shove that left me breathless, I forced it back where it came from. It barreled at Blanche, who stared in open-mouthed fear.

She dove out of the way as it crashed into the back wall. An eruption of droplets showered everything, the paper on the desk included.

Blanche was as spry as a woman half her age. She bounded up before I had time to blink, wrangling more water to her command. Luke stepped in, throwing manacles at her. They bumped against her wrists, clattering against something solid.

"Nice try, Magneton." Blanche smirked. "I came prepared." Her sleeves fell back to reveal two black cuffs. They gleamed in the sunlight. I had no idea what they were, but something in them repelled the metal Luke had thrown at her.

"What?" Luke stared at his hands, like they'd failed him.

"Anti-EM cuffs," Blanche said. "Courtesy of my employer, in case you got in my way. Carried in by my trusty pigeons—though one appears to work for Finch now."

Kenzie flapped wildly over my head.

"Davin's going to wish he'd stayed under his rock," I seethed. "What's he got on you, huh?"

"None of your business!" Blanche snapped, as she split a torrent of seawater and sent half at Luke, half at me.

I lifted my hands in time to control the incoming wave, but Luke was helpless. He twisted out of the water's way while I bent the deluge headed for me. I sent it from the room, and the water surged through the hole in the roof in a violent geyser.

"You can't trust he'll give you what you want," I said urgently.

"He promised me. I trust his word far more than yours!" Blanche spat. She flung another burst of water at me as she ran. The gush was evidently supposed to keep me busy. In the roiling wall, I saw the hazy outline of her sprinting figure. A glint flashed.

"She's got knives!" Luke yelled. He lifted his palms, trying to whip them from her hands, but nothing happened.

Blanche laughed icily behind the protective wall of water. "Ceramic knives, naturally, pilfered from the kitchens. As if I would be stupid enough to use metal with you around."

She's thought of everything! Yeah, this spy had picked up a few traits from her weaselly employer. He'd probably coached her on all of our skills, once he'd found out what she might be dealing with.

"I thought you had the formula." I dug in deep and concentrated on my Water power, my Esprit growing hot in my pocket as it channeled the energy. With a painful tug that left me shaking, I ripped the torrent aside and slammed it to the ground, the liquid following the movements of my trembling hands. I was in no state for this. Only Puffball, still on the desk, kept me going.

Fight... you have to fight.

Blanche prepared to pounce, knives drawn. "Who told you that?"

I shot a fireball at her chest, knocking her back. The Fire came out of me as crackling, red-winged spirits—the orange I'd eaten was still messing with my head. Even though she was the spy, smacking an old lady around didn't sit comfortably with me. But it was her or me, and I knew my choice. Davin wouldn't win this one, especially if he didn't have the decency to show his face.

"You did!" I barked, preparing a burst of Telekinesis. "In that note of yours. Davin gave you a list of possible formulas. You said you were close."

She staggered to her feet. "I lied."

"Then it looks like you're perfect for each other." I lashed the Telekinesis at her, sending her careening into the wall.

"On the stairs!" Puffball cried.

"What?" My head snapped toward the staircase. *Who's coming now?!*

Melody crept up to the platform, eyes wide with fear.

Luke rushed toward her. "You can't be here!"

"I heard noises," she replied, eyes flitting around the room. How quickly could that sharp mind of hers piece this mess together?

"Blanche!" Puffball squeaked.

I turned in time to see her propel a vast ball of Water at Luke and Melody. If it hit them, it'd wash them both down the steep staircase.

"Luke, behind you!" I yelled, whipping tendrils of Telekinesis to pull Melody out of harm's way. I wasn't gentle. I had no time to be. As I yanked the strands, Melody flew halfway across the room and hit the floor with a thud. She skidded for a moment, ending up right between me and Blanche.

Luke dove to the ground, the water pummeling the wall behind him and dousing him thoroughly. But at least it hadn't knocked him down the stairs. Without Air to cushion his fall, he'd likely have snapped his neck.

I sprinted toward Melody, but Blanche was a second faster. The torrent of Water hardened with a dose of Ice before hitting me full force. The pain left me speechless. Agony ricocheted through my ribcage, and my abdomen tightened to try to meet the impact. Digging my heels into the ground didn't help, as my legs were too shaky from the poison. The ice pounded me against the railings of the balcony, which looked down over the staircase below and the steep nothingness on either side of it. Sheer willpower made me grip the iron bars, or I would have flown over the edge.

As the ice splintered into shards around me, I wheezed. I'd taken a hell of a battering and felt every inch of it. I gripped the iron bars tighter, fearing I'd crumble if I let go.

Blanche set her sights on Melody, who struggled to stand. I tried to step forward, but my knees buckled. Pain jolted through my legs and back up my torso like a yo-yo of torture, every breath hard to take.

Luke sprinted for Blanche, dragging every piece of metal he could find out of the woodwork. He hurled pins and nails and even the knife that'd been set out for the oranges, but it wasn't enough. Blanche lifted her cuffs, and the metal bounced away, tumbling harmlessly to the ground.

A second later, she whacked Luke with a vicious explosion of Water. Only, it didn't slam right through him as before. This time, the water formed a bubble around him, and he was trapped inside. His pale face stared through the membrane, his mouth opening and closing in panic as bubbles rose from his nose.

He's going to drown.

Blanche held one hand up, her expression determined, keeping the bubble in place. "I'll kill Melody and Luke if you don't hand that notebook over."

"You're not getting it," I rasped.

"You might change your mind in a minute." She pointed her free hand at Melody and started to chant. "*Frange ossa. Sanguis tuus calidus est. Audite vocem meam. Frange. Hoc autem dolet. Audite vocem meam. Frange ossa. Sanguis tuus calidus est. Dolor sentiunt. Enim superveniet in te.*"

I'd heard a similar spell, once upon a Katherine. Blanche wanted to break Melody apart, making her bones shatter and her blood boil. Scarlet tendrils spiraled from Blanche's hands and hit Melody in the back, as she swayed on her feet. Her face turned toward me. I saw the exact moment the curse took hold. Or, rather, heard it.

Melody screamed, her veins lighting up. Silhouetted below her skin, I witnessed her bones starting to glow. Blanche continued chanting over Melody's increasingly intense screams. She would add magical pressure until Melody's bones broke, or until I gave up the notebook. Whichever came first.

Luke gaped inside the bubble. His hands frantically pummeled the membrane, but it didn't break. Blanche had him helpless. And now, she had Melody in her crippling curse.

Gremlin, what do I do? I can't even step forward...

"Destroy her," Puffball insisted, still perched on the desk, unseen by anyone but me.

I grasped every thread of energy I had left and staggered toward Blanche, lifting my palms. All the while, I struggled to ignore Melody's heartbreaking screams. Blanche was killing her. And I didn't know how much breath Luke had left.

"The notebook, or they both die!" Blanche screeched.

"He's not worth this," I gasped. "Davin will double-cross you once he gets what he wants."

Blanche smirked. "You won't talk me out of this. I'm getting my husband back. Davin will resurrect him in exchange for me giving him that. So, give me the notebook, or your friends suffer. Maybe you'll remember *their* faces, if you survive this!"

"You'll be lucky if you get anything more than a zombie!" I stared at her and formed a fireball. Both of her hands were occupied. All I needed to do was hit her, and both spells would break. She had no free palms to use more Water or Glacier abilities.

"Your lies won't convince me. Davin can do it. He's shown me he's more than capable," Blanche replied.

Stumbling forward, I sent the ball flying. She leaned back, the projectile whizzing straight over her head and crashing through the glass behind her. I tried to make another, but my body had other ideas. My knees gave way and I slumped to the ground, every body part in excruciating pain. One or two ribs were broken, and there was no telling what other damage she'd done with her ice wall.

"Smash her to pieces! Forget your knees, forget your ribs! Bones heal, so stop being a wimp and get her!" Puffball cried, hopping from foot to foot.

I barely lifted my head in time to see a shadow leap from the staircase. It darted across the room, tackling Blanche to the ground.

Mr. Abara had appeared from nowhere. He sank his knee into Blanche's chest as he snatched out his pouch of coal. Cupping some in both hands, he held her wrists down. Two half-circles of diamond spread from his palms, melding with the wood below. He'd trapped her, cuffing her wrists to the ground.

But the bubble held, and so did the curse.

On fumes, I managed to hobble toward her. I felt the burn of my Esprit in my pocket and channeled one last, potent blast of Telekinesis into her. As the blast subsided, Blanche's head lolled to the side and her eyes rolled upward. Unconscious.

The bubble exploded, and Luke tumbled down to the ground. He gasped and spluttered for air. I lurched. Mr. Abara was beside me in a heartbeat, his strong arm dragging mine over his shoulder to keep me upright.

"You all right there, boy?" He peered at me, worried.

I nodded. "I will be."

Melody screamed again. Somehow, the curse still had her in its grip. Her whole body glowed. I could see every vein, every bone, every sinew. Soon, those bones would start to crack, and those veins would open. These curses could progress quickly.

"We need to help her," I wheezed.

Mr. Abara half carried me to her. As I sank beside Melody, I put my hands on her arms, trying to feel out the curse. I could unravel some curses, but my cult days had been more about inflicting than undoing them. Tracking hexes and spying hexes and protective charms were easy. This… was anything but. I sensed the power of the curse bristling off Melody, whispering its secret strength.

"Can you do something?" Mr. Abara looked down at me.

"Careful, Finch," Puffball said, its small ears twitching. "Don't involve yourself. It's much too dangerous."

I shook my head and met Mr. Abara's concerned eyes. "It's powerful, and tricky. I can't undo it without knowing what curse it is, specifically." I paused. "Although, there's something I can try."

I hunched forward and awkwardly unbuttoned the top of Melody's musty-looking blouse. Not too far to be improper.

"What do you think you're doing?" Luke lurched over, soaked from the bubble.

"Trying to save her," I replied firmly. I shifted the left side of her shirt over to expose the top of her chest, enough to bare her heart. I'd learned a trick, way back, that'd act like a shot of adrenaline. It might be enough to reset her Chaos and push the curse out.

I paused at the sight of a red tattoo over Melody's heart, startled. It looked like it'd been burned into her skin. Not an Apple of Discord, thank Chaos. No, this symbol was composed of three dots with three long, triangular shards pointing toward it, like rays of light, all encompassed in three thin circles. I'd seen the symbol before. It was the symbol of "awen"—created around the time the Primus Anglicus came into being. It represented the trinities in the magical world. The three divisions of the soul: mind, body, spirit. The three realms earthly creatures inhabited: land, sea, sky. The cosmic divisions: underworld, middle world, upper world, a.k.a. the afterlife. It also supposedly represented love, wisdom, and truth.

I'd seen a symbol like that in my mother's books, when she set her sights on a woman named... It was right on the tip of my tongue. *Odette.* Yes, that was it. And that symbol was how Chaos had marked her, always discreetly placed and known by very few.

"She's the Librarian," I whispered. Now, it made sense why she had muscle with her. Now I understood why she needed Luke.

"What is going on here?" a voice boomed behind us.

I turned to find Etienne stalking forward.

"Blanche attacked us for the formula," I explained rapidly. Melody didn't have a lot of time. "She's working for Davin Doncaster. And she's put a curse on Melody. I was going to shoot Chaos directly into her heart, but if you've got any better ideas, I'd love to hear them."

Etienne glowered at Blanche, who lay unconscious on the floor. "That snake! I should have known he would try to find a way inside my monastery. I heightened the defensive shields to keep him out, but I ought to have looked within as well."

"Etienne, please!" Luke begged. "Help Melody."

Etienne ushered me out of the way and took over. "You had the right idea, Finch, but these things require more delicacy."

He pressed his palms to her chest and closed his eyes. White light pulsated from his hands into her, shivering along her limbs. It overwhelmed the curse's reddish glow, until only white light remained. Once it stretched from Melody's head to her toes, Etienne pulled away.

"Will she be okay?" Luke asked urgently. He looked shaken.

Etienne nodded. "I've unraveled the curse. All we have to do is wait. I managed to get here just in time, it seems. Any longer and her bones would have crumbled, or Finch would have killed her. Unwittingly, of course."

"How did you manage that? You didn't even know the curse." I stared at Melody.

"I am more than the master of this monastery and a former assassin. Although, the latter comes with its share of knowledge." He smiled proudly. "One can't be a successful hired killer without knowing their way around a wide variety of dangerous curses— how to inflict and how to undo. Fortunately, I know more than Blanche. It wasn't so difficult."

I sank back on my haunches. "Thank you."

"Yes, thank you." Luke nodded vigorously. "Thank you, with all my heart."

"Mr. Abara, would you put these on Blanche? While I rather like the diamond cuffs, they won't defend against her abilities when she wakes." Etienne took a pair of Atomic Cuffs from his jacket pocket and handed them to Mr. Abara. "She has violated the sanctity of the monastery, as has Davin Doncaster. Whatever it was they sought, they won't get it from here."

Mr. Abara took the Cuffs and made quick work of clapping them on Blanche's wrists, then dissolving his diamond.

"I thought he was your pal?" I asked, blinking away the fog in my eyes. Puffball had vanished, and so had most of the weird effects of the poison.

Etienne frowned. "Who?"

"Davin."

Etienne snorted. "That devil? I hardly think so. While it is true that I'm somewhat beholden to him, he is no friend of mine. Indeed, I will evade my obligation toward him to the end of my days, if I can." His eyes narrowed. "Although, I'm curious how you know of our former friendship."

I shrugged. "He might have mentioned you once, while I tried to rip his head off. Something about you owing him your life." It was a lie, but I still had to divert his suspicions.

"It sounds as if he is no friend of yours, either." Etienne cracked a half-smile.

"I guillotined him recently, if that gives you an idea of how I feel about him. But he managed to spring right back. You know how he is." I sighed bitterly. "He sided with Katherine. He tried to kill people I care about. I'd guillotine him again and wipe my ass with his fancy suits with no shame whatsoever."

Etienne chuckled darkly. "Then it looks as though you and I are of one mind."

So, Etienne wasn't in business with Davin. That caused a wave of relief, to find out Etienne's villainy had stopped at an assassin's past and not spread into the present.

To be honest, I was more pissed off that I'd suspected just about everyone except the one person who turned out to be the spy. *Go figure.* Blanche had evidently been learning from the Katherine-to-Imogene playbook. And it was obvious who'd taught her.

Luke pushed through us and scooped Melody into his arms. He cradled her like a little girl, smoothing back the sweaty tendrils of her hair. She was out cold, but the white light had faded from her body.

"Mr. Abara, if you could bring Blanche? We must see that she is securely incarcerated before I make the arrangements to have her dealt with." Etienne walked to the staircase without looking back. Mr. Abara followed, carrying a limp Blanche, her Cuffs clanking as they went.

I felt like a bit of a third wheel, left with Luke and Melody. But I couldn't just dive back into the map-making. The orange poison had worn off, by the looks of it. No melting dome of glass, no Puffball.

Melody blinked her eyes open. She stared up at Luke and me in surprise.

"You're awake," Luke whispered, his voice shaking with relief.

She nodded. "What happened? I don't remember anything after the curse hit."

"I'll tell you everything once you've rested." Luke smoothed his thumb across her cheek.

Awkward...

"Finch?" She managed a smile in my direction. "Did you save the notebook?"

"What do you take me for? An amateur?" I brandished it at her.

"Thank goodness. I was so worried." She sagged into Luke's arms.

"So, you're the new repository for all Chaos knowledge, huh?" I chuckled, while Melody and Luke exchanged a shocked glance. "A heads-up would've been nice. The Librarian, all wrapped up in a jacket made of teddy-bear hides. Honestly, I need to stop wondering if my life could get any stranger. The answer is always yes."

Never had truer words been spoken. But the spy was in safe

hands, the notebook and the formula's secret were still in mine, Etienne wasn't Davin's sidekick, and, you know what, I started to wonder if I might actually get out of this thing in one piece.

I began to laugh uncontrollably. And once I started, I couldn't stop.

THIRTY-ONE

Finch

———————

M elody blinked in confusion. "How do you know about me?"

"You can't know. Nobody can," Luke jumped in, on his white horse.

"Neat little tattoo on your chest, Melody," I replied. My body ached, and pain stabbed my chest every time I breathed, but it hurt no more than a bad cold would. Adrenaline still pulsed through my veins, which helped take the edge off. Once that was gone, the real agony would start. So, I had some time.

"My chest?" She scrambled to close her buttons.

"I only unbuttoned a few because I was going to jumpstart your Chaos in hopes it'd break the curse. Etienne undid it instead—the curse, I mean, not your shirt." My cheeks warmed under Luke's stern gaze and Melody's mortified face.

She nodded, visibly relaxing. "That doesn't answer my question. How would you know what it meant? It's not exactly common knowledge. I didn't even know about it until Chaos itself seared it into me."

"I've seen it before. I'd prefer not to say where," I said quietly. "I just know it was on the last Librarian. The symbol of awen, right?"

"That's right," she replied with a small, sad smile. "You know about it from your mother, don't you?"

I sighed. "Yes. She had her eye on the last Librarian. I only saw a few of her notes, but that symbol took center stage. Did you know the last Librarian? Is that how you took her place?" I scratched my head. "I don't know how Librarian succession works."

"I didn't know her at all. I didn't know such things as Librarians existed." Melody sat up and leaned against Luke's shoulder. "But, when Odette died, the whole knowledge of Chaos transferred into me. It happened in the middle of the night, during an Awakening episode. That's what they call it."

My eyes widened. This was some crazy stuff, even by my standards. "Who are 'they'? And what in the name of Frank Sinatra is an Awakening?"

She chuckled. "*They* are the soldiers of Chaos, who put the information in my head. The Children and demi-Children. An Awakening opens one's mind for a vast quantity of knowledge to be poured inside. I don't remember much, but it felt as if I lived a thousand lives in a few minutes. So, now, my mind is filled with all my memories, billions of thoughts and information from people I don't know, and knowledge from Chaos itself that I never knew existed. There are gaps, of course, but I know more than anyone living. I don't say that to toot my own horn—it's just the truth."

"That's why she struggles to know what to say and what not to say, while she's still learning how to be the Librarian," Luke interjected. "It's like trying to hold back a dam that has thousands of cracks in it. Things inevitably slip out."

"Exactly," Melody agreed shyly. "My mind has been overloaded, so it gets difficult to keep a lid on it sometimes. Words just... come out in bursts. Not the important, secret stuff, of course. That's under lock and key up here." She tapped the side of her head.

"My sister went through something like that, on a smaller scale." I remembered Harley in the New York Coven after pressing that handprint on the door to the Grimoire. A massive memory dump had surged into her head. I guessed that was a fraction of what Melody had received.

Melody smiled. "I know."

"You do?" I frowned.

"When information is drawn into a magical's mind, it feels like a book being checked out. I can trace it to find out who has it, if that makes sense."

I raised my eyebrows. "Fitting with the whole 'librarian' metaphor."

"I'd just become the Librarian then, so every sensation was fresh and overwhelming. I felt that information dump as if it happened to me," she went on. "That must have been about a year ago now, maybe slightly more."

"The timeline fits," I replied. "Is that when Captain Hothead started to work for you?"

Luke scowled. "And I was just starting to tolerate you."

"Aww, I'm touched." I flashed him a grin.

"Only a few people in the upper echelons of magical society know what I am, and they sent Luke to watch over me. It's essential that my identity is protected, or I'd be targeted in an instant," Melody explained, looking up into Luke's eyes.

Guilt twisted my stomach. "Like Odette, you mean?"

"Yes, like her. She didn't have anyone to protect her, not really. I suppose that's why the upper echelons decided to assign a bodyguard, after what happened to her." Melody looked back at me. "Even with Katherine gone, there are still dangerous people in this world."

"You don't have to tell me. We just handcuffed one of their minions." Davin wasn't going to like hearing that he'd been foiled. But at least we had Etienne protecting this monastery from his old pal. When we had to step outside the comforting shield, things might get hairy again.

"There are others, too, not just Davin. Wherever there is humanity, there is evil. Wherever there is power, there are those who would do anything to take it." Melody nestled further into Luke, as if being near him could save her from all of it. "And for someone like me, there will always be someone else who wants to use me for their own ends."

"That's rough." I stared down at the floor, uncomfortable. "You're still only a small fry. I bet you feel like your life's over, huh? Well, life as you knew it?"

Luke shot me a hard look that said, *What the hell is wrong with you?* Honestly, I didn't know. I guessed I had a case of verbal diarrhea, too. I blamed the poison and the adrenaline.

She nodded. "I'm still learning to cope."

Just then, the African gray flapped through the smashed-up ceiling. In all the insanity, I hadn't noticed Kenzie-the-pigeon leaving. But she must have, to slip into something a little more talkative. Unless the ordinary parrot had just snuck in.

"Kenzie?" I whispered to the bird as it landed beside me.

"Numbskull!" it croaked back. Yep, this was Kenzie all right.

I stroked its feathery head. "Thank you for bringing that note to me. I know you must've risked a lot to get it here."

"Are you going to tell us what the deal with the parrot is?" Luke asked suspiciously.

I cleared my throat. "Um, a friend of mine. A Morph friend."

Luke looked alarmed. "What, there's a *person* in there?"

"Sort of, but you don't have to worry about her. She's with me."

"Tick-tock!" the parrot chirped. "Last Unknown! Last Unknown! Last Unknown!"

"Huh?" I squinted in confusion.

The parrot cocked its head like I was an idiot. "Last Unknown!"

Erebus wants me to find the Last Unknown? I had to be clever, so as not to give the Erebus part away while I got some clarification. "I need to find the Last Unknown? Is that what you're saying?"

"Bingo! Genius!" The parrot nodded furiously.

Melody gasped. "You're looking for the Last Unknown, too? I thought you were looking for the Fountain of Youth."

"Uh... yeah, didn't I mention that? I need to find both places." My cheeks flamed. "Although, to be fair, I don't really know what it is. I just... uh... know I have to find it. A recent development." *Yeah, like two-seconds-ago recent.*

"It's the lost city with many names, like I told you before," Melody said excitedly, apparently forgetting her filter again. "It has so many that magicals have simply referred to it as the Last Unknown for centuries."

"What kind of names?" I had the Fountain of Knowledge right here. If anyone could give me clues about what Erebus was after, it was Melody.

Melody smiled excitedly. "The most popular name, which you might be more familiar with, is Atlantis."

"*Atlantis?*" I gaped at her. "Come on, everyone's heard of that—surely someone's found it by now."

Melody shook her head. "It's not that easy."

So, Erebus wants to find Atlantis... For some magical artifact in the ruins, maybe? Or to recover lost texts, perhaps, written by the

Primus Anglicus? Or a power source, to soup up his human body a bit? Who knew what went on in that shady mind of his.

"I'm honestly relieved someone else is looking for it—someone like you, at least," Melody added. "I might have all this knowledge, but you've proven you're more adept at this map-making business."

"I wouldn't say that." I avoided looking at Kenzie. "You're not annoyed that I'm after the same place?"

This couldn't be a coincidence. I didn't want to sound like a broken record, but coincidences were like the Tooth Fairy—they didn't exist. This had to be the universe, or Chaos, or both, bringing us together somehow. We'd arrived at the same time, in the same place, when we could easily have missed each other. She had the know-how; I had the chutzpah. Maybe we wouldn't make a bad team.

"That depends on why you want to go," Melody replied. "I'm not selfish, like those Basani twins. I don't desire it for myself."

"Then why *do* you want to go there?" I asked.

Luke frowned. "We shouldn't tell him *everything*, Melody."

"Why not?" She peered up at him. "He might be able to help us."

"I'm all for back-scratching, for the right reasons," I said.

"It's one of the few pieces of knowledge I didn't inherit from the last Librarian," Melody explained. "As I said, there are gaps. But this gap wants to be filled. It's like an itch I can't stop scratching. To me, it's foolish to have an entire chunk of a map that nobody knows anything about. Literally nobody."

I nodded. "That's not why I want to find it, if that's any comfort." It was time to be honest with Melody. She'd given up her deepest secret—a dangerous one, in the grand scheme of things. If nothing else, it meant I could trust her. "I want it to save myself from a lifetime of servitude, or very imminent death. My money's on the latter."

"You'll have to tell us more if you want to join forces with us," Melody said softly.

I huffed a sigh. She had a point. She'd given me all of her information, and I'd given her a tiny slice. "Erebus wants me to find it. No idea why, but he's promised he's not down with the global enslavement thing. I don't usually believe him, but I do this time. If that was why he put me on this task, he'd have already started his reign of domination. Whatever he wants Atlantis for, I'm pretty sure it's personal. It doesn't seem like his goals will hurt humans or magicals."

Melody smiled. "That's more like it. But, tell me, how did you get this far? Did you know Erebus would send you here?"

I almost choked laughing. "He's not exactly chatty about things I actually need to know."

"So, that would be a no?" Luke scoffed, clearly unimpressed by the direction of this conversation.

"Precisely," I replied.

"You wound up in his service as a trade for the ability to kill Katherine, if my Librarian sources are correct," Melody pressed, her eyes shining with interest.

I sighed. "You've told me how you came to be the Librarian. So I guess it's only fair I give you all the deets on how I ended up as Erebus's favorite stooge. It started with Katherine, yeah. I made a deal with Erebus to take over my body and end her. The deal was servitude with an undisclosed finish line. I've been working for him ever since, traveling the world, picking up items he asks for. A personal shopper for Darkness, if you like. I didn't know what he wanted these things for, naturally. Then he sent me to find... uh..."

Do I tell them?

"Uh?" Luke prompted.

I'd gone this far. Why not go whole hog? I had little to lose and a lot to gain. Besides, nobody could get their hands on the Fountain of Youth now, anyway.

"He sent me to find the Fountain of Youth. My friends helped me, and we led him right to the fountain. There, he… bagged himself a human body. So, if you see a godlike dude strutting around, it's probably him." I fidgeted nervously. "Once he had that, he caused a cave-in. He saved my friends and brought me to the monastery. That's how I ended up here. No details, just insistence that I get the job done. I picked up bits and pieces as I went along, but I still didn't know the place he wanted to find until… well, now."

"He's *human*?" Melody's eyes bulged.

"Well, he's a Child of Chaos in a physical body. I'm not sure if that counts as human," I replied.

"And he wants to reach Atlantis." Melody tapped distractedly at her chest, where her tattoo was emblazoned. She still looked horrified about a human-Child hybrid wandering about.

"Apparently." I shrugged.

Melody looked at me with big, sad eyes, her expression softening. "You've been through a lot."

"It was worth it to end Katherine and save my sister. And everyone else," I hastened to add, dropping my gaze. Even I knew that old line sounded insincere.

"At least, that's what you keep telling yourself?" The pity in her voice broke my heart.

My head lifted. "I'm worn out, doing all this by myself. I tried to keep everyone at arm's length for so long, and… I can't do it anymore. At least, not alone." The words spilled like Melody had opened a floodgate. "I need help. You can help me. I can help you."

"Melody…" Luke's tone held a distinct warning.

I straightened. "No, hear me out. Neither of you are involved with Erebus, and with Melody being the Librarian, she should be able to fly under his radar. Odette, from what I remember, was shielded from most people, and most entities. It didn't help her in the end, I know, but it kept her safe for a while. I'm just asking for a bit of your time—long enough to get this job done, for all of us."

"Melody," Luke repeated, firmer now.

"There's a lot you don't know, Luke." She turned to him. "That's not your fault. I wouldn't know, either, if Chaos hadn't singled me out. But Finch needs us. And we need him. We still need the formula. All the Chaos knowledge in the world hasn't helped me with that. What's the harm in putting our heads together?"

Luke stiffened. "A lot of harm. We're talking about Erebus. I know enough about Children of Chaos to avoid them. What if he tries to use your power against you?"

"Children of Chaos put this knowledge into my head. That means, in a weird way, we're all on the same team." Melody put her palm to his chest. "It also means I know how to keep us safe, as Finch said. A way to fly under their radar. Chaos made it that way I'm a lockbox they can't pick. It's an odd contradiction, I know, but it's the truth. And I know it's your job to protect me, but Librarians come with defenses of our own."

"This is too risky, Melody." Luke stood firm.

"Finding Atlantis is risky, but you agreed to help me," she replied. "I'd be dead if Finch hadn't interfered. I might have a big brain, but it would have gotten smashed to pieces on the staircase. We can trust him, Luke. He's in this situation against his will."

Luke pulled a sour face. "That's not our problem."

"I'm making it our problem." Melody pulled away from him. He looked lost without her. His hands twitched, like he wanted to grasp her and pull her right back to him. "Finch, we're going to help you, if you help us."

I nodded. "I can do that."

"I'll dig through my knowledge to see if there's some way to even the playing field against Erebus. As you can probably tell, I'm still coming into my own as the Librarian, but if there's something in the Annals of Chaos that can help you, I promise I will find it."

"Are you on board, Luke?" I asked.

Luke sank back. "We owe you for what you did back there. With that in mind... yeah, I'm on board. I go where Melody goes." He sucked in a sigh. "She's always had a thing for stray animals. I suppose you're not far off."

"I am pretty cute." I flashed a smirk to hide the twisting knife in my chest. Finch Merlin, the dumped puppy nobody wanted. *Way to play on my insecurities, Luke.* It was still hard to believe that people cared about me. I knew they were waiting, back home, but sitting here... they'd never felt farther away. And I didn't know if I'd ever get back to them.

"You know what you have to do, Finch." Melody grasped my hand.

My self-pitying reverie shattered. "Huh?"

She smiled. "You need to draw a map to Atlantis."

THIRTY-TWO

Kenzie

I flapped to the desk and squawked at the oranges. Being a bird sucked. If I'd been able to speak to him, this would've been so easy.

Finch frowned, then nodded. "Right. The oranges."

"What do you mean?" Melody asked.

"They're part of the map-making. You eat them, and they create a… bizarre mental state. According to Etienne, that's the stuff needed to make this work." Finch got up and hobbled to the desk. "The last one wore off. At least, I think it did, because the room isn't melting anymore. Must've been all that adrenaline and spy-catching."

"Are you sure you should eat another?" Melody sounded worried.

I concurred. Double-dosing probably wasn't good for his head.

He shrugged. "I have to, or we're not finding Atlantis."

My pal looked broken. Once his back turned to Melody and Luke, his new accomplices, he winced. A ripple of absolute agony crossed his face. He'd clearly forgotten to hide it from my parrot form.

"Are you okay to do this?" Luke chimed in. "I meant what I said about the infirmary."

Finch gritted his teeth. "I'll be fine once the poison hits. Just don't worry if I start screaming. That's all part of it."

"Numbskull!" I squawked. It was hard to show concern in this form.

He looked down at me. "I swear, I'll be fine."

He picked up another orange and peeled it, then swallowed segment after segment like he hadn't eaten for a week.

"Oh boy," he murmured, sinking down into the chair.

"Pain!" I croaked.

He shook his head. "No, not pain. The walls are melting again. And… yep, there he is. Crap, crap, crap, crap."

"Knock, knock! Who's there?" I cawed. What was he looking at? Finch stared intently at a spot on the desk.

"Nothing… it's nothing." He squeezed his eyes shut. Whatever it was, I guessed he wasn't eager to see it. A hallucination, maybe?

"You! For! Ear!" I squawked. He needed help, fast. Euphoria had helped Harley out in the past, from what she'd told me. Maybe it'd work here, too. I didn't know a lot about Euphoria, but it couldn't be too different from Morphing. You know, sinking your mind someplace else. Detaching from your body and leaving any weirdness behind.

Finch stared at me, his eyes swimming. "I… can see you."

"You! For! Ear!"

"What? You'll have to shout over the waterfall!"

"You! For! Ear!" I squawked louder. What waterfall? He must be seeing some mad crap, thanks to that orange.

"Euphoria!" Melody yelled. "Use Euphoria to break through whatever's happening."

He closed his eyes but gave no sign he'd heard us. "Ah… closing my eyes really doesn't help. Yeah, I know they're right, Puffball. I'm trying my best here! If it's so easy, why don't *you* try to concentrate while the world is turning into puddles of goo around you?"

Puffball? Puddles of goo? I didn't even want to know.

His back arched violently. A pulsating blue light throbbed in the center of his chest. That light shot up his neck to his eyes, and his lids flew open to reveal pools of bright blue. No irises, no pupils, just two eyeballs of raw light. Another ripple slithered down his right arm and into his hand, which spasmed. It didn't look like Finch was in control anymore.

His fingertips grasped a quill and dipped it in a pot of ink. The blue light spilled down his fingers and into the quill, turning the ink that same glowing, pulsating shade. His hands moved at lightning speed as the quill dragged across the paper. Lines, names, land, sea, filled the page faster than my parrot eyes could follow. The light left a trail of glowing ink in its wake as he moved on to the next part, and the next. Almost like automatic writing—a phenomenon I'd heard about on some late-night documentary while taking care of Mom. A person channeled their subconscious thoughts onto paper in an altered state. This definitely fit the bill. But way cooler.

The names he'd written, however, didn't make sense to me: *Μαύρη πέτρα. Νότια Αυγή. Γη των Πράσινων Φώτων. Η Θάλασσα του Σαπφείρου. Όπου συμβαίνει ο χορός των πνευμάτων. Η πύλη μεταξύ ζωής και θανάτου.* I just hoped he knew what they meant when he woke up from his trance.

I peered at the page. He'd drawn a large island, with a smaller island to the right. Dead center between them, he'd drawn a star that shone more brightly than the rest of his map. But the writing and locations were all Greek to me. The island could've been anywhere.

His quill traced lines, naming the islands he'd drawn. He drew one last island, a tiny speck, to the left of the smaller island he'd drawn. The final name: *Η πύλη μεταξύ ζωής και θανάτου*. He etched a second star and sank back. The blue light left him as quickly as it appeared. He blinked, and his eye color returned to normal. If I'd thought he looked exhausted before, that was nothing. He looked on the edge of total collapse. And I couldn't do anything to help him.

"Melody! Melody!" I chirped.

She came running, with Luke in tow. "Are you okay?"

He nodded blankly. "Just… tired."

"You don't look good." Melody didn't even glance at the paper. That gave her major brownie points in my book. She cared more about Finch than Atlantis. At least, for now. I still wasn't sure about these two. They seemed like decent folks, but that didn't mean I thought it was a good idea for Finch to team up with people he hardly knew.

"I'm sure." He took a sharp breath. "That was… an experience."

"Is this it?" Luke pointed to the paper.

Finch mustered a weak smile. "Yep."

"Where is it?" Luke pressed.

"Luke! Give him some space. Can't you see he's struggling?" Melody chided, pulling Luke away slightly.

Finch put his elbows on the desk and rested his head in his hands. "I just need a minute."

"Take however long you need," Melody insisted.

"Bingo! Genius!" I croaked. It hurt to see my friend so broken.

The orange poison had probably vamoosed with the blue light, leaving him to deal with all the injuries Blanche had inflicted.

Finch rallied shortly. "Atlantis is in the stretch of ocean between South Georgia Island and Antarctica. These names mean Black Rock, South Dawn, Land of the Green Lights, The Sapphire Sea, Where the Dancing of the Spirits Takes Place, and the Gateway between Life and Death." His fingertips traced the map, pointing out each one.

"What about the stars?" Melody glanced over his shoulder. "What do they mean?"

He gestured to the one between the smaller island and the bigger one—South Georgia Island and Antarctica, I guessed. "This is Atlantis." Next, he pointed to the second star, the one on the tiny speck island. "This is the Gateway between Life and Death. I'm not entirely sure how they work together, but I don't think you can just waltz into Atlantis. Which means getting in might have something to do with the gateway. That's what gateways do, right? They open into something else."

"You did it." Melody gasped. "You actually did it. Even if the gateway doesn't play a part in Atlantis, at least we know where to look."

He snorted. "And I'm feeling every ounce of the effort."

"I've got a question." Luke raised his hand, comically.

"What is it?" Finch replied.

"How powerful is this place, if Erebus can't get inside on his own?"

Melody cocked her head, thinking. I did the same. "Children of Chaos can't just wander around Earth as they please. So, he wouldn't have been able to get into Atlantis in his usual form."

"Hence the need for a human body," Finch interjected, before shuddering. "Since when do I use the word 'hence'? I've been around Etienne for too long."

"But why couldn't he have made a map himself? How come he didn't already know Atlantis's whereabouts?" Luke pressed. "This place has to be insanely powerful to keep a Child of Chaos out, in any form."

I'd been wondering that myself. Why put Finch through all of this? He wasn't the all-powerful deity.

Finch nodded. "From what I've seen, it seems he's not as powerful in human form. He's got limitations. Sure, he's still strong, but he can't delve into his Child of Chaos-ness the way he might want."

"That will work to our advantage." Melody grinned. "If he can't watch you all the time, he can't control you, Finch."

Finch smiled. "That gives me more hope than I had before."

"That said, it's best to err on the side of caution. Until we know what Erebus's limitations actually are, we should play it safe. He *is* still a Child of Chaos, as you said, human body or not. He has civilizations' worth of knowledge. Even in human form, he won't be easy to fool."

Oh, I like you, Melody Winchester. You can stay. Without even the pleasure of meeting him, she'd figured Erebus out. Maybe I was wrong before. By the looks of it, Finch couldn't have picked a savvier teammate. Well, except for me.

THIRTY-THREE

Finch

O h sleep, oh Morpheus, oh Hypnos... how I missed thee.
I still felt like a bundle of breakages wrapped up in a bruised patchwork of skin, but a decent night's rest made it more manageable. One of the monks had slipped me something, too, on my reluctant visit to the infirmary. One bottle downed and I'd finally slept last night. A curious purple liquid. No idea what it was, but I wanted barrels of the stuff.

Melody and Luke hadn't finished the formula. They didn't need to now. Midnight came and went without any of us realizing, and Melody had refused to leave me. And of course Luke stayed because Melody did.

Kenzie was safely hidden inside Melody's jacket, having also refused to leave my side. I didn't want Etienne seeing her. It was the same last night—I'd had to smuggle her into the infirmary under Melody's jacket, and then put her under the bed. I didn't know if she'd gone back to get some rest of her own while I'd been out cold. Still, she was stubbornly sticking with us now. And maybe that was for the best. Soon, if she hadn't already, she'd have to relay intel to Erebus. He'd want news. She was smart; she'd know not to say too much. But it worried me that I didn't know exactly *what* she might end up saying. Erebus had a way of prodding and poking to pry information out of someone.

"And how is the wearisome student today?" Etienne looked up from his desk as Melody, Luke, and I piled into his study. We'd decided to wait until morning to visit him, to give Luke and me a chance to recover, though Luke hadn't come out too badly. Part of me suspected he wanted to get some sympathy out of Melody.

"'Wearisome'?" I replied. "You sure that's the right word?"

Etienne smiled. "Yes, it is. How did the map-making go?"

"I don't really have a benchmark. I made a map, so I guess it went well." It had been a weird ride. My mind had pretty much flown out of my head, into some kind of astral state, and spread across the entire globe, led by Chaos. I'd had to fixate on what I wanted, where I wanted to go, and that precise channeling had done the rest. Hell, it took over completely.

"And what map did you draw? Where is it you plan to go?" Etienne pressed. "The Fountain of Youth, wasn't it?"

"Did I tell you that?" I squinted at him.

"I hear things, here and there," he replied.

"I thought you were here to teach, not pry," I shot back.

He shrugged. "It doesn't hurt to know what my students get up to, but you make a valid point. If you don't wish to tell me, that is your prerogative. However, I would say that I have a depth of knowledge that you might find useful, if you wanted to be forthcoming."

Since nobody knows much about Atlantis, that's a firm no to that, pal.

"What will happen to Blanche?" Melody interjected, saving me from the interrogation chair. "You said she'd be punished for her actions against the sanctity of the monastery. What will that entail? You don't do executions here or anything, do you?"

I smirked. "No, but I hear they throw a hell of a bar mitzvah." As per usual, I resorted to jokes to cover my discomfort.

"Very amusing, Finch." Etienne didn't laugh. "Blanche will be sent to Purgatory, where she will await trial for aiding and abetting a dangerous fugitive, and a former Cult of Eris member."

I arched an eyebrow. "Isn't that a little risky for you, bringing in the authorities? Wouldn't want you to be carted off to prison, now, would we?"

"No, we wouldn't. You have no need to fret. An influential friend is doing a favor for me by transporting Blanche to Purgatory and explaining the circumstances without mentioning me." He smiled smugly. Just how many friends in high places did this guy have?

"Where is she?" Melody asked.

"Where I can keep an eye on her." Etienne rose from his desk and crossed to a door in the side of his study. He opened it with one of his many keys to reveal another door, of iron bars. A cell, in no uncertain terms—Etienne's own private jail. Behind the bars, Blanche writhed, straining against a gag. Like she really wanted to say something.

You had your chance to talk.

"You can say your piece," Etienne said, stowing the keys away. "I have some business to attend to with the remaining students. I must contend with the collateral damage of their disappointment, though I'm used to such things by now. I will be back shortly, so I suggest you make your grievances snappy."

He left without another word. I supposed he didn't have to worry about her breaking out. The protective charms on the barred door thrummed with magical intensity. He'd used the good stuff.

"Anyone got anything to say?" I sighed sadly. In the cold light of a new day, this was a bittersweet victory for me. True, I'd found Atlantis, but that had come at the price of denying everyone else the opportunity to learn map-making. I'd kept it secret to stop Davin's spy from making progress. But she'd been found, and I still hadn't shared the love. I felt bad about it, if only for Mr. Abara. Melody and Luke, too, despite their insistence that it was fine because we were headed for the same place. The others could stuff it.

Luke shrugged. "I don't. I said it all yesterday."

"Relax, Luke." Melody's voice held warning. "Maybe it's best you don't go near her, if you're feeling like that."

"Like what?" I pried.

"He's having some dark emotions about Blanche." Melody went to Luke and took his hands in hers. "She isn't worth it. I'm alive, and I'm okay. You're alive, and you're okay. We're all going to be fine. There's no use bearing grudges."

Luke gazed into her eyes. "I thought I would lose you yesterday."

"I know, but she's going to be punished. You heard Etienne." Melody soothed the beast. "Let's just focus on what comes next."

I scouted Etienne's books while contemplating what to ask Blanche. It was my way of getting my questions in order. All the while, I absently toyed with the eye pendant around my neck. I'd almost forgotten it was there, I'd gotten so used to wearing it.

I glanced at Kenzie, who'd fluttered over to my shoulder. "Do you know what this thing is for? You put me through a lot to get it."

"Nope! Nada! Take! Just take!" she squawked. "Ball! Gold ball! Take! Just take!"

"For someone who loves the sound of his own voice, Erebus sure does keep his mouth shut about important stuff," I muttered. But it had to have some use, right? Erebus liked a laugh at my expense, but he wouldn't have sent me through that underworld for nothing.

I lifted the pendant from my shirt and held it up to the light. The symbols etched across the gold burned more brightly, but they didn't give anything away. I wasn't familiar with the markings at all. Which meant they had to be old school—from a time I hadn't bothered to study during my cult education.

"What's that?" Luke distracted me from the pretty item.

"A memento." I shot him a knowing look.

Melody squeaked, her hands flying to her mouth. "Did you *steal* that?"

"Stole, borrowed, took without asking… whichever floats your boat." I looked it over again. "Anyway, I didn't have a choice. Erebus wanted me to have it, so—" I froze, mid-sentence. A thin, curved, near-imperceptible line ran around the center of the orb. I hadn't noticed before, but this thing was made of two halves. Ignoring Melody's shocked stare, I pushed the halves apart, revealing what looked like an actual eye in the center of the pendant. The metal covering provided the lids to protect the eyeball. Immediately, the iris lit up white.

"Is it glowing?" Melody came closer.

I nodded. "Yeah. Have you seen something like this before?"

"No… I don't think so," she replied, clearly in awe.

"Have a sift around that mind palace of yours, see if anything comes up," I suggested. The iris flashed green when Melody came into its field of vision. Curious, I pointed it at Luke. Another flash of green. *Hmm…* I turned it toward Blanche, just to get the full array of experimentation. The iris burned red and glowed for longer than it had with the other two. I flashed it back at Melody and Luke and got the same burst of green. Then back at Blanche, just to be sure. Yep, red again. Words started to appear in the air before the eye: *All is not what it appears.*

"Does anyone else see that?" I asked. What the hell did it mean?

Melody peered closer, a gasp escaping her mouth. "Yeah, I definitely see that. All is not what it appears? What does that mean?"

"I guess it means all isn't what it appears," I replied, as Melody pushed me closer to Blanche, the red glow throbbing and the letters burning brighter. Blanche struggled behind the bars, her eyes wide. She rocked like a madwoman, her teeth visibly straining behind the gag to try and bite through, or tear it away.

"But why is it green for us, red for her?" Melody jittered.

"It probably knows she's a traitorous... never mind," Luke bit out savagely.

I frowned. "We should ask her some questions. Maybe this eye can sense her lies? And I'd sure like to know what Davin was after, in exchange for bringing Blanche's husband back."

"I don't think we should go near her. Red means danger or stop, where I come from," Luke grumbled.

"She's tied up and locked behind bars. What's she going to do—break through all these charms and walk out of here, scot-free?" I walked up to the bars, stuck my hand in, and tore off the gag before Luke could get a dig in.

A tiny ball tumbled from Blanche's mouth and hit the floor. My heart almost jumped clean through my chest. It looked like... no, it definitely was... an Ephemera.

"Thank Chaos... thank Chaos you came." Mr. Abara's voice said with Blanche's lips. "Etienne wouldn't remove the gag. I couldn't explain. I couldn't tell him... he locked up the wrong person."

My stomach churned. "What's this, some trick of yours?"

"No, boy. I am Mr. Abara. There is no trick from me, only her." His eyes darkened as his body morphed back into his own. "I was tasked with keeping an eye on that woman while Etienne went to tell the students what was happening. He left for a few minutes, but it was all she needed. She hit me with a hex—a green puff of smoke. Next thing I know, I'm waking up with an Ephemera in my mouth, bound and gagged."

My head spun. If Mr. Abara was here, then where was Blanche?

"She must have used a modified Ephemera to hold Mr. Abara in this form," Melody said, her voice tight with terror.

"I told you she was a vicious harpy!" Luke snarled.

I jumped into action, using everything in my arsenal to unpick Etienne's protective charms in double-quick time. Every unraveling curse I'd ever learned poured out of my hands to the charms. They glowed as they came apart. Luke bent the bars wide enough for Mr. Abara to get out. For a man his size, that was no easy feat. But every second we wasted, Blanche was out there, on her way to freedom.

Or somewhere else... I patted my jeans pocket to make sure the map was still there. Sure enough, it was.

An icy smack of dread hit me in the gut. Etienne hadn't seemed worried when he'd strolled out of here, which meant the monastery's outer defenses hadn't been triggered. If Blanche had escaped, it would've sounded the alarm. So Blanche must be nearby, lying in wait, preparing to pounce.

Now, I was fully convinced that Erebus's and Davin's goals were closely linked. Davin had been there at the Fountain, right before Erebus claimed his human body. He had sent a spy to the monastery precisely when Erebus had sent me. I'd have staked my left bum cheek—my favorite one—on it...

Davin wanted to find Atlantis, too.

THIRTY-FOUR

Finch

"Mr. Abara, tell Etienne what's happened," I instructed. "Melody, Luke, come with me. We need to find Blanche."

"What if she's already escaped?" Melody replied anxiously.

I shook my head. "She hasn't. She's after the map. Don't ask me how I know that, because it's a long story—longer than we've got time for. You'll just have to trust me."

"You've still got it, right?" Luke raised an eyebrow.

I patted my pocket. "Of course. Safe and sound."

"Then why isn't she trying to find *you*?" Mr. Abara asked.

"I'd say she's waiting for the right moment. If she doesn't know we know about you, Mr. A, that gives us an advantage. So, let's head out!"

I took off across the study and burst into the hallway. Melody and Luke ran after me, and the three of us tore through the monastery. Glancing back over my shoulder, I saw Mr. Abara veer off in the opposite direction. I waited for Kenzie to flap away, but she was nowhere to be seen. She was a crazy-smart girl—she'd probably flown out the window to scour the outside.

We sprinted along hallway after hallway, checking every room and alcove for Blanche. The prospect of scouring the entire monastery for her wasn't comforting. But she couldn't leave without the map, and I had that. Maybe that'd bring the old girl right to us. A dangerous tactic, but it'd speed things up a bit.

"I know what that pendant is!" Melody gasped as we searched another room, startling a bunch of monks in the middle of morning prayer.

"You shouldn't be here! It's sacrilege to interrupt!" one shrieked, covering himself like I'd caught him naked.

"Blanche is loose. I'm sorry, but you might have to put whatever you're doing on the back burner and get looking for her!" I yelled at them before heading down the next corridor. I turned to Melody on the way. "What, it just came to you?"

She nodded. "I've been searching my... mind palace, as you called it. It just popped into my head!"

"What is it?" Luke cut in.

"It's called a 'Revealer,' though it goes by another name, too. It's a rare, ancient artifact, filled with the Chaos of a Veritas magical," she explained breathlessly as we sprinted.

"A who-said-what-now?" I panted.

"A magical who can detect deception. They're extinct, but they used to exist as readily as, say, Mimics or Empaths. The pendant is made from the eye of one. Hephaestus, to be exact," she went on.

I frowned. "The burly blacksmith dude from Greek mythology?"

Melody nodded. "Exactly. Sometimes, he's pictured with an eye patch—most people presume that's because he was a blacksmith."

"That's not the case?" Luke replied, barely out of breath. He made me and Melody look bad.

"Blacksmiths used to wear an eyepatch over the eye that came closest to the smithy flames. But that wasn't the case with Hephaestus," Melody explained. "He actually lost his eye as part of an... exchange. His eye was the most powerful point of his Veritas magic, like a biological Esprit of sorts, and he gave it up in exchange for making Aphrodite fall in love with him."

"Who did he make that deal with? Seems like a lot to give up to make someone fall in love with you," Luke remarked.

Like you wouldn't do something insane to get Melody to love you. I didn't say it out loud. I needed Luke on my side, not battering me for my loose lips.

"Well, the thing is..." Melody began.

Creeping suspicion shivered up my spine. "Don't say it."

"No, go on. I want to know," Luke urged.

"It was—" Melody started.

I grimaced. "Don't say it!"

"It's important to know the origin of things like this." She offered me a sympathetic glance. "Hephaestus made the deal with Erebus. That's why it also goes by the name, 'the Eye of Erebus.'"

I balled my hands into fists. "Son of a—! That's why he got Kenzie to make me steal it! He's probably been waiting years for the right person to get it back for him." The memory of that flock of seagulls in Havana, grouping together in the shape of an eye, was seared into my head. The eye was his calling card, when he wasn't smearing bloody messages on people's windows or shattering perfectly good mirrors. Now his choice of symbol made sense.

"You've heard of it?" Melody peered at me curiously.

"You could say that," I hissed.

Melody's eyes shone. "Do you know anything else about it?

There isn't much knowledge left of it, so I'll have to keep digging in my head, unless you have answers."

"I didn't even know it was a physical thing with a backstory until now." An idea burst into my brain. "But don't worry about sifting around in your mind palace. I'll ask Erebus about it the next time I see him, since this thing is clearly so precious to him. That jackass has a whole universe of explaining to do next time I see his ugly mug, anyway, so I might as well throw that in, too." I kept running, with the other two trailing after me.

"You mentioned Kenzie—is she the parrot?" Melody called out.

I nodded. "She's not usually a parrot."

"Right, I mean Morph," Melody panted. "Is she working for Erebus, too? How did she know you'd need it?" Nothing got past Melody.

I channeled my anger into my legs. "Seems that way. I can't really deal with that right now, though, or I might put my fist through a wall."

"Noted." Melody pointed back to the pendant, continuing between breaths. "Why do you think Erebus wants it?"

"No idea. Those answers will have to come later—from the Prince of Darkness's own mouth. Right now, we need to find Blanche."

"I have an idea." Luke raised his hand.

"What?" I glanced at him.

"If she wants the map, and you have it, where's she most likely to go?" Luke came to a stop, and so did I.

I clenched my jaw. "Crap, you're right."

"Am I missing something?" Melody chimed in.

"My room," I said. "She'll be lurking there, I'd bet. She'll have ransacked my drawers already. By now she knows I have it on me."

"Then let's get going." Melody shot me an encouraging grin.

Retracing our steps, we raced through the labyrinth of hallways until we reached my room. There, we pulled to a halt. I lifted my finger to my lips and rested one hand on the handle.

They nodded, raising their palms for a fight. Luke looked worried, and he had every right to be. His skills hadn't worked well during our last encounter with Blanche, but we didn't have time to find weapons. He'd just have to hope the element of surprise would make a difference. Besides, he had Melody and me to help him out, and this time, we knew we were walking into a potential warzone.

I flung the door open. We were all fired up, wound tight and ready to come to blows. But the sight before us abruptly halted our attack.

Blanche stood in the center of the room behind a solid, floor-to-ceiling wall of ice. She'd drawn all the water from the creepy moat surrounding Hades and used it to build the barrier. The ice was so smooth, we could see her smirking on the other side.

"You had to sound the alarm, didn't you?" She tutted loudly. "Not that it matters now. You're too late."

I lifted my palms and forged a fireball, then pummeled it at the ice. "Is that right?"

She chuckled. "Poor thing, you were so out of it, weren't you? That's the trouble with monastic medicine—you only get the best stuff when you're here. They don't share it with the rest of the world. Potent sedatives and powerful healing serums. But they make you a little woozy, don't they?"

"What are you talking about?" I spat, bombarding the ice wall. It was deceptively thick, and the fireballs took time to make a dent. Luke stepped up beside me and wrenched a poker from the fireplace, using his Magneton powers to form a pick. He started to hack at the ice while Melody applied pressure with Air.

"You didn't notice your feathery friend disappear in the middle of the night, did you? That stoic sentinel needed to rest back in their real body, I imagine. And Melody and Luke couldn't stay awake forever. All I had to do was wait, and, as you know, I'm good at that." Blanche smirked.

My heart stopped. "What?"

"A concerned friend, coming to make sure you were okay. It couldn't have worked more perfectly," she went on. "Although, I confess, I'd have been out of here a lot sooner if you hadn't hidden your oranges so well. Very sneaky, to dose them with Shapeshifting energy to make them look like a laundry basket."

I glanced at the corner of the room, where I'd hidden the oranges before Melody and Luke finally dragged me to the infirmary last night. The fake laundry basket was gone... which meant the oranges were, too.

"You don't have what Davin wants," I insisted, surging more Fire into the torrent aimed at the ice wall.

"Oh, but I do, Finch. I was just on my way out when the sirens sounded. I couldn't resist seeing the look on your face when you realized you hadn't managed to stop me." Her smile never faltered.

My hand delved into my pocket, whipping out the map. "If you think you have the map, then what's this?" I brandished it at her.

"A blank sheet of paper," Blanche replied.

My eyes darted to the map. *Crap.* She was right. No directions, no locations, nothing marked the paper.

"I took it from you while you slept. Or, rather, Mr. Abara did— his form is very useful. Nobody questioned him." She leered through the ice, smug as anything. Her tricks had been so simple. Deviously simple.

"Davin isn't who you think he is." I returned to bombarding the wall, the ice finally starting to break. If this had been her way of buying time, she was running out of it, fast. "Whatever he's promised, he'll turn on you at the first opportunity."

Blanche snorted. "He told me you'd say that. And, besides, you don't have what he has. You're not a Necromancer. You can't bring my husband back."

"Give me the map, and we'll forget about this," I urged her. "He's manipulating your grief to get what he wants. He won't give up that much energy to bring back your husband, trust me. He betrayed *Katherine*! Do you really think he'll give a damn about betraying someone as insignificant as you?"

"Insignificant?" Venom dripped from her words.

"Just hand over the map and the oranges, and we'll figure this out!" I could feel the control slipping through my hands, as slippery as that ice.

She flicked the ice, and the cracks spread. "I have more reason to trust Davin than *you*. He betrayed Katherine because she was evil. He was playing her all along—he told me everything."

"And you believed him?! If you do, you'll end up with nothing. It's never too late. You can always change your mind." I was pretty much begging, at this point.

"My pigeons have already delivered the goods." She checked an imaginary watch on her wrist. "It's time for me to go." She turned toward the window.

NO! Closing my eyes, I gathered every Elemental and Telekinetic ability I possessed and formed a swirling ball of five powers. I'd never done this before, and my palms could barely contain the volatile energy. With a shove that stole my breath, I hurled the ball at the ice wall. It slammed into it so violently that the entire room shook on impact. In a split second, the ice disintegrated into a thousand jagged splinters.

"Grab her!" I yelled.

Blanche looked back with terror in her eyes as she scrambled for the windowsill. Mustering the strength I had left, I grabbed her around the waist with a tendril of Telekinesis, tugging her back into the room before she could escape.

"Let go of me!" she wailed as she hit the floor. I held her in place, but her hands twisted wildly in front of her. She sent daggers of ice flying toward us in a barrage of glinting projectiles.

I dropped the Telekinesis to create a barrier of Air, as did Melody. The combining air currents swept the icy shards back the way they came. They hit the far wall with a series of cracks.

Blanche ducked and covered her head, catching a few ice splinters in her forearms and back. Blood trickled down her arms and to the floor—wounded by her own weapons. As for her legs, the larger shards that struck her had buried in her skin, melting slowly from the heat of her oozing blood.

She recovered quickly, drawing up the last water from Hades's pool and turning it to a solid lump of ice. Her gaze fixed on Melody. Her breath went ragged as she lifted the ice block with her Chaos, her arms shaking over her head under the strain of holding it in midair.

"Don't you dare!" Luke howled, curling his hands into fists. The adapted poker he'd used to chip away at the ice flew at Blanche. It thudded through her chest with a sickening, wet sound. Her eyes went wide in surprise, and the ice block dropped to the ground. Tiny pieces and bigger chunks skittered across the floor, their target forgotten.

"What… did you… do?" Blanche stared down at the end of the poker, which was deeply lodged in her flesh.

"What I should've done when you first threatened Melody," Luke snarled back. Melody, on the other hand, stared in utter horror. She looked pale, like she might faint.

"Luke! Your girl's about to keel over," I warned.

He rushed to Melody, catching her as her knees gave way. Melody's eyes rolled back into her head, and she was down for the count. Luke held her close and sank to the ground with her in his arms.

I strode to face Blanche. She swayed like a poppy in a hurricane, her hands reaching for anything that might hold her up. She even looked at me in desperation, as if I would help her out.

"Finch... I... change my... mind. Just... help me," she pleaded. "Get me... to Davin. He's the... only one that... can save me. I don't want... to die."

I shook my head slowly. "I gave you a choice, and you refused. There's nothing I can do for you now."

"It might not be... too late." Blanche's eyes darted to the window. "Help me and... I'll get the map back."

I hurried to the window and stared out. Beyond, the Ionian Sea lay eerily flat except for one cluster of ripples, forming around a long shadow. A single boat rowed away from the island with a familiar figure sitting in the center, his arms pumping the oars.

Davin. Two dead birds lay on one of the empty rowing benches. Birds I recognized. Kenzie had Morphed into one to tell me about Blanche's deception. And, resting in a basket on the stern, were my oranges and, presumably, my map.

"You didn't need to get inside, did you?" I whispered, broiling with rage.

Davin and his boat waited in the water beyond the monastery and its protective shield. He hadn't even had to set foot on the island with Blanche doing all his dirty work. No need to risk setting off alarms or alerting Etienne. And those carrier pigeons had delivered everything to him. Kenzie must've tried, too late, to

Morph into one again to steal the items back... but Davin had killed them.

Even now, a vicious seagull circled the boat, divebombing it. With one bolt of Necromantic Chaos from Davin, it plunged into the ocean, dead as a doornail. Fear spiked through my anger. What would happen to Kenzie if her Morph vessel died? If she'd already made her way through three, hopefully that meant she'd be okay, but I couldn't shake the dread that pulsed in my veins.

But that dread stemmed from more than my worry about Kenzie. The oranges were gone, the map was gone, and Blanche had collapsed behind me, the light gone from her eyes. Up ahead, I could've sworn I saw Davin grin back at the monastery. A moment later, he snatched up his stolen goods and vanished in a dark puff of smoke. It enveloped him whole, leaving the boat empty, bobbing on the water.

"Finch?" Luke called out.

I turned slowly, on the brink of a panic attack.

"What happened?" he asked. Melody was still out.

"Davin... got away." I clenched my jaw, my teeth squeaking.

Luke furrowed his brow. "What are you going to do? Should we go after him?"

"He's already gone." I shook my head, wanting to scream at the top of my lungs.

"What does that mean? What can we do?"

I glanced back at the empty ocean. "It means I'll have to draw that map again, from memory. And that Davin might beat us to Atlantis."

THIRTY-FIVE

Finch

T he door of my room opened, silencing a whole tirade of filthy words about to trip oh-so-elegantly off my tongue. Etienne burst in with a cluster of monks. Mr. Abara wasn't among them.

I pushed the pendant under my T-shirt, since it was stolen goods. Well, someone had swiped it from Erebus, and I'd swiped it back, but that was a distinction that Etienne probably wouldn't appreciate. I'd gone snooping for it, after all. That would likely be enough to punish me, even if I explained why.

Melody stirred in Luke's arms, blinking in confusion. "What happened?"

"An incredible offense to myself and the monastery is what happened!" Etienne cried, his cheeks purple with fury.

"Mr. Abara found you, then?" I sighed, edging past Blanche's body and the blood pooling across the floor.

"Yes, he did. He is leading another team through the monastery as we speak," Etienne replied tersely.

"No need. Blanche gave everything to Davin, and he's gone. And she's... well, you can see what she is." I gestured to her lifeless form. Luke did what he had to, but death was never something to jump for joy over.

Aside from yours, Davin. When I finally killed that slimy, evil, devious, wormy little... it wouldn't have been polite to use the word I wanted to. Nevertheless, when I finally killed him, there'd be fanfare and a friggin' festival to mark the occasion. Fireworks, free candy for everyone, and effigies of that devil burning on pyres across the whole damn world!

Etienne looked ready to explode. "Davin Doncaster has made an eternal enemy out of me over this sacrilege! I don't care if I owe him a life debt. If I ever see his face again, I'll rip it off with my bare hands! All of this, because he failed to learn the skill of map-making himself, years ago. All of this, because he wasn't intelligent enough to gain the art of his own accord! So, he sends a *spy* to steal the craft, instead!"

"Wait, what?" I narrowed my eyes. "Davin tried to learn map-making?"

"Yes, and he couldn't, and now he's done this! It's the height of vulgarity!" Etienne paced. I could've sworn I saw steam coming out of his ears.

The news brought a sickening "aha!" moment. Davin trying to learn the art had to have something to do with Erebus. I already knew there were some crossovers in my work for Erebus and Davin's involvement with the Child of Chaos. The Fountain being the first, and this being the second. There were definitely some connections between the two of them, but this revelation made me realize that Davin's and Erebus's paths might have been inter-twined for a lot longer than I could've guessed.

"Well, now he has the map, and those oranges, to boot. So, I'm back at square one with no poison to send me on a magical mystery ride." I kicked a chunk of ice, wishing it were Davin's severed head.

"What of that? It's the act of thievery that appalls me. But you're not back at square one." Etienne turned to me, visibly calming himself.

I frowned. "I'm not?"

"Do you think the art of map-making relies solely on oranges? That's nonsense and would be a highly inefficient skill. Mapmakers aren't always going to have a potted orange tree handy, now, are they? They were just a method of channeling Chaos. Now that you've drawn your first map, you can do it again without the help of such fruits."

"I can?" I gaped at him.

Etienne sighed. "Think about it logically."

"Well… I guess it *would* be pretty inefficient if you always needed to have orange trees around," I replied.

"Precisely. You can still draw the map without the poison; it will just take you longer to achieve the end product," Etienne explained dryly. "A few days instead of an hour or two. Inconvenient, perhaps. Unattainable, no."

"How come it takes longer?" I pressed.

"Think of it like caffeine and writing an essay while tired." Etienne gestured to an empty mug on my desk. "You can still write the essay without the caffeine, but you will write it a great deal quicker if you have the caffeine to sharpen your mind and keep you focused. The oranges provide the added stimulus, in this scenario."

Just then, Hades started to move, the statue stretching like it'd come out of a thousand-year coma. *Ah crap… not the time, Erebus!* Etienne would lose his mind if he realized I really was in cahoots with a Child of Chaos, after everything I'd told him to the contrary.

The statue's head twisted to me, the limbs glitching—freezing and starting as if running on a low frame rate.

"Boy, there you are!" Erebus boomed. "Kenzie's mortal form has grown weak. Too weak to remain here, so I've come to you myself. I see you have company. Nevertheless, I must speak to you. You are needed. Return to where Kenzie lives so I don't have to repeat myself. We have work to—"

The statue crumbled suddenly, pieces breaking away and tumbling into the now-empty pool around Hades's feet. Erebus's communication spell had failed again. And poor Hades had taken the brunt of it.

Etienne pinched the bridge of his nose. "All of these constant violations!" I opened my mouth to explain, but he cut me off. "Don't bother with excuses, and I won't ask whom you were speaking with. The sooner I can have you all out of my monastery, the better! I must prepare for the next batch of potential students."

If that's the worst of your problems, you've got it easy. I had to deal with Erebus. And, by the sounds of it, my overlord was already in a foul mood. *Oh, goody...* Just the temperament I wanted him in when I told him we'd lost the map and that Davin probably had it.

I was a little surprised that Etienne wasn't ripping my head off about Erebus's sudden arrival. It clearly meant I'd lied about my ties to the Child of Chaos. Maybe Etienne cared more about stopping Davin than he did about my servitude to Erebus. Or maybe it just wasn't clear enough that Erebus had taken over old Hades.

"So, I can really draw the map again?" I said, to test the waters. At least I'd have one glimmer of optimism to share with General Shady.

Etienne rolled his eyes. "Yes. Would you like me to say it until I'm blue in the face?"

"Does Davin know I don't need oranges?"

Etienne paused. "No… I don't expect he would. He never made it past that stage, so he should have no reason to believe that."

Small mercies...

"Now, if you don't mind, I think it's past time you were on your way." Etienne gestured to the mess of Hades on the floor. "Trouble clearly likes to follow you around. I would feel more comfortable if it followed you away. And if you never returned."

I raised a hand. "One problem with that."

"Oh, for Chaos's sake, what now?" he moaned.

"I'd be out of your hair in a heartbeat, but you've got all your protective mumbo-jumbo," I replied. I took my trusty stick of charmed chalk from my back pocket and waved it at him. At least Blanche hadn't gone riffling through my pants for that. *Ugh...* I had to wonder what else she'd copped a feel of while I'd been out.

"Very well, I'll lift the magical restrictions for a moment or two so you can leave as quickly as magically possible." Etienne huffed an irritated sigh and raised his hands. Bronze light burst out of his palms.

"Wait! We're coming with you!" Melody jumped up, apparently recovered.

I frowned. "You sure?" I had half expected Melody to change her mind after that last fight with Blanche and all the dangers surrounding Davin.

"I doubt Etienne wants us around, either. Isn't that right, Etienne?" Melody smiled sweetly at him.

"You are precisely right. If I had my way, I'd evict every one of you from this island, but Mr. Abara has asked to remain awhile, to discuss some matters that do not relate to map-making, and he seems to be less trouble than you three. I imagine he may stay until next month, when the trials will begin again. As for the others… I'll see how I feel about them in due course," he said stiffly.

"They can take the trials again?" I hadn't expected that, though I supposed there was no reason not to give second chances.

Etienne shook his head. "Ordinarily, no, but Mr. Abara was unfairly thwarted on this occasion, as Blanche utilized his body, and I do feel somewhat responsible. For that reason, I may offer a second attempt to him, though I will be altering the trials, for variety's sake and to prevent advantage."

I supposed this was Etienne's way of dealing with the fallout. If he gave Mr. Abara a second try, then Mr. Abara wouldn't be able to call him out for being unfair or suggest that Etienne's failings were the reason he couldn't complete the trials. After all, if Blanche hadn't stuffed that Ephemera in Mr. Abara's mouth and made him look like her, he might've had time to finish off the poison trial.

"Sounds like the right thing to do." I looked at Melody, ignoring Luke's stern gaze. They might be given that second chance, too, if they asked nicely. "Are you sure you want to come with me?"

"We've got plans, remember?" She flashed a wink.

I smiled, relieved. "That we do."

"Fetch your belongings, then leave," Etienne said firmly.

"On our way, *mon capitan.*" I had nothing to collect, so I waited for Melody and Luke to return with their things.

Two backpacks, and the rest of the challengers later, and we were good to go. The others weren't coming with us—at least, I hoped not—but Melody had apparently fetched them, wanting to have some tearful farewell. Well, there wouldn't be any tears here.

"Later, taters." I gave the Basani twins and Oliver a cursory wave.

"Yeah, good—" Shailene replied, with Fay coming in to finish the job.

"—riddance."

I smiled. "Cheaters never prosper."

"Excuse me?" Shailene frowned.

I had to get one last jab in. "I'm just saying, maybe the two of you should brush up a bit more on your Morse code next time you feel like getting some outside help."

Fay paled. "How do you—"

"Don't say a word," Shailene hissed at her sister.

"Morse code?" Etienne came into the conversation.

I nodded. "You might want to keep a closer eye on what happens outside your protective shield. Morse code, carrier pigeons, Davin Doncaster. It doesn't do you justice, Etienne."

"You little creep!" Shailene looked about ready to lunge, but Fay held her back.

"It doesn't matter now," she muttered.

Etienne scoffed. "I should say it *does* matter, and we will be having words when Finch has finally departed. So much rule-breaking. I will have to rethink everything!"

Oliver laughed at the anger of the Basani twins. "Take care of yourself, Finch. Looks like you'll be leaving a legacy here, even if it's just making these trials harder for everyone who comes after."

"I do what I can." I smiled back at him. "Right then, I'd say it's go time. It's been wild, guys. All the best, and all that."

"That is not how we say goodbye where I come from," Mr. Abara boomed. He pushed through the insipid trio and walked to me, pulling me into a bear hug so tight my rib almost popped.

"It was nice knowing you, Mr. A," I wheezed, as I hugged him back. "I mean it."

"Maybe one day, if I fail again next month, you'll draw a map for me?" He pulled away, eyes glinting with tears.

I nodded. "I'll find you when I'm finished with my stuff."

"Thank you." He scooped me in for another squeeze before

inflicting the same love on Melody and Luke. Luke tried to wriggle free, squirming with all his might.

"Don't fight it." Mr. Abara chuckled. "Embrace it."

With our goodbyes over, and Etienne getting more impatient by the second, I walked to the nearest wall and sketched a doorway, whispering the *Aperi Si Ostium* spell to Kenzie's apartment.

The lines fizzed and crackled as they sank into the wall. Turning the handle, I opened it into Kenzie's apartment and ushered Melody and Luke through. With a quick tip of the proverbial cap to Etienne and the others, I followed, shutting the door behind us. Despite the crapstorm that had gone on at the monastery, I was going to miss that view… and that food.

I'd been ready to shower Kenzie with a truckload of gratitude, but that faded as I stepped into a very weird scene. Kenzie sat on the couch, her shoulders hunched, holding a blue bottle with glowing lights inside. They looked like trapped fireflies.

She jumped in fright, then settled down when she saw I wasn't a robber or worse. "Finch!"

"In the flesh," I replied, trying to be funny. I didn't like seeing her so sad.

"You're back… you're actually back." She looked conflicted, like she wanted to run and hug me or burst into uncharacteristic tears. A few already trickled down her cheeks, but not because I'd scared her. She also looked pretty tired, like she was on her last legs. I glanced at the bottle in her hands.

"Did you Purge?" I blurted. She'd been through a lot, passing messages to me and guiding me through lava-filled underworlds. Was that why she looked exhausted?

"No… it's not a monster." She brushed her fingertips over the bottle, fresh tears brimming in her eyes.

"Then what is it?" I came closer to get a better look. The lights were so beautiful.

"My mom and sister," she said quietly.

"*What* did you just say?" I stared at the bottle, watching the lights swirl in growing horror.

Ryann stepped through the far doorway, looking pale and awkward. And behind her... Erebus himself. I should've been terrified, but that seemed like a waste of energy. What else had I expected?

THIRTY-SIX

Finch

"I have to give you credit for promptness." Erebus sauntered across the apartment, while Ryann made a break for the couch. Our eyes met for a fleeting moment, but I saw only fear. I wondered what she and Kenzie had been through in my absence. Was Ryann part of some deal with Erebus? I'd already come to the sickening conclusion that Kenzie was... but Ryann? It broke my heart to think she might already be in danger.

"You called, I answered. Isn't that how we roll?" I put on a bit of bravado. I didn't want to give him ammunition by showing weakness in Ryann's presence. Maybe she was just helping out. Maybe she wasn't trapped in a deal. And that meant I had to pretend I didn't care.

Erebus grinned eerily. "I suppose it is. What do you have for me? Kenzie returned and said something had occurred, but she didn't know what. Pathetic, mortal fatigue brought her back before she could observe. Humans have a woeful lack of stamina, I must say."

"Nothing wrong with my stamina, thank you very much." I stepped forward, sandwiching Melody between Luke and me. I really hoped she and I had been right about her ability to fly under his radar. "As for what happened… it's not all good. Let me just slap that preface on what I'm going to tell you."

Erebus stiffened. "Start talking."

"We thought we caught Davin's spy, after this blazing fight. She was craftier than expected, though, and she tricked us." I rattled the info off as quick as I could. "She managed to get the map to Atlantis, which I'd gone to all that effort to draw, and took the oranges that helped me draw it. She delivered them to Davin before we could stop her, and Davin did his usual disappearing act."

A literal black cloud collected, swirling over Erebus's head. His eyes glinted furiously.

"But before you start flinging El Niño about, there's one bit of good news." I held up my hands. "I can redraw the map without the oranges, but it just takes a bit longer. Etienne said it'd be a few days instead of an hour or so. If I'm guessing right, the oranges were just a way to open up my mind, and now it's so open, my brain might fall out."

The black cloud evaporated. "Hmm… that doesn't solve every-thing, though, does it?"

"You mean Davin?" My anger flared again at the mention of his name. "Yeah, he's still a massive problem. He has the map now, as well, which means we're racing the clock. And it's going to be tight."

"Do you have a silver lining for me regarding that?" Erebus glared at me.

"Maybe. The map gave the names of places, but it didn't actually define the way into Atlantis. It's more of a suggestion. Davin is still going to have to figure that out." I tried to remember how it had felt when I drew it. "Being the creator of the map, I got the feeling that the overall directions were... I don't know, linked to me somehow. If that's true, that gives us an edge. An overarching sense of the place that isn't on the paper itself."

Erebus pursed his lips. "You'd better hope you're right."

"It was also written in a rare language which Davin will have to decode. It made sense to me while I was writing it, but I don't know what it was." I offered him another silver lining, to try and placate him further.

"It will be Atlantean, I imagine," Erebus replied.

"Right... Atlantean. Of course." I held my nerve. "Can I ask something?"

"As if anything I said would stop you." Erebus sighed. "Go on."

"What's Ryann doing here?" Kenzie had mentioned her while she was parroting around, but she hadn't had the voice-box to give me the details. I didn't want to show Erebus I cared for Ryann, but he'd have smelled a major rat if I'd underreacted about her part in all of this. I hoped I was giving friendly, platonic, "I don't want humans getting hurt" vibes instead of "I'm totally lovestruck and trying to be a hero" vibes.

Erebus shrugged. "That has nothing to do with me. Ask your pet thief."

"I'm nobody's pet anything," Kenzie shot back. Her eyes were rimmed red, as if she'd been crying. That alone made terror pulse through me. Kenzie never cried. At least, I couldn't remember ever seeing it. She was tough as old leather.

"Kenzie?" I prompted, trying to keep cool. I could see she was having a hard time, due to that blue bottle in her hands. *Her mom and sister... were they part of her deal?*

"I needed help," Kenzie said simply. "Ryann came by, and she wanted to be involved in bringing you home. Being human, she was a good choice. She's already agreed to have her mind wiped after, so no harm done."

I stared at Ryann in disbelief. "You agreed to have your mind wiped?"

"It's the only solution," she replied, eyes shimmering. "Anyone else would've been too risky. Don't worry, though. Nobody knows I'm here, or what we've been up to. They're all at the SDC, freaking out about your disappearance from the Jubilee mine."

I shot a hard look at Erebus. "Yeah, thanks for that. You could've at least let me tell everyone I was okay."

"Why would I have done that?" Erebus cocked his head, genuinely baffled. "You're alive, aren't you? That should be enough. Telling them you were okay would have piqued their curiosity and invited them to track you down. That is not conducive to my needs. You will have time for weepy reunions once your work for me is done. A prolonged absence will simply make your return all the sweeter."

"So you haven't pulled these two into a deal?" I pressed.

Erebus's dark eyes glinted. "Kenzie, yes. Ryann, no. Although I could, if you wanted me to."

"No!" The word came slightly too quickly. "Getting Kenzie involved is bad enough. I wouldn't want you accidentally backpedaling on your sentiments about human enslavement."

Ryann managed a very subtle smile in my direction—so subtle it might've been my imagination—though it vanished a split second later. I realized she was mirroring my actions, trying to show nothing on her face in case Erebus picked up on it. But seeing her again and seeing that ghost of a smile... not showing how I felt might've been the hardest task I'd been given thus far. All I wanted to do was vault the couch and hug her. I wanted to kiss her, as well, but that was a no-fly zone. A hug would've been enough.

"Oh my... that *is* powerful." Melody poked her head around my arm. "Such worry, confusion, guilt, and... affection? Hmm, no, that's not it. It feels a bit like love, but love is so complex, and the emotions are so conflicted. Dearie me, they're all fighting for superiority. It's like a battleground of feeling. Ryann, was it? Is that your name?"

Ryann froze. "Uh... yeah. That's me."

"Not now, Melody," I whispered back. Any other moment, I'd have punched the air and beat my chest like a gorilla at the news that Ryann had conflicted emotions about me, and something that felt a bit like love. But with Erebus here, I couldn't enjoy it. It made her vulnerable. I didn't want that.

Melody's cheeks reddened. "Sorry, I did it again."

"It seems you've found a sweet little Empath on your travels." Erebus leered at our party of three. "How charming."

I waited for the Librarian penny to drop, but Erebus didn't seem to notice anything out of the ordinary.

"An Empath?" Ryann choked. "So, she was... reading my emotions?"

"She does that, but it's rusty, so she doesn't always get it spot on. Right, Melody?" I gave her a pointed stare.

She nodded effusively. "Yes, that's true. Sometimes I get people's emotions all mixed up, and they sort of tumble out of my mouth in a jumble of collective feeling. I imagine I got a bit of Kenzie's worry in there, and a bit of Luke. He cares about me, so the affection probably came from him."

Luke's jaw dropped. "Melody..."

"Sorry, Luke." She gave a hopeless shrug. Someone had to be the scapegoat.

"Actually, Erebus, I wanted to ask you something else." I switched the subject before an awkward silence settled in.

He smirked. "Color me intrigued."

I tugged the pendant out of my shirt collar. "I wanted to know why you had me traipse through a literal hell to get this? Don't get me wrong, it came in handy. We wouldn't have known Blanche escaped without it. But why's it so important to you?"

"It's mine," he said with a shrug.

"And?" I already knew most of the story from Melody, but I wanted Erebus to fill in the gaps.

"Etienne acquired it many moons ago, and I knew where he kept it stashed. I wanted it back so it might assist you in your task, though it's good Etienne doesn't know it's missing. He would be beyond livid. It's one of his prized possessions, though he had no right to it." A note of irritation bristled in Erebus's voice. "Although, if you have already used it, you cannot use it again."

I frowned. "How come?"

"It contains the right eye of Hephaestus, plucked by my own fair hands. When detached from the living body, the organism lies dormant—dead, for all intents and purposes. To use it again, it must be imbued with rare ingredients that will resurrect the eye and its properties. It must be 'refilled' each time. A nuisance, I agree, but that is the truth of it." Erebus scanned his nails absently, as if he'd just asked me to pick up some groceries.

"But the Eye belongs to you, right? Don't you have those ingredients?" I replied, annoyed.

"Why would I? I haven't seen that pendant in a long time. I would hardly have the ingredients lying around to resurrect the Eye. If you want to use it again, you will have to find the ingredients yourself. They won't be easy to come by, by any stretch of the imagination, but you are a resourceful and determined creature. I'm sure, if you are eager enough, you will find the means."

You mean you want me to do all the hard work... again.

"Then take it back, if it's just going to be useless." I started to take it off, but Erebus stopped me.

"No, keep it. It is a special item, and you may discover the wherewithal to make it work again, if you are desperate enough." He smiled strangely. "Chaos has a way of putting things in the right places for those curious and willing enough to locate them. Perhaps the ingredients will fall under that category, as Chaos positioned the pendant for you to find. Perhaps Chaos wants you to have it."

Or a Child of Chaos. But why? If it was now just a piece of jewelry, why was it so important that I held on to it? I didn't bother to argue—I just didn't understand his logic.

"Let's not get sidetracked." Erebus straightened, though his posture was as rigid as steel. "For your next endeavor, Finch, you will need all the tricks you can tuck up your sleeve."

I raised an eyebrow. "Are you going to elaborate this time, or leave me hanging?"

He grinned a wolfish grin. "A bit of both, but you should know the stakes in this game. You will proceed, and if you succeed in the next task, Finch, I will consider releasing you from your servitude. However, if you cross me, all your friends will die, and you will follow them. The same goes for Ryann, as she has decided to pledge her allegiance to your cause."

"You leave her—" I started.

"These are the stakes, like them or not." He glowered at me.

I held my tongue, and he turned to Melody and Luke. "The same applies to the two of you. Finch knew better than to make friends in my service. A friend of my servant is nothing but a pawn. Obey the rules, and everyone has the chance to live. Disobey, and everyone dies."

THIRTY-SEVEN

Finch

———————

Your friends will die...

Erebus's ultimatum echoed in my head. I had to succeed in these next tasks, but in order to do that, I needed more information.

I dug my fingernails into my palms, steadying my nerves. "I've got no problem drawing the map again, but I need some clarification. You left me on the edge of a cliff last time, and that's not happening again."

Erebus narrowed his eyes.

This was risky, but I had an ace to play. "You're going to tell me why you want to reach Atlantis and how long you're going to drag me along on this ride."

"You are in no position to make demands of me," Erebus snapped.

Time to play it... "I'd say I am, for once. You've still got strength, sure, but I know you're not nearly as powerful in your shiny new meatsuit. That means you're going to give me some answers, because you can't dangle your 'I'm a Child of Chaos, hear me roar' thing over my head this time."

"Finch… this isn't a good idea," Melody whispered frantically. "Remember what I said."

"Finch is right," Ryann said from the couch, fire in her eyes. "You couldn't have done any of this without us, Erebus."

"Seriously, not a good idea." Melody gripped my shoulder, but I didn't turn.

Luke came to my side. "And if you're involving Melody and me in this, we deserve to know why."

"Give us the truth. Now." My face twisted in anger.

Kenzie stayed where she was, staring at the bottle. "Don't, Finch."

Erebus sighed. For a fleeting moment, it looked like he might relent. But I should've known better. His hands shot up, his palms pushing outward. A thundering wave of pure energy barreled into us. My feet went out from under me as I hit the floor, his furious Chaos pinning me to the ground. Luke and Kenzie collapsed, and Melody fell behind me with a thud. Ryann fell too, pinned to the couch by the same force.

"I will let this attempt at mutiny pass, just this once." Erebus stooped over me, glowering into my eyes. "Get to work and draw me another map. I will be back by the week's end to collect it. You are not my only port of business. I have places to be."

I strained against the invisible grip that held me, but it was too strong.

"But, since you've performed so well prior to this attempt at defiance—here's a morsel for you." He leaned closer, his breath freezing my face. "You're right about Davin needing more than a location, which is why you are still breathing. It means you still have time to remedy your mistake. Getting to

Atlantis won't just require a map. A gateway must be unlocked."

He vanished a second later, his grip disappearing with him. I sat up, dragging in eager breaths. For a slice of truth, he hadn't given me much. Likely, he'd given me all he thought I deserved.

After I rose shakily, I made a beeline for Ryann. She picked herself up, her whole body trembling. I helped her but couldn't stop my lips from flapping. Everything I'd wanted to say came out in a torrent... just not the stuff I *really* wanted to say.

"What were you thinking?" I asked, my hand on her shoulder. "Why didn't you keep out of this? I told you I didn't want you getting near Erebus, and now you're right in his sights. You might as well have painted a giant target on your back."

She stared at me. "I stayed here to help you. You never would have made it through the poison trial if it wasn't for me. I got you that formula. I couldn't have kept out of it, even if I'd wanted to."

I reeled back, surprised.

"I should yell at you for not asking Harley and the others for help. But Erebus would use them, in any and every way possible. I, on the other hand, can have my mind wiped, which will stop Erebus from trapping me in any kind of deal. I can be made to forget as far back as necessary, to prevent it. So, rant all you like about me being a target. I already know the trouble I'm in. I wouldn't leave you to do this alone, even if I *could* go back and stop myself from knocking on Kenzie's door."

I blinked. I didn't know what to say.

"Oh, now you go quiet on me?" She rolled her eyes.

"What do you mean, Kenzie's promised to wipe your mind?" I found my voice.

Ryann's expression softened. "We discussed just pretending to wipe my mind, at first, but then we wondered what might happen if we had to do it in front of Erebus. Kenzie told me she can deposit memories into an animal's mind, as a backup, should it come to that. So, it'd be more of a temporary forgetting situation."

"We just wanted to make sure we had all bases covered." Kenzie leaned across the back of the couch. "And she's right—you'd have been screwed without her. Frankly, so would I. She might be my new SDC favorite."

Ryann nodded. "So, don't harp on about me being involved. We can't change that now. All we can do is look forward."

My gaze fixed on the blue bottle with swirling lights. "That's really your mom and sister?"

Kenzie gritted her teeth. "Yeah."

"Was that part of your deal?" I asked.

"No, it wasn't," she replied bitterly.

"I'm sorry Erebus came to you." I looked at my old friend. "He chose you because you know me. I got you all into this. Who knew a person could be vulnerable by association, huh?"

Kenzie shoved me in the arm. "Don't get all wallow-y. I don't blame you for this. I got something out of it, even though it might not look like it." She nodded to the bottle. "Erebus broke my mom's curse. Yeah, he stuck her in a bottle right after, but that was partially my fault. I ran my mouth, and that was the price I paid."

"Even though we can't bring in the others, we'll make this work together," Ryann chimed in. "What else are friends for?"

Ouch... still in that bittersweet friendzone. They might as well call it the Finchzone.

"How did he cure your mom?" I segued away from my embarrassment.

"We found the source of the curse," Kenzie explained, before diving into a wild tale of portals, blood magic, a surprise uncle stalker, and dilapidated warehouses in rural Shreveport. She also went into detail about how her mom and sister ended up in the bottle. That part made me want to spit in Erebus's face. To have what she'd always wanted in her grasp, only for it to be ripped away… I couldn't imagine the pain. And I hated Erebus all the more for doing that to her.

The bottle on the table drew my attention as the sparks inside expanded rapidly. White light filled the glass. A moment later, the whole thing shattered violently, the shards sending everyone for cover. Everyone except Kenzie. She stared in horror, no doubt fearing the worst.

The two glowing lights spiraled through the air and came to rest on the floor. The light stretched out, growing limbs and solidifying, until two physical bodies lay on the ground. Kenzie's mom and sister, still and unmoving.

Kenzie sprinted to kneel between them, pressing her head to their chests one after the other. "They're breathing! They're alive!"

"They are?" Ryann hurried to help, checking their pulse and airways. No doubt a trick she'd learned from Dr. Feelgood.

"He said our deal would be a one-time thing, and I kept my end of the bargain." Tears trickled down Kenzie's cheeks. Something I'd never get used to. "I guess he kept his. I w-was so sure he would k-kill them."

Ah, Erebus, just when I had you in the unmitigated evil category, you go and do this.

"Are they okay?" Melody approached the two figures.

Ryann nodded. "They're out cold, but alive. We might have to wait until they wake up to find out more, but everything's physically working."

"He kept his end of the deal," Kenzie murmured, clutching her mom and sister's hands. "He kept his promise."

"Why don't we get them into their beds, so they're more comfortable?" Ryann suggested.

I picked up Inez, surreptitiously choosing the lighter party, though their mom looked so frail that there probably wasn't much difference. Meanwhile, Luke scooped Kenzie's mom into his arms. Together, we carried them into Kenzie's mom's room and laid them on the carefully made bed.

"I'll stay with them," Kenzie said. "You guys have a lot to talk about. I'll tell you when they wake up."

I smiled at her. "If you need anything, you know where we are." She didn't hear me—too busy staring at her mom and sister, who were alive and hopefully well. I couldn't blame her. She had them back. That had to mean everything.

We stepped back into the living room.

"If I'm getting out of my deal, I should get started on redrawing this map." I stood to the side of the couch, staring at the broken glass shards.

"Do you know what Erebus meant about the gateway?" Melody sat on the floor cross-legged.

I shook my head. "No idea. The map called it the Gateway between Life and Death, but that doesn't sound like a door you just walk into. If anything, that sounds like a door you stay away from."

"I wonder if it'll become clearer when you redraw the map, like a second draft of a book." Melody tapped her temple in thought.

"Only one way to find out, I guess," I replied, glancing at Ryann. "Before I start ransacking my brain for that map... I want to tell Harley and the others I'm okay, but I don't know if it's a good idea to go to the SDC and tell them face-to-face."

Ryann smiled. "Already handled. Harley got antsy a day or two ago when I hadn't come back—you know how she is. I told her I was with Kenzie, and that she'd gone out to try to find you in

Morph form, so I had to stay to watch her body and family. In a day or so, once you're in the middle of redrawing the map, I'll send her another message to let her know you've been found, and that you're okay. Maybe we could say you're searching for an artifact for Erebus?"

"That could work." I smiled back. She really did have all the good ideas.

"She also said that if you or I need anything, we could call her any time."

I snorted. "Yeah, I know the drill by now."

"If you're going to redraw the map, may I suggest more comfortable surroundings?" Melody cast a conspiratorial look at Luke. "This apartment is nice, but we're all going to need rooms. And I imagine Kenzie will want some privacy, now that her mom and sister are back. As the SDC appears to be out of the equation, why don't I host you all at the Winchester House? It's roomy, and there'll be plenty of quiet spots for Finch to get his thinking cap on."

A gunshot rang out in the street below. Another chorused back.

"You know what, that might not be a bad idea," I replied, with a nervous laugh.

"Scared of a little shootout?" Ryann grinned at me.

I raised a sarcastic eyebrow. "It might interrupt my concentration on redrawing a super-complex map to Atlantis."

"Then it's settled!" Melody chirped. "You're all coming home with Luke and me. And, while you're busy recreating that map, Finch, I'll stick to my promise. I'll rummage through this brain of mine to find a way to free you from Erebus."

Oh Melody... why did you have to say that? Honestly, it felt like tempting fate.

A vast horizon of uncertainty lay ahead of us. Atlantis beckoned, we'd have to race Davin to it, and, just to make things extra difficult, we needed to unlock a gateway we knew nothing about. It seemed insurmountable. But, as I looked at the motley crew around me, I drew some courage from their determined faces. Sure, this journey would be hard and strange and dangerous... but I wouldn't face it alone.

What's next?

Dear Reader,

Thank you for reading *The Lost Map!*

See the details for the next book, *Harley Merlin 12: Finch Merlin and the Djinn's Curse*, after the following announcement:

I'm excited to reveal my brand new fantasy called **Darklight**, which releases September 8, 2019. All-new characters, an exciting, all-new world... I've included a sneak peek of the first 3 chapters in this book, so keep turning the pages if you're curious! (P.S. And I hope you like the cover.)

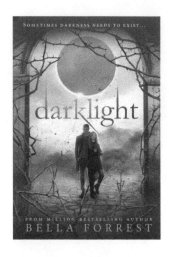

Blurb:

"Vampires don't exist. At least, not anymore..."

I celebrated when vampires were declared extinct.

Those monsters had preyed on humanity for millennia, committing senseless, brutal murders. Like the rest of my colleagues at the Occult Bureau, I looked forward to a world where we could all sleep at night—where constant cover-up jobs were no longer required to keep the public calm and unaware.

But the end of vampires wasn't the end of our problems. It was only the beginning.

Other blood-sucking creatures began to lurk in the night. As soon as I turned twenty-one, I became a ground agent at the Bureau because I wanted—no, *needed*—to join the fight.

And then Dorian Clave burst into my life—turning everything I thought I knew into quicksand. Vampires like him were killers who devoured humanity's inner darkness until shadows danced beneath their skin. Yet there was more to him than that.

He showed me that light cannot exist without the dark, and that trying to fight this balance would have consequences our human minds couldn't even comprehend.

Because sometimes darkness needs to exist.

Darklight Chapter 1

I focused on the five dark silhouettes perched atop the Ferris wheel of Navy Pier Park. The ride was closed for renovation, but crowds of tourists bustled on either side of its boarded-up enclosure: a steady stream of warm targets.

"Team A, be ready," I breathed into my comm, and glanced to my teammates behind me within the wheel's perimeter. Six helmeted heads nodded back, their hands tightening around silver barrels.

"Team B is going in," came the low, confident voice of my brother and second-in-command.

A large helicopter whirred overhead, drawing closer to the wheel and slowly circling it.

I glanced at my watch. "Greta, you should be in position."

"Yup, and waiting for your command, Lyra," came the clipped voice of Team C's leader.

"Start the haze," I replied.

The hiss of decompressing gas filled the cool spring night, and

Greta boomed through a megaphone: "Please evacuate the pier. This is an emergency. Head for the children's museum. You will receive further information there. I repeat, please evacuate the pier."

Beyond the enclosure's walls, a semi-dense fog billowed from the ground, covering the crowd. Shouts and cries rang out, followed by a stampede of panicked footsteps. I refocused on the wheel's apex, ignoring the guilt that panged in my chest at the sounds of alarm and confusion. The smokescreen could be inconvenient and frightening, but ultimately it would prevent the tourists from being targeted.

The silhouettes started shifting, clearly noticing the helicopter and the commotion. I caught the rustle of an opening wing.

Placing some distance between myself and the base of the wheel, I raised my gun, and my colleagues did the same. "All right, Team A. On my count. Three, two, one…"

I aimed for the largest shadow and fired, my entire body vibrating from the force of the bullet's release. I heard the creature's rasping cry, as guttural and grating as a vulture's, followed by four others as my teammates hit their marks.

But the shadows barely jerked. Instead, their massive wings shot out, and they launched into the air so fast that I lost them in the darkness.

It was far from my first encounter with the strange avian species, but I still shivered when the light from the nearby Wave Swinger attraction touched their sleek, ink-black forms. In many ways, each resembled the common stork—long and graceful, with an extended beak, broad wings, and thin, dangling legs. But these weren't the kind you'd see carrying babies on greeting cards.

At least three times larger than the biggest earthly stork, they soared through the sky like dark omens, propelled by unnatural speed and a craving for blood. Their talons resembled an eagle's, while their beaks were sharp and strong enough to puncture metal —they could suckle a human dry in three minutes if they found a main artery.

There was a reason we called them "redbills."

"Zach, get to work!" I yelled.

Gunfire exploded from the helicopter, peppering the birds with artillery. It took more than a single shot to bring them down—even with bullets specifically designed to deliver their death.

"Spread out!" I ordered my team. "Don't let them dive!"

The redbills began to circle the aircraft. The chopper was their greatest source of aggravation, and, judging from the way their beaks angled toward it, they were preparing to strike back. I leapt onto the wheel's frame and pulled myself up the metal skeleton for a better angle. I fired a round at the largest predator.

"Focus on the biggest!" I shouted. "But don't let the others get close enough for a snatch-n-fly." *Rookie mistake of the year.*

My team fired, angry streaks of laser-blue cutting through the darkness. At least ten bullets struck the creature from my team's direction, in addition to a round fired by one of the chopper's gunmen. The redbill's wings beat violently but held its flight. I'd never seen one so large, and with its massive size came extra resilience.

After another onslaught, it finally floundered, an unearthly shriek ripping from its throat and spurts of dark blood raining from its body. It backed down, swerving shakily toward the water at the end of the pier. It would probably be underwater in moments.

My team's focus switched to the next target, a redbill spitting nasty hissing sounds which reminded me uncannily of curses. It darted right up to the aircraft, its powerful beak close to ramming the tail.

Swearing under my breath, I pulled myself higher up the wheel and leaned a little farther out of my comfort zone to get a better shot. I fired, my artillery joining my team's focused stream. Shots pummeled the bird's underbelly, but it didn't falter. It took two intense rounds before it fell away, hissing loudly as it plummeted with a crash into the roof of a snack joint.

"Good job!" I shouted. "Three more to go!"

I released three bullets in swift succession at our third target, then leaned out even farther to attempt a shot at its neck. My finger was on the trigger, pressing—

"Lyra, watch out!"

Something clamped around my waist. My feet slipped from the frame as an impossible force yanked me to the right like I was a rag doll. The gun flew from my hands and the breath left my lungs— then I was flying.

The pier bled rapidly away beneath me, and a mass of shimmering dark water replaced the ground. My eyes stung. I couldn't hear my breathing over the roar of the wind.

I winced as I felt the cold, painful press of armor against my flesh, as if it were closing in on me, and glanced down. Two blood-speckled claws engulfed my waist, the giant talons squeezing tight.

I didn't glance up, because I didn't need to. All but one bird had been in my peripheral vision before I was snatched. Clearly the first hadn't been as injured as it looked—or it had somehow recuperated and flown back with a burst of energy.

Either way, it didn't matter. If this redbill squeezed any tighter, it was going to crush me even before its deadly beak could gouge me.

Those realizations hit me within moments, flying disjointedly through my brain as my reflexes finally kicked in. I yanked my knees toward my chest and fumbled in my boots to reach the knives strapped there. I pulled both out and slashed them across the creature's claws, hoping it would drop me.

Its legs retracted, shifting me into a more vertical position, but the bird's grip barely loosened. Instead, it shrieked and thrust down with its beak, catching my right thigh. My suit dented into the muscle with a pain like being punched, and I gasped in both pain and anger. If it hit the same place twice, it'd cut right through.

Time for plan B. There was no time to replace the blades in their sheaths. I let them fall, then pulled out a small rectangular pulse patch from a sleeve in my suit's right shoulder while keeping my eyes on the creature holding me. As the bird thrust its beak down at me again, I jerked my head to the side, narrowly avoiding a second strike. I slapped the patch onto the bird's right ankle and pressed the center of it, hard. The patch glowed bright blue for a split second, then beeped.

The effect was instantaneous. The creature's talons loosened as the device sent a powerful surge of energy rushing through its body. My suit was specially insulated, but if it were damaged enough, the pulse would've killed me, too. Which was why the patch had been the backup plan.

My stomach dropped as the stunned bird and I hurtled down in freefall, the black, choppy waves rising to meet us at breathtaking speed.

The impact jolted every bone in my body, and though the ice-cold water didn't reach me through the suit, my skin prickled at the instant drop in temperature. I struggled against the instinct to gasp, preserving the precious air within my helmet.

I opened my eyes to a swirling confusion of bubbles, wingtips, and pale shafts of moonlight, and thrashed to put some distance between myself and the redbill. It was still alive, though it seemed to be struggling to get to the surface.

The surges created by its writhing body made it hard to fumble for another patch—especially with my suit dragging me down. I managed to pull one out and kicked back toward the bird. An insanely risky move, but I managed to catch the tip of its wing as it curved through the water. I held on for dear life, slapped the second patch on with my left hand, pressed hard, and let go.

The violent currents subsided a moment later. Lungs burning, I prayed that the redbill was finally dead while I struggled to remove my helmeted suit, the heart-stopping cold engulfing me as I kicked to the surface. The pulse was over, and I didn't have the energy to sustain the suit's weight.

Then again, hypothermia might kick in soon. But I trusted my brother to fish me out before that.

Breaking the surface, I heaved a gloriously deep gasp of air while I reached for my comm and wiped my eyes.

Two redbills hurtled toward me from the sky above, their razor-sharp beaks angled to strike.

My heart lodged in my throat, and in one motion I gasped again and dove hard and fast, bracing myself for beaks to slice through the water. I should've expected them. It was Bill Behavior 101. The birds saw their companion take down prey (or so it looked from a distance), and they wanted a piece of it. A snatch-n-fly had never happened to me before, so I wasn't as prepared as I should've been. Simulations only took you so far.

I wouldn't be able to survive this kind of attack even with a suit. The only idea I had was to get as deep as possible, rely on the water to hide me, and resurface far enough from them to get away, all before my lungs gave out. It sounded impossible.

It never came to that. The redbills didn't follow me. There was a commotion above the surface: two deep, echoing booms followed by a bright flash. Two enormous splashes disturbed the water around me.

I rose back to the surface to breathe, blinking furiously when I reached air. Our aircraft hovered in the sky. A tall, broad form dangled from its extended ladder, a wide-barreled grenade launcher gripped in one hand.

"Lyra!" Zach bellowed, his head swiveling wildly as he scanned the waves.

"I-I'm here," I managed, almost choking on an incoming wave. I raised a hand and flailed.

I could've sworn I heard his sharp exhalation even from this distance, and the helicopter moved closer. Slinging his gun over his shoulder, Zach climbed to the bottom of the ladder as it swung directly overhead. He reached his hand out to me, and I kicked hard to grasp it, allowing him to haul me up.

I swung around to the side of the ladder opposite him, both of us clinging to the same rungs, and met my older brother's brown eyes with a deep inhalation. His lips stretched slowly, the sheer panic I'd seen in him only moments before melting into his signature devil-may-care grin.

"Having fun?" he asked, reaching through the rungs to smooth back my sopping wet bangs.

"A friggin' ball." I batted his hand away and started climbing before I froze in the harsh wind.

Zach followed me up. "Are you hurt?"

"Mostly shaken. A few bruises. I'll survive." My teeth chattered.

"Not gonna lie, you had us all crapping our pants back there. I don't think any of us saw that sucker returning for more... At least all's well that ends well, eh? You gave me a chance to use this baby."

He was referring to the grenade launcher. We weren't supposed to use heavy explosives unless a location was cleared of citizens, which was why we'd started with weaker gunfire at the pier. Out here, though, we could blow things up to our hearts' content.

Something Zach enjoyed more than was probably healthy.

"You're welcome," I replied, my voice dryer than the Sahara.

As I reached the top of the ladder, a pair of strong hands grabbed me and hauled me up. The warmth of the aircraft's interior enveloped me like a sauna. Our captain—and our *real* first-in-command—stood before me, his sharp blue eyes narrowed in scrutiny. But before he or I could say a word, someone attacked my head with a towel.

"Better get you warm fast, Lyra." A familiar voice came from behind me, muffled by the towel scraping my ears as it swiftly transformed into a turban. Hands spun me around until I stood face-to-face with my brother's girlfriend. "Come and get changed," Gina said firmly. Her light amber eyes were concerned and relieved as she took my hand and led me to the back of the aircraft.

"Yes, get changed, Sloane." Captain Bryce's thick Scottish voice sounded from behind. "And then we all need to talk."

"That sounds ominous," I muttered.

"Pretty sure it's the usual drill." Gina sighed.

Passing Teams A and B, I saw that everyone was unsuited and wore relieved expressions, though some had a tinge of thinly veiled amusement, similar to my brother's expression on the ladder. I threw a playful scowl at those faces.

No, it hadn't escaped my crew that their first-in-command (albeit *in training*) had been the one to fall into what our trainers labeled Rookie Mistake of the Year.

But come on. This one had been different. After all those injuries, I couldn't have expected the bird to be that fast or stealthy. I needed more experience with bills of that size.

A set of warm, dry clothes had been laid out in a makeshift changing room. Gina waited outside while I peeled off my wet uniform.

"You got rid of all the birds, right?" I called through the curtain, realizing I'd only seen two come after me, which left one unaccounted for.

"Yeah. Once you got lifted, Captain gave permission to override grenade protocol so we could deal with them faster and get to you. Team C had mostly cleared the area by then, anyway. Pilot's taking us back to base now."

"Good." I caught the reflection of my face in a small mirror while reaching for the dry clothes. My hazel-brown eyes were bloodshot, my usually sun-kissed skin still pale from the cold. But after wringing out my ponytail and pulling on a cozy, fleece-lined getup, I felt much better.

I stepped back into the corridor.

"Now for some hot chocolate," Gina said. She turned and made for the front of the chopper, and I followed, watching the back of her short, blonde bob and ignoring my smirking colleagues on the way back. I sank into the seat next to my brother in the center of the common area while Gina fixed me a drink in the mini kitchen unit.

Captain Bryce's eyes lighted on me from the front of the room, and a moment later, he cleared his throat.

"We'll commence the Stripping, then," he announced, every syllable tart and sharp.

I recoiled involuntarily and felt the whole room do the same around me.

A verbal *stripping* for each of us was what it would be—there really was no other term to describe the *very* detailed performance breakdowns Bryce gave his trainees after every mission. Nor was there any way to prepare for them.

I flinched when his eyes turned to me, but then, apparently changing his mind, he strode to the seats on the far left, the first of which was occupied by Colin Adams, a member of Team B. Bryce stopped less than a foot in front of him and crossed his arms over his chest.

"So, laddie. What made you think popping your first bullet before Zach's command was a good idea? Did you think you'd earn an extra point for enthusiasm? Were you wanting to get ahead of your colleagues? Naturally trigger-happy, are we? Or is there some great intellect in that hard helmet of yours that I'm missing?"

His blue eyes bore intensely into the Chinese-American, whose face flushed furiously.

"N-No, sir. I'm sorry. I was just... nervous," he mumbled.

"You might want to take something for that twitchy finger then, eh?"

Colin nodded, swallowing hard.

Bryce moved along to the next trainee: Sarah Lammers, also of Team B and the youngest of our crew.

"And you, Sarah. What made you think it was a good idea to skip to the loo in the middle of a firefight? Couldn't you have gone a few minutes beforehand? Were you paying no mind to my words before we took off?"

"I just realized that I... really needed to go." The eighteen-year-old's cheeks rapidly turned a blotchy pink.

"You should've done it in your knickers then and changed later. You put your colleagues' lives in danger."

"I-I'm sorry, sir."

"This isn't high school anymore, folks, in case you needed reminding. When you're out on a field mission, your first priority is each other's safety. Anything else is secondary. Your action this time might not have had significant consequences, Sarah, but in even a slightly different scenario, it could have had very serious ones."

Bryce moved on to the next Team B member.

"And you, Grayson. What made you think it was a good idea to keep glancing at Louise while you were supposed to be fighting? Do you have a crush on her or something? Didn't realize the best way to ensure you can *keep* looking at her is to focus on getting the both of you back to the ground?"

A mortified silence fell over the room. Louise's eyes were fixed stiffly on the floor, while Grayson's looked close to popping out. "I-I wasn't looking at her, sir," he stammered. "I'm not sure what you're talking about."

A wily smile cracked Bryce's leathery, suntanned face. He laughed, heartily. "You think I was born yesterday, son? You were ogling her like she were some sorta rice puddin'. Might as well just tell her you fancy her now, so you get it out of your system. Don't want your poor little heart getting us all killed next time we're in the air now, do we?"

Bryce moved on, leaving Grayson looking like he was choking.

The captain worked his way systematically through the rest of Team B's members, breaking down in brutal detail transgressions both small and large—he gave the same attention to both—and thoroughly dismantling all (of the few) objections he received. If he appeared to spare most of my Team A colleagues, it was only because his all-seeing eye hadn't quite extended to the ground where they'd been most of the time. But the closer the captain drew to Zach—and to me—the clammier my hands became around my cocoa. I doubted I'd be exempt.

Zach held his breath when Bryce finally stopped in front of him.

"And you, *Second-in-Command* Sloane." He paused, furrowing his brow, deftly drawing the tension out. "You were a bit too keen to get that grenade launcher out for my liking. Yes, we had an emergency, but if I weren't here, I suspect you would have been looking for any excuse to jump on it. That's not the way of a good soldier. You shouldn't be driven by personal preference in any way, only by what is objectively best for the situation, and of course your superior's orders. You're one of the older folks here, and I expect to see that maturity. I suggest you work on honing your objectivity."

He paused again, then spoke in a lower tone, as though it were meant only for Zach's ears. "And maybe play a bit less with your father's toys, eh?"

"Got it, sir," Zach breathed, visibly flustered, though obviously relieved his reprimand hadn't been worse.

Bryce started to move on, and then his head snapped back. "Also, get a damn haircut. I can hardly see your eyes anymore through that brown mane."

A titter of laughter broke out amongst the group. I couldn't help but smirk too, knowing how much Zach hated the super-close, cropped shaves the captain advocated. His aversion was likely due to the well-meant, yet categorically awful, home haircuts our parents used to give him when they didn't have time to take us on a trip to the salon. Which was most of the time.

"Oh, sir." Zach clutched his chest, feigning hurt. "That's a low blow. *Gina* likes it wavy."

Bryce gave him a stony, narrow-eyed look but said nothing. He continued on to Gina… skipping me entirely.

I frowned, unsure of whether I should believe my luck. *Maybe I'm getting off the hook after all?*

Bryce stared down at Gina intensely, his expression inscrutable. The hum of the aircraft was the only noise around us for several long moments, until he sighed softly.

"Ah, this one. What can I really say? She's an angel." A rugged smile tugged up the corners of his lips.

The room exploded in mock outrage.

"Come on, sir! I'm sure you could think of something!" Zach protested, leaning around me to poke his girlfriend playfully in the shoulder.

"Yeah, Captain. That's just straight-up favoritism!" Roxy complained.

Bryce whirled on the tall, burly girl from my team sitting behind us, his eyes flashing.

"What did you just accuse me of, lassie? *Favoritism*, you say? Aye. Well, I'd *favor* all of you if you showed the same damn work ethic, situational awareness, and efficiency as this young lady. When the rest of you have developed those qualities, I'll throw a bloody rave!"

Gina's freckled cheeks darkened as she tried to roll her eyes and shrug off the attention, while Bryce's gaze roved over the seats, daring anyone to protest. When nobody did, his eyes snapped back to... me.

Crap. I braced myself, tightening my grip around my cup as he returned to stand before me, fearing I *had* gotten my hopes up too soon.

But then I realized he didn't look like he was about to deal out a stripping. If anything, he looked... concerned.

His gaze held mine for several heartbeats, and then he shook his head slowly.

"Eh. Lyra gets a free pass, too. I'll be very honest with you all about something: I didn't see that bastard returning for more either, not after the battering we gave it. I've never encountered a bill as tough as that."

Vindicated! I felt like saying the word aloud and giving a little fist pump, but the seriousness of our captain's expression stopped me.

"Do you think it was just a one-off?" I asked, eyeing him. "Some genetic fluke?"

Bryce shrugged. "I sure hope so. Definitely wouldn't do us any good if they started breeding stronger."

He glanced around at us darkly, and I knew what he was implying. The Bureau was stretched to the max for personnel as it was.

There'd been an increased number of redbill sightings over the past year, around North America particularly, for reasons that were still unclear to the Bureau. It was as if the birds had spiraled into a breeding frenzy. Recruitment agents, my mom among them, were working overtime to keep up with the demand for new officers, and younger, less trained recruits were starting to be allowed into ground missions as a result. Which explained our motley crew.

Some state and city departments simply didn't have enough people. Our branch here in Chicago, for example, sometimes had to send out squads as far as Oklahoma to help deal with threats. It was lucky that tonight's sighting had been local… well, not so lucky for the revelers of Navy Pier Park.

A secondary, albeit unrelated, factor didn't help the Bureau's staff problems. The demand for soldiers, and law enforcement workers in general, had grown slowly but steadily over the past half-decade or so, thanks to a slight but continuous rise in the regular human crime rate. It meant there was a smaller pool of officers the Bureau could recruit to their specialized force, since more soldiers were out dealing with ordinary human problems.

I just hoped things would smooth out sooner or later, for all of our sakes.

"*Anyway,*" Bryce said, casting another strong look around the room. "Don't any of you take this as an excuse to start whining. Even a bird thrice the size of that one is nothing like the bloodsuckers *we* used to hunt."

"I find that hard to believe," Roxy mumbled from behind. *Too loud.*

Bryce spun on her again. "And what was that, my wee lass? Care to speak a bit louder, so we can *all* hear your precious thoughts?"

Roxy gave a soft sigh. "I find that hard to believe," she replied sullenly. "There's no way vampires were as strong or dangerous as these freaking monsters."

Bryce's lips formed a hard line. "Mm-hmm. And what, precisely, makes you say that?"

I turned over my shoulder to glance at Roxy's half-flustered, half-incredulous expression. She didn't know how wrong she was.

"I mean, how could they even compare?" she started. "Vampires didn't fly, for one thing, so it couldn't have been half as difficult to catch them. They had small fangs, compared to huge, snapping beaks. They kept way more to themselves, too, from what I've heard, and weren't a big threat to public places. Plus—"

"And what about their brains?" Bryce interrupted.

Roxy stuttered. "Their... brains?"

"Their brains," Bryce repeated, his eyes widening.

Roxy's brow furrowed. "Well, yeah. Vampires were smarter. But still—"

"Exactly." Bryce took a step back, shoving his hands into his pockets. "Vampires were cunning devils. They could outsmart a human in almost any situation, and usually the only way to match one was to put many human minds together. Bills are just dumb brutes, and any comparison is frankly offensive."

He gave an almost wistful sigh and sank back into his chair, facing us. His eyes grew distant.

"Honestly, if vampires hadn't been such a menace, I would've been sad to see them go. Watchin' them was like... pure poetry in motion... put any martial artist to shame. They could distract you by just the sheer skill and speed of their movement, and the way they used your own strength against you, you'd barely realize you were bleeding until it was too late."

He tugged at his collar and pulled it down to reveal the beginning of a massive scar on his upper chest.

"Aye." He grinned, watching our stunned faces. "This was done with my own weapon. But I'm not going to lie. As risky as the job was, it was more of a thrill hunting a vampire. You never knew what could happen. Would they lure you into a trap? Attack the moment they saw you, or wait a while, and lull you into a false sense of security? Or maybe they'd do neither and instead slip away into the night, let you try to trail 'em some more until you tired out... But they were worth the chase. And when you finally caught one? Oof. The thrill was indescribable."

He finished with a crooked smile, and the whole room stared in rapt silence; even Roxy's brow had softened.

I'd heard plenty of tales of vampire chases before, but I'd never seen this side of Bryce. He spoke with such awe of the creatures that had snuffed out so many innocent lives, it was almost hard not to wish I'd seen one, too... even if they were the reason my uncle needed a permanent walking aid.

After all, Zach and I had grown up expecting to track the predators, just like our parents had done in their early careers. But by the time I turned sixteen, vampires had disappeared.

"It *is* weird how they died out so quickly," Zach mumbled, as if he'd followed the same line of thought.

Bryce leaned back in his seat, nodding slowly. "Aye. It was unexpected for a lot of us. Guess there couldn't have been as many as we thought there were to begin with, and once all countries started cooperating, we managed to drive them to extinction. Amazing how destructive we humans can be when we put our minds to it." He chuckled, though it sounded halfhearted.

"Where do you think they came from, Captain?" I asked. The origin of vampires was more of a mystery than their disappearance, and everyone and their mother had an opinion about it. I'd never heard Bryce's before, and I was genuinely curious.

The captain puffed out his cheeks. "I'm not sure what you're expecting to hear from me, when an entire research department couldn't come up with anything better than 'they just existed'. The honest answer is I don't know. But if you held me at gunpoint, I'd probably say the same—they just always existed. A so-called 'supernatural' creature living among us, perhaps since the dawn of time, for one reason or another. Who knew? Bram Stoker was on to somethin'."

I nodded, having basically come to the same conclusion. Some folks liked to swerve toward fictional vampire lore and present theories about vampires' ancestors having once been humans who went on to—*somehow*—develop unnatural abilities. But the science simply didn't back that up. Vampires had been caught, dissected, and studied in labs, and there was no proof that they were ever part of our gene pool, or that they could spread their condition to others. They actually showed no genetic commonalities with any earthly creature. Which led to *others* suggesting they could be a species from another planet. I wasn't even going to get into that.

"And what do you think about the redbills' origin?" Grayson muttered. "Given there's no record of their existence anywhere up until half a decade ago."

We all turned to glance at the blond man. It was the first time either he or Louise had spoken since Bryce's... exposé on Grayson's feelings—a fact that the captain's sardonic smile not-so-subtly acknowledged.

"Aye," Bryce replied. "We all thought vampires were an anomaly, the only species of their kind out there, until the redbills came along... right around the time vampires stopped showing up. I'm not going to *try* to speculate about that one. All I know is they're somehow made of the same stuff as vampires. Not natural."

"Do you believe in reincarnation, sir?" Zach asked.

My brother's smile clearly indicated that it was a joke, but Bryce's expression looked oddly strained.

"Not sure about that, lad. But karma, maybe? I mean, it is odd, isn't it, that we get rid of vampires, only to be saddled with this other huge, heaving problem." He cast Roxy a look. "Not that it's necessarily of the same caliber. But it's a problem nonetheless. And it appears to be getting worse."

He finished on a quiet note that seemed to infect the room. My brother and I exchanged glances, and the tension in Zach's jaw reflected what I felt in my gut. *Hopefully not too much worse.* Or at least, not too quickly. We struggled to keep pace as it was.

Unlike vampires, redbills could not be concealed from the public. Vampires had been discreet, and they had always attacked in seclusion—one on one. They rarely left witnesses. That had been the government's major advantage in preventing the mass fear and panic among citizens which would surely have followed a declaration that vampires walked among us.

With the redbills, the authorities had been able to get away with explaining them as an abnormal breed of stork, a strange fluke of nature—possibly even the result of past nuclear plant accidents— and that research was ongoing to determine their origin and the best way to subdue them. But if they bred too much and attracted too much attention, that explanation would become harder and harder to swallow. Our saving grace was that they hadn't spread to other countries yet—or at least, there'd been no reports.

We needed to keep it that way.

"Landing in five." The pilot's announcement broke through the quiet.

I shifted in my seat, wanting a distraction, and glanced out the nearest window as the aircraft tilted. I watched the thousands of lights of downtown Chicago rise to meet us. The evening felt so clear and calm, so comfortingly *normal*, that if it weren't for my still-damp hair and sore thigh, it would be hard to believe we'd just been battling monsters.

This was what we were fighting for, I reminded myself. A world where we could all sleep peacefully at night, where families could vacation without fear, where couples could enjoy their late-night dates and children could play out on the streets. *The world as it should be.*

I was among the first to unbuckle when the aircraft touched down on the roof of our base. I stood up slowly, testing out my right leg, and winced slightly. It hurt more than when I'd sat down, probably due to swelling where the beak had caught my suit. I was going to have one ugly bruise. But it could have been a lot worse. Like, no-leg-at-all worse.

"You okay?" Gina asked from beside me, obviously noticing my grimace.

I nodded. "Yeah. I can still walk and run. I just need some rest."

I moved toward the door, wanting to get ahead of the crowd. I was definitely looking forward to resting. It wasn't that late, but my little swim had taken more out of me than I'd realized.

The door drew open, letting in a chilly waft of air, and I was on the verge of leaving when Bryce called, "Hold up, folks."

We all turned to see him staring down at his comm screen.

"We've just had another summons," he announced.

My breath caught. "Another one?" Our team had never had two calls in a single day.

"In Chicago?" Sarah asked incredulously.

"Nope. Washington, D.C. They're short-staffed because New York State borrowed from them. They're requesting any recruits available." Bryce glanced up at us. "Satellites flagged an unnatural frequency at a closed church, and the D.C. chief needs a team to investigate. Suspicion is there's a bird trying to nest there, because it hasn't posed a threat yet."

"And we have to leave *now?*" Roxy asked.

"First thing in the morning," Bryce replied. "They're keeping an eye on the building for the moment, but I need you all here by four a.m. sharp. Go to bed as soon as you get home, and you'll be bright and fine." His face twitched in a dry smile.

I glanced at my watch—*21:45*—before Zach grabbed my arm and pulled me down the stairs after him.

"No rest for the wicked, eh?" Gina murmured from behind us as she followed.

No… No, I guess not.

Darklight Chapter 2

Captain Bryce gave us his usual cold "goodbye" grunt as my team-mates and I hopped from the chopper to the air pad. He stayed behind to discuss the next morning's strategy with the pilots.

We entered the Bureau through sliding steel doors and were greeted by familiar obsidian-black walls. The tired shuffling of our boots echoed from the vaulted ceilings. After a night like this, the main hallway always seemed never-ending.

Everyone stayed silent until we reached the elevators. Roxy hit the down button.

"Have a good night," I called in her direction.

"Yeah, sweet friggin' dreams," she muttered. The rest of the crew shook their heads, trying to laugh through their sighs.

As they filed into the elevator, my brother, Gina, and I split from the group, heading toward the giant metal door that always reminded me that my bed was close.

Zach pulled his ID from his suit's breast pocket and pressed it against a dark gray pad on the wall. Three low beeps rang out, and a *clunk* sounded through the hall as the door unlocked. I reached to pull down the handle, but Zach slapped my hand.

"Take it easy, gimp." He grinned.

I rolled my eyes while he pulled the massive door open, and we started down a much smaller hallway into the residential staff apartments. *I wonder if Mom and Dad are still awake.*

The narrow white walls of the base's family housing were lined with sporadically placed numbered doorways. Zach and Gina pulled ahead of me. Whether I wanted to admit it or not, my pace was a little slower than usual.

Gina glanced back over her shoulder. "Want an arm?"

"I'm good," I assured her.

We finally reached 237. Zach once again pulled out his ID, pressed it to the pad, and opened the door to our family's apartment. I faintly smelled casserole. Zach made a beeline for the kitchen and started making himself a plate.

"I'll have a bite and then head to my apartment, if there's enough," Gina said, unlacing her boots beside me in the entryway.

"Mom always makes a full tray. Lyra, you want a plate?" Zach called.

"Not really hungry," I said, carefully bending over to untie my own boots.

Gina eyed me. "You need to lie down."

I nodded to acknowledge her concern but said nothing—I didn't want her going into mothering mode.

She half-smiled. "You and your brother. So damn stubborn. I'll see you at the ass-crack of dawn, Lyra," she said, accepting the plate of casserole Zach handed her.

I waved over my shoulder as I headed toward my bedroom, assuming my parents were asleep.

I was aware that most twenty-one-year-olds in America didn't live with their parents, but most people in America didn't grow up as second-generation OB agents. Bureau base housing was limited, so until Zach and I had families of our own, we shared quarters with our parents. Honestly, we were all so busy that we didn't see much of each other on a daily basis.

Halfway down the hall, I noticed a light shining under the closed living room door—and heard voices.

The sound of my mother's sharp tone halted my breath and footsteps. She rarely spoke above a gentle hum, albeit a hum that commanded respect. When I could hear her through a closed door, something was wrong.

I couldn't make out her words, so I inched closer. I heard my father's voice interject, lower and slower than my mother's, but just as severe. I held my breath, now able to make out the words.

"I don't understand how the Board hasn't taken action on this yet," my mom snapped. "It's unacceptable. This is not how the Bureau is supposed to conduct itself."

My heart jumped at another familiar voice, calm and thick as caramel. Uncle Alan. "Don't be so quick to judge, Miriam. We're dealing with something we don't understand yet."

It was hard to hear what they were saying over Zach and Gina chatting in the kitchen. *Quiet. Quiet!* I squeezed my eyes shut and focused on the living room door—after all, it wasn't like I could shush my brother and his girlfriend so I could snoop better.

Uncle Alan dropped his voice, and Zach's fork scraping his plate from the kitchen drowned out my uncle's words. Several moments passed, but I remained frozen.

My mother gasped. "Unbelievable." My heart pounded so loudly in my ears that her higher timbre was the only thing I could distinguish.

Uncle Alan raised his voice an octave in response to my mother's concern but then cleared his throat and returned to his hushed tone. "These are the facts we have. Like I've explained, even these vague details are strictly secret."

My mother didn't like her brother's response, apparently, because her voice peaked again, cracking this time. "People's lives are at stake! How could the Bureau keep something so dangerous a secret?! You and your damned red tape—papers and signatures aren't more important than human lives!"

This time my father joined in. "How many more soldiers need to throw themselves at these monsters before we get this under control? These are our *children*—your niece and nephew, Alan."

"Miriam, Russell," Uncle Alan replied calmly. "We all know why the Bureau has to do this. Something like this getting out could be catastrophic. I understand your concern. But letting this information reach anyone else's ears is out of the question. There's a reason it took me so long to tell *you*. And that only happened because of your promotion last month, Russell."

I bit my lip, and my eyes widened. My father was the new Head of Defense Technology.

"You are the only ones not on the Board who know anything about this at all," my uncle offered.

A heavy silence fell in the room. I started to feel lightheaded from holding my breath.

Uncle Alan continued, his usual sweetness now turned slightly rigid. "Stability and calm are the most important things for the Bureau, this country—and the globe—right now."

Guilt knotted my stomach. I was beginning to get uncomfortable about eavesdropping for so long.

I cleared my throat and knocked softly on the living room door. My mother's voice became a hurried whisper, and my father called out, "Yes, we're in here."

I pushed the door open to reveal three weak attempts at smiles. "Hi, everyone," I said cautiously.

My uncle sat in the armchair to my left, across the coffee table from my parents. His platinum hair was slicked back in its usual fashion, his trim gray suit predictably impeccable, even at this late hour. He whisked two papers from the coffee table and into the depths of his shiny leather briefcase, but not before I recognized the emblem in the header—Bureau non-disclosure paperwork.

"Lyra! We weren't expecting you home so early," he said warmly, and I couldn't help but smile back at him. No matter how tired I was, I always had extra energy for Uncle Alan. "A successful operation tonight, I hope?" he asked, wavering slightly as he stood with the help of his cane.

The memory of crashing into frigid water jolted my mind. "Mostly."

My parents weren't as good as my uncle when it came to pretending nothing was wrong. I met their worried eyes, looking at each of them in turn. "Is everything okay?"

"Yes, Lyra, we're fine," my mother said, her usual tenderness returning. She smoothed over her pixie cut with a hand. "Come and sit with us."

I moved to join my parents, teetering lightly—but mostly from exhaustion at that point.

My father eyed me with concern. "Are you hurt?"

"Nah, she's just being a baby." Zach followed me into the living room. "Big Bird got the best of ya tonight, didn't he?"

I shot him a glare and eased onto the couch. My muscles sighed with relief as I sank into the cushions.

"Lyra enjoyed her first snatch-n-fly tonight, didn't you, sis?" Zach smiled.

"Are you okay?" my mother asked.

"Oh, she's totally great." Zach leaned a hand nonchalantly on the back of Uncle Alan's chair. "She and birdie even went swimming together!"

If my knives had still been attached to my leg, they would've gone flying. I kept my eyes locked on my smirking sibling, glaring the daggers I couldn't throw, while I explained to my horrified parents. "We'd hit the target multiple times, and I thought it was eradicated, but it bounced back and caught me off guard. It was the biggest redbill I've ever seen."

My parents tried to stay stoic, but they exchanged a glance. Zach's grin faded, and his eyes darkened. Uncle Alan wrung his hands.

"I need to get to bed," I said, breaking the sudden quiet I'd created.

"The Scottish ogre is calling us in at 4 AM," Zach said, stretching his arms toward the ceiling.

"Special summons in D.C., apparently," I added, rising from the couch.

My mother sighed. "It's always something these days."

"Get plenty of rest, you two," Uncle Alan said.

I smiled again—entirely for my parents' sake this time. They suddenly looked fragile... older than I'd ever seen them, and so much smaller than they did when addressing soldiers and coworkers at the Bureau.

I steadily lumbered down the hall to my bedroom. The mere sight of my bed was pure bliss. The weight of the day had finally taken over. I was thankful that the ache from my leg had started to quiet.

Too exhausted to change, I slid into bed in my uniform fleeces. I'd had to sleep in much less comfortable uniforms, that was for sure.

But I didn't sleep. All I could manage was staring at the ceiling, counting the circles of my ceiling fan and listening to the nighttime hums of our residence. Every time I closed my eyes, I felt the redbill's claws wrapped around my body, saw the dark feathers looming as I tilted my head back... and all I could hear was my mother's protest. *Papers and signatures aren't more important than human lives...*

I didn't know exactly what I'd overheard in the living room, but something didn't feel right.

Darklight Chapter 3

Our seats vibrated as the chopper carried us over the still-sleeping territory below. The tiny window behind my head offered only dimly lit veins of highways and the deep violet and bronze of sunrise.

We'd transferred off the Bureau plane outside of D.C. and would only be in the chopper for a few more minutes. The team was in our usual circle, though somewhat cramped in the smaller aircraft, listening silently as Captain Bryce gave us the rundown. His tone was sharp—even at six o'clock in the morning.

"We'll split into three teams once we reach our destination," Bryce barked. "All three teams will be on the ground; Teams A and B will enter the site, and Team C will be posted outside the church. Team C—Sarah, Grayson, that's you. If anything comes in or out of that church, it's your problem."

I glanced around, finding most eyes glued tensely to the chopper's floor. Grayson's knee was bouncing.

"Team B. Zach, Colin, Roxy, Louise, Greta. You will split into groups, enter the church from the west windows and main door, and cover the first floor." Bryce pulled on his gloves as he walked around the circle. "You will not leave that floor unless I *tell* you to. Only necessary use of comms inside the site. I shouldn't hear more than a mouse fart in my earpiece. I'll be on the floor with you, so any chitter-chatter will answer to me—and I promise you'd prefer the redbill."

We rarely had the captain on the ground with us. Sweat dampened my palms, and I hadn't even heard my station's details yet.

"Team A." Bryce paused to clear his throat, his icy eyes glancing down momentarily. "Gina, Lyra. You two will enter through the east wall's window. The site has multiple levels, and you will be the first to head up. Silence is golden, lassies."

I nodded, holding Bryce's gaze. Gina sat to my left, and I watched her hands clench.

"The main floor is somewhere around thirty-thousand square feet," our captain continued. "We haven't placed the target yet, so step lightly. Redbills' sense of hearing isn't nearly as sharp as their eyesight, which is why I'm permitting an airdrop. But don't take anything for granted once we're in a closed space."

The head pilot's voice came through our earpieces. "Three minutes to site."

"Three minutes and fifteen seconds to drop," Bryce replied into his comm.

Zach cracked his knuckles from across the circle.

"Once we locate our target, you know what to do." Bryce tightened his artillery belt. "Safeties off when your little feet hit the ground. Understood?"

"Yes, Captain," the entire crew resounded loudly.

Bryce moved to the cockpit. Our comms were silent. He'd

turned them off, but I could see his lips moving rapidly as he gesticulated to the pilots.

For the short time until the drop, our eyes remained locked on the tips of our boots. No one said a word. The droning of the chopper intensified, and my stomach lurched as the craft descended. I closed my eyes. *Breathe.* At least my thigh was feeling much better than last night. The rest had done it a lot of good.

I glanced up briefly in the silence and caught Zach looking at me. His mouth formed a small smile. He winked.

"Line up, children," Bryce snapped, returning from the cockpit. "Look alive, why don't ya?"

The group bolted from their seats, the sound of our steps blending with the chopper's hum. Gina and I locked eyes, then shoulders. We made our way to the open door. The tops of trees became clearer in the now-pale-violet morning light.

The church came into view from the doorway, just to the north. Its spire had shattered; what remained was a spike of pale gray wood pointing at the sky. The shingles were scattered about the roof, some stacked together like forgotten piles of papers. The air battered my cheeks. The thrumming of the blades above battered my eardrums.

"Thirty seconds to drop!" Bryce's voice bit through my earpiece.

I looked over my shoulder. The teams were paired and lined up behind us, facing the exits. I braced my weapon tightly against my side.

"Ten seconds!" the captain shouted behind me.

The main doors of the church were visible below, and the chopper now hovered in place just behind the trees encircling the building. Someone dropped the two lines on each side of the doorway, and they slithered down toward the ground.

Gina reached over and gripped my arm for a split second.

"Drop, teams!"

Sucking in a breath, I crouched alongside Gina, gripping my line, and the chopper floor disappeared from beneath my feet. Weightlessness overtook me. The speed blurred my vision, and the friction of the line whizzing through my gloves warmed their damp fabric.

Treetops surged closer, then branches, trunks—ground—

Gina and I hit the soil in tandem. We dropped our lines and stepped away silently, unlocking the safeties on our guns and moving into position. My peripheral vision showed the other teams landing behind us and filing toward the church. The building's walls may have been painted once, but all that remained were thin streaks of gray on the rotting wooden boards. It was taller than I'd expected, its roof reaching far above us amongst the treetops.

Gina led the way. The back window—our entrance—was at shoulder level. Pinecones crunched under my boots, so I lightened my steps.

We reached the window. Gina eyed the windowsill—no glass left, totally busted out—and swiftly lifted herself up and through the flaking wooden frame. I waited three beats and followed suit, heaving myself inside.

I landed quietly on the old floorboards. In front of me, Gina scanned the room, gun butt against her chest. The edges of the main sanctuary were entirely dark. The altar's giant cross loomed above us from the back wall. The window we'd entered was one of two lighting the room—crisscrossed boards covered the others, except for the one Zach and Roxy were crawling through on the west wall. Dust floated through the few beams of light we had.

Must and earthy mildew filled my nose. The now-distant and

barely audible murmur of the chopper was the only thing I could hear besides my clipped breathing. Most of the pews were in scattered pieces, and old hymnals were strewn between them.

I followed Gina as she crept toward the altar. We knelt on either side of it, squinting through the haze. *One, two, three, four...* I counted my teammates as they shifted through the darkness, covering the perimeter of the sanctuary. Everyone was accounted for. Bryce's behemoth frame stood beside one of the massive, cracked pillars. I couldn't see his mouth moving, but I heard the gravel of his whisper in my comm: "Team B, say the word when all four corners are covered. Team A, stationary."

Zach and Roxy scouted the west wall, and I could see Colin and Greta securing the darkness framing the main door. I glanced above, mentally repeating my next orders. *You will be the first to head up.*

The vaulted ceiling was so tall I couldn't tell where the walls ended and it began.

"Team A, have you located the stairs?" Captain growled.

"Stairs near corner of altar and west wall, confirmed," Gina whispered. My eyes darted to the narrow staircase.

"Ground floor secure," Zach said softly in my ear.

"Right. Team A, visually secure the stairs. Then head up. If I've got your bearings right, there should be a balcony beyond that," Bryce instructed.

There wasn't much visibility up the staircase, but the next landing was clearly far up. Some of the slatted steps were cracked... some not there at all. Gina's gaze caught mine, and she nodded to reassure me.

"Stairs clear. Light steps, Lyra," Gina breathed over the comm, holding my eyes with hers.

"Team A, move up," our captain grunted.

Gina instantly responded, stepping delicately as she ascended. I left several steps between us as we climbed. My eyes bounced between her feet and the steps emerging from the dark above us.

A step groaned under Gina's left foot, and we instantly froze. She looked back at me, a warning to be careful. I nodded. Despite my care, the same step creaked under my weight, but it held.

Cobwebs latticed between the railing and the steps. I glanced at them for just a second, and I heard a step whine and then snap —*crack*—Gina's right foot was falling, and she was going down with it.

I snatched the back of her belt and threw my weight back as hers pulled me forward, my muscles straining. The broken wooden step clattered on the floor below, echoing off the east wall.

"*Freeze!*" Bryce hissed in my ear.

Gina's sharpened breaths were the only sounds that followed. I held on tightly to her belt; she gripped the railing, taking most of her weight off me. Her eyes closed in relief, but only briefly. She flashed a thanks to me with a glance. All remained still.

"Team A. Secure?" It was Zach.

"Secure," Gina replied.

"Continue," Bryce ordered.

Gina exhaled and turned back up the staircase. Shaking just slightly, I found my breath and followed her.

We covered over a dozen more steps, accompanied by one or two more creaks but thankfully no more collapses, until we finally found ourselves entering what looked like an attic—not a balcony. There were scattered wooden pillars, piles of old furniture, and a window in the wall far ahead. Another glowed behind us. The windows' light haloed above us from the opposite ends of the room, relieving the gloom just a little. We moved off the stairs and carefully tested the wooden floor with our feet.

"Next floor confirmed, Captain," Gina said quietly on her comm. "It's an attic. Moving forward."

Something pale moved in the corner of my eye and I jumped. The tip of Gina's gun darted toward it. We halted. It didn't move again. I squinted, making out a sheet draped on an old table. Inches of dust covered every surface. It fluttered again in some unseen draft.

I nodded to Gina to move forward. *False alarm.*

We silently passed other tables and chairs, all enveloped in cobwebs. The attic was dead quiet. We peered around, our forms casting even more shadows in the extending darkness.

"Western stairwell visually confirmed," Zach whispered.

"Zach, Roxy, take the stairs. Hopefully you can confirm a balcony," Bryce said.

Gina and I planted our feet and held steady. The room was motionless, soundless. If there was a redbill here, it was the quietest I'd ever encountered, that was for sure.

Our eyes continued scanning the dark. I reached up and slowly picked a spiderweb off my chin.

"Balcony confirmed," Zach murmured over the comm. "No movement."

Gina stepped forward, and I looked behind us for any stirring. Still nothing.

She signaled me with her hand, and I followed her deeper into the thick beams and abandoned furniture.

Thwap, thwap.

The sound tore through the silence. Gina and I spun toward it. I planted my heels to secure my stance, the slick metal of the trigger under my finger.

A sudden, bright thrashing and whirling engulfed Gina's head. I jerked back and adjusted my aim, trying to get a bead on the cloud flailing above Gina's shoulders—until I heard a quick, flustered cooing.

"Pigeon," Gina gasped. She swatted at the bird, and it tumbled down to the wooden floor then bobbed off, its feathers mussed, vanishing into the gloom.

I pulled the tip of my weapon back up and away from my teammate, my hand instinctively pressing against my breastbone. My heartbeat throbbed in my ears. *Holy hell…*

The two of us stayed there for a moment, catching our breath. In the resumed quiet, we peered around for any other movement.

Zach spoke again. "Moving to western balcony."

After scouting the rest of the room, Gina gestured toward the staircase. "Attic clear," she whispered into her comm.

I watched my feet as I followed her, to avoid kicking a table leg or brushing any dust-choked sheets. I glanced around in search of the staircase we'd come up, when Gina stopped abruptly. I nearly walked into her and quickly side-stepped. Then I saw why she'd stopped.

A figure stood directly before the staircase, blocking our only way out.

As I stared, I realized I could barely call it a figure—it was more a blanket of obscurity. No clear shape to the body. An empty space of jet black, only finding form against the slightly subtler grays of the room it stood in.

My eyes strained to trace the outlines of the figure's shadowed face.

"Hello?" I called out, my voice reverberating through the attic, seeming to fill every jagged crack and crevice.

Silence. Stillness.

That was the only response from the living shadow in front of us.

The hair on the back of my neck rose as I felt a chill, thick and contagious. It spread down my spine, gliding through my extremities with a frigid wake. Still, I gave a small wave, beckoning Gina to follow me forward.

Thoughts tumbled through my mind. *It's not a redbill. That much is obvious. And we're highly trained. If it's a squatter, or some psycho, we can defend ourselves.*

Not to mention, this was our only way out.

Gina stayed two steps behind me as our boots crept closer to the figure and our exit point. A few feet away, I saw a face begin to take shape amidst the darkness of its boundaries. *His* boundaries, I realized. And his eyes... My heart froze in my chest. Something about his eyes was so familiar, yet so foreign, that I felt my brow furrow, my mind scrambling to understand. I couldn't make out their color from here, but there was... something about them.

I felt my body tense suddenly—some primordial instinct that somehow pieced the puzzle together and hardened before my brain had a chance to do the same.

Then his hands were on me.

And despite his impossible speed, I felt it happen in slow motion. Like an almost-lucid dream, one where I was a full participant but couldn't respond fast enough. My gun flew from my hands and clattered to the ground, the sound echoing off the thick, wood-slatted floor. My comm was ripped from my ear and my body was heaved over his shoulder.

In the time it took me to gasp, he crossed the room. So light and fast it felt like we were floating, then, without warning, angling upward. I saw it in a blur—the window. He was *scaling the wall to the window.* I regained my voice, shrieking frantically into the attic space, and heard Gina's voice yelling back. A gunshot rang out, but the man didn't falter. My screams grew stronger as Gina's grew farther away, and I was plunged into empty space with only the body beneath me to cling to.

We were freefalling. As we plunged toward the ground, he made a sound—a sharp, guttural growl—and a huge shape appeared out of nowhere.

Broad wings and thin, dangling legs. An extended beak that had featured in my nightmares a few hours before. A redbill.

It swooped under us, catching us with a heavy shudder as the man straddled it and hauled me in front of him.

What is happening?

I didn't have time to ask myself anything beyond that. To think. To wonder. I barely even had time to breathe. Because a moment later, the redbill accelerated to cut through the air like a torpedo. I knew redbills could fly fast. But this—*this* was beyond comprehension.

The world screamed by in a blur, too fast and jumbled to be anything but a mix of faint colors and the meshing of space and time. My helmet detached from my suit and I gasped, choking on the wind. I felt the skin on my face being pulled backward. My eyes burned. And I clutched his cloak with everything I had.

Until, at some point, I realized we'd slowed. We weren't clipping through space anymore. I blinked, willing my dry eyes to moisten enough to function. To figure out where we were and what was happening. The surrounding shapes took form just as the redbill landed with a brain-rattling jolt.

Cliff, I grasped. *We're on a cliff.* My senses darted in every direction, trying to take everything in. Gray skies splayed out in front of me. Clouds rolled and tumbled in the sky, churning—matching how my stomach felt, tossing and twisting inside me. I heard the roaring of waves as they crashed into the cliff, salt spray cutting up into the air.

The man slid gracefully off the bird. The wind billowed through his dark cloak, causing it to flare behind him. He turned to me, and I remembered what I'd pieced together before he'd grabbed me. Before the power and momentum and speed swept all thoughts from my brain. My eyes flew to his face. To his *eyes*. Wondering if what my instincts had jumped to in the milliseconds before he snatched me could possibly be correct.

The wind swept through his dark hair, and strands of it skated across the pale, yet strangely shadowed flesh of his forehead. I gasped as my gaze caught his once more. I could see his eyes better now that we were free from the dimness of the church attic. Yes, they were blue. But not *just* blue. They were an icy, crystalline blue that seemed to shift and melt in his very irises, tinges of silver and gray surfacing with them. Like glacial waters, haunting and bottomless.

I knew what those eyes meant. What they were. The depth—the darkness. The shadows. I knew what they were from every story Bryce had ever shared about his past. I was reminded of them every time I saw the cane Uncle Alan still had to use—an ever-present connection to his days as a ground agent, the dangers he'd faced. I knew them from every whisper between my parents. I knew them from so many of the people who had done everything possible to prevent those eyes from ever seeing a human again.

And yet, here I was. Staring at them.

I felt it then: fear. Thick and dark, its talons sinking deep into my core. He reached out, his hands latching onto me. And for a split second, I wondered what it would feel like when he sank his teeth into me. Would it feel like his hands, the strong pressure I felt in them as they clutched me? As though his skin had melded into mine and I could no longer tell where I started and he ended… Or would it be fierce and fast, an anchoring of fangs in my flesh without warning?

Improvise. Adapt. Overcome.

The dizzy thoughts flashed through my head one after another until he jerked forward, and I felt my training kick in.

As he swept me downward off the redbill, I prepared to roll, assuming he meant to throw me to the ground; I wouldn't go down without a fight. Instead, my feet landed on solid rock. My fists clenched. I saw his lips part. Barely. And just when I gathered the energy of fear and anger coursing through my body, feeling it surge into the fist I was going to throw his way, he spoke.

His words rolled around us, deep and resonant, as though they'd ridden in on the waves crashing against the cliff behind us.

"Ah," he sighed. "I always prefer to have a conversation one on one."

Ready for more?

Darklight releases **September 8th, 2019.**

Visit www.bellaforrest.com for details.

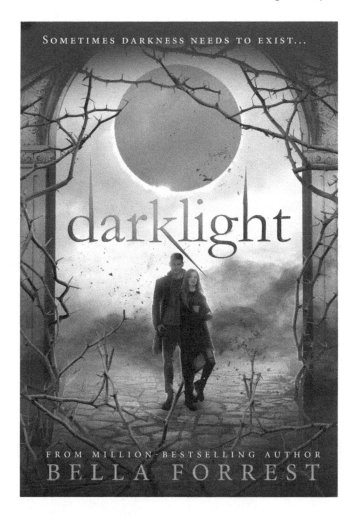

Thank you for reading, and I'm excited to see you there!

And keep turning for the next Merlin book...

Love,

Bella x

HARLEY MERLIN 12: Finch Merlin and the Djinn's Curse

Dear Reader,

Harley Merlin 12: **Finch Merlin and the Djinn's Curse** releases **September 30th, 2019**!

Visit www.bellaforrest.net for details.

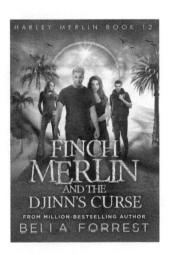

I'll see you there…

Love,

Bella x

P.S. Join my VIP email list and you'll be the first to know when I have a new book out. Visit here to sign up: **www. morebellaforrest.com**

(Your email will be kept 100% private and you can unsubscribe at any time.)

P.P.S. Feel free to come say hi on **Twitter** @ashadeofvampire; **Facebook** www.facebook.com/BellaForrestAuthor; or **Instagram** @ashadeofvampire

Read more by Bella Forrest

DARKLIGHT

(NEW! Fantasy)

Darklight

HARLEY MERLIN

Harley Merlin and the Secret Coven (Book 1)

Harley Merlin and the Mystery Twins (Book 2)

Harley Merlin and the Stolen Magicals (Book 3)

Harley Merlin and the First Ritual (Book 4)

Harley Merlin and the Broken Spell (Book 5)

Harley Merlin and the Cult of Eris (Book 6)

Harley Merlin and the Detector Fix (Book 7)

Harley Merlin and the Challenge of Chaos (Book 8)

Harley Merlin and the Mortal Pact (Book 9)

Finch Merlin and the Fount of Youth (Book 10)

Finch Merlin and the Lost Map (Book 11)

Finch Merlin and the Djinn's Curse (Book 12)

THE GENDER GAME

(Action-adventure/romance. Completed series.)

The Gender Game (Book 1)

The Gender Secret (Book 2)

The Gender Lie (Book 3)

The Gender War (Book 4)

The Gender Fall (Book 5)

The Gender Plan (Book 6)

The Gender End (Book 7)

THE GIRL WHO DARED TO THINK

(Action-adventure/romance. Completed series.)

The Girl Who Dared to Think (Book 1)

The Girl Who Dared to Stand (Book 2)

The Girl Who Dared to Descend (Book 3)

The Girl Who Dared to Rise (Book 4)

The Girl Who Dared to Lead (Book 5)

The Girl Who Dared to Endure (Book 6)

The Girl Who Dared to Fight (Book 7)

THE CHILD THIEF

(Action-adventure/romance. Completed series.)

The Child Thief (Book 1)

Deep Shadows (Book 2)

Thin Lines (Book 3)

Little Lies (Book 4)

Ghost Towns (Book 5)

Zero Hour (Book 6)

HOTBLOODS

(Supernatural adventure/romance. Completed series.)

Hotbloods (Book 1)

Coldbloods (Book 2)

Renegades (Book 3)

Venturers (Book 4)

Traitors (Book 5)

Allies (Book 6)

Invaders (Book 7)

Stargazers (Book 8)

A SHADE OF VAMPIRE SERIES

(Supernatural romance/adventure)

Series 1: Derek & Sofia's story

A Shade of Vampire (Book 1)

A Shade of Blood (Book 2)

A Castle of Sand (Book 3)

A Shadow of Light (Book 4)

A Blaze of Sun (Book 5)

A Gate of Night (Book 6)

A Break of Day (Book 7)

Series 2: Rose & Caleb's story

A Shade of Novak (Book 8)

A Bond of Blood (Book 9)

A Spell of Time (Book 10)

A Chase of Prey (Book 11)

A Shade of Doubt (Book 12)

A Turn of Tides (Book 13)

A Dawn of Strength (Book 14)

A Fall of Secrets (Book 15)

An End of Night (Book 16)

Series 3: The Shade continues with a new hero...

A Wind of Change (Book 17)

A Trail of Echoes (Book 18)

A Soldier of Shadows (Book 19)

A Hero of Realms (Book 20)

A Vial of Life (Book 21)

A Fork of Paths (Book 22)

A Flight of Souls (Book 23)

A Bridge of Stars (Book 24)

Series 4: A Clan of Novaks

A Clan of Novaks (Book 25)

A World of New (Book 26)

A Web of Lies (Book 27)

A Touch of Truth (Book 28)

An Hour of Need (Book 29)

A Game of Risk (Book 30)

A Twist of Fates (Book 31)

A Day of Glory (Book 32)

Series 5: A Dawn of Guardians

A Dawn of Guardians (Book 33)

A Sword of Chance (Book 34)

A Race of Trials (Book 35)

A King of Shadow (Book 36)

An Empire of Stones (Book 37)

A Shade of Dragon 3

A SHADE OF KIEV TRILOGY

A Shade of Kiev 1

A Shade of Kiev 2

A Shade of Kiev 3

A LOVE THAT ENDURES TRILOGY

(Contemporary romance)

A Love that Endures

A Love that Endures 2

A Love that Endures 3

THE SECRET OF SPELLSHADOW MANOR

(Supernatural/Magic YA. Completed series)

The Secret of Spellshadow Manor (Book 1)

The Breaker (Book 2)

The Chain (Book 3)

The Keep (Book 4)

The Test (Book 5)

The Spell (Book 6)

BEAUTIFUL MONSTER DUOLOGY

(Supernatural romance)

Beautiful Monster 1

Beautiful Monster 2

DETECTIVE ERIN BOND

(Adult thriller/mystery)

Lights, Camera, GONE

Write, Edit, KILL

For an updated list of Bella's books, please visit her website: www.bellaforrest.net

Join Bella's VIP email list and you'll be the first to know when new books release. Visit to sign up: www.morebellaforrest.com